The

The Hijack

Duncan Falconer

sphere

SPHERE

First published in Great Britain as a paperback original in 2004
by Time Warner Books
Reprinted 2004
Reprinted by Time Warner Books in 2006
Reprinted by Sphere in 2006
Reprinted 2008
Reissued in 2010 by Sphere

A CIP catalogue record for this book
is available from the British Library.

ISBN 978-0-7515-4472-5

Typeset in Bembo by Palimpsest Book Production Limited, Falkirk, Stirlingshire
Printed and bound in Great Britain by Clays Ltd, St Ives plc

Papers used by Sphere are natural, renewable and recyclable
products sourced from well-managed forests and certified
in accordance with the rules of the Forest Stewardship Council.

 Mixed Sources
Product group from well-managed
forests and other controlled sources
www.fsc.org   Cert no. SGS-COC-004081
© 1996 Forest Stewardship Council
FSC

Sphere
An imprint of
Little, Brown Book Group
100 Victoria Embankment
London EC4Y 0DY

An Hachette UK Company
www.hachette.co.uk

www.littlebrown.co.uk

To my Palestinian friend,
my Israeli friend, my Russian friend
and my dear English friend

1

The approach to the English Channel, two hundred miles due south of the Devon coastline, was the furthest from home Abed Abu Omar had ever been in his life. At forty minutes past midnight it was wet and gloomy, but, despite the constant drizzle that had gradually soaked him and his men since they left the Spanish coast the afternoon before, the desert in winter had sometimes been much colder, and he had spent many nights during his younger days without wood to burn or food for his belly.

The cloud was low but allowed visibility in all directions for several miles. The heavy swell that had arrived with the setting of the sun contributed to the conditions, making them perfect for the mission. Allah was indeed smiling down upon the twenty Arabs huddled under their glistening army-surplus ponchos, equally divided between two wooden, open fishing boats tied alongside each other and holding position, their engines silent. The signal-strength indicator on Abed's GPS flickered as it struggled to maintain a link with the navigational satellites through the cloud. The last positive reading indicated they were some five hundred feet off the proposed rendezvous point, but that was not a great concern to him. With this particular target he could afford to be much further from its track without fear of missing it.

The day before, Abed had received a message on his satellite phone informing him the vessel had been sighted passing Gibraltar and the Pillars of Hercules where it entered the Atlantic. Short of a mechanical breakdown, or some other unforeseen incident, it would soon be in sight.

Everything had so far gone to plan: the secret training in the desert camps of Lebanon, Syria and Jordan; access to the various ships owned by sympathisers in the Persian Gulf; the procurement of equipment; the preparation of the two second-hand boats purchased in Spain; and the arrival of the men from various places in Europe, America and the Middle East. The easiest part had been the acquisition of their weapons: not a gun, bullet or explosive device among them. Each man carried a Spanish garrotte, a dagger and a scimitar – the latter imported into Spain as antique artefacts – and they could use each of them with practised skill. For twelve months they had prepared and trained together for this moment, although it did not become a certainty until four months ago. Even now, with the time measured in minutes, there was still a possibility the operation could be aborted. That could happen right up to the point of no return, but Abed believed it was now unlikely. The sheiks, the masters, were as committed to the operation as Abed and his men.

He had not spent all of his short life, twenty-eight years, like so many of his people, waiting for the day he could serve Allah against Zion and its supporters and, if need be, make the ultimate sacrifice for the cause. Nor was his decision finally to take up the sword because he had been born and raised in the largest prison in the world, the Gaza Strip, or because so many people he knew had been killed or incarcerated. They were not the reasons he was here, although they had contributed over the years to the smouldering ember of hatred in his heart that one night burst into flames.

Abed's place of birth was Rafah, a Palestinian refugee camp in the south of Gaza along the border with Egypt. Up until just over a year ago, when he was smuggled out to begin his training for this mission, he had spent his entire life on the narrow strip of land eighteen miles by five that was the most densely populated place on earth. Gaza was surrounded on three sides by a narrow strip of no-man's-land, heavily fenced and razor-wired, and watched over by towers manned by lookouts and heavy machine guns. Like the Berlin Wall during the Cold War, or an American high-security prison, it meant death to anyone who tried to penetrate the perimeter day or night. The graveyards were littered with those who had made the attempt. On the map, Gaza looked like a long, crooked rectangle surrounded by desert on three sides and the Mediterranean Sea, constantly patrolled by naval gunboats, F16s and helicopters, on the fourth. Only a privileged few, those who had foreign passports or special permits, were allowed to leave Gaza. Several thousand Palestinians were admitted through the Erez

Crossing in the north into Israel on work days as cheap labour for the Israeli factories the other side of the border, but their passes were for twenty-four hours only and did not allow travel beyond the place of work. To be caught outside Gaza without a proper permit meant imprisonment, often for many years.

Abed lived with his mother in a breezeblock terraced hut with dirt floors in all but the main room, which was concrete. This was also the only room with electricity, when it was available. They had their own running-water supply – a tap in the unroofed entrance – and since the Israelis blew up the sewage works at the beginning of the current intifada, the toilet was a bucket behind a curtain at the end of the hallway which was emptied into a large hole in the ground in a derelict house near no-man's-land fifty yards away. Despite the conditions they were well-off compared to most others in the camps. The average income of a refugee family was ten US dollars a month. There was little industry left in Gaza, certainly nowhere near enough to provide work for those who were able. The population was more than a million, half of which was under fifteen years old, and a meagre living was scraped any way one could.

Abed was eleven years old when it occurred to him that his mother regularly received money although she never worked, but it was not until his teens that he asked her where it came from. He loved and revered his mother who had always cherished and cared for her only child, her one reason for living in this vile jail, something she often said to him after kissing his forehead each night before he went to sleep. The day he asked about the money she sat him down and explained how she came by it, also revealing for the first time the truth behind another great mystery of his life: his father. Her story was disappointingly brief for one of such importance, sketchily describing how Abed's father had escaped the country by fishing boat to Cyprus soon after Abed was born, and from there how he made his way to England where he settled to live and work. The plan behind the escape was that one day Abed and his mother would follow him and they would all be together again, away from the poverty and humility of the camps. However, his father had failed to get the necessary paperwork and visas, or perhaps the Israelis had refused to recognise them; Abed's mother was never clear about these kinds of facts and did not seem particularly interested in the smaller details. As far as she was concerned, they were trapped in Gaza, his father was in England, and that was that.

Like most of the older generation in the camps, she had grown to accept her way of life and had long since given up the dream of one day being free to live like those in other countries, in a proper house with utilities, a garden and the freedom to go where she wanted. The camp was over fifty years old, established in 1948, when the first people were forced out of their homes from towns and villages all over Palestine and herded like cattle into dozens of camps in Gaza and the West Bank, to live in crowded tents without proper medical facilities, food or sanitation. In time, they started up basic industries, made bricks and built small huts; these were closely packed together as their numbers grew, and only temporary abodes for they all hoped and believed that one day they would return to the farms and land they had owned for hundreds of generations. Her dreams, like those of most others, had withered with time. She had been born in Rafah camp, in an old British army tent barely a hundred yards from the hut she now lived in and where she knew she would die. Whatever the reasons for Abed's father's failure to get them out, the fact was they could not leave to join him, and he could not return without having to remain in Gaza for the rest of his life. He had chosen to stay in England where he could earn enough money to send them some each month so that they could live more comfortably than most.

The money arrived in his mother's bank account promptly until Abed was twenty years old, then shortly after his birthday it stopped. His mother was philosophical about it, supposing Abed's father had died and that there was nothing they could do about it anyway. That part of their lives, the more comfortable times, was over. She had always seen it as a bonus and now they would live like everyone else in the camp: almost solely dependent on help from the United Nations.

Abed remained curious about his father and asked her many questions about him: where he lived in England; if he had ever written to her; and if he was still alive the reasons why he might have stopped sending money. Abed's mother showed no interest in discussing the subject. Then one day he pushed her too far and demanded he had a right to know about his father. She lashed out at him with a venom he had never seen before and yelled that it pained her too much to talk about it and she didn't want him to mention his father ever again.

He did not.

Abed left university that same week and found work with a nearby metalsmith where he earned enough money to subsidise the UN rations, without which everyone in the camps might starve.

If he ever suspected his mother's stories about his father were lies, it never prepared him for the day he learned the dark and terrible truth, the same day he was smuggled out of Gaza, a truth that was like a cut across his heart he would always feel.

Abed had been asked many times to join the ranks of the local freedom fighters such as Fatah, Hamas, or factions like the Al Aqsa Martyrs Brigade. He always respectfully declined. His family was Christian Orthodox, a tiny minority among the Muslims, although it was not strange to find a Christian fighting for the Jihad, only unusual because of their small number. Abed was Palestinian and shared the torment inflicted upon his race that did not distinguish between Muslim and Christian, but his heart did not allow him to join the fight. It had not been wounded enough, not yet.

Abed showed above-average intelligence and athleticism in college and it was noticed by those who watched how patient he was. He was a listener more than a talker and did not display the characteristic hysteria that most Palestinians expressed after an Israeli raid and during the funeral that immediately followed a death, or when the futility of it all became overwhelming. There was something interesting about him, though most could not say with precision what it was. He was not a follower, and even though as a boy he rarely joined in the ritualistic, almost daily, stoning of the occupying army, which for some meant paying the ultimate price, he was never taunted for being a coward. It was obvious to everyone he was not, even though he had never done anything brave. Patience is a revered virtue for the Arab, especially among those who live in the camps. The men who watched were confident he would turn one day. Some men will always offer the other cheek and others never. And some, and they expected Abed to be of this type, might offer it once or twice before something pushed them over the edge. This could be relied upon in Gaza because there was no shortage of pushing by the enemy, and much was expected of Abed when that day came.

What changed Abed's mind about joining the Jihad, what pushed him over the top to take an active role in the struggle, was relatively sudden, although it was the straw that broke the camel's back. Some picked up arms out of despair, sometimes strapping explosives to their bodies and blowing themselves up along with as many of the enemy as possible. Others joined out of sheer anger, frustration and hatred. Abed best fitted this latter category, though he didn't discuss his innermost feelings with anyone, not even his mother. It was not a desperate act and he would certainly never throw his life away on a suicide bomb attack.

The event that wrenched open his heart and ignited the embers happened during the week he turned twenty-six years old, the same week he opened a metal shop of his own. The peace for him ended late one Sunday night during an Israeli incursion into the Rafah refugee camp.

These attacks were not unusual by any means and happened nearly every night somewhere in Gaza; raids by tanks, armoured personnel carriers, and Apache helicopter gunships, deep into the towns from any one of the numerous military outposts that surrounded the Strip. After the 1967 war, the Israelis decided they wanted Gaza for themselves and gradually carved chunks out of it by building settlement fortresses for their own people to occupy. By the time Abed reached his twenties, almost 50 per cent of Gaza had been confiscated to house only a few thousand Israelis. The explanation for the nightly incursions was to protect the settlements and discourage the Palestinians from attempting to expel them.

The first clue that danger was in the wind that night for the people living in Rafah camp was a cessation in the sporadic bursts of machine gun fire in no-man's-land along the border a street away. There was always a burst every ten minutes or so. A saying in the camp was that one slept with the gunfire and was woken by the silence.

Abed sat up in his bed, his ears searching to confirm the sounds he was as familiar with as the wind whistling through the date trees and the waves crashing on to the beach. When he was sure the distant creak and rumble was that of tanks and APCs, he put on his jeans and trainers and went to the front door, opening it just enough to peer carefully into the dark street. As the metallic clatter grew louder, there was the unmistakable crunch of a nearby building being crashed through. It appeared that Abed's neighbourhood was the night's target. That was not new, of course. Rafah had been attacked dozens upon dozens of times in the past few years, but there had not been an incursion into Abed's immediate neighbourhood for several months.

He was tempted to make his way down to the corner of the block to the main street that led to the marketplace to take a look and confirm what by now was obvious, but the snipers would most likely already be on the prowl, and if he was seen he would be shot. They were not the only unseen danger; the Apache gunships would also be hovering high above, their engines cloaked by noise suppressors, watching through night vision aides for anything living to show itself in the battered streets below. Many residents, regardless of age or gender, had died with a bullet to the chest or brain because they had been too curious and had not fought the urge to look out of their window during such times.

There was another loud crash from the opposite direction, followed by the guttural revving of a massive engine: another tank. They were penetrating from several directions. Whatever their area of focus was, Abed decided his home must be close to it, if not directly in it.

Suddenly the house at the end of the street crumpled and a tank brushed aside the front of it as if it were made of sugar blocks. A burst of machine gun fire followed as the tank continued past Abed's block and on to the next.

There was another long rattle of machine gun fire from behind the house which was very close. Then came the sound of someone running down the street towards him. The next burst of fire was different, lighter. Abed knew it was not the enemy. It was erratic and had the desperate characteristics of the hunted, not the hunter.

Abed could make out two men in his street carrying AK47 assault rifles, an easily recognisable weapon since they were often on display in Gaza City during the daytime when the Israelis rarely attacked. Israeli soldiers carried mostly American M16s or Canadian versions of the same model. They never used AK47s.

The men paused outside Abed's house looking uncertain about where to go next, with little time to decide. Abed remained still, watching them from the shadow of his door, which was slightly ajar. One of them sensed Abed and looked straight at him, and for a moment Abed wondered if they were considering an escape through his home. If the enemy suspected, it would mean the end of his home, literally, and possibly his incarceration. Despite the dangers, Abed opened his door to offer them entry.

'Close your door,' the man said. 'Stay out of sight.' He was tall and lithe and gripped his rifle close to his body, his finger through the trigger guard, ready to use it in an instant. Abed did not know him although he looked vaguely familiar. The man was not from Rafah camp. Perhaps he was from Khan

Younis, the larger town just north of Rafah. The man tapped his partner who was covering the other direction and they ran down a narrow alleyway opposite Abed's front door.

A moment later he heard more running in the direction the men had come from, and he instinctively closed his door and carefully drew the bolt across without making a noise. There was a roar of engines and the sound of masonry crumbling; one of the buildings behind Abed's home had gone down. Then many footsteps charged past his front door and gunfire erupted, followed by shouts in Hebrew. Everyone in the camp would be wide awake by now. Families would be huddled together in fear, praying their door would be passed by, that they would be among the lucky ones tonight.

A helicopter roared overhead drowning out all other sounds. Abed froze in the darkness as the helicopter's searchlight shone through gaps in the corrugated roof above the front door sending shafts of light across his face. As the helicopter moved on, a voice speaking in Arabic came over a hand-held loudspeaker.

'This is the IDF. All men from the age of fourteen to sixty come out of your homes with your hands raised!'

Abed was immediately filled with concern. The last time a callout happened in his neighbourhood he was eighteen. He had been made to line up along with a dozen other men, a few older but mostly his age or younger, and they were searched and ordered to remove their shoes. Several boys were slapped about, two beaten quite severely for not co-operating quickly enough, but Abed had received little more than a few shoves, the most severe one accompanying his dismissal when he was pulled away from the wall, pushed up the street and told to go home immediately without looking back or he would be shot. He obeyed them to the letter. The IDF, the Israeli Defence Force, was not to be trifled with. They were ruthless jailors, without compassion, and punished severely those who did not obey them, and just as often those who did. The rules of Gaza at night were the rules of the jungle, and the IDF had all the teeth and claws.

The loudspeaker's message was repeated over and over in all directions. Abed remained behind his front door unsure what to do. If he went outside he feared it would be different this time. He was a man now and adults were often beaten and nearly always taken away and interrogated, which usually lasted a couple of days. He still had a lot to do to get his new metal shop ready to open for business, with supplies due to be delivered in the morning, which he had to be there to receive. But if he did not go outside and the IDF decided to search his home, he might be shot or accused of colluding with terrorists. The latter meant immediate imprisonment without trial for God only knew how long. Some men had been gone for years without even being charged. But compliance did not ensure safety either. There were endless stories of men, and also boys, who had left their homes as ordered in just such a situation, and been shot or beaten and left for dead. The least Abed could expect was to be half-stripped and taken to a holding area, or driven to another part of the Strip and left to find his own way back without money for food or transport. Being beaten was inevitable. It would be down to the mood of the troops as to how badly. If one of their own had been killed recently then it did not bode well for anyone. Resistance was out of the question, and to defend one's home was to die as a terrorist. Many Palestinians had guns but few who lived in the camps. The most common was the AK47 but some had M16s, and there was even the occasional British GPMG, a heavier belt-fed machine gun. But guns were expensive in Gaza.

Ironically, most of the weapons smuggled in were not from other Arab countries, which in truth gave little support to the Palestinians. The Palestinians bought their weapons from the Israelis themselves, the so-called Israeli Mafia mostly; they passed through the settlements to be sold by the settlers themselves, the very people the guns might be used against. An AK47 could cost from three to five thousand US dollars, making Palestine the most inflated weapons' market in the world – in Baghdad an AK47 could be picked up for as little as thirty-five dollars. Some of the weapons originated from the West Bank, captured or found by Israeli soldiers during raids and then sold on to the Mafia. Weapons captured in Gaza were usually recycled back to the Palestinians at the going rate, a poignant example of commerce rising above conflict.

The loudspeaker voice came again, this time warning that any man found hiding would be guilty of terrorism. Abed had to go. Staying was a much greater risk. He quickly removed his trainers and put on an old pair of shoes since there was a good chance he would lose his footwear and the trainers were new.

As he reached for the bolt, he heard something behind him and looked over his shoulder. His mother stood at the corner of the hallway in her sleeping gown looking at him. He could not see her eyes in the darkness but he knew she was filled with fear.

'Don't go out there, Abed,' she said in a soft voice. 'Please don't go, my son.'

His stomach began to churn as his own fear grew. 'I must,' he said.

He reached for the bolt again and drew it across.

'Abed. Please. Don't,' his mother pleaded again, her voice trembling.

'Go back to your room, Mother.'

He started to open the door then paused as he remembered something. He pulled his shirt over his head and dropped it to the ground so that he was naked from the waist up. Some people had died because the soldiers feared they were wearing an explosive belt. At least he would remove that excuse to shoot him, not that they needed one; he was Palestinian and that was reason enough in their eyes.

'Abed, don't go,' his mother begged one last time, then she broke into tears knowing her son would do what he had decided and nothing she could say would change his mind.

As he opened the door he looked back at her, but she had her head in her hands, unable to watch him go. He stepped out into the street and raised his arms.

There were half a dozen soldiers a couple of yards away and they quickly trained their rifles on him. 'Come out!' one of them yelled.

An officer stepped forward, a large man no older than Abed, dressed like the others in a khaki uniform, a harness with weapons pouches about his chest and wearing a helmet, the straps tight under his chin. 'Forward!' he shouted as he closed in, his rifle aimed directly at Abed's face.

Abed walked calmly forward keeping his hands high. The officer reached for him and was immediately joined by another soldier who grabbed Abed harshly as if he might fly away, pulled him up the street and slammed him against a wall. Another soldier joined them to search Abed's trousers and legs while the officer stepped back.

'Take your trousers off,' the officer shouted.

Abed did not move quickly enough for their liking and one of the soldiers slapped him brutally across the face and repeated the officer's command. 'Take your trousers off!'

Abed was still too slow, refusing to give up all his dignity, arrogance his only weapon. He lowered his hands to unbutton his trousers and received another fierce slap across his face. 'Move when we speak!' shouted the soldier who hit him. Abed flashed a look at him; he was no more than eighteen years old. He appeared to be nervous. This was probably his first incursion, or first close contact with the enemy in a hostile situation. The soldier's uniform was a size too large for him and his weapons pouches were worn and undone. Abed glanced at the others as he pulled down his trousers. They were all filled with the same hate and eagerness to kill the vermin that lived on their promised land. As he pulled a trouser leg over his shoe, the soldier who had slapped him grabbed it and yanked so hard he pulled Abed's feet out from under him and Abed fell back against the wall, his backside hitting the street with a thump. He had grazed his back on the wall but he ignored the pain. The soldier continued to pull hard on Abed's trousers, tearing at them until one of the legs popped over the shoe, the other shoe coming off with the last tug of the other trouser leg. He tossed the garment aside and kicked Abed.

'Get up,' he shouted. When Abed did not move straight away he kicked him again. Abed's fear was growing by the second. The blood lust was in their eyes and he could feel they wanted to kill.

The soldier helped Abed up by his hair and Abed lost control for one second, pushing the man's hand away. The soldier could not believe the animal's audacity and clenched his jaw as he raised the butt of his weapon to strike, but the officer grabbed the soldier's webbing and pulled him back.

'So, we have a spirited one . . . What's your name?'

'Abed Omar.'

'You live in that house?'

'Yes.'

'Who else is in the house?'

'Only my mother.'

'Let's go and see if you're telling the truth.'

'I am telling the truth.'

'I wouldn't believe you if you told me it was night

time,' the officer said coldly. As he stepped towards the house, Abed was filled with dread. He could feel himself about to move and charge to protect his home and his mother even though it would probably be the last thing he ever did in this life.

Shots suddenly rang out nearby, followed by an explosion in the next street. The officer stopped and glanced in that direction, the activity reminding him he had work to get on with. He looked at Abed thoughtfully and then changed his mind. 'Bring him along,' he barked as he turned from the door and headed up the alleyway.

Abed was grabbed and held firmly between two soldiers as they marched him briskly behind the officer.

They turned a corner to where several soldiers stood outside a metal door that was the entrance to a breezeblock hut. The officer stopped to talk to them and after a brief discussion faced the door and banged on it loudly.

'You have been ordered to open up. If you continue to refuse we will open the door ourselves,' he shouted in Arabic.

He did not wait for a reply and barked an order to his men. Two of them hurried to the door and hung a small canvas pack the size of a brick on the handle. Wires were quickly led from the pack back up the street and all the soldiers except the officer and the two men holding Abed took cover.

'You have fifteen seconds to open the door or we come in,' the officer shouted then turned to the soldiers holding Abed and jutted his chin at them.

They moved tightly behind Abed, pressing one side of him against a wall while keeping him facing the door like a shield. Abed could still see part of the charge, the wires trailing from it along the ground and past his feet. Only then did it dawn on him that the soldiers intended to blow the door while he remained exposed. He tried to twist away but an arm reached around his throat and held him in a firm chokehold.

A woman's voice called out from inside the house that she was coming.

'Standby,' the officer said.

The woman called out once again, oblivious to what was going on, her voice growing louder as she walked along her roofless hallway to the door.

If Abed could hear her then the soldiers could too but none of them responded.

'Standby,' the officer called out again.

Abed became frantic. This was madness. 'She's coming to the door,' he tried to call out but his words were stifled by the arm about his neck.

'Now!' the officer shouted.

The explosion was deafening and the shock wave and bits of debris struck Abed's body sending him back into the soldiers holding him. Something hit him in the face and stomach and burned for a few seconds, but he did not have time to think about any of it. He was quickly pushed forward towards the hut, the point man of a Roman wedge. The door had been blown completely off, and he was rushed into the hallway and along it, the soldiers remaining tightly behind him in case a desperado within fired upon them. He almost tripped on something on the dark floor. It was a body. But the soldiers held him up and pushed him on. When they reached the end of the narrow passage that opened out into a small yard, the soldiers in the rear rushed past him and quickly entered the rooms. A woman screamed and furniture was smashed, then two young girls were dragged crying from a room and thrown to the ground in the yard where they grabbed each other in utter terror.

Abed was released, his employment as a human shield over for the time being at least, and he looked back up the hallway to the entrance where the body lay beside the fallen door. It was the woman who had called out. The device must have exploded as she reached for the bolt. Her right arm had been blown off above the elbow and half of her face was missing. He knew her. She was the mother of the two girls on the floor holding each other. Her husband was a security guard in a petrol station on the edge of the town. He was probably there tonight. No one would go and tell him until morning when the soldiers had gone and it was safe. Abed was horrified and looked away.

The soldiers could find no one else in the house and after some terse commands from the officer, Abed was pulled back out into the street and held against a wall. He glared at the officer barking orders as the screaming girls were pulled out of the house and taken away. The majority of the soldiers moved on up the street to carry on with their search and the officer faced Abed who was staring back at him with hate-filled eyes. Blood trickled down his face from a cut on his forehead and ran over his nose and mouth, and he wanted nothing more than to tear the officer's throat out with his teeth. The officer stood in front of Abed, slightly taller and looking down on him.

'You look angry,' the officer said calmly. 'Have we upset you in some way?'

The anger welled uncontrollably inside of Abed and he jerked his head forward as he spat blood into the officer's eyes. The soldier grabbed Abed by the hair and slammed his head into the wall. The officer wiped his eyes clean with his sleeve and then, taking his time to aim while the soldier held Abed, punched Abed in the stomach so hard it took every ounce of breath out of him as his knees gave way. The soldier did not let Abed fall and gripped his throat to keep him against the wall. Abed could barely recover the air he had lost as the officer wiped the rest of the bloody spittle from his face, took a pace backwards and brought the barrel of his M16 level with Abed's heart. The soldier held Abed as far away as he could to avoid being splattered with blood. Abed believed his time had come and he calmed himself ready for the bullet.

The officer stared into Abed's eyes, savouring the moment. He had every reason in the world to kill this Palestinian having lost three of his company in the last month: two to a landmine and one sniped in the back at a checkpoint. The pressure for revenge had come from his men, all conscripts, one of whom had recently lost a sister to a suicide bomber in

Jerusalem. But he did not need encouragement. He loved this land more than anything, enough to die for it, and certainly enough to kill those who had promised not to rest until every Israeli was gone or dead. The officer removed the safety catch and curled his finger around the trigger.

'Wait a minute.' A voice came from behind the officer. A rugged, tough-looking man in grubby civilian clothing whose face had not seen a razor in weeks stepped from an alleyway with a similar-looking partner who remained in the shadows while the first man, holding a notepad, came over to the group.

The officer lowered his gun and looked at the intruder with guarded contempt. He knew these men were Mossad and although he did not like them, he had no choice but to tolerate them. They called the shots on operations like this one. What the officer resented was the way they made him feel like a lackey of Mossad. His family had spent five generations in Israel having moved to the land before the Second World War. They had fought in just about every battle of survival since then and his father had been an officer during the Yom Kippur war and commanded a company under Sharon during the invasion of Lebanon, taking part as an observer in the infamous massacre by Phalangist militia of hundreds of Palestinian men, women and children in the Sabra and Shatila refugee camps. He was an army man through and through and proud of it, and resented these spooks lording it over him.

'What's his name?' the Mossad agent asked the officer.

'I don't know and I don't care.'

The agent looked at him, guarding his own contemptuous feelings about the officer, which were not very different from the officer's perceptions.

'What's your name?' the agent said to Abed.

Abed hesitated, still in shock from his near-death experience and suffering from the torture of knowing it was only a temporary reprieve.

'I asked you your name,' the agent said without any malevolence.

'Abed Abu Omar.'

The agent checked his notepad and then looked at Abed as if with a fresh pair of eyes.

'Let him go,' the agent said.

The officer's mouth opened like that of a fish. 'This has nothing to do with you.'

'I said let him go,' the agent repeated calmly.

The officer knew he was stepping into a fight he would not win. Mossad had the last word in virtually everything and if he disobeyed, he would pay a severe price. His career would be over for one, and that alone was enough to keep him in check. He lowered his gun and relaxed his shoulders in reluctant deference.

Another burst of gunfire came from a couple of streets away. The agent let his eyes linger on the officer's long enough to hammer the message home that he was in charge, then disappeared up an alleyway with his partner.

The officer spat on the ground in the direction of

the agents and mumbled an obscenity before returning his attention to Abed. 'Why did they spare you?' he asked.

Abed was even more surprised than the officer, and was feeling almost high with relief. 'I don't know,' he said.

'You think I give a shit what he said?'

Abed's relief went screaming into reverse.

'This isn't over,' he said. 'I'm going to save you for another time, make you sweat a little.'

The officer removed the magazine from his M16, cocked the weapon and caught the bullet that ejected from the breech. 'You see this,' he said holding the bullet up to Abed's face. 'This is yours . . . Kiss it.' He pushed it against Abed's bloody lips, grinding it into his mouth, cutting his gums.

'There, it has your kiss. Now, listen carefully. This is what I'm going to do with it. I'm going to give it to one of my snipers – he's the best in Israel – and I'm going to tell him to give it back to you one day. Maybe in a week, maybe in a month, but one day, you'll get it back. Right through your head. Or perhaps I'll just do it myself.'

The officer let the threat sink in, stepped back and placed the bullet in a breast pocket. He pushed the magazine back into its housing on the weapon, pulled the cocking arm until it was all the way back, then released it on its spring to load a new bullet into the breech with a slam.

'Take him away,' he said. The soldier yanked Abed down the street and around the corner to a waiting truck where a dozen other men from the camp were pressed inside, some of them bloody, all looking frightened. Abed's hands were bound behind his back and he was pushed up and into the truck. Two soldiers climbed in, shoving their prisoners further along, the tailgate was slammed shut and the truck drove away.

Abed was kept in a holding cell for a week along with several other prisoners before he was removed for interrogation. He was questioned for an hour after which he was returned to the cell. Two days later he was unceremoniously released, wearing the shirt and jeans from a Palestinian prisoner who apparently would never need them again.

When he opened his front door, he stopped in the doorway. Strewn about the hallway and small yard was their household furniture and belongings, or what was left of them. Anything that could be broken had been. A pile of clothes in a corner had been defecated on. Filled with immediate concern for his mother he hurried down the hallway to the entrance of the main room where he saw her huddled in a corner wrapped in a blanket. When she looked up and saw him, he could feel the relief gush from her as she leapt to her feet and ran into his arms, sobbing uncontrollably. He held her close, stroked her and kissed her head. 'It's okay, Mother. I'm all right.'

She would not let go of him and after a minute or so he gently pushed her away to look at her. 'Are you okay? Did they hurt you?' he asked.

She shook her head and tried to smile as the tears ran down her face, then took hold of him again as if he were a dream which might disappear any moment. 'It's okay,' he assured her. 'It's all okay now.'

But he was wrong. The officer was true to his word and made sure Abed did not forget there was a bullet with his name on it. The first reminder came a couple of weeks after the incursion as he stood in the street outside his front door drinking a bottle of Coke and taking a moment to feel the sun on his face. The bottle shattered in his hand as a single shot rang out from no-man's-land on the Gaza–Egypt border a hundred yards away. He dived back into his house, his hand bleeding from a cut caused by the shattering glass and wrapped a cloth around it to stem the flow. The sniper had missed him, but Abed knew it was not through lack of skill. The IDF snipers were far too good to miss someone standing still from that range. They had plenty of practice. The shot had been a reminder, a message that Abed had not been forgotten and his day would soon come.

A week later he was open for business in his new metal shop situated on the corner of a block near the marketplace only a few hundred metres from home. After finishing welding a metal framework for a door he turned off the acetylene torch and accidentally knocked a tool off the bench. As he bent down to pick it up a shot slammed into the wall behind him where his head had been a second before and ricocheted off several metal sheets in various parts of the shop before lodging itself in the ceiling. People in the street outside scattered with practised alarm and Abed flung himself to the floor behind his bench just as another shot slammed into one of the metal table legs in front of his face, splattering him with flakes of rust and dirt. The adrenaline soared through his veins as he realised the day of his execution had come and the sniper had so far been unlucky. He could not stay where he was and crawled as fast as he could across the floor, heading for a corner out of view from the street. Another shot rang out but no bullet entered his shop. It sounded different, louder, as if fired from close by. Abed remained tight in the corner unable to see out of the shop, which hopefully meant the sniper could not see inside.

He lay there for what seemed an age, contemplating his situation. The bottom line was it was only a matter of time before he was killed as the officer had promised. If he was going to stay alive, he had to do something radical and he spent the next few hours mulling over his options.

By the time Abed got to his feet he had come to a decision, which was not difficult since he had only one choice.

That night he asked a friend who had connections with the Islamic Jihad to arrange a meeting for him. He was asking to join the cause. The truth was he still did not truly want to be a part of the armed struggle, despite all that had happened, but he could not stay in Rafah, and since he could not leave Gaza he needed to relocate to somewhere else in the Strip. But that was not easy. Gaza was not a big place and if he and his mother moved to another part, they would have to find somewhere to live in an already overcrowded place and begin the equally difficult task of finding work. Abed was not exactly sure what the freedom fighters could do for him but he had to find out. Of equal concern was what they would ask him to do for them. He hoped they might hide him in one of their secret compounds, but if so, what about his mother? She could not live with them. If she remained at their home in Rafah and the IDF learned he had joined the Jihad they might retaliate by destroying the house and quite possibly killing her too.

To his surprise, when he eventually met with the council he did not need to explain any of his concerns to them. The council, who remained secretive about their names and everything else that did not directly concern Abed, had already decided what was best for him. He was told nothing other than they would take care of everything and after the meeting was taken directly to a sparse apartment in the middle of Gaza city and told to stay inside it and not to go out for any reason whatsoever. Food was provided and he was assured his mother would be told he was well and not to worry about him, and that they would also take care of all of her needs. There was no formal induction ceremony or briefing, no indication that he was now a part of the organisation other than this security blanket, but it appeared he was now a member of the group, but what group he did not know. There were many factions within the liberation struggle who often squabbled and fought between themselves, each with a different view of how the ultimate fight should be conducted, politically and militarily. It was a valid concern since he would owe someone for this service and the cost could vary from one group to another. He also had his own views on the situation and being Christian Orthodox did not necessarily share those of the extreme Islamic fundamentalists who had taken advantage of the intifada, the current war with Israel, and risen to control Gaza. Abed decided that since he had given control of his destiny to others, and that there was nothing he could do about it for now, he would gratefully accept the security and wait to see what developed. His only plan was to regain control of his life as soon as he could, although he was well aware that this would come at a price.

For a month Abed saw no one except Hasim, a teenage boy who was responsible for providing food and domestic supplies. Hasim was always very polite and humble but provided hardly any conversation. Abed soon decided Hasim was not so much close-lipped for security reasons as he was dim-witted. Television and books were Abed's only way of passing the time and he soon began to feel like a prisoner although the doors were not secured from the outside and he could leave if he wanted to.

The fifth week a man arrived with Hasim and introduced himself as Ibrahim. He was the same age as Abed, slightly taller and thinner, and had a thick beard. After a formal greeting, Hasim left the two men alone and Ibrahim set about making some tea without saying another word. Abed chose not to speak either. After taking a cup of the sweet drink together Ibrahim eventually broke the silence. He told Abed in an economical manner that they were going to leave Gaza together. Abed's first question was where were they going and his answer was a warning look. Ibrahim was physically strong and hardened but his manner was gentle and non-confrontational. The look had no malice behind it and was intended as a tuition.

'Your first lesson, Abed, is never to ask questions. The sheiks know everything. All will be taken care of. You will never be told the next step until after completion of the one before.'

Abed understood and sat back looking at Ibrahim, suspecting he knew more and would reveal it when he wanted to.

'It was not always this way,' Ibrahim continued. 'We used to be more relaxed . . . and more stupid. Traitors infiltrated us and many of our leaders and best fighters were killed. So now we work in cells, isolated from all other cells. No single person knows where each cell is or who is part of it. Not even the sheiks. Each cell can be contacted, but only through its single contact. In this way traitors can also be found out more easily.'

Ibrahim poured them both a fresh cup of tea and they sat back in silence for a while longer. Abed was enjoying this in a bizarre way. It might not be conversation per se, but it was interesting communication: informative about Abed's future with the hint of more to come.

Ibrahim eventually smiled at Abed. 'They say you are intelligent and brave. Did you really spit in the face of the officer? Some might say that was more stupid than brave.'

Abed did not answer and simply stared at Ibrahim. Ibrahim's smile broadened. 'They are right. You will learn fast.'

Ibrahim got to his feet and casually looked out of each window, checking not only the street below but the rooftops that surrounded them and the sky too. He then opened the front door and took a look outside. 'One must always be careful,' he said as he closed the door and sat back down in front of Abed. 'There are those who would sell our lives just for a permit to escape this prison.'

He poured himself some more tea and filled Abed's glass. 'We leave Gaza tonight,' he said without a hint of drama.

Abed did not show his surprise. While he had considered many ways in which the council might employ him, he had never thought they might get him out of Gaza. It seemed far too great an effort to go to for such a small fish. He immediately began to imagine where he might go and what it would be like outside of the Strip. His imagination was limited since he knew so little about the world. Instead of excitement at the prospect, he found himself feeling nervous, but he was not clear exactly why. Maybe it was the passage through the perimeter, which was notoriously dangerous since many more had died than had succeeded. But it was better than staying in Gaza and he could not have hoped for more under the circumstances. Then another thought entered his head, the true source of his concern.

'There is one thing I must ask,' Abed said.

'My rank is not above yours, Abed. I can tell you everything I know, which is not much more than I've already told you.'

'It is not information. I must see my mother.'

'Ah. That has already been taken care of. I told you the sheiks think of everything. We leave as soon as it is dark and go to Rafah where you will have time to see your mother.'

'Back to Rafah? Is that wise?'

'We must. That is the way we will leave Gaza.'

'The Rafah tunnels into Egypt?' Abed asked. The tunnels were legendary, though their location was as secret as the cells. In design they were much like the famous tunnels dug by inmates of the World War Two prisoner of war camps, and they were used to smuggle contraband into Gaza, including weapons and explosives or the ingredients to make them. The IDF would on occasion discover one and destroy it, but another was soon dug to replace it. Rafah was the obvious place for a tunnel because it bordered Egypt, although that did not necessarily mean it was safe to arrive in that country either. The Egyptians were no friends to the Palestinians and were quite capable of handing them over to the Israelis if they were caught in their country without the proper permits. However, it was far less of a risk than escaping into Israeli territory where one had to run the gauntlet of dozens of checkpoints to get to Jordan, Syria or Lebanon.

'Concern was also my first thought,' Ibrahim said. 'We will find out tonight.'

Ibrahim grinned and Abed finally smiled for the first time in a long while.

'We are going to have an adventure,' Ibrahim said. 'I don't know for sure, but I believe it is true. We are destined for glory, my new friend.' Ibrahim offered up his glass and the two men toasted the adventure and their new friendship.

That night Hasim came to the apartment and led Abed and Ibrahim to a car parked a block away. Hasim said goodbye and left. Abed and Ibrahim climbed into the back. Two men were seated in the front, the passenger holding an AK47. Not a word was spoken as they drove through the city and down on to the beach road. They turned south past Hotel Row, the Riviera of Gaza, except that now most of the hotels were empty, some even burned down since the intifada by the fundamentalists as punishment for serving alcohol. Several miles further on they headed inland from the beach to avoid the Israeli settlement of Gosh Ghativ and stopped several hundred yards short of the Salah ed-Din road, the main highway that ran the length of Gaza, right through the centre from north to south. The highway was not safe to drive on at night – the IDF would shoot at any vehicle that moved along it during darkness.

The passenger signalled Abed and Ibrahim to get out. The driver remained and as Abed and Ibrahim followed the passenger off the road and into a ditch, the driver turned the car around and headed back the way they had come. The passenger waited silently for a moment, checking there was no movement anywhere about them, then moved off for several hundred yards across rugged, open terrain, stopping to listen every now and then, until they reached the outskirts of the town of Khan Younis. They climbed into another car that was waiting for them, manned by only a driver, which took them into Rafah a mile or so further on.

The car stopped at the far end of Abed's street, the driver turned off the lights and engine, and they all waited in silence for several minutes.

'You have half an hour to visit your mother,' the passenger said finally, speaking for the first time. 'No longer. We will wait here for you.'

Ibrahim smiled at Abed and nodded, conveying his good wishes.

'There are snipers out tonight,' the passenger added. 'Keep to the shadows at all times and don't pause. Go directly to your house and stay inside.'

Abed climbed out and headed down the street towards his house, keeping against the wall until he reached his door. There was no one else about and he could see the glow from a small light within. He carefully opened the door and went inside, quietly bolting it behind him. His mother never bolted the door while he was not home, and even though he had not been there in over a month obviously she had remained hopeful he would return.

He found her sitting in the main room, sewing by candlelight. She looked up at him, and after her initial surprise she put down her sewing and stood up. He had expected her to run into his arms, but she did not. She was unhappy about something and there was a trace of anger in her eyes.

'What do you think you are doing?' she asked. There was no mistaking the anger in her voice. 'Men have come and given me money for food and told me you are well. I know who they are.'

He realised what her concerns were and that he should have been prepared for them. He walked over to her and took her hands in his. 'Sit down, Mother,' he said.

'No,' she said. 'Have you lost your senses? I know what you are doing and you are mad. You will be killed.' She had no idea what he was doing, only that he had joined the cause, but that was enough.

'I have no choice, Mother. What am I to do? If I try to live a normal life I will be killed.'

'The IDF will kill you if you join those fools. This is not the way to get back our homeland. The Jihad are worse than that fool Arafat and his thieves in the Authority.'

'My concern right now is not for my homeland. It's to stay alive, and keep you alive.'

'No. You will not join them. I did not stay on this earth to raise you so that you could die like a bandit with a gun in your hand.'

He grew suddenly angry and intolerant of her ignorance. 'Then what should I do? Eh? What is your solution? I cannot stay here without being shot, and I cannot leave Gaza without their help.'

His words only heightened her fears. 'You are leaving?' she gasped. 'You are leaving Gaza?'

He calmed his voice, aware that the news was breaking her heart. 'Yes, I am leaving Gaza, Mother. And you will remain here and be taken care of. It is all arranged and nothing you can say will stop me. It is final so don't talk of it any more. Come. Sit. I don't have long. Let us spend some time together. Make some tea for us.'

'If you leave Gaza it will be the end of my life,' she said, but his reply was only to stare at her with a look of kindness as well as hopelessness. It was as if for the first time she could see the determined man instead of her determined small boy. He had grown up so quickly. It seemed like only the other day he rode his little tricycle up and down the street outside the house, and was it as long as twenty years ago when she first dressed him in his new, clean school uniform and packed him off with his little satchel of books on his back? But even as a young boy, when he said it was final, then it was. She had been proud of that strength in him then. Now she wished he was weak and feeble and that she could dominate him as some mothers could their sons. But that would never be. He was master in this house and always had been.

She took her hands out of his and went to the small fuel cooker on the floor, lit it with a match and placed a pot of water on it. She started to place tea in the pot and then stopped as if exhausted, unable to carry on.

'I will never see you again,' she said, without a doubt in her prediction.

He could not pretend to her that what she said was not true. He was not the kind of man to say anything for the sake of appeasement if he did not truly believe it himself, and so he remained silent.

She looked at him, her expression solemn, her eyes fixed. The emotion seemed to have faded and neither sadness nor anger remained.

'Sit down, my son,' she said softly. 'There is something I must tell you.'

The way she looked at him and spoke the words compelled him to obey. He could not recall ever seeing her this way before.

Abed sat in the only chair in the room and she came over and knelt on the rug in front of him at his feet. She looked like a small, fragile little girl and he looked down on her.

Her lips suddenly began to quiver and when she looked up at him her eyes were filled with guilt. 'You have never lied to me your entire life. You have been a good son . . . I have not been a good woman. I have lied to you all of your life.'

Abed did not move, his eyes fixed on her. He could not begin to imagine what she was about to tell him.

'You will never want to see me again once I have told you my secret. But I must tell you. Perhaps it will make you change your mind about this new course you have set yourself. Or perhaps it will only strengthen your will to leave, for you will have nothing to come back to . . . Whatever, I must tell you. I cannot go to my grave with this secret . . . not from you, although it fills me with fear.'

She took a moment to compose herself and then began.

'When I was a young girl, the camps were different from how they are now. There was not so much violence between our jailors and us. They were not all bad, as they seem to be today. There are good and bad hearts everywhere . . . among them, among us . . . The soldiers would come into the camps, but not always to hurt people. They were just soldiers, many of them as young as me. I was on my bicycle one day, coming back from school, and I had an accident. I hurt myself and my bike was broken. Some Israeli soldiers were nearby and they came and helped me. They dressed my wound and one of them walked me to the corner of our street. He was very polite and kind and there was no trace of hatred in his young, innocent heart. He was just a boy, and I was just a girl. The next day, when I left my house for school my bicycle was leaning against the wall outside the house and it had been fixed. A few days later my mother sent me to the shop for something, and on my way back the young soldier was in the street doing his job. He came over to me and said hello. His name was David and he walked me back to the corner of my street. It was dark and no one saw us and so we talked for a while. He hated the conflict between our people and said he dreamed like us for it to end . . . And that was our beginning. I saw him many times after that. In such a hate-filled world where our peoples were killing each other every day, we became friends. Secret friends, of course. He would leave me notes behind a loose brick in a house at the end of my street and we had a secret hiding place where we would meet.'

Abed shifted uneasily in his chair but his eyes, beneath a deeply furrowed brow, never left her lips.

'We became more than just friends,' she continued, taking a deep breath, the words becoming more difficult to release. 'I became pregnant.'

'No,' Abed cried as he leapt to his feet and walked to the other side of the room.

Her eyes followed him but she remained on her knees like a slave in front of her master.

'Don't tell me any more,' he said. 'I don't want to hear.'

'You must, Abed. I must tell you everything. I told my parents it was a boy from another town. They were horrified and said my life was over. I was nothing more than a whore. Had I been Muslim I would probably have been killed. Had I told them the father was an Israeli soldier nothing would have saved me. But I loved him, Abed. You were not born without love.'

Abed screwed his eyes shut.

'You are the son of an Israeli soldier,' she continued, gushing out the truth after holding it prisoner for so long. 'By the time you were born he had had to leave Gaza. But he did not desert us. He came to see you many times when you were a baby. He held you in his arms and caressed you with love. Every time he came here he risked his life just to see you.'

Abed clenched his fists so tightly they began to shake.

'We both knew in our hearts it was hopeless. We could never be together. He could not get me out of Gaza and obviously he could not stay. And he could not keep coming to see you. It was more and more dangerous for him each time, and for you too. There are those who would have killed you if they found out. You were two years old the last time he saw you. He brought you some presents and you played together while I kept watch from our secret place. I have never seen him or heard from him since that day . . . He is the one who sent us money all those years. You have no father in England.'

He kept his back to her while she wept, her face in her hands.

After a long silence between them, she looked up at him. 'Abed?'

He could not answer or look at her.

'Abed . . . You cannot join the Jihad,' she cried out in desperation.

Abed spun around to face her, his eyes on fire, and then headed for the door. She lunged forward, throwing herself to the floor to grab his foot but missed. 'Abed!' she cried, her face in the dirt, but he was gone. She sobbed uncontrollably, repeating his name.

Abed walked to the front door and paused before opening it, exhausted by what he had heard. He gripped the handle wishing he could rip it off its hinges and throw it aside. A million thoughts were spinning inside his head and he was unable to grasp any one of them. He wanted to beat his head against the wall and knock the memory of what his mother had told him out of it. He unbolted the door, pulled it open and stepped out into the centre of the street facing no-man's-land as if in hope that a sniper would see him and take his shot. He was breathing as if he had run a mile at full speed. He wanted to tear open his chest and rip out his Israeli heart, for the heart comes from the father. And then he screamed so loud it rocked his feet. It wasn't a word, just a despairing yell until he was breathless. When Abed was spent he remained panting where he stood. Abed's mother lay where he had left her, holding her hands tightly over her face.

He did not hear the running footsteps behind that stopped short of him, but he recognised the voice.

'Abed?' It was Ibrahim. 'Abed. What is it?'

Ibrahim came around to face Abed, afraid to touch him, as if he sensed some evil had taken hold of his new friend and might attack him too. 'Abed?' he asked once more.

Abed shook his head. Ibrahim looked towards no-man's-land, concerned with their exposure in the middle of the street.

'We should leave here, Abed. It is dangerous.'

Ibrahim raised his arms to take hold of Abed's shoulders but Abed knocked them away. He turned from Ibrahim, and walked up the street towards the car. Ibrahim looked at the open gate to Abed's house, at the light glowing inside, and could only wonder what had gone on between Abed and his mother.

Abed spoke to no one for a long time, not even Ibrahim, other than when necessary. In the early hours of the morning, before first light, they passed through the tunnels of Rafah into Egypt and several days later arrived in Lebanon by boat and then on to a secret base camp in the desert where they spent the next three months training with fifty other Arabs from around the world before moving to another secret camp in Syria. He not only learned about weapons and explosives, but land and sea navigation, computers and other technologies, and how to drive a car, truck, tank and various kinds of boats. Some of the teaching was in classes, but most was by computer using CDs. Abed immersed himself in the work, pushing to learn all he could as well as testing his physical limits. It was a way of dealing with his secret curse. In the eyes of the others, he was a serious fellow and obsessed with the Jihad, and his promotion was swift and uncontested. He spoke only when he needed to and his temper was short, especially with those who made mistakes. He did not demand perfection, only that those who could not achieve it kept away from him. Ibrahim often spoke in Abed's favour when men talked ill of him, assuring them that he was a fine man, and for those more difficult to convince he would explain that something had happened with his mother the night they left Gaza which made him unhappy. But Ibrahim was privately saddened. Abed was not the same man he had met in the safe house in Gaza. That first day in the apartment he was sure he had made a bond with Abed and had met a friend for life, but he did not know the man he left Rafah with.

By the time they were ready for the final phase of training in the Persian Gulf just twenty of the men were selected to go forward, and Abed was to be their leader, which they accepted without question. Whatever they feared or disliked about Abed, it was agreed he was an exceptional warrior. Besides, not one of them would have wanted the position of leading Abed.

'It comes, Abed,' said Ibrahim.

Abed slipped out of his thoughts and looked to the horizon. He knew exactly where it would be as soon as he heard the words.

The ship was brightly lit and matched the signature of the photographs they had studied; however these were the busiest waters in the world and many ships of similar design sailed in them. Abed would not be certain it was their target until they were close enough to read the name on the side, and by then they would be well into their boarding procedures. They would also be in danger of a crewmember seeing them and Abed did not want to take that risk with the wrong ship as there was a chance a warning might be sent to the coastguard about two unidentified small boats in the area. Crews were more aware these days as piracy was on the increase, and also because of the new United Nations-led international ship security codes implemented since the September Eleven attack. But then again it was extremely rare in these waters and part of the reason Abed and his men were here. They were going to carry out a waterborne version of the 9/11 attack by bringing the fight into the enemy's front yard.

The men came out from under their ponchos, all dressed in the same black one-piece combat suits, each with a dagger attached to a belt at his waist and a scimitar strapped across his back. Everyone looked towards the vessel as it drew closer, and the bright yellow-and-white blur, like a fat, sparkling Christmas tree, began to take shape as individual lights became discernible. It was clearly a supertanker. The largest mass of lights was in the stern; this was the five-storey tall superstructure containing accommodation, galleys, messes, hospital, control rooms and bridge. A thin line of lights from the superstructure outlined the long uninterrupted deck, as wide as a runway, and led to smaller clusters of lights in the bows which were the anchor and cable winch houses and entrance to the bosun's locker.

'Start the engines,' Abed said. 'Head towards its track.'

The men responded like a well-oiled machine and took their positions along the gunwales as the engines clattered into life. The lines connecting the two boats were untied and the coxswains gradually increased power and picked up speed. As they headed into the swell, the boats rose over the peaks and dropped down into the troughs in a big-dipper fashion with the occasional larger wave breaking over the bows to drench the men. At no time were they concerned about capsizing because they had practised the procedure many times, at night and in harsher conditions in preparation for these notorious waters. Abed was grateful for the heavy seas because it would be almost impossible for the tanker's radar scanner to pick out the small wooden boats. Furthermore, a tanker's primary fear in the English Channel was running into another ship large enough to cause damage, so all attention on the bridge would be focused on that major concern. The harsh weather would also deter crewmembers from stepping outside where they might look out at the water, though even if they did, it would be near impossible to see anything in the blackness from within the glow of the bright lights that enveloped the ship.

'Stay on this heading,' Abed said to the coxswain sitting astride his saddle-seat beside him, one hand on the steering wheel, the other gripping the throttle. The other boat maintained a parallel course metres away.

Abed looked through his binoculars and could now make out the funnel markings, a white star on a blue background. The superstructure was white and the body of the ship was grey, the colours he was expecting.

'More to the right and speed up a little,' Abed said. Timing was essential and once in position they would have only minutes to make any adjustments before the next phase.

The coxswains obeyed and the boats speeded up, loping over the waves as the men crouched, hanging on to the sides. Each man rehearsed his individual tasks in his mind, things they had practised endlessly until they had become instinctive. No one considered the tanker's crew to be a serious threat since the carriage of arms on board was not permitted. The captain was English, the chief engineer Russian, the first officer Egyptian, the other seven officers a mixture of Croatian, English and Scandinavian and the seventeen-man crew Philippine. These men were not a threat physically: a handful might use the limited workout facilities on board the tanker but would be nothing compared to the combat readiness of Abed's men. The chief concern was getting on to the main deck and moving into position to carry out the assault without being seen. If this was not achieved, surprise would be lost, and the crew was not entirely without some forms of defence. The ship had high-pressure fire hoses which crews had used in the past to repel would-be boarders. During normal ship's routine few of the doors on the deck and superstructure were locked because of the fire risk since the greatest concern for an oil tanker's crew was its ability to escape quickly in case of such an event. However, if the crew suspected an attack was imminent they could batten down the hatches, making it very difficult to gain entry, and Abed's men had not brought any special equipment with them for forcing steel doors.

Abed's eyes never left the tanker, gauging the distance and angle to its bows. As they drew closer to the ship's projected track, the lights on the super-structure narrowed and it took on a broader and more uniform shape as it squared to Abed's position.

'All stop,' he said to Ibrahim.

'All stop,' Ibrahim called out so that both boats could hear. 'Connect up,' he then said as they slowed.

The coxswains played the engines in and out of reverse to slow the boats and manoeuvred them around so they were facing each other, nose to nose. Two large boxes, one in the prow of each boat, were opened and the ends of strong nylon lines, laid neatly inside so that they would not tangle when fed, were threaded through heavy metal rings fixed to the point of the bows of each. The ends of both lines were then shackled together, connecting the boats at their noses.

'Snag line connected!' came the call.

Abed never ceased assessing the tanker's track to ensure the bows were on a precise collision course with the boats while everyone waited for his command.

'Prepare the snag,' he finally said to Ibrahim.

'Pull back,' Ibrahim called out immediately to the coxswains who then gently slipped their gear levers into reverse and slowly revved the engines. Both boats backed away from each other, a potentially dangerous operation because if they went too fast or caught a wave they ran the risk of being swamped. There were no water-draining pumps, and moving in reverse defeated the normal method of draining water through a non-return valve in the stern which utilised forward momentum to suck it out.

As the boats moved apart, the lines from both boxes uncoiled and paid out through the metal rings in the bows. A wave suddenly crashed over the back of Abed's boat and Ibrahim called out for bailers. The men were already armed with small buckets, waiting for such an incident, and began to scoop up the water and toss it overboard.

The tanker drew relentlessly closer. Abed never took his eyes from it, leaving the running of the boats to Ibrahim who used a walkie-talkie to talk to the other group who were already difficult to see in the blackness, the nylon line connecting them the only indication of their whereabouts.

The tanker's enormity grew with every passing second. The vastness of the beasts never ceased to amaze Abed even though he had trained on a dozen of them. He had never seen this one before but he knew its every detail. The keel had been laid in Ulsan, Korea in April 1994 and it was launched in October the same year. It was of single hull construction, 332 metres long by 58 wide with the bridge deck 30 metres from the water at full load. It weighed 313,000 tons when carrying its maximum capacity of 2.9 million barrels of crude, putting the keel 22 metres below the water and the main outside deck 11 metres above it. It had a brake horsepower of 31,920, and fully fuelled could travel at a maximum speed of 15 knots for 71 days without stopping.

The man in the bows of Abed's boat whose job it was to monitor the line as it paid out shouted a warning to the coxswain to stop, but he was too slow. The large bolt attached to the end of the line leapt out of the box and jammed in the rings, as it was designed to do, but not quite so violently. The boat jolted harshly to a stop and several men lost their balance and fell backwards. Abed kept hold of the coxswain's console to steady himself and kept his eyes fixed on the tanker as Ibrahim chastised the line watcher for his incompetence.

The next awkward part was ensuring the middle of the 200-metre line between the boats was central to the cutting edge of the tanker.

'Towards us,' Abed called out quickly to Ibrahim who immediately relayed the order into his walkie-talkie.

Abed's boat backed up while the other boat shunted forward. The tanker loomed less than half a mile away.

'Hold,' shouted Abed, his order echoed by Ibrahim.

The tanker's bow lights began to reveal more details of the ship. The anchors fixed either side could plainly be seen, and beneath them the tapered scars of grease and rust which ran down the sides to the water. Individual windows and portholes in the superstructure could be made out, some lit, some with blinds half closed, others in darkness, and then the rails that lined the deck became clear.

'Keep the line tight,' Ibrahim shouted to the

coxswain who touched the revs just enough to pull the boat back and maintain the line on the surface.

The superstructure started to disappear from the point of view of Abed's boat as the massive bows loomed above to block it out. The side of the tanker became the predominant view, cutting through the water like a vast screen of steel that seemed to have no end, and the name came into full view: Orion Star. It was the final confirmation this was their boat.

Abed picked out various points of interest on the tanker: the black silhouette of the crane against the back glow of lights halfway along the deck, the boarding ramp secured at rail level and hanging over the side and the vast network of pipes that grew out of the pump house immediately forward of the superstructure and ran the length of the deck to the bows.

Another few seconds and they would be exposed under the arc of the bow lights. If any of the crew happened to be looking over the side they might see one of the boats, but the chance of that at this time of night was slim. Most of the crew would be tucked up in bed or watching a movie in the entertainment quarters. The engine room might already be empty and running on automatic alarm systems. There would be no more than three men on the bridge, two officers and a watch keeper, and the captain would be in his quarters or watching a movie with the rest of the officers in their own mess. That was normal routine at least, and hopefully there was nothing unusual happening aboard this night.

The verticle edge of the bows sliced easily through the water between the two small wooden boats and the deep hum of the enormous engine began to filter through the noise of the wind and the engine of Abed's boat. The snag was seconds away. There was no danger of the line slipping under the tanker because of the depth of the snub-nosed bow breaker beneath the water that extended several metres ahead of the furthest visible point of the bows above water. The coxswains kept the nose of the boats pointing towards the front of the tanker so that when the line was snagged they would move forwards and not jerk to the side.

Everyone crouched and held on, waiting for the sudden acceleration. Abed kept a firm hold of the console, all the time searching the deck of the tanker and bridge wings for any sign of life. He could make out a figure moving on the bridge but nothing on deck or on the external stairways of the superstructure. All seemed well.

The line suddenly snapped taut as a violin string as it whipped out of the water and the ring in the bows creaked under the strain, but the boat did not immediately move. During one such training exercise, the line snapped and whipped back with such force it took one of the men's ears clean off. This line was stronger, but there would always be doubt until they were under way. The bolt suddenly clunked as it moved into another position in the ring, almost giving the man directly behind it heart failure, then as the line reached its full stretch the boat lurched forward as if it had harpooned a thunderous whale. They matched the speed of the tanker within seconds, moving at an angle to it and drawing closer to the side.

A hundred metres of line brought them alongside the tanker just less than a third of the way down from the bows. The boat thumped against the side of the vast steel wall that went up to the heavens and the men quickly unfastened four fibreglass poles secured in the bottom of the deck. Using a technique they had practised endlessly, the ends of two poles were connected with bayonet fittings and then fed back so that the next one could be attached to the end. As the pole got longer, it became a more difficult task to perform. Abed's boat was four metres long but since the pole had to be eleven metres in length it meant that most of it was allowed to extend over the stern and into the water while the last sections were attached. The final piece of equipment was a hook slotted into the end of the pole which had a large coil of lightweight caving ladder fixed to it. The idea for the device was taken from Indonesian pirates. Once the pole was constructed, the end with the hook was raised into the vertical position against the boat as the ladder unfolded and pushed up, the aim being to place the hook on to the edge of the deck or rails. The combination of gusting wind, rain and swell made it difficult to control the flexible pole and stop it from swinging about. This was where the endless training paid off. When the teams first practised the technique on dry land in perfect conditions they had many failures such as losing control of the pole completely or the hook and ladder falling off the end. When they progressed to doing it at sea in a rocking boat many thought they would never ever be able to manage it first attempt, as Abed had demanded. But in time they became proficient and confidence soared. They only brought one set of ladder and poles per boat for this mission and therefore failure to hook on meant the failure of the entire operation. After several minutes of extreme effort, and one very close call where they almost lost control of the pole completely, a supreme push to keep it vertical saw the hook snag on to the edge of the deck and the pole was pulled down and allowed to fall into the sea.

'Abed,' Ibrahim called out, waiting for the order.

'Go,' Abed said, and Ibrahim was first up the ladder, his scimitar dangling from his back. When he was halfway up the next man followed. Abed went next and quickly pulled himself up the rungs, his arms and legs working in tandem. Eleven metres is a long climb on a caving ladder, especially when the climber is being blown about and banged against the side of a steel wall, but they had done it so many times they ran up like gibbons.

When Abed reached the deck, he swung over the rail and joined Ibrahim and the other man lying flat on their bellies by a thick pipe, taking a moment to rest their exhausted arms while at the same time scanning the area. As the fourth man arrived, Abed and Ibrahim got to their feet and made their way down the deck to the halfway point where a workshop was located a few metres inboard close to a heli-pad. Abed moved to the corner of the workshop from where he could get a look at the superstructure fifty metres away. There was no sign of life other than on the bridge and judging by the relaxed movement of those inside, the crew were unaware of the intruders.

Within a few minutes the rest of the men were gathered against the wall of the workshop which was large enough to hide all nine of them comfortably. The coxswain remained with the boat, which he kept tight alongside.

Abed personally checked his men were all accounted for then signalled them to move. They followed him at the crouch across the open deck towards the spine where the vast collection of pipes some ten feet high ran the entire length of the centre of the ship. With cover from view from the super-structure, they made their way along the pipes towards it.

They arrived at the pump house just in front of the superstructure and stopped, waiting for the other team which should have been mirroring Abed's on the other side of the tanker, but there was no sign of them. Ibrahim crouched to look under the wall of pipes, hoping to see feet moving on the other side. The contingency plan if the other team failed to make it was to complete the mission, even though nine against twenty-seven increased the chance of failure.

'Ha! They come,' Ibrahim whispered excitedly but not without some relief.

Shadows moved towards them on the other side of the pipes and the team leader looked around the corner and gave Abed a solid thumbs up indicating all his men were with him.

Abed gave the signal and the two groups moved

off in opposite directions, Abed's team heading around to the starboard side of the superstructure while the other went to port.

He paused at the corner of the superstructure, checking once more that it was clear, before making his way to the main deck entrance that faced starboard. His men gathered in a line against the bulkhead while he studied the heavy steel entrance door which was closed. The door was evenly surrounded by six dogs – heavy clips – all in the unlocked position except one, the centre dog opposite the hinges. He carefully pulled the lever down, unlocking it, and jerked the heavy door open just enough to look inside. The entrance was a weather-lock, a small chamber with another door a few feet away, but that was fully open and the broad corridor beyond was brightly lit, immaculately clean and empty. This was the first real indication that the ship was at security level one, its lowest level, and the security officer was expecting nothing in the way of danger.

Abed checked his watch. It was 2 a.m. He expected the task to be complete and the teams heading back to the boats by 3 a.m.

'Allah is great,' Ibrahim said to Abed as a way of wishing them luck. 'And so is Jesus too,' he added as an afterthought, remembering Abed was a Christian.

Abed checked the faces of his men who crouched watching him, waiting anxiously for the word.

Abed opened the door fully, stepped inside, stood in the weather-lock and looked down the corridor to the door at the far end some thirty metres away.

It opened and the leader of the other team stepped inside to face him.

Abed then did something the men were not expecting: he stood for what seemed a long time in the doorway as if locked in a trance. Ibrahim at first thought Abed had heard or seen something, but there was nothing.

'Abed?' Ibrahim whispered. 'What is it . . . Abed?'

Abed did not respond. Ibrahim stepped through the door, reached out and took Abed's shoulder. 'Abed,' he said again.

Abed turned to look Ibrahim in the eyes. For a moment, Ibrahim thought he saw fear in his face. He had always believed Abed did not know the meaning of the word and was suddenly filled with concern. His own orders, privately conveyed from the sheiks, was that if anything happened to Abed, he was to take charge of the mission, and if any member of the team had a change of heart, for whatever reason, he was to be instantly killed. They had never said as much but that would include Abed.

Ibrahim's hand tightened on his scimitar and slowly started to draw it from its scabbard. But whatever was going through Abed's mind seemed to pass and he lowered his eyes and faced the corridor again.

He drew his scimitar, adjusted his grip around the haft and stepped from the darkness of the weather-lock into the brightness of the ship, followed by Ibrahim and the others.

2

Stratton stood in the arched entrance of a grand Elizabethan country house set in ten acres of manicured gardens, looking down on to a spacious, groomed lawn where a hundred well-heeled guests were enjoying an official morning garden party: VIPs, the titled, ambassadors, statesmen and ministers of various levels. He had arrived with his four-man team at dawn to carry out preliminary security checks, search the grounds and scan the extra staff, caterers and valets as they arrived. The guests had started trickling in around 10 a.m. and an hour later everyone of importance had arrived.

It was a fresh, sunny day and Stratton was dressed in a smart jacket and tie, his dark hair shorter than it had been in many years, and he was bored as hell. This was not his usual employment by a long shot but he knew why he was here. His bosses in the Special Boat Service thought they knew, but they did not. The mandarins in Whitehall, far above his superiors at the SBS headquarters in Poole, had retired him, thrown him out and back into 'normal life', a relative term for life in Special Forces could never be described as normal. It was not a punishment though, far from it. In their eyes, they had done him a favour.

Bodyguard work was the most boring job for anyone, let alone an SF operative. It meant long hours hanging around doing nothing but watching and waiting, in cars, restaurants and always at the whim of those they looked after. It was true that a lot of Special Forces work was also spent waiting and watching but, for Stratton at least, bodyguard work had some features that qualified it as the most loathsome of assignments in his business. He hated working for civilians, and the work felt like nothing more than glorified servitude.

Civilians and soldiers mixed like oil and water in their working modes: there was no mystery about being a civilian since all soldiers had been one, but few civilians could truly understand the life of a soldier. There was an even bigger chasm between civvies and Special Forces; a civilian might scratch the surface of understanding life in SF by reading every book available on the subject, but they could never begin to fathom the mentality of an operative. There were civilian parallels – sportsmen, firemen and police armed-response teams for instance – which touched on aspects such as the team ethos, but the lifestyles and working conditions did not begin to compare with those who fought side by side in a war and weathered the dangers of operating alone on under-cover operations. The job created bonds for life.

Within this microcosm, Stratton was an anomaly; he was highly respected for similar reasons to those of civilians who respected SF: they did not know what he did. He was a regular SF operative, but he was also a favoured agent for military intelligence and had often been called upon to carry out assignments independent of his parent unit, the SBS.

His unusual relationship with MI5 and MI6 began in Northern Ireland many years before while working against the IRA. Like many others, he had first been noticed as an intelligence gatherer with the Northern Ireland undercover detachments. It became evident to his masters in London that his Special Forces combat skills, intelligence and aptitude for working alone made him a versatile tool that could be utilised to a far greater degree. Before long he was brought into the inner sanctum of military intelligence and exposed to the more deadly undercover front-line fight, beyond the awareness of most senior military officers and ministers, let alone the general public. Even his own bosses in the SBS did not know where he went or what he did when the request came to 'borrow' Stratton.

Initially, Stratton had embraced this new side of specialist military work. It suited him perfectly. He preferred to work alone and revelled in the dangers and high degree of autonomy. He never questioned the assignments at first even though there were occasions when his conscience warned him he was moving into a darkness in which he might one day lose his way. His first assassination had been justified as far as he was concerned, as indeed they all appeared to be at the time, but he gradually began to feel like an executioner, an image he did not like. His work was not all killing though, and he felt he could control his conscience with some practice. But Stratton was living in denial which came at a price, one he was not aware he was paying until greatly in debt. Like a cancer creeping through his body, Stratton realised something ugly was happening to him when it was almost too late. In a few short years he was no longer the young man who had enthusiastically joined the military in search of excitement and adventure. The hubris was gone. He was weathered and dented and the shine had disappeared from his eyes.

This change had not gone unnoticed by the man who gave him his assignments; the voice on the phone that beckoned him to London to receive orders for his next piece of work. Stratton had come to loathe that voice, but, like a drug addict, or someone hypnotised, he always trotted off to do his master's bidding.

Then one day the calls stopped. It took many months of silence before Stratton began to accept he had been beached, and a year had now passed since Sumners had made his last contact. He should have felt relieved, but the disturbing truth was that deep down he was not. Perhaps he had not yet learned to live without his fix, or perhaps it was something else; he didn't know. It didn't matter any more though; he would have to learn to move on. Perhaps it was the sense of failure that hurt him most, for that was the only reason he could think of why they did not call. He was no longer good enough for them.

Jobs like this one did not help. They gave him far too much time to examine himself. He watched the people on the lawn chatting politely, nibbling their cakes and sandwiches, the women in their bright hats and dresses, the men in their expensive suits, the car park beyond filled with Bentleys, limousines and other such cars. Rich trappings did not touch Stratton though. He had no interest in the lifestyles of these people who appeared dull and mundane to him.

Morgan, a large black guy with a distinct blend of African and European features, wandered over to Stratton. His father was Jamaican and his mother Antiguan, and he described his looks as Caribbean with a bit of whitey thrown in. He was in his early thirties and his broad, heavy-boned and powerful body was not designed for formal dress. He looked plainly uncomfortable in his borrowed jacket, shirt and tie, and kept sticking his fingers inside his collar in futile attempts to stretch it to stop it digging into his neck.

'Can't wait to get this bleedin' gear off,' Morgan said, pulling up the sleeves that ended at his knuckles. 'Didn't realise Foster's arms were so bleedin' long,' he said, referring to the SBS lad who had loaned him the clothing at such short notice. 'Never seen so many toffs together in one place before. 'Ow the 'ell did we get cobbled into this job?'

'I happened to walk by the RSM's office just as he was looking for someone to palm it off on. Sorry.'

'I thought the cops usually did this bollocks.'

'They do, but apparently someone in MoD especially asked for Special Forces. There's a lot of high-powered people here.'

'Lotta wankers too.'

An attractive woman who looked to be in her late teens walked from the lawn and up the steps towards

Morgan and Stratton who parted to let her through. She was wearing a pink frilly outfit with a low-cut neckline that was on the side of brazen for such an occasion.

She smiled coquettishly as she approached the two men and let her eyes linger on Stratton's just a little too long as she squeezed between them to enter the building.

'Hello,' she said.

'Hi,' Morgan said enthusiastically to the back of her head, keeping his eyes on her rear as she moved down the hallway and out of sight. 'Sweet,' he drooled. 'I'd crawl through an 'undred yards of minefield just to 'ear 'er fart down the end of a field telephone.' Morgan was known for his basic sense of humour.

'She's probably never had an offer like that before,' Stratton said dryly, his attention caught by a shrill scream from a clump of bushes; a very young girl in an expensive dress ran out pursued by an even younger boy in shorts, short-sleeve shirt and tie, wielding a water pistol.

'I don't think she was into a bit of black though. A bit of old white more like.'

'Money has mature taste,' Stratton said.

'She's probably a Lady Somethin' or Other,' Morgan went on. 'Bet she wouldn't piss on the likes of us if we were on fire . . . Mind you, that's the very type who just might, and we wouldn't need to be on fire either,' he added with a chuckle. Morgan was also known for laughing at his own sick jokes, loudly and often alone.

'Where's Smudge?' Stratton asked.

'Down at the main gate,' Morgan said. 'And Bob's the other side of the marquee. I think 'e's actually enjoying this. He likes rubbin' shoulders with this lot. Have you noticed he even starts talkin' like 'em? And the bloke's from bleedin' Luton.'

'I'm going to get a wet,' Stratton said as he headed inside.

'Grab me a sarnee would ya – cheese and pickle if they've got any. I'll go and do another round of the walls . . . I'll start climbin' the fuckers if this thing goes on much longer.'

Morgan headed off and Stratton walked down the hallway. As he reached a corner at the end, a man's voice called out from behind him.

'I say. Excuse me.'

Stratton looked back to see a young man in a white suit and red tie that appeared a little extrovert for this gathering. 'Would you get me a Buck's Fizz, old boy?' he asked with a smile.

'What?' Stratton said, looking irritable having heard what the man had asked him.

'A Buck's Fizz. Orange juice and champers, old thing.'

'I'm not a waiter.'

'You're staff, aren't you? Be a dear and run along and get me one.'

Stratton controlled an urge to say something he would regret and forced a smile. 'Sure. Anything else?'

'No, that would be lovely,' the man said with a warm smile. 'I'll be outside.'

Stratton walked around the corner and along a corridor that led to the kitchen. 'I'll shove a champagne bottle up your arse if you call me dear again,' he muttered to himself.

The pretty young woman was standing in a doorway as he passed by it. 'You'd probably lose the bottle with that one,' she said.

Stratton paused to glance at her. 'Sorry, I was talking to myself.'

She smiled as he carried on into the kitchen.

Food and drinks were everywhere; a chef was preparing sandwiches, a waitress headed out of a door into the garden carrying a tray full of strawberries and cream while another returned with dirty crockery. Stratton picked up a jug of orange juice, filled a glass and took a sip. He picked a sandwich off a tray and opened it – roast beef; there did not appear to be any cheese and pickle, but then Morgan would eat anything anyway. He wrapped it in a paper napkin and placed it in his jacket pocket. As he took another sip of his juice, the pretty girl walked in.

'Would you pour me one?' she said. 'Please,' she added, emphasising politeness.

Stratton picked up another glass, filled it and handed it to her. She took it from him and held it, looking at him, still smiling, obviously wanting to chat.

'That was Pippy, Lord Branborne's son,' she said. 'He only asked you for the drink because he fancies you.'

Stratton ignored the remark.

'He likes a bit of rough now and then,' she added.

Stratton sighed inwardly and took a sip of his drink.

'Are you not going to make him his drink?'

Stratton gave her a tired look.

'Oh, that's right. You're not a waiter ... The rumour is you're one of those roughy-toughy special soldier types. I've heard about people like you. I thought you only ran around places like the desert shooting nasty terrorists. Must be a nice change to do something like this, standing around doing nothing all day.'

'Yeah, we all jumped for joy when we heard.'

She didn't miss the sarcasm but it did not appear to bother her because she moved closer to him, head slightly lowered, eyes looking up at him.

'Do you have a gun?' she asked. 'I bet you're well armed.'

Stratton studied her eyes and all he could see was a rich tart.

She prodded his chest close to where his gun would have been holstered if he were left-handed.

'Can I see it?'

'No.'

'You probably don't need a gun though, do you? I expect you know all that kung fu business.'

Stratton was looking for a polite way out of this conversation and the kitchen. She was cute but not enough to have to listen to her crap.

'What would you do if a dozen terrorists came over the wall right now and attacked us?' she went on, moving closer still, her ardour obvious. Stratton was uncomfortable being hit on so aggressively at a professional venue and unsure quite how to handle it in a polite manner. The watchword for jobs such as this was diplomacy in all matters.

'I'd hide in the cellar.'

64

'Really? I know where that is if you'd like me to show you.'

The waitress behind the woman glanced at Stratton and rolled her eyes before leaving with a tray of sandwiches.

'Isabelle,' a man called out from inside the house as footsteps came down the corridor. She frowned at the interruption. Two smartly dressed men came into the kitchen. Stratton noticed the tiny army badges both had pinned to their lapels. He couldn't tell which regiment they indicated but considering the calibre of people at the function, the cut of their suits and their bearing, they were not only officers – a non-commissioned officer had a snowball's chance in hell of being invited to a gig like this unless he was titled.

'Ah, there you are,' the taller one said on seeing the girl, then paused as his eyes fell on Stratton who was far too close to her to be considered polite. His smile was replaced by the kind of cold expression a male displays on seeing another coveting his female property. 'We're going into London for lunch,' he continued, talking to her but eyeing Stratton warily. 'Where's your coat?'

She rolled her eyes for only Stratton to see before turning to face her boyfriend. 'Do we have to go now? I'm enjoying myself.'

'It's a bit of a bore, darling, and we've shown our faces,' he said. 'What are you doing in here anyway? Annoying the staff?'

'This nice man was telling me how he is prepared to lay down his life to protect us all if terrorists should come over the walls in their hundreds. I'd introduce him to you but he won't tell me his name – the strong secretive type, don't you know?'

Stratton finished his drink and put the glass down. 'Nice talking to you,' he said as he turned to leave.

'Yes, why don't you run along,' the boyfriend said with an attitude.

Stratton stopped and looked back at the man whose tone he found offensive. The other man was also staring at Stratton in support of his friend, like a pair of elegant wolves.

'You're not here to hang around the kitchen chatting up ladies,' the friend added.

Both men saw a flicker of danger behind Stratton's grey eyes, but they were too well bred to heed any warning from a mere ranker.

'I'm Captain Brigstock, Life Guards, and this is Captain Boyston. I know you're not an officer so why don't you consider it an order. Off you go,' he said, and topped it off with a chin-jutting, superior smirk.

The girl put her arm through her captain's, switching allegiance like the fickle wind. 'Ooh, you do excite me when you get bossy, Charlie.'

Stratton sighed, turned about and continued to the door. They were not worth the effort.

'I don't know why we have to have these mindless thugs as security,' Brigstock said to his friends but intentionally loud enough for Stratton to hear.

Stratton paused in the doorway without looking back. The officers were beginning to test his self control. He raised his eyes to the skies as if looking for divine help and stepped outside. As he walked away laughter came from the kitchen.

He folded them from his mind and paused on the green to survey the area wondering how much longer this party was going to go on for.

'Stratton? I say. Is that you?' a man called out.

Stratton saw a stout, grey-haired gentleman in his sixties the other side of the green heading towards him with his hands in his jacket pockets, a classic affectation of the upper class that the man wore comfortably.

The woman and her two young officers walked out of the kitchen. 'Isn't that your uncle?' Boyston asked Brigstock.

'Yes,' Brigstock said, suddenly fluffing up and putting on a broad smile as he waved. 'Hello, Uncle.'

The old man noticed him as he approached and looked immediately disjointed on recognising his nephew. 'Oh, Brigstock. How you doing, lad?' he said blandly.

'Fine, sir,' Brigstock beamed while Boyston, also smiling broadly, took a large step forward to stand beside his friend. The old man was obviously very important and it wasn't what you knew but who you, or your closest friends, were related to. 'This is my friend—'

'Excuse me a moment, would you?' the old man interrupted easily. 'On my way to see an old friend.' He breezed past them and headed for Stratton.

'I thought it was you,' he said to Stratton as he stopped in front of him.

'Hello, Ambassador,' Stratton said, genuinely pleased to see the man, and they shook hands warmly. He was the former British ambassador to Algiers.

Three years before, Stratton turned up at the embassy on his own to propose an evacuation plan for the staff during an uprising in the country by Islamic fundamentalists that threatened their safety. An SAS contingent had arrived the day before and was pushing a proposal to cut down all the trees in the embassy grounds so that helicopters could land and evacuate everyone to the airport where a military transport aircraft would take them out of the country. But since the embassy was near the sea, Stratton had been sent from the SBS headquarters with an alternative plan. His idea was to take a short drive to the beach under heavy guard where fast attack boats could ferry the staff to a waiting Royal Navy frigate.

The ambassador's wife happened to love the trees in the garden and was horrified at the thought of seeing them cut down but had conceded them as an unavoidable price one had to pay for the safety of the embassy staff. When she heard Stratton's proposal she nudged the ambassador and whispered in his ear that she would divorce him if he didn't go with the boat idea. The ambassador liked the waterborne option anyway since he happened to be an ex-Navy man and fancied stepping aboard a war ship once again after so many years. However, the four SAS men were officers and Stratton was only an SBS colour sergeant; diplomacy was required so as not to ruffle SAS feathers. As the ambassador fumbled through the pros and cons, racking his brains for a justifiable way out of the air option, Stratton had interrupted politely, informing them that recently the Algerians had acquired some Stingers – hand-held ground-to-air missiles – and that using aircraft to evacuate the area might not be a wise option.

The SAS officers knew Stratton had outmanoeuvred them, and the ambassador was pleased with Stratton's timely advice which gave him the room to close the matter.

'How have you been?' the ambassador asked Stratton, genuinely interested. He had never been impressed with rank alone and was far more inclined towards people of substance. Brigstock and Boyston were within earshot and horrified that the security man had a higher priority than them.

'Fine, sir,' Stratton said shaking his hand. He liked the old man who had filed a most complimentary report on his return to England about the SBS's handling of the embassy situation.

'You must say hello to Angela. She's over there and would love to see you. You know she often mentions that time in the embassy, and not only her trees that you saved. You outflanked the SAS in one other area. You were the only military chap thoughtful enough to bring some English newspapers and tea.' He laughed heartily bringing a broad grin to Stratton's face. 'So what are you doing here? Must be god-awful boring for the likes of you. What idiot put people of your calibre on duty at a garden party?'

'We have to take the rough with the smooth, sir.'

'Yes, I suppose so.'

The ambassador caught his nephew hovering over his shoulder and reluctantly acknowledged his presence. 'Brigstock. You met Stratton?' The old man didn't want to share Stratton with his nephew but these parties were all about meeting people of influence.

''Em, not exactly sir,' Brigstock stammered.

'Special Boat Service. One of the top operatives in the country, and that's not just my opinion.'

Stratton ignored the two men who started to offer their hands but changed their minds when they realised they would not be taken. Brigstock's girl-friend smiled at Stratton as if she had always been on his side.

Stratton's phone vibrated in his pocket. 'Excuse me a moment, sir,' he said as he took it out, checked the screen, pushed a button and put it to his ear. He heard a loud noise that sounded like interference. 'Scouse. That you?' he said loudly, trying to compensate for the noise.

'Stratton,' a voice shouted.

'You in a chopper?' Stratton asked.

'Yes. Where are you?'

'Lord Balmore's estate. We're covering a garden party.'

'I know that. I'm towards your location. This isn't a social call.'

Stratton then heard the throb of a helicopter and looked to the skies. It sounded like it was coming from the south but a wood bordering that side of the estate concealed anything flying low from view.

'Get your arse into the open,' Scouse shouted. 'We're coming to pick you up.'

'What's going on?'

'Something big.'

The helicopter suddenly roared out from the treetops, right over the lawn, putting an abrupt halt to every conversation, and banked low over the estate. It was an SBS Super Lynx, a nine-seat jet assault helicopter.

'Get yourself a marker,' Scouse said.

'I'm on it,' Stratton said, then to the ambassador. 'Gotta go, sir.'

'Something come up?'

'Looks like it,' Stratton said.

'That's more like it, eh?'

Stratton scanned around for something bright and saw it draped over the shoulders of Brigstock's girl-friend.

'May I?' he said to her as he took her pink jacket.

'Oh. Yes . . . um . . .'

Then Stratton was off, jogging to a clear part of the lawn.

'Look after yourself,' the ambassador called out to him.

The man in the white suit stepped out of the building as Stratton went past. 'I say. Where's my Buck's Fizz?' he said, then noticed the circling heli-copter. 'Oh, my word.'

Stratton held the phone to his ear as he swung the pink coat around his head. 'Scouse, I'm waving pink.'

'Seen,' Scouse replied, and the Lynx continued its spiral back to the lawn. It headed directly for Stratton rapidly losing height and then a few metres from him tipped its nose up to halt its forward movement, levelled out and dropped rapidly on to its trolley wheels as Stratton ran towards it. The marquee took a pounding from the rotors, as did the nearby guests, tables and ladies' hats, which went flying.

The side door was already open and Stratton jumped in. The Lynx rose quickly, nose dipped dramatically, and accelerated forward and up, engines screaming and the blades carving hungrily into the air as it gained height. The pink jacket came flying out of the door and landed not far from the two officers. Brigstock's girlfriend ran to pick it up and then waved farewell with it as the Lynx thundered over the house and was out of sight and sound in seconds.

Morgan and Smudge came running on to the lawn amid the whirling debris in time to see the helicopter go.

'Lucky bastard,' Morgan said looking thoroughly pissed off.

Scouse slid the door shut, closing out the wind and some of the noise, and Stratton regarded the five SBS operatives who shared the cab behind the cockpit. They were all dressed in black assault clothing, with bulging chest harnesses filled with various pieces of equipment and ordnance, leather gloves, helmets on laps, throat mics, MPK5 sub-machine guns and P226 semi-automatic pistols strapped to their thighs. Scouse, sat beside Stratton, slid a heavy-duty black holdall along the floor and dumped it on top of a large coil of heavy thick rope at Stratton's feet, one end of which was shackled to a strong point in the ceiling near Stratton's door.

'Here's your kit,' Scouse shouted over the shrill of the engines.

Stratton took his jacket off and started pulling at his tie. 'What is it?' he asked.

'Possible hijacked supertanker. Sometime before dawn. It's way off course and doesn't respond to any radio calls. The coastguard's alongside but it's too high for them to climb on deck. They have a chopper in the area but they've been told not to board her. The bad news is it's heading for the coast at top speed, towards the Torquay area, and it's full to the gunwales with oil.'

'How long've we got?'

'It's gonna be tight. By the time we get there I reckon we'll have about fifteen, twenty minutes to take it.'

'Anything on the bad guys?' Stratton asked as he pulled off his shoes and trousers and dug his one-piece fire-retardant assault suit out of the bag.

'Helicopter reports no sign of life on deck and the bridge looks empty.'

'Where's it from?'

'It's an Aralco oil company boat. One of their big ones. Last stop was Sidi Kerir oil terminal off the coast of Egypt in the Med where it took on its load. It was on its way to Rotterdam. Last known contact was with its headquarters in Dubai one a.m. this morning.'

'What's the plan?'

'Two under-slung VSVs are on their way by Chinook. We'll take the bridge as the lads hit the main deck. A bunch of bio-chem and nuclear special-ists are on their way.'

'Who's in the VSVs?'

'Jacko's got Alpha in VSV one, Stevens has Echo in two. And you've got us.'

Stratton looked at the other faces: Fred, Nick, Tip and Foster. 'All right, lads?' he asked. They gave him a thumbs up. Stratton didn't know them very well though he had worked with Tip a couple of times. Because Stratton had spent so much time away from the squadrons he hadn't rotated through the various teams as much as other seniors such as Scouse. Now that he had been back almost a year he was getting to know most of the guys again and meeting the new ones. Everyone knew him, of course, even the new operatives who had just joined. It was generally considered, although it was not a subject particularly discussed, that Stratton was the SBS's top operative, and often other operatives' first choice of team commander if an operation was going down. That was influenced by the fact that Stratton was often the operations room's first choice for the more difficult tasks. Senior officers acknowledged he had the gift of inspiring those he worked with.

'Hey, Stratton,' Foster said, leaning towards him. 'Morgan 'asn't fucked up my jacket by any chance?'

'Why'd you lend it to 'im if you're so worried?' Tip asked.

'Either 'e went with the jacket or I did,' Foster stated.

'He said something about trimming the sleeves a bit,' Stratton said poker faced.

Foster studied Stratton, wondering if this was a bite, but he didn't know him well enough to call him on it.

'Did that to a pair of trousers I lent him,' Tip added.

Foster looked at Tip, still unsure, and sat back to mull over the future of his jacket.

Stratton struggled to pull the suit on over his torso, pushed his arms into the sleeves and zipped up the front to his throat. He strapped up his boots, pulled on his harness, sorted out his weapons, put his helmet on his lap and clipped his throat mic around his neck. The final piece of clothing was a pair of leather gloves, which he pulled on tightly, sealing the Velcro around his wrists. He was ready.

He leaned forward to zip his civvies inside the bag when he thought of something. Remembering Scouse's great appetite he took the sandwich out of his jacket pocket and offered it to him. Scouse took it, looked inside and stuffed the entire thing in his mouth.

'Thanks,' he said, munching it. The others looked at him. 'What?' Scouse said with an innocent expression, still chewing, spitting a bit of bread out as he spoke. 'It was only one bite anyway.'

The Lynx flew at maximum speed 5,000 feet above the countryside and it was not long before the coast was in sight. They passed over Exeter and followed the River Exe to the sea.

'CTC,' Scouse said, indicating the Commando Training Centre on their left, the camp at Lympstone where they had all joined the Royal Marines as recruits, some much longer ago than others.

Stratton looked down on the huge complex and picked out the Tarzan course, weapon training huts and the route up to Woodbury Common and the endurance course. Memories of life as a young, innocent recruit scrolled through his mind, a time when he could never have even begun to guess what the future held for him. He had lived from day to day through the six months of arduous training while the vestiges of civilian idiosyncrasy were gradually stripped from him to be replaced with those of a soldier. Then as soon as it was over and he had earned the title Royal Marine, it was not enough. He wanted more intensity, tougher goals and a smaller, more exclusive group, and so he applied to join the SBS. As he looked out of the window he thought about his life since then and what he had achieved. He could think of nothing now that seemed worthy though some had at the time. He often doubted his chosen career. As he got older he began to believe that soldiers throughout history had never really achieved much. If the definition was true that the quality of a war was judged by the resulting peace then he had failed in everything. The wars he had been involved in were in the same old places against the same old enemy and fighting for the same old thing: power and control, and the soldiers fuelled the war machines.

Stratton felt a tap on his shoulder and looked away from the window to see it was the co-pilot. They were moving beyond the estuary and he was indicating ahead. Stratton took a headset off the panel beside him and put it over his ears.

'There it is,' the co-pilot said, pointing.

Stratton looked below the horizon to see a tiny

cluster of ships still quite far out to sea. The tanker was easiest to make out and the other specks were no doubt the coastguard and some police boats.

Scouse was listening on his SBS network radio and nudged Stratton. 'Team Bravo and Charlie are in the water and closing on the tanker. They're waiting for us.'

'I want the other boats out of the way,' Stratton said.

'They're getting the order now,' Scouse said.

There was a possibility of an explosive device on board and there was no longer a need for the boats to be there anyway. The thought of a greater threat such as an atom or even a dirty bomb had occurred to most but that was not worth talking about at this stage. If there was a serious device they wouldn't know anything about it a second after it went off.

Stratton leaned forward to get a look at the pilot but didn't recognise him. 'Who's the pilot?' he asked Scouse. The pilot and co-pilot could only hear him if he spoke through the intercom headset.

'Ah. One small problem,' Scouse said. 'He joined the branch a couple of weeks ago and he was the only pilot available at five minutes' notice.'

'You're kidding me.'

'He's obviously good or he wouldn't be here.'

'Has he done an eagle feast before?'

'One, and not at max speed.'

'I wouldn't describe that as a *small* problem, Scouse.'

An eagle feast was part of a simultaneous two-pronged assault on a ship at sea: one from the water, the other from the air. To approach from the air unnoticed a craft had to be high, but then to take part in the assault it had to cover the distance down to the boat in the fastest possible time. The best way the Special Forces naval pilots had come up with was simply to take the wind out of the rotors and let the helicopter drop like a stone. The hard part was controlling the drop and getting the wind back into the rotors at the end of it.

Stratton put his cabin headset back on and pushed the mic in front of his mouth. 'Pilot? What's your name?'

The pilot glanced back for a second. He looked very young. 'Robert,' he said into his own mic. He was an officer but had been around long enough to know it was first-name terms among all ranks in the SBS working at the sharp end, including attached ranks such as he was.

'Good to meet you, Robert. I'm Stratton. Is that right you've only done one eagle feast before now?'

'Yes, a week ago,' he said, doing his best to sound confident, but Stratton was not so sure.

'You happy with the procedure?'

The pilot paused a moment and Stratton thought he caught a slight change in his expression.

'Well . . . to be honest, not really,' he said. 'Wish I'd had the chance to practise a couple more before my first live one.'

Stratton glanced at Scouse who was listening through another headset and wearing a concerned expression, which was more put on than genuine – cavalier humour was the norm in the SBS, especially when tension was mounting. But there was something to be worried about since there was not any room for error on the manoeuvre.

'Too late to worry about that now,' Stratton said to the pilot.

'Rubbish,' Scouse chimed in. 'There's plenty of time to shit yourself.'

'They're waiting on us,' Stratton continued. 'Let's get to the drop height.' Then aside to Scouse: 'He can only get it wrong once.'

'True enough,' Scouse said.

The pilot eased up the blade pitch control and the Lynx started to climb.

'How long to eighteen thousand feet?' Stratton asked him.

The pilot glanced quickly over at Stratton, looking more worried. 'You mean twelve thousand feet.'

'I like to come in from eighteen. Hardly any chance of being seen or heard at that height. How long?' Stratton asked again.

The pilot glanced at his co-pilot who shrugged helplessly. 'Em . . . three minutes,' the pilot said awkwardly, his mind starting to race.

'What's six thousand feet between friends,' Stratton said to Scouse. 'Where are the boats?'

'A mile in rear of the tanker,' Scouse said.

'Tell them to start their run now.'

Scouse relayed the order as the Lynx shuddered, straining to climb as fast as it could.

A mile behind the tanker the pair of 22-metre-long grey-and-black VSVs cruised gracefully through the water at quarter speed. They were unusual boats, shaped like a cross between a slim wedge of cheese and the nose of a Concorde supersonic jet, and virtually undetectable by radar due to their stealth construction. The boats were designed to cut through the waves not ride over them like every other high-performance speedboat, and in rough conditions they could pierce a swell and disappear beneath the surface for a short period of time. The boats were fully enclosed with a cabin capacity of twenty-six operatives packed tightly together and an optional pair of twin 50-cal. machine guns in the bows. Their maximum speed was confidential and far in excess of the maker's advertised 60 knots.

The coxswains pushed their throttles forward and the massive twin 2,000hp diesel engines roared deeply as the boats accelerated powerfully through the water. The forty operatives, twenty in each boat, were dressed identically to Stratton's team but with added specialised equipment for getting on board a large ship. The VSVs cruised a few metres apart and within half a minute were at near maximum speed and closing on the tanker like surface torpedoes.

The Lynx shuddered and levelled out. 'Eighteen thousand feet,' the pilot said, and sounding none too confident about it.

'We right behind the tanker's stern?' Stratton asked.

'It's directly below us,' the co-pilot said, making some checks on his instrument panel.

'Hold until I give the word.'

'Roger that,' came the co-pilot's reply, glancing at his nervous partner as inexperienced as he was.

The pilot released the controls one hand at a time to clench and unclench his hands and get the blood flowing through them. His anxiety was growing. Under normal circumstances, the training for this procedure was taken in gradual steps to allow the pilot to get the feel for it, a few hundred feet first before working up to a couple of thousand, the speed building each time. He had put troops down on ships many times in the past but never from an eagle feast. When they called him in the mess during breakfast that morning, told him about the operation and asked if he could do it, he said he could without hesitation. His response had been partly macho but mostly because he didn't want to pass on the opportunity of a lifetime to do a live operational ship attack with the SBS. There were more pilots than there were opportunities to take part in a job like this one and it would be a big chalk up on his record. But now, hovering at eighteen thousand feet, the tanker looking quite small far below, he was having doubts and questioning his gung-ho eagerness. It was not just his life at stake, there were seven more in his hands. Here he was getting ready to do what until a few years ago only a handful of highly experienced pilots had attempted. Only the best were allowed to even try. He was one of the best, but if he screwed this up, well, he would not be around to get chastised for it, that was for sure. It was too late to change his mind now. He would rather crash the helicopter than live with the life-long disgrace of backing out of it.

'Two hundred metres,' Scouse relayed from the VSVs. 'One hundred . . . Slowing . . . Alongside.'

The two VSVs approached directly behind the stern of the tanker and then broke swiftly to come along either side. Meanwhile in the back of the boats, the hook-men, two in each, were already on their feet and in harnesses designed so they could stand and hold the skyward-pointing launchers on their shoulders without falling over, even in rough conditions. When the coxswains reached a point alongside the tanker just behind the superstructure and inches from the wall of steel, they dropped the power off quickly then hit reverse thrust for a few seconds to hold their position and match the ship's speed. Without a word of command the hook-men fired their air guns and four grapnels flew high into the air, trailing lines to land on the deck. Operatives quickly pulled the lines back until the grapnels caught hold. This was where a little luck was required since the hooks were out of sight. They had to grab something solid. If the hook did not it could spring loose and once the line had the climber's weight on it, drop him. Often the hook did come loose, flew back until it snagged something else such as the rails, and dropped the climber into the water so he had to carry on climbing from there. A much worse scenario was if the hook flew over the rails and out to sea. The climber would fall into the water and there was a danger of him going under and being sucked through the props. Four grapnels meant the odds were almost certain a hold would be taken somewhere, and one, although not ideal, was all they needed at a push.

'Go!' the operatives pulling the lines shouted as they felt the hooks bite hold.

The climbers attached their climbing devices, activated them and shot out of the boat. The secret to this manoeuvre was to keep facing the ship and run up the side. Each climber carried three lightweight caving ladders rolled up and clipped to his hips. They stopped just short of the lip of the deck, keeping out of view in case they came under attack, unclipped the first ladder, hooked it to the lip, and let it unravel down to the boat. They repeated the procedure with the other two ladders then remained where they were with their weapons aimed up at the rails while operatives started to climb from below. When the first three reached the deck they in turn hooked two more ladders on to the lip and let them unroll, and then this first wave of four men climbed over the rail on to the deck to secure a bridgehead. In less then two minutes from first hook-on, both teams were aboard. They divided up and headed towards their designated targets.

'They're on!' shouted Scouse.

'Go!' Stratton said to the pilot who took a breath, dropped the pitch of the blades, removing all the lift, and nosed the craft forward. The Lynx quickly picked up speed and plummeted like a bird of prey going for a kill. Everyone experienced the drop in the pit of their stomach as the blood rushed to their head causing momentary dizziness. It began like the scariest fairground ride in the world, but the real fun part was to come.

After two thousand feet the Lynx was near vertical and Stratton could see the bows of the tanker through the windshield. The craft started to shudder as it reached terminal velocity. Stratton, Scouse and Tip beside him were held facing forward in their seats by their seatbelts while the other three could only sit back and look at them. The pilot increased his grip on the controls as they began to shake more violently, his eyes glued to the altimeter. Fourteen thousand feet. It was not the ideal time to ask himself the question, but when dropping from twelve thousand feet he knew he needed to start pulling out of the dive at two and a half. The question was, when dropping from eighteen thousand, did he have to pull out sooner? Surely not, he thought. Terminal velocity was terminal velocity no matter what height you started from. Then the Lynx gave a violent jolt with a force the pilot had never experienced before. Eight thousand feet. There was another equally violent shake as if a bus had rammed into their rear. He wondered if the rotors were buckling. Perhaps his nose was too far down. He had to maintain a steep angle, but not completely vertical. He had to keep air under the rotors to force them away from the helicopter's body. If he went too steep and air got on top of the blades, it could force them down where they would chop a piece off the helicopter as they turned. Another bang. If any part of the blade broke away it wouldn't function properly and they'd never pull out of the dive.

'Now remember, we want the top floor, not the basement,' came Stratton's voice over the pilot's earphones. The pilot did not find the comment reassuring. The controls shook in his hands. His eyes flicked from the instruments panel to the window for a second and saw it was filled with the enormous tanker, laid out in front of him like a runway, except he wasn't approaching like a plane but in a flat dive headed straight for the poop deck. He then started to experience a most frightening phenomenon, not uncommon in situations like this, known as ground rush. His eyes started picking up minute details of the ship giving him the horrifying impression of being only yards away. Inexperienced free-fallers sometimes had similar illusions which could cause panic and premature pulling of ripcords. For a few seconds the pilot believed they were about to slam into the deck like a kamikaze aircraft. He almost panicked and was about to pull back when he forced his eyes to find the altimeter. Three thousand feet. He still had five hundred feet to go. He forced himself to hang on for two more seconds. Two thousand and five and he pulled up the pitch lever with one arm while at the same time dragging the stick back with the other. The craft did not respond immediately and he pulled the controls as hard as he could as if trying to rip them out of the floor. The Lynx shook so violently it felt like it was going to fall apart. Then suddenly, the nose began to lift. Everyone sunk into their seats, compressed by the enormous G-force exerted upon them. The pilot no longer used the instruments to fly and stared at the superstructure. It was in full view and they were heading straight towards it. He held the controls back with all his strength and then heard a voice saying: 'Come on. Come on . . .' It was his.

There was one last horrendous shudder and the

superstructure disappeared as the nose came up and there was nothing but blue sky in front of them. He'd done it – but it wasn't over yet. Due to his inexperience he forgot to relax his pull quickly enough and the nose came up too far. He jammed it forward but overcompensated and for a moment the Lynx did a rodeo dip and pitch. He quickly brought it under control, levelled out and looked out of his window. The port side of the bridge was forty feet below and to the side, exactly where he needed it to be. It was only then he realised he had been holding his breath for God only knew how long and exhaled heavily as sweat streamed down his face.

Stratton snapped his seatbelt away, slid his door open and pushed the heavy rope out. He watched it cascade to the bridge deck which extended from the port-side bridge door all the way across the width of the ship. Before the end of the rope hit the deck Stratton was out and sliding down it, closely followed by Scouse. The team left the Lynx so quickly the operative above Scouse was almost touching Scouse's hands with his feet.

Stratton hit the deck and moved swiftly away to avoid being landed on by Scouse who was not a small man. He ran to the bridge door with his MPK on aim and looked inside. The bridge was virtually surrounded in glass and it was plain to see there was no one home. Scouse, Nick and Tip joined him while Fred and Foster headed down the outside steps to the deck below.

Meanwhile, on the main deck far below the bridge, teams were spilling into the engine room, auxiliary generating room and steering locker to gain control of the ship, while others headed into the superstructure and fanned out to clear every room on each deck. Two pairs sprinted along either side of the length of the deck to clear the workshops and then headed on to the bosun's locker. All the while they were checking for booby traps, and, of course, the enemy. But as yet not a shot had been fired. The radios buzzed with commands and locations as they were cleared but there was no reference to a contact.

Stratton pulled a small charge from a pocket of his chest harness and stuck it on the glass on the door while Scouse, Tip and Nick moved to the side. Stratton pushed himself flat against the bulkhead just as it exploded with a sharp boom. A second later he stepped through the jagged hole where the window used to be and the others followed him inside.

They fanned out, checking every corner including cupboards and under the map table, but it was empty of life. Stratton went to the internal door, which was slightly ajar, and stepped through. He pushed open the door to the small radio shack to find a man lying face down at his desk, a large pool of dried blood around his head and on the floor. Stratton inspected him to find the man's throat had been sliced open.

A voice came over the radio. 'Alpha three in the engine room. I've found nine of the crew. All dead. Not a pretty sight.'

'Echo one in the control room. Seven dead crew here.'

'Alpha four, sickbay. Five dead.'

'Echo one. Captain's quarters. I've got three dead. Looks like one of 'em's the old man.'

'Stratton,' Scouse said. 'We've got a slightly bigger problem right this moment.' He was staring out of the front plate-glass windows. The others moved to have a look.

'Shit!' said Tip. They all had similar comments on their minds.

Torquay was not much more than a mile or two away and they were heading towards the bay at full speed.

'Any ideas anyone?' Scouse asked.

Stratton's mind was racing.

Scouse headed for the controls. 'Shut down the engines.'

'No. Wait,' Stratton said, putting out an arm to stop him.

'For what? We'll be halfway into the town in a couple of minutes.'

'These things take a few miles to stop in a straight line fully loaded, and we don't have that far.'

'Let's at least slow the bleeding thing down. Put it in reverse.'

'The result won't be much different.'

'So let's just stand here and ride it in,' Scouse said sarcastically, his tension rising.

'A tanker captain once told me that in theory you can stop one of these in less than half a mile if you swing it hard over,' Stratton said.

'What?'

'He'd never actually tried it with a full load but I think a new ship does a fast turn as part of its sea trials.'

'You *think*?'

'We're gonna find out, Scouse me old friend,' Stratton said as he pulled his weapon sling over his head, placed the gun down on the map table and took hold of the wheel.

'Maybe there's a reason no one's tried it full of oil. What if the bleeding thing tips over?' Scouse asked.

'Our options?' Stratton asked.

'Torquay'll be fucked, literally,' Tip said.

'We haven't signed for the boat,' Stratton said. 'Something to tell your grandchildren if nothing else.'

Scouse looked between them. The others' expressions suggested they were all siding with Stratton's idea.

'Bollocks,' Scouse said. 'Let's do it then.'

Stratton took a moment to check the instruments to see if there was something obvious he had overlooked. He couldn't think of anything. 'Better warn the others,' he said as he placed his hands on the wheel and took a firm grip, like a trapeze artist about to attempt a dangerous feat.

'All stations, this is Charlie One,' Scouse said into his throat mic. 'Get your arses out of the ship and on deck. I say again, get out of the ship and on deck. Stratton's about to try a handbrake turn and you might wanna be where you can get overboard if it doesn't work. I say again, get out on deck and make ready to go overboard. VSV one and two, back off now.'

'Here we go,' Stratton said as he spun the wheel to the left, all the way around until it could go no further and held it there.

The ship immediately started to turn. Scouse, Tip and Nick stood looking out of the front window in expectation. One way or another, something exceptional was going to happen.

'I wouldn't 'ave missed this op for the world,' Nick said. Scouse and Tip nodded in agreement.

As the massive ship started to turn, it gradually began to tilt over to the right. 'Like I told you,' Scouse said, spreading his feet to keep balance. 'It's gonna roll like a canoe!'

They all grabbed hold of something as the floor began to slope.

'You sure about this, Stratton?' Scouse asked as the ship leaned further over.

'Course I'm not bloody sure. How many times do you think I've done this?'

In the engine room and steerage locker, operatives were scurrying up stairs, along gangways and through doors, spewing out of the various exits and to the side, all eyes on the town not far away and speculating the outcome.

A dozen steel pipes, several metres long and big enough to crawl through, which were stacked in the centre of the main deck, snapped their bindings and rolled with a chiming clatter down the deck to burst through the rails and spill into the sea.

'She's going over,' Scouse said in a raised voice as the boat continued to lean and started creaking eerily.

But as it took the tight turn it appeared to reach its maximum pitch and hold. Stratton kept the wheel hard over, his eyes never leaving the coastline.

'She's holding,' Scouse murmured, not sure if he was correct. 'She's holding,' he said again, this time a little more certain. 'Come on, baby. Turn you big, fat bitch.'

The end of the tanker moved away from the town and along the coastline like the second hand of a clock.

'Christ! She's gonna clear it,' Scouse said, excitement creeping into his voice. 'She's gonna clear!'

Then suddenly the tanker began to jolt violently as a terrible deep creaking came from below, as if the ship were moaning in pain. The wheel shuddered in Stratton's hands and the massive jerking motion worsened. Then as the ship started to lurch to one side it was suddenly obvious.

'We're running aground!' Stratton shouted.

'She's gonna rip open!' Scouse said.

Then as if enormous brakes had been brutally applied, the boat jolted to a stop and those on deck not holding on fell forward.

The tanker had ground to a halt broadside to the town which was little more than a mile away. The propellers continued to turn as the engine hummed sending vibrations throughout the ship, but it was stuck fast.

Tip stepped through the door on to the bridge deck and walked to the rails. 'Holy cow,' he shouted. 'Take a look at this.'

'She's broken in half,' Scouse called out, guessing the worst as he followed Nick outside.

'Bloody hell,' Nick exclaimed as he got to the side.

'Stratton!' Tip shouted.

Stratton grabbed his weapon, hurried on to the wing, and even his jaw dropped when he saw it.

The huge ship, 330 metres long with 22 metres of its sheer sides below the water, had been slipping its vast tonnage sideways against the ocean as it turned. This was effectively how the tanker had reduced its speed so quickly, by transferring its forward cutting energy to its long broadside where it was slowed by millions of tons of water. But energy doesn't disappear, it just turns into something else; in this case motion, in the shape of a very, very large body of water. The tanker had become an enormous wave-making machine.

'It's a bleedin' tidal wave,' Scouse said.

The wave was the entire length of the tanker and spreading, six or seven metres high, and heading directly for the Torquay coastline.

'Two boats,' Tip shouted.

Stratton pulled a pair of binoculars from a pouch and looked through them. 'Fishing boat . . . the other looks like a tour boat.'

'They're fucked,' Scouse said.

Stratton pushed away from the rails and ran as fast as he could down the exterior staircase as he talked into his throat mic. All heard his communication as he hit 'C' deck and ran around to the next stairway.

'Zulu one. Come alongside now! And I mean now!'

Scouse and the others followed, not knowing what Stratton was planning.

Stratton hit the main deck and ran to the rails where other operatives stood watching the wave. He looked over the side to see one of the VSVs coming around the stern. Stratton climbed over the rail and, without a pause, continued over the side, dropping feet first. Scouse arrived in time to see him hit the water. The VSV slowed as it approached and Scouse suddenly realised what Stratton had in mind.

'Stay here,' Scouse said to the others then sprang over the rails and plummeted to the sea.

Scouse hit the water a couple of metres from Stratton and when he surfaced the VSV was alongside. The crewman, Jab, a young corporal SBS operative, grabbed Stratton's arm and helped him aboard.

Stratton pushed aside the heavy rubber flap that covered the entrance to the cabin and went inside.

'Jock?' he shouted, recognising the coxswain at the controls.

'What's up, Stratton?'

'Other side of that wave are people in boats. We're gonna get them.'

Jock was an experienced SBS sergeant and immediately understood, although he blew a soft whistle to himself at the audacity of such an attempt. He kept his thoughts to himself for the moment, aware that time was of the essence, and checked to see Scouse was on board as he grabbed the throttles.

'Hold on,' Jock shouted in his West Coast Scottish brogue that twenty years in the SBS had hardly softened, and he pushed the throttles forward, easing the engines to half power as he turned the boat away from the side of the tanker.

Scouse and Jab entered the small cockpit, gripping the roof support bars to hold themselves against the powerful acceleration. The inside was like any military vehicle: basic, zero comforts, all struts and hard surfaces and jammed with communications, radar equipment and other technology. It was solid and confined.

The wave was visible through the narrow cockpit windows. Even though it was moving relatively slowly, it was only several hundred yards away.

'Round the end or through it?' Stratton asked.

'The sides. I ain't tried surfing this bitch yet and today ain't the day for it,' Jock shouted above the engines as he increased power. 'Where's the boats?'

'Straight out from the tanker's side. Less than a mile.'

'You reckon we'll make it in time, do you?'

'No idea. You?'

'Doubt it,' he said, glancing at Stratton for a second. 'Trying to make me as mad as you?'

'We're all bonkers in this business, Jock.'

'Aye, true enough.'

The VSV roared like a fighter jet on the water as the engines increased in power, the two tachometer needles pushing towards the red zone. The sheer thrust could be felt in the confined metal space, the vibrations echoing along every surface.

The end of the wave was soon visible, tapering off to flat water. Jock suddenly decided not to wait until they reached it and turned the boat sharply to face the back of the wave. It leaned over like a Formula One racing bike and straightened out as it cut into the slope at a slight angle. It pierced the hump, partly submersing for a second, and dropped down the other side before levelling out on the flat.

All four men glanced back at the mountain of sea that towered behind them, all thinking the same thing. If they carried on they would soon be trapped between the wall of water and the coast and there was going to be only one way out of it. Stratton scanned ahead for the boats and quickly saw them in the calmer waters of the bay. The fishing boat was heading towards the mouth of the walled harbour, its three-man crew oblivious to the encroaching danger. The tour boat was further away from the wave and looked as if it was carrying a dozen people or more.

'What do you want to do?' Jock asked as he aimed for the nearest boat.

'We won't have time to empty both,' Stratton said.

'Be lucky if we empty any,' Jock murmured.

'Give the fishing boat a heads up and go for the other one.'

Jock sounded his klaxon as he started to turn away from the fishing boat.

The fishing boat's captain stepped out of his small booth to investigate the horn and his mouth dropped open when he saw the wave less than half a mile away. His two crewmen, folding nets on the deck, also looked up and froze in horror. The captain quickly spun one-eighty degrees to find the entrance to the walled harbour several hundred metres away, his mind racing to calculate if he could make it in time. The harbour was made up of two stone sea walls that curved out from the land and overlapped where they met out to sea with a gap between them wide enough for a large boat to pass through. Inside was a calm harbour housing hundreds of yachts.

He ran back inside his booth and pushed the throttle fully home. The increase in power was barely discernable. Keeping a hand on the wheel, he stepped out of the booth to take another look back at the wave as his mates dropped what they were doing to join him.

'My God,' he murmured.

The tour boat was also heading for the harbour but it was much further away than the fishing boat and would never make it in time.

A woman passenger taking photographs of the horizon was the first to notice the wave through her lens. She put the camera down, hoping it wasn't what she thought it was.

'Ken. What do you think that is?' she said to her husband.

Within seconds the twelve other passengers were on their feet staring at it.

'It's a tidal wave!' one of them shouted in horror, and panic immediately swept through the boat.

The pilot glanced over his shoulder at the sound of the klaxon and blanched. He quickly gauged the distance to the harbour mouth and, his engines already at full power, knew they would not make it.

Stratton looked at the fishing boat as they moved away from it. If it had a chance, it was a slim one. The VSV could get to the tour boat before the wave. The question was could they unload it in time?

He was prepared to leave some people behind if he had to.

Jock looked back at the wave as they closed, mentally preparing himself for what was going to be a delicate procedure. He assessed it would be at the tour boat in less than a minute.

'We've got about twenty seconds to load that lot and I'm pulling away,' he said.

'Understood,' Stratton said. 'You got the next bit worked out?'

'Nope.'

Stratton patted him on the shoulder and headed for the back of the VSV.

'Stratton,' Jock said. 'You're a good man. But if I don't get the chance to tell you later, you can also be a real arsehole at times.'

Stratton stepped through the rubber door flap to join Scouse and Jab outside.

All eyes in the tour boat fell on the strange vessel approaching at speed wondering if it had come to help, but as the VSV bore down on them, for a tense few seconds it looked as if it was going to smash right through.

Jock gauged the distance perfectly and half a dozen boat lengths away he slammed the engines into full reverse at the same time turning the VSV hard over. As it halted its forward progress it slammed broadside into the tour boat and Stratton immediately yelled at the passengers.

'Get aboard. Now. Go, go, go!'

They needed no encouraging as Stratton, Scouse and Jab formed a chain and grabbed the first person, a woman, and pulled her violently on to the VSV and into the cabin.

'Move yourselves!' Scouse shouted. 'Or we'll leave you behind!'

It was enough to shift any doubters into top gear. They piled out of the boat as quickly as possible. A woman tried to jump on to the front of the VSV and slipped, landing brutally hard on the side of it, cracking several ribs, but managing to hold on. Jab scurried along the side, grabbed her unceremoniously and hauled her back and inside the cabin despite her groans of pain.

Stratton jumped on to the tour boat and pulled a man clutching his frightened wife up on to the side and across the small gap between the boats where Scouse took over and virtually rammed them inside the cabin.

Stratton snatched a look at the wave now only two hundred metres away. The VSV's engines gunned, a message from Jock he was leaving any second.

The passengers fell into the VSV like lemmings. A man slipped out of Jab's grasp and landed face first on the deck, his nose exploding on the metal surface.

When the wave was less than a hundred metres away, there were three people still in the tour boat: the pilot and his only crewmember, wrestling with a hysterical woman. The pilot finally punched her in the face and, as she staggered under the blow, with the help of his crewman threw her over the side and into Scouse's arms.

The wave was now close enough for them to hear

the deep lashing sound of tons of water rising up and curling over the frothing peak, coming on relentlessly and hungry to roll and crush the boats to pieces.

Stratton leapt off the tour boat and on to the VSV. 'Go for it!' he shouted back at the pilot and his crewman.

As the back of the VSV started to rise with the front of the wave it powered away and the crewman and pilot took Stratton's advice and leapt into the growing void. Jab grabbed the crewman's hands as they slapped on to the back of the VSV, but the pilot missed and plunged beneath the water. Scouse and Jab pulled the crewman in as the VSV screamed away from the tour boat, which angled up the slope of the vast wall of water into the vertical before flipping over. It tumbled once, pieces flying off it, and was then consumed by the wave.

The fishing boat was three lengths from the staggered mouth of the harbour when the wave hit it like a hammer coming down on a toy. The two crewmen leapt over the side in desperation just before it struck but the old captain remained in the doorway of his booth, holding the wheel, defiant to the last. The wave picked up the boat and threw it against the wall where it shattered into a thousand pieces. The two crewmen suffered a similar fate, their bodies smashed against the granite and obliterated by the tons of water that followed. The vast harbour wall held and the sea shot vertically into the air along its length. Those inside could only freeze in horror as the wave shook the wall with a thunderous roar and the spent monster gushed over the top.

Jock held the VSV's engines at full power and headed towards the beach half a mile away as if he intended to drive up it. Stratton stepped into the cabin, past the shattered people seated in the neat rows of plastic chairs and into the cockpit.

'Well, Jock?' he asked.

'Only one option,' Jock shouted as he gradually turned the wheel and the VSV leaned steadily over. The frightened people in the cabin held on to the boat and to each other, aware that they were far from out of danger.

'I think the trick will be not to hit it too fast,' Jock said. 'Our problem isn't going in, it's getting out the other end before we sink. Get everyone to hold on. We might tip so be ready to get the fuck out.'

The VSV turned around smoothly until it was facing the wave. 'Come on, you bitch,' Jock shouted as he held the power steady and they closed on it. Stratton wasn't sure if he was talking to the boat or the wave. 'Have some of this, why don't you,' he added.

'Hold on!' Stratton shouted to the civilians.

Scouse grabbed the hysterical woman who was weak with shock and clamped her between his body and the side. Jab helped a father hold his son fast to the deck. Stratton remained standing in the doorway of the cockpit, looking out of the front window which was filled with nothing but a wall of water running vertically.

Jock throttled back allowing the boat to ride up the slope a little instead of going straight into it, which might put them too deep underwater. As the nose of the VSV started to rise, he opened up the engines again and cut deep into the wall. As they disappeared inside everything went instantly dark. The sea engulfed the back and thumped hard against the rubber flap, bending it inwards in an effort to get inside where, if it did, it would flood the boat. The flap was nothing more than a sheet of reinforced rubber designed to fall back against the opening to create a seal in the event the VSV went underwater, but that was envisaged to last no more than a few seconds, and at no great depth. As the VSV penetrated the mountain of water the pressure soared and the flap was barely holding, and way beyond its spec.

Stratton looked around at Jock who was standing doing nothing but looking out of the window and praying for daylight. 'Jock?'

'This isn't a submarine,' Jock shouted. 'It's not meant to be anyway. I can make it go left and right but I can't make it go up!'

To make matters worse the boat started to tilt. The civilians were horrified enough and might have been more so if they knew it was not meant to happen quite this way.

Scouse was staring at the flap that creaked gradually inwards. Water started to leak through one side of the seal and he turned to Stratton. An ounce more of pressure and it was going to break. Seconds later they would flood and sink.

Suddenly the water around the front of the cockpit was not as dark as the sides and then daylight flooded in through the windows as the boat punched its way out of the sea and skyward with the grace and power of a killer whale. For an instant it was airborne and the propellers speeded up, the engines roaring without the resistance to stop them. Jock remained standing, holding on to the wheel and throttle like a rodeo rider. As the VSV came back down, slightly on its side, Jock throttled back, and as the stern dropped into the water he turned the wheel hard over and applied full power once more. The belly of the boat flopped heavily to level out and as it continued its roll, Jock powered into a tight turn. The VSV responded and Jock then turned the wheel in the opposite direction until the boat straightened up. He immediately throttled back, put the engines into neutral, and the boat slowed until it gently bobbed on the calm surface.

Jock looked back at Stratton with an exasperated expression. Stratton nodded a compliment and turned his attention back the way they had come.

Jock followed Stratton, Scouse and Jab out on deck where they could get a better view of the wave as it pressed on towards the Torquay coastline.

The focal point of the wave once the left flank had passed the harbour, was the coast road where people had already seen it and raised the alarm. Those on foot ran away from the beach to higher ground. Several elderly people shuffled away as fast as they could, some fortunate enough to get help. People stepped from shops to investigate the commotion only to take immediate flight.

The wave rolled in relentlessly, sweeping moored boats along with it. As it hit the beach and rolled up it, it gushed over the sea wall bringing several of the boats with it. The wall took much of the force but there was still power enough to roll cars parked or driving along the sea road. The last vestiges of thrust were spent slamming into buildings across the road where several shop fronts were shattered, and then, suddenly, it had expended its energy and the threat disappeared.

Seconds after the water subsided, the front was strangely quiet and void of life. It was absurdly surreal; a clear, sunny day, the seagulls cawing above and little evidence of the weapon which had struck the mighty blow, other than soaked streets and the carnage it had caused. Upturned and shattered hulks of boats lay on the road, one almost inside a building. Not everyone escaped with their lives. A handful of bodies lay unmoving, twisted amongst the debris.

People began gradually to surface, tentatively at first, unsure, then quickly to help the injured and search for those who might still be alive.

'Poor bastards,' Scouse muttered.

'Hey, over there,' Jab shouted, pointing towards some wreckage, all that was left of the tour boat. Someone was in the water, hanging on to a piece of deck, waving weakly. Jock hurried inside and hit the throttle, shunting the VSV forward. It was the tour boat pilot and somehow he had survived. He was as surprised to see them as they were him.

As they headed back to the tanker, a Sea King flew past, circled and came in to hover over the tanker's heli-deck in preparation for landing.

'That'll be the nuke and bio-chem specialists,' Scouse said.

Half an hour later Stratton and Scouse were back on board the tanker. Several tugs were on their way to pull it off the sand bar as soon as the incoming tide allowed and if that didn't work then some of the crude would have to be pumped off. But there was a lot of speculation the tanker might have broken its back already, and if not would probably do so when they tried to pull it off. So far there was no sign of an oil leakage but no one was calling this a success yet. Stratton had doubted the wisdom of his action as soon as he had done it. He had caused the deaths of those fishermen and God knows who else in the town. It was an on-the-spot decision, and it was always luck if those ever turned out to be fault-less. He hadn't known the depth of the sea here, and what damage and loss of life might have occurred had the tanker carried on into town. He pushed it out of his mind.

Another Sea King had landed on the tanker, which was now crawling with various specialists, forensics and bomb-disposal experts scouring every nook and cranny.

The operatives had done their job and were hanging around as security while they waited for a Royal Navy frigate to arrive and take over.

Stratton was carrying out his own inspection of the boat, more out of curiosity than for any other reason. He had never seen anything quite like this before. So far there was no sign of any devices of any kind. It was a well-carried-out assault, execution of the crew, a successful withdrawal and then the tanker itself was turned into a weapon. There was no evidence of the perpetrators, but the scale, organisation and target all suggested a powerful anti-West terrorist group was behind it.

After seeing the dead officers and crew in the superstructure, he headed along the length of the deck to his last stop, the bosun's locker in the extreme bows. He stepped in through the narrow doorway between the massive winches that raised and lowered the enormous anchors, and walked inside to the end of the short balcony at the top of the stairwell from where he could see to the bottom of the ship. The cargo holds on a tanker end some ten metres short of the pointed bows and the remaining area is used as a store for things like ropes, chains, cables and rat-guards. A hundred feet below Stratton could see two operatives chatting beside what looked like a couple of bodies.

He made his way down, his feet echoing on the metal steps inside the white and brightly lit steel cavern. As he reached the last bend in the stairs before the bottom he could see the two bodies in blue over-alls were the Philippine engine-room workers. They were lying where they had been found and would be removed when the forensic officers had inspected them. When the initial reports of the dead came in, the number totalled twenty-four, which left three unaccounted for. Because of its distance from the superstructure the locker was the last place searched and when the tanker looked like it was going to run aground the front of the boat, especially below the waterline, was not a place anyone wanted to be. It was Jacko, leader of team Alpha, who had reported finding the last three crewmembers.

The two operatives glanced up at Stratton and one of them pointed to a far corner the other side of the stairwell. Stratton looked to see Jacko staring up at a man lying across several pipes above him.

Stratton stepped down on to the lowest point of the ship and walked over to him.

'Stratton,' Jacko said, greeting him. They both stood and looked up at the body a few feet above them, all evidence suggesting it had fallen from some height. The man, a Caucasian, was wearing white overalls indicating he was an officer. He looked tall, more than six feet anyway.

'Chief engineer, I think,' Jacko said. 'Him and the other two must've made a run for it and tried to hide in here . . . At a guess I'd say the bastards threw him off there,' he said, indicating a midway stairs landing. 'They've all been razored. Throats slit. I don't think any of 'em 'av been shot. The two Filipinos look like they put up a bit of a fight. They've got slashes and stab wounds all over 'em.'

Stratton looked around, trying to picture what had happened. He saw a wallet on the floor directly below the man on the pipes and picked it up. Inside were some US dollars, an identification card and two photographs. One was of a woman and two children and the other was the dead man with another man, slightly broader and harder looking, but very likely his brother, perhaps even his twin. The engineer's name was Vladimir Zhilev, a Russian from Riga,

Latvia, and he was the chief engineer as Jacko had said.

'Any clues as to who did it?' Stratton asked.

'Nothing so far. Got to be Al Qaeda or one of those lot. Who else would do this?'

Stratton took a plastic evidence bag from a pouch and was about to drop the wallet in it when he noticed a piece of paper stuffed into its side. He pulled it out and opened it up. There was something scrawled on it and a red stain. The writing looked Arabic and on closer inspection the red stain was a thumb print in blood.

'Where's this shit gonna end?' Jacko said.

'It's only just started,' Stratton said as he folded the paper, replaced it in the wallet and dropped it into the evidence bag.

'Give this to forensics when they get down here. It's his,' Stratton said, indicating the engineer and handing the bag to Jacko. 'Navy'll be here in twenty minutes. I'll see you up on deck.'

3

A grey, ten-year-old Saab Estate covered in a couple of weeks of dirt and grime drove slowly along a residential street on the outskirts of Riga, Latvia, cutting through several days' old, grey slush. The suburb was two miles across the river from the old city and this part of it was not as unpleasant on the eye as others built during the Russian occupation. More brick and wood than concrete had been used to construct the buildings in this street, most of which were houses and bungalows. The grey, soulless, depressing apartment blocks the Russians were famous for building throughout its former empire were at the other end of the housing estate and practically out of sight from this street. The winter snows did much to hide the ugliness but the sun was now shining brightly through a patchy sky to shrink back the heavy downfall that had fallen a week before.

The car pulled up alongside the kerb, stopped and the engine was switched off. It was a quiet neighbourhood, the houses comfortably spaced with street-parking guaranteed.

Mikhail Zhilev climbed out of the vehicle and registered pain on his granite, Slav face, which was covered in a two-week-old beard, as he stretched his six-foot-three, fifty-year-old body until his spine cracked. He had been determined to finish the last eight-hour leg of his two-day drive without a stop but his stubbornness had not come without a price. The old twinge in his neck which had plagued him for the past twelve years had throbbed continuously since leaving the mountain road and in the last hour or so had become almost unbearable. When anyone ever asked him about his discomfort he always explained it away as the result of thirty-five years of Sambo wrestling, a Russian self-defence discipline, in particular the last few weeks of those years when he pushed himself hard in the hope of finally winning the heavyweight division of the Russian Army Championship, a hope dashed in the semi-finals when a bad fall almost left him with a broken neck. But the few people who truly knew him, all old comrades in arms except for his brother, knew the real culprits were the Russian scientists and their damned experiments, and also the OMRP (Detachment of Marine Reconnaissance Point – Naval Intelligence) and their bosses in the GRU (General Intelligence Department) who allowed the ridiculous practice of using the military's finest as medical guinea pigs.

Zhilev let his head fall gradually forward and then, with a grimace, forced his chin the last few inches on to his chest until the vertebrae in his neck also cracked. It gave him a little relief although he knew from experience it would not last long. He thought of the bottle of Temgesic tablets he always kept in his pocket, heavy-duty painkillers, but only for a second before dismissing the notion. He carried them for much the same reason some former smokers keep a packet of cigarettes, as a constant test of resolve and willpower. Soon he would be sitting back in his armchair, his feet up, a towel rolled behind his neck, relaxing and taking the weight off his shoulders, the only sure way to relieve the pain. In his philosophy, painkillers were for the weak, and no one who knew him had ever described him as being weak. One glance at his tall, slightly stooped demeanour, his rock of a head and determined eyes, his powerful shoulders, long arms, gnarled fingers and oaken bones bound in old iron muscles and there was no doubt that this man had spent his entire life in physical hardship. His career may have prematurely aged him but only a blind fool could fail to sense he still had a great capacity for physical destruction.

Besides, there was a much deeper truth behind his disdain for pills. Zhilev had a psychosomatic aversion to any form of drug, and for understandable reasons.

Zhilev opened the back of the car and pulled out an old canvas A-frame rucksack which had a military-style web-belt, pouches and a knife secured to the top. He pulled it heavily on to one shoulder, ignored the pain as he straightened up, steam shooting from his mouth and nostrils as he exhaled the frosty air, shut the boot and trudged up his garden path. He stepped on to his porch where snow remained against the house, sheltered from the direct sunlight, and pulled a bunch of keys out of his coat pocket. He unlocked the front door and stamped his boots on the wooden decking before stepping over the small drift that had moulded solid against the door and entered the house. A pile of mail littered the entrance and he crouched to pick it up before closing the door and walking down the sparse, creaking hallway and into the kitchen.

The house was clean, tidy and organised, the furnishings basic and austere, and noticeably void of a feminine touch.

He placed the letters on the wooden kitchen table, bare except for a half-burned candle in a saucer, dropped the rucksack on the clay-tiled floor, hung his coat on a hook on the wall and gave his neck a brief pressure massage. As he brought his head forward to stretch the vertebrae, he opened his eyes and they fell on a black-and-white framed photograph, twenty-five years old, on the wall by the door. It was of a dozen young, athletic men in black-rubber diving suits posing casually for the camera, some wearing unusual-looking diving sets which did not have air tanks. Some carried underwater mines magnetised to metal sheets strapped on to their backs, others held small flotation boards with compasses and depth gauges attached. Behind the men, on a specially built trailer, was a black 'Proton' type underwater two-man tug, or miniature submarine, some twenty feet long from nose to rudder, a red hammer and sickle sten-cilled on the side. The men were smiling, some of them shyly as if unused to cameras, or perhaps caught unaware by the photographer. Beneath the photo was the badge of the Russian Combat Swimmer, a para-chute with wings either side and a diver on an under-water tug across the base of a parachute.

Zhilev stared at the picture as his thoughts went

back to those glorious days. He looked at himself in the photograph, the handsome youth in the centre, clean-shaven, straight-backed, short hair parted neatly at the side, a proud warrior of the highest order in the prime of his life. The nostalgia washed over him and he remembered the day the photograph was taken as if it were yesterday and, as always, found it hard to believe so much time had gone by so quickly.

Zhilev disconnected from the picture which always managed to fill him with despondency and loss rather than pride. He turned to the task of cleaning his kit, the first thing a good soldier did as soon as he returned from the field, and hung the belt with its attached pouches and knife on another hook beside his coat and opened the rucksack to empty it. Everything had an old army surplus look about it: no bright colours, earthy, sturdy and practical. The last items at the bottom were a sleeping bag and poncho. He pulled out the poncho and put it to one side, picked up the rucksack and carried it to a cupboard under the stairs. The small space was crammed with military equipment that looked more suited to a museum than any modern Western army. Hanging on hooks or placed neatly on a shelf were items such as compasses, maps, flashlights, a folding spade, knives and a pile of rations. There was also a variety of camouflage outfits, boots and cold and wet-weather gear. Several semi-automatic pistols were laid out neatly on a shelf with their magazines and boxes of cartridges beside them: a Tokarev, a more recent Makarov and a WW2 Luger, all in fine condition. He draped the sleeping bag over a line, hung the rucksack on a nail and closed the door. He put the poncho on a chair by the back door since it would need hosing down before it was put away. There was no tent. Zhilev preferred to sleep on the ground in the open no matter what the conditions and under a poncho only when it snowed or rained. In the field he liked to travel with the bare necessities and sleep with all-round visibility. It was a behaviour he had formed after years of operating in small intelligence-gathering teams, often in the most inhospitable weather and terrain.

Satisfied his gear was sorted out and organised, he filled a chipped enamel kettle from the sink tap and placed it on an old stove. He lit the gas that gushed from the ancient cast-iron ring and sat down at the table to sort through his mail.

The majority of it he tossed into a bin without reading beyond the first clue that it was junk, and when the sorting was complete he was left with three letters of any significance. That was about average for the two weeks he had been away walking in the hills.

Zhilev went alone on long camping expeditions at least twice a year, sometimes three. He had left the military twelve years earlier, medically discharged as unfit for duty, and even though he was often in great discomfort he refused to become a 'soft civilian'. His legacy of pain from those days of service to his country was accompanied by an unhealthy level of hate and loathing for those who had caused it. Looking back, he had loved his life in the Spetsnaz, Russian Special Forces, but he had been cheated out of at least three more years of active service, and perhaps more importantly the opportunity to work with naval intelligence as a rear-echelon field adviser, a posting ideal for older, experienced men, and one that could have kept him employed in a special forces capacity into his sixties. The doctors had given him a zero physical rating in his final report with the added comment that his damaged neck could one day cause him paralysis and perhaps, due to the extent of the damage which was close to his skull, even death. Zhilev refused to accept it and pleaded with them to let him prove they were wrong and that he was strong enough to do any task they set him. But they refused to even consider his plea and furthermore warned him to discontinue any strenuous physical activity for the rest of his life. There was no measure of how much he loathed those fools for first using him like a guinea pig and then, after almost killing him, deciding he was no longer good enough even to teach new recruits from the vast pool of experience he had gained over twenty years and countless operations in the service.

The National Scientific Research Institute of Experimental Medicine of the Defence Ministry of the Russian Federation was the lofty banner these scientists operated under, and they often used Spetsnaz to test their concoctions designed to do a variety of things such as raise physical endurance, remove the feeling of fear, increase tolerance against harsh environments and allow a soldier to operate for up to a week without sleep. The experimental drug that poleaxed Zhilev was a serum created to delay death after receiving a lethal dose of radiation such as during a nuclear attack. Whereas an untreated person would collapse within hours as their brain and internal organs swelled and rapidly degenerated, and their skin blistered and broke apart causing an horrifically painful death, the drug allowed a soldier to operate almost normally for up to four days, giving him the strength to carry out his mission before suddenly dropping dead.

Zhilev was given the newly developed drug in pill form, one every four hours, and ordered to conduct a gruelling map march with forty kilos of equipment over mountainous terrain to test its effects. After two days he became delirious and fell down the side of a crag fracturing his neck. He would have died of exposure had he not been found that evening by his comrades after he failed to make a checkpoint. He lay in a hospital bed for six weeks recovering from the fall and the effects of the drug. When he learned he was to be kicked out of the military he wanted to blow the entire experimental medicine institute to bits. He might have done so too, for Zhilev was certainly a most vengeful man and he had the knowledge and training as well as access to the explosives and equipment necessary. The only reason he did not was because he was not completely certain the door to the service was shut to him. He had high hopes that his colleagues would succeed in an appeal against the decision.

It took more than a year, while Zhilev moped around his brother's house, before he learned the appeal had been denied. Only then did he accept finally that his career was truly over. He had been thrown out and tossed on to the scrap heap like so many before him. He always knew it would happen one day, but when he was old, not thirty-eight and in his prime.

After his unceremonious dismissal from the service, a hero of the now Russian Federation, he was given a small amount of money in compensation as well as his pension which, even though it was one and a half times that of a regular soldier, was not much to live on. It was Vladimir who gave him the money to buy the house he now lived in. Not having to pay a monthly rent meant his pension could go a lot further. His brother had been a vital crutch for him in the years immediately after his untimely retirement and the only voice of comfort and reason. Zhilev would be in a military prison had it not been for Vladimir who spent an entire night talking him out of his planned demolition raid against the medical institute.

Zhilev tried to remember when his brother said he might be home. There was never a firm date. So many factors could delay him, the most common ones being the weather and late arrival of his replacement. He checked the cheap plastic clock on the wall. As soon as he was finished with his chores, he would call on Vladimir's wife. They lived only a few miles away in a nice, large house that backed on to a wood where their children loved to play. Vladimir would have telephoned from the ship and told her when he was coming home. But first, he would go to the shops and buy some meat and potatoes for the supper she would insist he stayed for, and then some toys for the children who loved to see Uncle

Mikhail, if for no other reason than he always had a gift for them.

Zhilev held up the letters and read the return addresses. One was from the bank, a statement no doubt, since it was due about now. The second was a gas bill and the third was from the oil company his brother worked for, based in Dubai. Zhilev thought it strange the letter from the oil company was addressed to him. He had never had anything to do with it. It was possible the letter was from his brother, but the address was typed, not handwritten as usual, and besides, Vladimir was not in Dubai. He flew to his ship wherever it was in the world then, three or four months later, he would get off at the first available port and fly back home to Riga.

Zhilev opened the envelope from Dubai that contained a single sheet with the company's letterhead and no more than a few typed lines. His heart skipped a beat and he filled with dread as he saw the first few words: *I regret to inform you . . .*

When he got to the part that confirmed his fear that his brother was dead, he put the letter down and spread his hands out either side of it to steady himself. He started from the top again and read it through slowly, and when he got to the end, he lowered his head into his hands and began to gently weep, his heavy shoulders shaking.

Zhilev remained at the table for a long time after he had stopped crying while steam gushed from the bubbling kettle on the stove. When he eventually got to his feet, he went to a cupboard and took out a mug, placed a spoonful of instant coffee into it and filled it with the boiling water, stirring it slowly as if in a trance. All he could see and hear were memories of his brother.

Zhilev was a year younger than Vladimir although most people thought they were twins. They were inseparable throughout their youth. Vladimir was the quiet, intelligent one while Zhilev was the adventurer and very much the risk-taker. When Zhilev accepted a bet one day from fellow schoolboys that he could not ride his bicycle off a ramp and over a ditch from a culvert that gushed vile black water from the old generating station, it was only because Vladimir had inspected the width of the ditch, the angle of the ramp, the mechanics of the bike and told his brother it was possible. The first time they were apart was the day Vladimir was called up to serve his mandatory time in the military. Vladimir was more fortunate than most since, as a gifted engineer, he went directly to an engineer battalion and spent virtually his entire three years in an armoured depot on the outskirts of Moscow thus missing active service. Zhilev considered his military career just as fortunate and for quite the opposite reasons. From the day he joined he dreamed of a future filled with adventure and exciting operations behind enemy lines, gathering information and carrying out direct action.

The day after Vladimir left home for the army, Zhilev walked into town and joined the local military youth school where he learned to scuba dive. By the time his call-up papers arrived a year later, he had some idea of what he wanted to do and even a vague plan. Rumours abounded of special units that carried out clandestine operations in enemy lands and every youth soldier and conscript had at least one exaggerated story he had heard of their derring do. What nobody seemed to have a clue about was where the mysterious groups were based and how a person joined them. It was generally understood that they came to you, but for that to happen a man had to stand out in some way, be different, exceptional. Zhilev had learned from his old diving instructor in the youth military school that the best route to 'special forces work' was through military intelligence. That would open many doors for anyone who was successful in that department. First Zhilev had to get through the basic military-training course and then take it from there.

The three-month induction training was easy for him and made him all the more determined not to end up serving with the kind of men he had joined up with, most of whom were unmotivated and got drunk at every opportunity. All he could think of was getting to the end of the course and applying for a specialist aptitude test which, if he passed, would allow him to attend a selection process for military intelligence. Within a week of completing basic training he was invited to take the week-long series of mental aptitude tests with some short map marches thrown in to assess the recruits' physical condition. He passed the course with ease and received orders to study radio communications under OSNAZ, the Special Forces unit of the Intelligence Directorate of the Navy, in Kiev. This was the first big step towards his goal but he still had no idea how he was going to break into the actual operational units. Zhilev spent a year at the vast old concrete complex built after the Second World War under Stalin's directive, learning radio technology and how to operate the various 'special' radios used by Special Forces and field agents – or spies for want of a better term – learning their construction and the many complex coding systems.

At the end of this course he sat a final test and passed with honours. His intelligence as well as Sambo skills, which highlighted his physical abilities, did not go unnoticed and a week after the exams he was called to see his commanding officer who personally handed him a military assignment, voluntary in nature, which was simply two words: marine intelligence. The brevity of the offer suggested it was far beyond ordinary military duty. In fact, it was a career directive and, as the commander pointed out, a great honour to receive. There was one slight obstacle Zhilev had to clear before he could accept the offer: he could not embark on an intelligence career as a conscript and would have to sign up for twenty years, which also included signing a contract that stated he understood the punishment for disclosing official secrets was death. These were not even issues for Zhilev and he promptly signed on the dotted line. He was finally on his way to realising his childhood dream and within days was on a train to the Black Sea where he would join the OMRP and one of the legendary and highly secret reconnaissance and sabotage units that came under the general banner of

Spetsnaz, which simply translated means 'of special purpose'. He knew his life was going to change in every conceivable way and he marched eagerly, albeit blindly, into it.

Had he known where the great adventure would eventually lead he would have remained in Riga and become a metal worker like his father, marry, and have a family and take holidays in Yalta once a year like everyone else in the factory. But he did not.

Zhilev took the two hundred mile train journey south from Kiev to the city of Ochakov on the Black Sea, a hundred miles north of Sevastopol, the head-quarters of the Black Sea Fleet, which was to be his parent command. From Ochakov, he was taken in an army truck into the wilderness to eventually arrive at Pervomayskiy, an artificial island at the mouth of the rivers Dnepr and Bug. Called Mayskiy for short, the island was a stone fortress constructed in 1881 and used as such until World War Two. It was taken over by the Spetsnaz in the 1960s and the interior reconstructed to provide classrooms, a small hospital, helicopter pad, sports facilities and accommodation for two hundred and fifty men, and included a water-processing plant and enough food and supplies to comfortably sustain the men inside its walls for up to a year without contact with the outside world in the event of a nuclear attack. This was the home of the 17th Brigade of the OMPR and where Zhilev was to be based for much of his career.

The following two years were spent training extensively in all forms of intelligence gathering, both technical and physical, as well as advanced small arms and sabotage. He learned Special Forces diving skills, which included the use of bubble-less re-breather diving apparatus as well as mixed gas options for deep-water operations, and how to drive and navigate a number of different miniature submarines. He studied intensively a variety of Western commercial and military targets, from oil platforms to missile silos, so that he could report on them as well as mount sabotage operations against them. This was where he also learned to use several different kinds of chemical, biological and man-portable nuclear weapons or suitcase bombs.

The only negative aspect of that period was he could not see as much of his brother as he would have liked. When either of them were on leave, and that was rarely at the same time, they would make their way to the other's nearest base town, in Vladimir's case, Moscow, and in Zhilev's, Ochakov, and spend as much time as they could together. By the time Zhilev's two-year training programme was complete, Vladimir was a civilian once again, and with Zhilev's probationary period over, it was easier for them to meet. In fact Zhilev spent every leave period back in Riga with his brother, attended his wedding as best man, and was at every one of their three children's christenings.

During Zhilev's operational years he took part in missions and so-called rehearsals all over the world from Cuba to China, England and America, and was involved in the training of several renowned terrorist groups and the passing of weapons to, among others, the Palestinian Liberation Organisation. The day he realised his career in Spetsnaz was over was the worst in his life, until the arrival of this letter. Nothing in the world meant more to him than his brother, not even his own life. He would have given it gladly if it meant Vladimir could come back home.

Zhilev's thoughts went to Vladimir's wife and daughter. He wondered if they knew. Vladimir had elected Zhilev as his next of kin in the event of an emergency because there was no one in the world he trusted more. As an engineer on an oil tanker travelling all over the world, there was always the chance he might have an accident and he wanted his brother to be the first to know before his wife and children.

Zhilev decided to drive over to the house and tell Marla, Vladimir's wife, the grave news. But first he had to recover a little more himself. She would be devastated and he wanted to have full control of his own emotions so that he could concentrate on comforting her.

He checked the letterhead for the phone number of the office in Dubai. Before going over to see Marla he would make arrangements for his brother's body to be brought home for burial, and also find out how he died. Then he noticed the date at the top of the letter.

'My God,' he murmured. Vladimir had been dead for more than a week.

4

Stratton was hunched over a desk reading a book in the office of C Squadron's operations' hangar, situated on the edge of the Special Boat Service's sprawling headquarters camp a quarter of a mile from Poole harbour. The book was about the Templars, the military order established after the beginning of the first crusades, the invasion of what is now known as the Middle East at the end of the tenth century. He'd had the book for more than a year, having come across it in the television room of the south detachment undercover operations HQ in Northern Ireland and, not having had the time to read it due to a sudden increase in operational developments, it had ended up in a box of odds and ends that he brought back with him to England after prematurely finishing his tour. The book had surfaced only the other day during a much-needed sort through of the spare room of his cottage in the quaint village of Lythchet Matravers just outside Poole, and he began reading it there and then. The book actually started centuries before the famous knights and opened with the story of Abraham and Isaac, about as far back as Christian, Jewish and Muslim history went. Since the chronicles of the Templars intertwined with the beginnings of the present-day conflict between the Middle East and the West, it seemed an apposite read.

The only clue inside the hangar that it was raining outside was the faintly audible staccato of droplets hitting the metal, insulated roof. The office, tightly packed with filing cabinets, computers and monitors, various phone and communications links, the boss, 2IC and sergeant majors' desks, plus a table devoted to tea and coffee making, had scant room for little else. It had no exterior windows just those looking down into the cavernous hangar's interior, which also had little in the way of spare room and was a soldier of fortune's Aladdin's cave. The hangar was divided up into the various SBS tasks and terrains they operated in: arctic, jungle, desert and maritime, including all-terrain vehicles, snowmobiles, an assortment of inflatable craft, canoes, parachutes and diving equipment. Add to that the operatives' personal lockers and the place was veritably jammed.

Morgan, the only other person in the office, was seated at the 2IC's desk behind Stratton gurning as he plucked hairs enthusiastically out of his nose with his large fingers, a task that required some vigorous excavating. The two weeks following the buzz with the supertanker had been quiet ones with much of the squadron away catching up on leave owed since playing games in Iraq. As acting sergeant major of the squadron, Stratton was manning the fort while the boss and 2IC attended a briefing in London, which meant he couldn't stray far from the camp until they got back in case something of an operational nature came up. He did have some work to do, namely preparing a training programme and the stores and transport requirements for a mini-submarine-borne assault exercise against an oil plat-form in the North Sea, but he was putting it off for a day because he was not in the mood. He could practically write it in his sleep anyway, but the truth was he found the book so interesting and enlight-ening he wanted to keep on reading it.

'I was always led to understand,' Morgan said nasally, a finger deep in his nostril, 'that if you plucked hairs instead of cutting them, after a while they didn't grow back, but I think that's a load of bollocks. Been plucking these bastards for years and there's more than ever . . . Christ, that's a long one,' he said, lift-ing it up to the light to inspect it. 'Look at that,' he said, holding it out for Stratton to see. Stratton looked over his shoulder at the hair that, at some two inches, was indeed unusually long. 'It must've been growing out of me bleedin' sinus,' Morgan said as he placed it on the desk to study it further. 'Perhaps it was an ingrown eyebrow,' he pondered.

Stratton went back to his book. The choice between a conversation with Morgan about his nasal hairs and the Templars was not a difficult one.

'One thing is true,' Morgan continued. 'It doesn't hurt like it used to. The more you pluck 'em, the more it seems to numb the nerve endings. Know what I mean?' Morgan knew he was being a nuisance and was enjoying it.

Stratton turned the page while Morgan, having mined his nose to exhaustion, directed his attention to the hairs inside his ears.

The phone rang. Morgan wiped his fingers on his sleeve and picked it up. 'C Squadron,' he said. 'Yeah,' he said looking at Stratton. 'Who is it, please?' Morgan listened a moment then held out the phone to Stratton. 'Some bloke named Sumners. Sounds like a rupert,' he said using the affectionate nickname for an upper-class-officer type.

Stratton looked at the phone without allowing the surprise to show on his face. He never expected to hear from MI5 or MI6 again in his life, let alone Sumners, his former taskmaster. It was strange how, after all this time, the call sent a quiver of anticipation through him as it did in the early days working for MI. The calls always meant Stratton was off somewhere, usually alone, and to do something interesting, except when it came to terminations. That was ultimately why the relationship had ended. The number of those kinds of assignments seemed to be growing and Stratton began to develop an anathema for the calls and the mere mention of Sumners' name. Now, a year since the last time he had spoken to the man, Stratton's reaction was strangely mixed. There was without a doubt that old sense of anticipation, but there was also a residue of trepidation. He had healed in some ways but not completely. It didn't mean he was prepared to pick up where he had left off but he was nevertheless curious. He couldn't tell where the sudden expectancy was coming from. Perhaps it was due to the comparatively dull employment of the past year, not that he had been exactly idle. There were a few breaks in the travelling and training, and the year had not been without action, specifically in the Gulf and Far East. But something had indeed been missing from his life since he returned to the SBS. Perhaps it was being part of a team again after spending so long working alone. It had taken him several years into his Special Forces career to accept the fact that he preferred working by himself. But loners were contrary to the team ethos of the SBS. To some extent, they were even shunned, which Stratton agreed with wholeheartedly in theory. Nevertheless, he could not help the way he felt. Teamwork was something he always preached to younger members in training while at the same time trying to resist the lure of the antithesis. He might never have known how much he liked working alone had he not been invited away from the core work of the SBS to spend several years assigned to military intelligence.

It was not possible Sumners was making a social call. The man was all business all of the time. He was a purebred, classic, British intelligence officer: cold, logical, manipulative and intelligent. Any social skills were an act which arose out of a need for diplomacy. Sumners did have some redeeming qualities; Stratton had always felt he could trust the man, within the boundaries of the job, of course. Sumners would not stick his neck out for any operative who strayed from the task in hand and was more than capable of deserting one who did. But Sumners also understood the job required resourcefulness and a high level of initiative and had always supported Stratton's decisions in the field even though on more than one occasion he had not agreed with them. The operative on the ground had the implicit advantage when it came to judgement and intuition and Sumners gave him the benefit of the doubt in most cases. It had to be said this subtle understanding was an unusual quality for an MI operations officer, especially for one like Sumners who had never set foot in the field or had any dirt-on-the-hands involvement in an operation.

Whatever the meaning was behind the confusion of warning bells and anticipation, Stratton could not resist and took the phone from Morgan and put it to his ear.

'This is Stratton.'

'Would you like to do a job for us?' Sumners asked.

That was typical, Stratton thought. They hadn't spoken in a year and Sumners couldn't even begin the conversation with a hello or how have you been.

'I'm fine,' Stratton said.

'I only ask questions I know the answer to of people I don't trust. What I don't know is if you would like to do a job for us?'

Stratton didn't answer, his mind racing over a variety of considerations. He wanted to know what the job was but also knew that asking would be a waste of breath. It wasn't for operatives to pick and choose their assignments like fruit in a market. Taskmasters wanted to hear the word 'yes' and quickly too. That opened the door to the next stage of the game, which was the briefing. But Stratton wasn't a robot. Nor was he the neophyte of several years ago, trusting and eager to do any assignment handed to him. He was already an old sweat even though he was relatively young in this particular field of special operations that valued experience, ingenuity and guile above all other qualities. He would be open to just about any assignment but he was also prepared to blow off Sumners if there was any clue the job was an assassination.

'I know what you're thinking,' Sumners said. 'I wouldn't have called you if it was a job I didn't think you would approve of.' There was a hint of patronage in his voice, which was understandable since he did not like offering jobs. That made it quite flattering. But Stratton was not satisfied by far and, perhaps inspired by the subtle compliment, chose to push a little further.

'Why me?'

'Let's be clear on one thing, shall we? You're still in my book as an MI operative and I'm offering you an assignment. It's as simple as that.'

The comment put Stratton off balance. He did not believe his name had remained in Sumners' book, but then again he had telephoned him. 'You haven't called me in over a year,' he said.

'You were fatigued. It was quite obvious. You needed a break. I'm not entirely insensitive,' he added.

Bullshit, Stratton thought. Nevertheless, he couldn't help feeling pleased he had not been dumped entirely. It had done some damage to his ego and self-esteem when it became obvious MI no longer considered him worthy of them. He knew Sumners was telling a partial lie though. The truth was they had let him go at the time but kept him under scrutiny. That was standard procedure for all retired operatives purely from a security point of view – MI didn't want to see any of its valuable intelligence finding its way into the marketplace. But in Stratton's case they had also been assessing his fitness and he had obviously been cleared for operational work once more. But what kind of work was the question. Sumners knew why Stratton had burned out and that he would not go down that same road again. The man would have put all the pieces together and decided Stratton was ideal for this new task, whatever it was, despite the past. He had hinted at it with his comment about the job being one Stratton might approve of. Stratton wanted back in, there was no doubt about that, but not under the same old circumstances. He wondered if he should make that understood right now. If he did not it would eventually surface, and probably at a time inconvenient to the both of them. But would his demands scare Sumners away? Stratton would have to take the risk. If Sumners didn't like it then that would be it and Stratton would certainly never hear from him again. Ultimately, Stratton's sanity meant more to him than the work.

'You know the kind of job I'm not going to do for you again,' Stratton said.

'And you know this employment can have no constraints from operatives,' Sumners parried.

They remained silent for a moment. It was an obstacle both wanted to pass through without giving way. But the ball was clearly in Sumners' court.

'I need someone with maritime knowledge,' he finally said. Sumners had decided to make the pass around the obstacle. 'Frankly, I don't know any more than that at the moment, other than it has to do with the tanker you recaptured.'

That immediately sparked Stratton's interest. Whatever was behind that strike was international and major league. It had preyed on Stratton's mind ever since, the brutality and arrogance of the assault, but he never expected to hear anything more about it.

'Would you like the job, yes or no?'

'Yes,' Stratton said automatically.

'I need you in London as soon as you can get here. Your boss is on his way back to Poole and you're cleared to leave right away. You know the Grenadier?'

'Yes,' Stratton said. That suggested a lot to Stratton already. MI5 was north of the Thames close to Westminster and dealt with the country's internal security. MI6 headquarters was the other side of the river and dealt with the rest of the world. The Grenadier pub was just a few streets from MI6 and frequented by its personnel.

'Seven p.m. then.'

'Fine.'

The phone went dead and Stratton returned it to its cradle.

He took a moment to take it all in. He was on the move again. Suddenly the SBS was once again a place he only hung out in while waiting for the phone to ring. It felt good. There was a new adventure to be had.

He opened his desk drawer, took out his passport and put it in his breast pocket. He looked around to see if there was anything else he needed. It was purely a reflexive action. He knew there was nothing. Everything he would need for whatever the job was, he'd get in London. And if there was anything the SBS had that he might need, it would be delivered to him.

Stratton realised Morgan was watching him as if he knew something was up that did not involve the Service. He had heard Stratton's strange side of the conversation and seen him collect his passport. Add that to Stratton's bizarre past of always disappearing and it was obvious he was going somewhere again.

'The boss is on his way back,' Stratton said. 'I'm checking out.'

'You be gone long?' Morgan asked.

'No idea . . . Take care of yourself.'

Stratton headed for the door.

'Stratton?'

Stratton paused in the doorway to look at him.

'How . . . what do you have to do to . . . you know . . . get in the job?' Morgan asked, unsure how to form the words. It was a sensitive subject that due to protocol allowed no questions, but he felt he knew Stratton well enough to dip a toe into it.

'They call you.'

'And if they don't? I mean. Is there any way I can get them to call . . . let 'em know I want in?'

'I can't help you, Morgan.'

Morgan nodded, disappointment on his face. He understood, or thought he did. 'See ya, then.'

Stratton left the room.

Morgan sighed as he sat back, put his feet up on

the desk and tried to imagine what on earth Stratton did when he went away on his private little trips. His hand subconsciously moved to his ear and searched inside it for a hair to pluck.

Stratton headed down the stairs, crossed the hangar floor to the main entrance and stepped out into the rain. In his opinion, Morgan, because he was black, had a better chance than most of getting a call. MI6 was short of dark-skinned operators. The job was dangerous, but Morgan was canny and more than capable of handling himself. He wondered about putting in a good word for him, then decided against it. If anything bad ever happened to Morgan, Stratton didn't want it on his conscience.

Two and a half hours later Stratton walked out of Waterloo Station and paused to look at the taxi rank. The queue was some twenty long with more people tacking on to the end every few seconds, although taxis appeared to be arriving in an endless stream to cope with the demand. He checked his watch. There was plenty of time to walk the mile or so to the meeting place, which he preferred to do anyway. He would spend the time thinking about his return to military intelligence. Savouring it might be a better description. There was no doubting the mild euphoria he was now feeling. He fastened the front buttons of his old leather jacket, shoved the Templars book he had read throughout the train journey into a side pocket, pulled up his collar against a chill wind and headed in the direction of the Thames.

At five minutes to seven, Stratton paused in a quiet back street a couple of blocks from the main road.

It was several years since he had been to this location. There was a small park across the street and in its centre was the little knoll from which the Real IRA had fired an RPG7 antitank missile at the MI6 headquarters building quite visible a quarter of a mile away. It struck a window halfway up, doing little more than smashing some glass and scarring a wall inside. The media had billed it as a bold demonstration of the Real IRA's willingness and capability to take over from the Provisional IRA and to carry the conflict directly into the heart of England and military intelligence. MI saw it as a perfect illustration of how pathetic the fight with the IRA had become: in the grand scheme of things, the best they were now capable of was smashing a window.

Stratton left the railings that surrounded the park and continued on to the pub.

The high-ceilinged bar was spacious with that characteristic turn-of-the-century feel. The thirty or so people spread about gave it a busy atmosphere but it was by no means crowded. A quick scan revealed Sumners at a table on the far side of the room beside another man who was well-groomed, intelligent looking and wearing a Savile Row suit. They had not yet seen him. Stratton thought Sumners had aged more than expected in the year since he last saw him. His hair had always been white-grey but his face was more drawn and his eyes darker. Perhaps he had pulled a few late nights lately. The difference between the two men sitting together was interesting. Their body language said a lot about them. The other man had an air of superiority and not just by the cut of his clothes. It was the way he was sitting: legs crossed, hands flat together on his thigh, back straight, chin slightly raised, eyes looking down his nose and staring straight ahead as if he were royalty. He was definitely the private-club type and did not look as if he frequented alehouses such as this one. Sumners on the other hand had his hands in his coat pockets, chin against his chest, feet apart and on the ground and brow furrowed in deep thought. He stared at nothing but in the same direction as his companion. The half full glasses on the table in front of them both contained ice and a slice of lemon.

It was not unusual for spymasters to meet in a public place for a pre-briefing, especially in the evening, before moving on to a secure place to conduct a more thorough brief. Stratton checked his watch. It was exactly seven.

He walked over to the table. Sumners spotted him just before he arrived and got to his feet.

'Ahh, Stratton,' Sumners said, offering his hand. His smile was thin and as cold as always. Stratton shook his hand, which was also cold despite being in his pocket. 'This is my department chief,' he said.

The man produced his own version of a smiling mask and offered his hand without getting to his feet.

'Stratton,' he said. 'Heard a bit about you. Glad you could come along. Can I get you a drink?'

'I'm fine, thank you,' Stratton said, and took a seat at the table. Sumners moved around to form a triangle.

'How was your journey up from Poole?' the unnamed man asked cordially. Talking to people much lower than him was a part of his profession and he oozed confidence. Stratton wondered what the man was doing here. He doubted Sumners needed him to give his brief. It was just possible he happened to be in the bar for another reason and since he was Sumners' boss, Sumners had joined him. Stratton wondered which type of MI officer he was: either one of the brilliant ones snapped up from a top university to be groomed for the higher echelons, or titled and just doing his stint in MI, which was a very traditional pastime for some families. If he was the latter there was a chance he was an idiot. Some things didn't change in jolly old England and fools could still find their way into the inner circles of power simply because of their birth or connections. Judging by the cut of his suit and his expensive watch, he was independently wealthy. That was not at all unusual. No one joined MI6 for the money. The pay scale was about equal to the regular army. In Stratton's case, because his parent unit was Special Forces, he was paid far higher than any MI5 or MI6 operative. He probably earned more than Sumners, who was not independently wealthy and obviously did the job purely for the love of it.

'Do you go to Lulworth Cove much?' the MI officer asked. 'Delightful part of the country.'

'Nice place to dive,' Stratton said.

'Clams,' the man said. 'Very good clams.'

'One of the reasons we like to dive there.'

'Very sensible.'

The conversation paused there and a silence hung between them. It was for Sumners' boss to lead the talking and so Stratton and Sumners sat quietly, waiting for him to continue. The man leaned forward to pick up his glass and took a sip. He inspected the contents for a second then put it back on the table. Stratton wasn't sure if he caught a faint look of disapproval.

'Are you superstitious, Stratton?' the man eventually asked.

'Superstitious?' Stratton echoed. He expected the man to get on with the operation pre-brief but it sounded as if he was still making idle chit-chat. 'You mean walking under ladders and breaking mirrors?'

'That sort of thing,' the man said.

'No.'

'What about the supernatural?' the man asked.

Stratton glanced at Sumners wondering where this line of questioning was leading but his old boss was firmly in the back seat and keeping quiet, staring straight ahead deep in his own thoughts as if he were not part of the conversation.

'You mean ghosts?' Stratton asked.

'If you like. How do you feel about ghosts? Do you believe they exist?'

'It's like the question of life on another planet. I don't give it much thought.'

'But you're not opposed to the idea. Things like ghosts. You don't believe it's all a load of rubbish?'

Stratton was tempted to ask what this was about but decided to play the man's game. These types weren't known for wasting much time on idle talk, especially with the likes of Stratton, a mere field operative. The questions had to have something to do with the op but Stratton couldn't begin to imagine what.

'I wouldn't say it was rubbish, but I wouldn't argue in its favour,' Stratton said.

'What about clairvoyants? Do you believe they can get in touch with the afterlife and learn about things that have happened or are about to happen?'

'I've never met one. I've heard stories from police officers who've used them on occasion.'

'Oh? What sort of stories?'

'I was told how a clairvoyant helped find the body of a little girl who had been murdered and then she, the clairvoyant, directed the police to clues that led them to who did it.'

'And do you believe that was what happened?'

'I believe the officer who told me the story believed it.'

'You mean you would have to see it for yourself to believe it?'

'I think if I bet money against it being true I would lose, but that doesn't mean I'm a believer . . . Can I ask what this is all about?'

The man smiled slightly then checked his watch, leaned forward, picked up his drink and took another sip. He put the glass down and stood up to pull on a heavy, dark-blue wool coat.

'You can go ahead, Sumners,' he said. 'I'll see you tomorrow.'

'Right, sir,' Sumners said without getting up.

The man smiled thinly at Stratton again. 'Good luck,' he said, and walked out of the pub.

Stratton watched him go then looked at Sumners for an explanation. 'What was that all about?'

'After I tabled your name for the job, he asked me how broad-minded you were in the area of the supernatural and I couldn't give him a satisfactory answer, not knowing you that well. So before we went ahead with the brief he wanted to ask you himself.'

'Well that's made it all perfectly clear,' Stratton said.

Sumners finished his drink and stood.

'You're saying that was a test,' Stratton said, his expression conveying that if so it was a strange one.

'If you like . . . Let's go for a walk,' Sumners said as he stood and headed for the door.

Stratton sighed, got up and followed.

They stepped outside and Sumners put his hands in his coat pockets and at a slow pace walked towards the river where a cold mist was starting to form.

'He simply wanted to know how open-minded you are.'

'I'd have thought assassinating people required an open mind.'

'Not as much as this job I fear,' Sumners said tiredly, as if he wasn't quite as open-minded as the task required. 'If you thought this was going to be on the front line I'm afraid you're going to be disappointed.'

'You said it was to do with the supertanker.'

'In this world of global terrorism no source of intelligence can be ignored, no matter how far it stretches the boundaries of reality, or our concept of it. As you know, no form of intelligence gathering is one hundred per cent reliable. That's why we employ a great variety of methods to acquire it.

To corroborate and substantiate, analyse and cross check.'

Sumners walked a little further in silence, gathering his thoughts. 'You're going to meet someone,' he said. 'A man. He works for the CIA.'

'A field operative?'

'No. Not your idea of one anyway.'

Stratton pondered why a member of the American Central Intelligence Agency would need a Brit MI6 operative assigned to him. 'Is this some kind of local bodyguard task?' he asked, praying it was not.

'Not exactly . . . You're going to be doing some decoding.'

'Decoding?'

'He will provide information and you will decode it.'

'Have you forgotten who and what I am? This is Stratton. I'm a thug, which is what you turned me into by the way. I used to see myself as an intelligence gatherer and a sophisticated direct-action operative, until you made me into a murderer.'

'That's a bit over the top, Stratton. Unlike you.'

Stratton realised he was much more flippant with Sumners than he used to be. That was not so much to do with familiarity as with experience. Even though it had been a year since they last talked, Stratton felt he knew the man better.

'Decoders have large brains and sit in comfortable offices,' Stratton said.

'It's not quite that kind of decoding. You'll understand better when you meet him.'

'So who exactly is this person?'

'You've heard of psychic spies?'

Stratton's brow furrowed. 'Is that what all the supernatural questions were about?'

'I empathised with your analogy about not betting against its existence but then not quite being a believer. I would have described this man to you as a kind of clairvoyant but when I suggested as much during the initial brief I received from the CIA I was told that was not at all correct. Ever heard of "remote viewing" in an intelligence-gathering term?'

'Wireless video?'

'Imagine being able to do exactly that, see something miles away but without any technological aids.'

Stratton furrowed his brow again. This was becoming bizarre.

'What about precognition?' Sumners asked.

'Seeing into the future?'

'Yes. This is where my understanding of it all starts to get a bit foggy. I apologise. I'm not sure if precognition is the same as remote viewing . . . The example they gave me was PanAm flight 103 that crashed into Lockerbie after terrorists blew it up. A few hours after it happened, remote viewers apparently saw the bomb that brought it down inside a music box. They also saw a back-up bomb; an Iranian woman who lost her family when the Americans shot down that Iranian airliner from one of their missile frigates had explosives strapped around her waist. If the music box hadn't gone off she would've detonated hers. For decades the CIA has used psychics as intelligence gatherers. Apparently we've been quite heavily into it ourselves. This is the first time I've ever had anything to do with it. The difference between clairvoyants and remote viewers is clairvoyants use the supernatural whereas remote viewers use alpha waves. I suppose one is spiritual and the other scientific. Remote viewers are able to focus on things, the other side of the world if need be: people, objects, smells, colours, emotions. The thing is they don't always understand what they see. The information they gather has to be analysed, or decoded. Apparently, a remote viewer was tasked to access Osama bin Laden's mind after the Twin Tower attack to learn his mental state – was he worried or feeling good and secure, that sort of thing. The viewer saw him in a cave, but which cave and where in the world was it? That's the decoding part.'

Stratton stopped walking and looked at Sumners, trying to control a growing suspicion of the man's motives for calling him in.

'Is this some kind of a joke?' Stratton snapped, more irate with Sumners than he had ever been before. 'Stratton's all burned out so we'll give him the crap at the bottom of the barrel. Is that what this job is? Looking after Harry Potter's dad? Well, thanks very much, Sumners, but no thanks. You can shove this one up your arse.'

Stratton started to walk away.

'Calm down, Stratton. Listen to me. This is important . . . He saw the tanker assault,' Sumners called out to him, then checked to make sure the street was empty, which it was. 'He saw it being captured and the crew butchered.'

Stratton slowed to a stop and looked back at him, his curiosity piqued.

'My boss hates the Grenadier,' Sumners continued. 'I assure you he wouldn't have come down here to see you or anybody if he thought the job was the bottom of the barrel.'

'The tanker was hit around midnight,' Stratton said. 'If someone knew about it why did we hit it at the last minute half a day later?'

'That's what I've been trying to tell you about the decoding side of it. There are thousands of tankers sailing the oceans of the world at any one time. The viewer couldn't see its name or tell where in the world it was. The decoders didn't have enough knowledge or information to decode what he saw.'

Stratton faced Sumners. The hook was going in.

'And what am I supposed to do, hang around with him until he has another vision?'

'They're not visions. Look upon them as searches. He's already found something and apparently it scared the hell out of him. I'm afraid we've not been able to decode it either. We need someone on the ground with him all the time, asking questions, clarifying the information. Decoding teams will also be on hand as usual. Different viewers are sensitive to different things. This one sees locations but he's also sensitive to emotions. So far he's described what he's seen or felt as an enormous danger but he can't tell what that is. To use his own words, he's never felt anything so horrific in his life.'

'If this is so big, why me? I mean, this isn't exactly my job description.'

'Right now our intelligence resources are stretched thinner than they've ever been in our history.

Wonderful though remote viewers may sound in theory, they are greatly flawed. Much of their information cannot be accurately decoded. It's often misleading. On average they're rated at six per cent accuracy. Your rating as a field operative for instance is ninety-two per cent. What you see and report back is real and usually easily verifiable. But the six per cent the remote viewers give us that is successfully decoded is worth the fortune it costs the CIA to run its psychic department – according to them at least . . . These recent viewings are related to the tanker. That's what this particular viewer has been concentrating on ever since it was attacked . . . And that's why you are here.'

Sumners had done a good job stroking Stratton's ego and expectancy back into shape. There was some importance attached to the assignment and it was interesting.

'He's here then, in England?' Stratton asked.

'Yes.'

The two men faced each other in the dark street, neither sure of where they stood in this most unusual and possibly ridiculous task. All their years of training in their respective disciplines had not prepared them for an operation like this.

'Okay,' Stratton finally said. It was bizarre, but why not? What else was going on?

Sumners took a photograph from his pocket and handed it to Stratton. It was a headshot. The man appeared to be in his late fifties, had short grey hair and was refined looking. Sumners took the picture back after Stratton had studied it for a few seconds.

'He's described as sensitive with occasional unstable tendencies but not violently so. He's also paranoid and perhaps even schizophrenic.' Sumners took a package from his coat pocket and handed it to Stratton. 'Cell-phone and charger. My numbers are programmed into it as well as others you might need. There's also five thousand pounds expenses money, a credit card and your MI6 ID. The routine hasn't changed. Expenses must be justified, all fares economy and I'll need receipts for anything over five pounds. He's at the Victory Club under the name of Gabriel Stockton, room 534.'

'The Victory Club?' Stratton asked. It was a hotel around the corner from Marble Arch, a basic discount hotel for currently serving and former members of the British military and their families.

'Where did you expect us to put him up? Claridge's? He's expecting you tonight. I've reserved you a room next to his. I look forward to hearing from you.'

Sumners turned and walked away.

'How come he's expecting me when you didn't know I'd take the job?'

'I must be psychic,' Sumners said without looking back and walked past the entrance to the pub and disappeared around the corner.

Stratton frowned and then weighed the package in his hand, his mind already searching ahead. He was used to automatically planning as many aspects as he could of a new assignment immediately after a briefing, and sometimes during it, but this one left him with little else to contemplate other than how to get to Marble Arch.

He pocketed the package and headed down the street, his philosophical old self surfacing once again. There was never a dull moment in MI6.

Stratton's taxi pulled up outside the Victory Club, half a block from the corner of Edgware Road, and he climbed out and handed the fare to the driver.

'Can I have a receipt, please?'

The taxi driver handed him a blank receipt and drove away.

'Good evening, sir,' a cheerful Eastern European in a doorman's uniform bid Stratton as he opened the front door for him. Stratton returned the greeting as he walked inside and headed for the reception desk.

After checking in, Stratton walked around a corner to the elevator, stepped inside and pushed the fifth-floor button. A few seconds later, he exited the elevator on the fifth floor and headed along the corridor, passing a dozen or so rooms bearing brass plaques dedicating them to an assortment of British regiments, until he reached room 534.

He placed his ear close to the door but couldn't hear anything, no television or movement.

He knocked.

A creaking sound suggested someone was getting off a bed, then came a voice: 'Who is it?' a man said with a hint of an American accent.

'It's Stratton.'

'Who?'

Stratton wondered if someone had already screwed up and forgotten to give the guy his name. 'Stratton. I was told you were expecting me.'

There was a moment's silence. 'One second,' the voice eventually said. Stratton could hear more movement. A moment later the door was unlatched and opened wide enough for the man to look out. Stratton recognised him from the photograph though he was taller than expected, perhaps an inch or so on top of Stratton, his hair had more silver in it and he had a far more distinguished look in the flesh.

Gabriel studied Stratton with what appeared to be suspicion for an inordinately long time.

'Stratton?' the man asked, looking unsure.

'That's right,' Stratton said as he looked at both ends of the corridor, checking to see they were alone.

Gabriel opened the door and Stratton walked into the simply decorated room which was barely large enough to allow anyone to move around the double bed without scraping the walls. It had a small television on a swivel bracket bolted into a corner close to the ceiling, a dresser with an electric kettle, two cups and tea and coffee and a tidy en-suite bathroom with a bath, sink and toilet ergonomically fitted into the most confined of spaces. Stratton stood in the gap between the room entrance and the bathroom as Gabriel closed the door behind him, locked it and remained standing, apparently not quite finished with his examination of Stratton.

'Everything okay?' Stratton asked, forcing a smile, doing a bit of inspecting himself. Gabriel was conservatively dressed in a wool jacket, striped shirt, plain tie, wool trousers with a razor crease and brown brogues. He looked like a schoolteacher. His build suggested he had been athletic in his younger days but not any more. Everything about him, the cut of his cloth, hair, fingernails and neatness of his belongings suggested he was meticulous. He looked tired though, his eyes red and sunken, the lids blinking lazily indicating a thirst for sleep, and they flickered in harmony with his gravel voice as if sensitive to the coarseness of it.

'You're British military intelligence?' Gabriel said, more a statement of doubt than a question.

'And you're Gabriel,' Stratton said, ignoring the attitude and putting it down to paranoia. 'You settled in all right?' Stratton asked, practising his polite tone. 'How was your trip?'

'Tiring. I don't like travelling.'

'London can be a zoo.'

'I've been here before,' Gabriel said. 'I'm not much of a fan . . . Excuse me,' he said, looking Stratton in the eye as he took a pace towards him. Stratton moved aside and Gabriel walked past and into the bathroom where he packed his toothbrush, toothpaste, soap and comb into his ablutions bag, and walked back into the bedroom to the window where he collected more of his personal effects and placed them into a small holdall.

'I take it we're going right away?' Gabriel asked as he picked up a pair of slippers off the floor and put them carefully into the bag so that the soles were uppermost and not touching any clothing.

'Going where?' Stratton asked as he watched Gabriel pull a quilted jacket on having apparently decided they were indeed leaving.

'They didn't tell you?'

'Tell me what?'

'I told them this morning and nothing's changed,' Gabriel said sounding irritated.

Gabriel was obviously not the friendliest of people. Stratton wondered if this was his permanent mood or if a night's sleep would reveal a more gracious side to him. As for the information Gabriel had given 'them', Stratton could only wonder what he meant.

'Why don't we sit down and talk for a moment,' Stratton suggested. 'Get to know each other a little. Whatever it is you told them you can tell me,' he continued, waiting for Gabriel to sit on the side of the bed before he took the seat by the door.

Gabriel remained standing looking unsatisfied with Stratton's suggestion, or perhaps it was the patronising tone in which he spoke to him. 'I can't work here,' he said. 'That's why I don't like being away.'

'Away from where?'

'Virginia. I work better there.'

'You live in Virginia?'

Gabriel gave him a look as if Stratton should have known the answer. 'You *are* from MI6, aren't you?' he asked in a superior tone difficult to hide because that is how he felt. This thug was not what he had been expecting. He had imagined a man in a suit for a start, or at least a jacket and tie, not in what looked like nylon trousers with zipper pockets on the sides, boots of some description and a leather jacket that appeared to have survived World War Two. Gabriel suddenly wondered if there might have been a misunderstanding and that this man was simply a driver or escort.

Stratton could sense Gabriel's discomfort with him but he was no stranger to being underestimated because of his looks. 'I was brought on to the job in a bit of a hurry,' Stratton said. 'They told me a little, but who better to tell me about the job than you?' He now wished he did know more about Gabriel and thought it was unlike Sumners not to brief him thoroughly, but since he had not, there was probably a reason behind it. Still, it had made his introduction appear amateurish. 'Why don't we take a moment and you can tell me everything I need to know.'

Gabriel frowned, disappointed this man was to be his 'assistant', but he was used to disappointment in this business. His own intelligence agency did not impress him at the best of times, and although he had never worked with the British before he did not expect they were likely to do so either. If this character was anything to go by, the Brits looked like they would prove to be dismally worse. When he heard British intelligence was sending over one of their people to assist him, he assumed he would be like the type he had met in abundance at CIA HQ, Foggy Bottom, Virginia. Normally he had nothing to do with the 'labourers' as his department referred to the CIA's regular field agents. They occasionally sat in on meetings, usually in the form of familiarity briefings at the wacky spooks or psychic department, part of the tour for new agents. They came in all shapes and sizes and nearly always smartly dressed, but Gabriel had never met one like this before. He was not what Gabriel would have described as a big man, by American standards, although he did have an aura of toughness about him. Add to that his battered leather coat, dishevelled hair and a day's growth on his face, overall, his look was unkempt to say the least. There was something else about him though, something Gabriel had never been so keenly aware of in a person before, agent or otherwise, not at first glance. If he were pushed to describe it, he would have to say there was a darkness around the man that his forced smile could not disguise.

'Why'd you come to England then?' Stratton breezed on. 'If you work better in Virginia, that is?'

'Too much interference. I couldn't see clearly. Distance shouldn't make a difference, but location sometimes does . . . my location . . . Sometimes where you are, the atmosphere and surroundings, are not conducive . . . The danger is here, anyway. I know that. This is the best place to be.'

'Danger?'

'That's what I said.'

'What danger?'

'I don't know.'

'I mean, is it—'

'I don't know,' Gabriel said, cutting him off brusquely as he went back to packing his things. 'As soon as I got into the taxi at the airport and headed into London, I saw the air base as clearly as if I was there myself.'

'What air base?'

'I told them all about the air base,' Gabriel said, looking at Stratton with unguarded suspicion. 'What *do* you know about me and what I do?'

'Look . . . I just came in from the outside. There

wasn't time for a proper brief. Let's just accept I know nothing about you, what you do, or what this is all about. In fact, I don't really have much of a clue what my part is supposed to be in this operation.' If that's what it is, he thought to himself. 'So can we just cool it a little and accept I know nothing?' Stratton's sullen, unmoving eyes remained fixed on Gabriel's.

Gabriel could sense the Englishman was no pushover and decided he liked being here as little as Gabriel did. If the Brits worked anywhere near the same way as the agency, they were stuck with each other, for the time being at least, and so to that end Stratton had a point. Gabriel was aware he was acting irritable and short tempered but he was never very good at dealing with pressure even when he was aware of all the mitigating circumstances. He was not naturally an ill-tempered man and did not like feeling that way.

Gabriel took a breath and made an effort to bring himself down. 'I saw an American air base,' he said, somewhat slower and calmer than he had been speaking previously. 'I'm certain of that. There was a large wood nearby, a forest I should say. Soldiers use it. There are open spaces in the woods and I could see soldiers with guns and in combat fatigues.'

Stratton suddenly felt awkward listening to Gabriel as if he was providing serious information. It was one thing to try and accept that there were people who could see things as if they were able to transport themselves to another place on the planet, but to actually have to communicate with one as if everything they said was a fact made Stratton feel self-conscious, as if he was having a conversation with a mad person just to humour them.

'You're saying this American air base is in England?' Stratton asked, ignoring his discomfort and doing his best to take this seriously.

'Yes.'

'Why?'

'What do you mean, why? Why they put it in England?'

Stratton added another mental note about Gabriel. He was literal. 'No. Why do you think it is an American air base in England?'

'I can't see signposts. It doesn't work like that. If you were to think of a place, anywhere in the world, that you have been to, or even just heard or read descriptions of, a beach, a mountain range, a living room, whatever the images you had in your head, that's what I would see. I can't hear voices or the words in a person's head, just images and emotions. Do you understand?' Gabriel was beginning to sound like a teacher talking to a young student.

Stratton did not, but at least Gabriel was talking. 'You can read anyone's mind then?' he asked.

'It's not mind reading. I don't know who I can access or why I can access them. In this case it seems to be connected with something very evil.'

Stratton didn't know what to make of Gabriel. Clearly the man believed in himself, and obviously several people high up in British and American intelligence did too. That negated whatever Stratton thought of all this. All he could do was get on with his job, once he had identified what that was. 'So why an American air base in the UK?' he asked.

'Because it was filled with American personnel, soldiers, airmen, US flags.'

'But what puts it in England?'

Gabriel went back to his packing. 'The vehicles, the trucks and the cars, were driving on the left side of the road,' he said as he neatly folded a shirt before placing it into another compartment of his holdall.

'Why not Japan?'

'Red phone boxes,' Gabriel said. 'There are some things I am able to work out for myself,' he sighed. 'You ever decoded remote viewers before?'

'No.'

Gabriel shook his head. This was becoming more amateurish by the second. 'Decoding is everything. You're here because of your local knowledge. Your job is to interpret what I see.'

'And you don't have any hint of what the danger is?' he asked.

'I said no.'

'Then how do you know there's danger?'

'Because *he* does. He knows it's dangerous. It's the danger itself that I've tapped into, more than anything physical. That's why it's so strong. It's the most dangerous thing he's ever done in his life, and he's done many dangerous things. I can feel it in him, burning like a furnace.'

'He?'

'I don't know who *he* is either.'

Stratton guessed that might be his answer. 'You know where this danger is?' he asked, pressing on.

'No. It's not with him. He's looking for it, or at

least he was last time I viewed him. He believes he knows where it is and how to find it, and he is determined to succeed. All I can tell you about the danger is that he's touched it before but never experienced it.'

'Do you know anything about him at all?' Stratton asked, starting to treat it as a game to keep his interest up.

'He's foreign. I'm certain of that. I can't hear voices or discern languages, just the emotion. Emotion has no language barriers. Yes, some races are more emotional than others, but I'm looking at an individual. He's introvert. Lonely I think. He's interesting. And dark, of course. Very dark. Dark and deep as an abandoned mine. And dangerous. I could get lost looking inside his head . . . There's a lot of fear there . . . anxiety. Sadness too, and anger. He's tormented, that's for sure.'

'How do you know it's a man?'

'He has the desires of a man. They're different than the desires a woman has for another woman. You understand that much at least.'

Arsehole, Stratton added to Gabriel's mental notes. However, the man was genuinely afraid of something and fear alters a person. 'What do you think he's afraid of?'

'That's the part that's most confusing. Some of the fear is mine. I'm having trouble controlling it. It's getting in the way.'

'Why are you afraid?'

'I don't know.'

Stratton looked away, doing his best not to appear

unconvinced, but Gabriel was far too sensitive to scepticism to miss it.

Gabriel smirked, more at himself or the situation than at Stratton. 'You think I'm full of it, don't you?'

Under different circumstances, Stratton might not have denied it, but considering the powers that sent both of them here to work together it would have been inappropriate. 'I was told there might be a connection with the supertanker.'

'You don't want to be here,' Gabriel said, ignoring the question and feeling his temper rising again. 'I can't see the point in you getting involved if you don't have any faith.'

'Maybe someone more suited to this will take my place tomorrow, but right now you've got me.' Stratton hoped that was true about being replaced, and decided he was going to insist on it at the first opportunity. There was nothing about this assignment that fitted his job description.

Gabriel sat down on the bed heavily, exhausted, and held his head in his hands. 'I need to rest,' he said, and then immediately appeared to wrestle with himself and got to his feet again. 'No. We must go. We have to identify the location.'

Stratton studied Gabriel as he pondered the situation. On an immediate basis, getting out on the ground and doing something appealed to him. He did not like stagnancy and preferred being on the move. Also, on a professional level, there was nothing worse than wasting time when there was an opportunity to make ground, and since this was the start, as far as Stratton was concerned at least, moving anywhere was a step forward. Besides, he needed to break the ice with this man, and it did not look as if he was going to get far stuck in this hotel room.

Stratton took his mobile phone from a pocket, scrolled through the phone list and hit the send button. A moment later the call was answered. 'Stratton here. Two five eight. I need a car, self drive . . . Stratton, two five eight,' he said, repeating his Military Intelligence number, but the person on the other end could not find any record of him. As soon as an operative was assigned to an operation, every department in MI was supposed to receive a notification e-mail. Not all areas were open to his discretion, such as requesting a private jet, which depended on his priority rating. A car should have been well within his allowances but the procurement department could give him nothing if he was not on the assignment roster. No doubt he was tapping into the system before Sumners had gotten to a computer. Stratton could hear voices at the other end and a moment later the person dealing with him came back on the phone. Stratton was about to ask him to get in contact with Sumners when he was told the assignment roster had just that second been updated and his request was already being processed. Stratton's faith in the system returned. 'Thank you,' he said and put the phone back in his pocket. He checked his watch.

'A car's on its way,' he told Gabriel who nodded and picked up his bag. 'It'll take a few minutes.'

Gabriel looked around the room to check he had everything.

'Do you normally have help decoding your viewings?' Stratton asked.

'A vast research department usually.'

'Back in Virginia.'

'And Stanford, the research institute.'

'That's a university.'

'The first remote-viewing protocols were synthesised at the institute. The programme was partially funded by the agency who monitor the security issues. But, of course, it's better to have local knowledge if you're looking for places, which is why you're here.'

'I understand the part about the local knowledge,' Stratton said.

Gabriel believed him although he remained doubtful the Englishman was any closer to taking it seriously.

They stood in silence for a moment. Stratton had to admit he was mildly fascinated with the concept of being able to 'see' other people's thoughts and wanted to ask Gabriel how he did it, but decided this was not a good time. 'Let's head down to the street,' he said, opening the door. 'It shouldn't be long.'

Gabriel walked out of the room and Stratton followed letting the door swing shut.

They went down the stairs to the lobby, out through the hotel entrance and on to the street, where they stood apart in silence. A few minutes later a dark blue four-door Rover turned the corner from Edgware Road, cruised along the street and pulled to a stop in front of them. A man climbed out of the driver's side leaving the engine running, looked at Stratton and gave him a nod. Stratton walked around the car to the driver's door.

'This got comms?' Stratton asked the driver.

'Na. It's clean.'

'No support kit in the boot?'

'Nuffin. I was told you needed a sterile car just for a run around.'

Stratton understood – they were in good old England on a safe op – but he always liked the support of comms, a medic pack and a weapon or two, out of habit if nothing else. Safe ops held bad memories for him. The last one he ran was in Paris and he had lost a US Navy Seal operative to the Real IRA. 'Thanks,' Stratton said to the man who nodded and walked away up the street.

'This is our ride,' Stratton said to Gabriel.

Gabriel climbed into the back while Stratton got behind the wheel and shut his door. He turned to look at Gabriel pulling his bag beside him and resting his head on the back of the seat as if preparing to sleep.

'Where're we going?' he asked as he turned back to familiarise himself with the instruments and check the fuel gauge.

'That's your job,' Gabriel said tiredly.

Stratton suddenly felt like a chauffeur but held back any sarcastic comment, reminding himself this was a game and a temporary one at that. Gabriel had the clues and Stratton had to piece them together. It might even be fun. What else was going on?

'An American air base near a large wood with soldiers in it?' Stratton asked.

'I have nothing more to add to that at the moment,' Gabriel said.

Stratton pulled his seatbelt on, put the car into gear, drove round the corner at the end of the street and headed for the Bayswater Road.

The only American air bases in England he could think of were Mildenhall, Lakenheath and Fairford. There were a few others the Yanks shared with the RAF in some way or other and Gabriel had given no clues the bases were not dual nationality. But Mildenhall and Lakenheath were the biggest US bases outside of the States and both were close to Thetford Forest, which had a large Brit army training area. That was north east of London, two hours or so. It was a start, and if it was a negative, he would have to make a few calls to get information on other locations.

M1, M11 or A1, he wondered? The M11 sounded good from what he could remember of trips into Norfolk.

Stratton suddenly felt hungry. He had not eaten supper and only a sandwich for lunch. 'You hungry?'

'No.'

Stratton decided to get out of the city first and then stop somewhere, on the motorway perhaps, and grab a bite. He looked in his rear-view mirror. Gabriel had his eyes closed but did not look asleep.

'Is it some kind of mental gift?'

'What?'

'Remote viewing.'

'I'm told most people can be taught to view.'

'You can be taught to look inside people's heads?' That sounded even more far-fetched.

'It's all about clearing one's mind and getting into a pure alpha state.'

Gabriel did not elaborate further and Stratton was beginning to find his attitude irritating. 'Gabriel, I'd like to know more about it . . . Yes, I'm sceptical, but you can understand that.'

Gabriel opened his eyes slightly to look at Stratton. He remained silent for a moment deciding whether or not to bother trying to explain any further. 'The brain basically operates in four mental states: alpha, beta, theta and delta. Delta is deep sleep and the best place to receive viewings, but you can't interpret them if you are asleep. Theta is light sleep and also a good place to view, but you can quickly drift into delta. Beta is normal consciousness, such as where you are now, but it is almost impossible to view because the mind is too crammed. Alpha is the mind state between theta and beta where you can clear your mind but remain awake. It's a form of meditation. The rest is practice and being able to interpret what you see. It's really that simple. If you want to know more about it, you'll have to get a book. I do it, I don't teach it.'

Stratton rolled his eyes. He had got what he asked for but was none the wiser.

'Do you believe in God?' Gabriel asked him.

'I don't know.'

'Because you haven't seen him.'

'Because I've never needed him,' Stratton said, then wondered how true that was. He was reminded of something he had thought of that afternoon on the train while reading his book about the Templars and the crusades, which was how many men went to war and fought for God or in search of him.

'Interpreting . . . That's where it always falls apart,' Gabriel said. 'Like those cards psychiatrists hold up with nothing but black blobs on them and they ask you what you see. One person sees a butterfly, another sees Abraham Lincoln. Eventually someone has to make a choice, and then all the other choices have to hang off that one. You start wrong, then every-thing else is usually wrong.'

Gabriel closed his eyes.

'You make much money as a viewer?' Stratton asked, trying not to sound flippant, although he was being a little. Gabriel didn't answer. Stratton glanced in the mirror. He was either asleep or didn't want to talk any more.

A sign indicated the M11 was a few miles ahead. Stratton checked his watch. They could be in the area in an hour and a half.

An all-too-familiar feeling suddenly enveloped him, a deep sense of pointlessness, as if he should be doing something more useful with his life. What that was he had no idea but the frequency of the feeling seemed to increase the older he got. He often wondered if he would get more out of life doing something like diving instruction on some Caribbean island, living in a palm-covered lean-to on the beach and wearing flip-flops, shorts and brightly coloured shirts. But then, who was he kidding? A week of that and he would start turning crazy. He suspected the answer to his idea of a meaningful life was close by but he had always been skirting around it, not brave enough to make the leap. For the moment Sumners dictated his life for him until he could find one of his own. And fate, of course.

5

Zhilev stood in the darkness of a forest surrounded by a dense, brittle army of black slender pines, their heads shuffling in the breeze. He was completely still, listening to the sounds of the night. It was some thirteen years since he had last stood in this wood, on the same spot, also in darkness, but that time he was not alone. He had been with three other members of Spetsnaz, all Combat Swimmers, all from the unit on Mayskiy Island. They had been dropped off the night before by a Russian 'fishing boat' in the Norwegian Channel, ten miles off the coast of East Anglia, where they then motored the rest of the way to the coast in a small rubber inflatable. The relatively quiet beaches west of Cromer had been chosen as the point to come ashore where it was also easier to carry the boat up the gently sloping sand and into the hinterland at high tide, deflate it and bury it with the engine and fuel bags in a sand dune. They then made their way across country and just before dawn arrived at a small wood a mile in from the coast where they laid up for the rest of the day. One of them remained on watch at all times in case of farmers or children while the others slept, ate, or serviced their gear, then the following evening they crossed several fields to an agent contact point in a quiet country lane. The agent was a Sandringham game warden who had done this many times in the past ten years. He drove them across country in his Land Rover to the other side of Thetford Forest and from there they walked through the wood to the point where Zhilev now stood.

He remembered how the pines were younger and thinner then but still dense enough to give cover from view from the light, night-time traffic that cruised the A1065, 75 metres away, where it cut through this part of the forest. During his military service he had imagined returning to this place, but never as a civilian.

Zhilev had been standing still for almost an hour, the recommended minimum amount of time to watch and listen before proceeding to the next phase. Throughout his career, Zhilev had been a perfectionist and stickler for protocol. His reconnaissance and target survey reports were always detailed and supported by sketches, photographs, charts or maps, with samples of local soil and flora where possible, and Zhilev kept a copy of everything except the samples. It was an offence to do so but wise and worth the risk if your chosen career in the military happened to be with an arm of the KGB, which Special Forces ultimately were even though Zhilev's unit came under the direct command of the Navy. One never knew where one's career might lead and a detailed record of one's past exploits was essential, even though it could be a double-edged weapon.

The tide of power in Russia was a turbulent one and long before the wall came down those in privileged places knew a storm was brewing from within. Zhilev decided early on in his career that keeping such information and never needing it was better than the reverse.

There was a chill in the moist air, still not as cold as Riga at this time of year, but his well-built Russian boots protected his feet from the damp ground and his shaggy old sheepskin coat, a present from his brother to use on camping trips, kept his body warm. The only activity he had detected while standing in the wood was a handful of foraging muntjaks, the short-legged, plump little Asiatic deer that roamed these woods. Zhilev had not taken his original route across the forest from the old agent drop-off point but had walked through the wood, keeping parallel with the road, from the garage on the roundabout three-quarters of a mile away where he had left his car parked among many others so it would not be noticed.

It had been a tiring journey from Riga to Ostende but he had managed to snatch a solid hour's sleep during the short ferry crossing to England. Apart from his usual aching neck, he felt quite good. Perhaps it was the rush of being on an operation once again, even though it was not an official mission sanctioned by his government. But it would be the biggest operation he had ever undertaken, by far; much bigger than ferrying agents into Europe through Swedish locks using mini-subs, or a bodyguard to Gorbachev in Reykjavik and Malta, or ferrying weapons and explosives into Palestine and

Lebanon and operators into Afghanistan. This mission had not been planned and prepared by him but by Spetsnaz, and was a long-standing operation which had been in position for the past thirty years, and maintained and trained for in the event it was needed. Zhilev had some variations to the plan, of course. The target for one.

It had taken him no more than a day to adjust and update the operation to his needs after thoroughly going over the report he had kept, along with several others, in a large metal box under the stairs. The only factors that could pose a problem were changes caused by time, erosion and, of course, by the FSB, the Federal Security Service which had replaced the KGB after the end of the Cold War. It was possible that operations of this nature had been dismantled but Zhilev considered it unlikely. There were clues that operational commitments against the West had not changed, comments he had heard on television or read in newspapers and on the Internet from politicians and high-ranking military personnel, which suggested many attitudes and suspicions about the West remained for the most part unchanged. The West appeared to have fallen under the illusion that with the end of the Cold War, Russian espionage and war and counter-war plans had been shelved or dismantled. To the contrary, if anything, there had been a general increase in spying and military planning and contingencies immediately after Yeltsin took command. If people in the West thought that because the wall had come down and a fledgling democracy was growing in Russia, it had changed its mind about

Western greed and expansionism and no longer suspected its duplicitous and underhanded ways, they were sadly mistaken. In the old days, expansionism was about land and the fulcrum of political control. Now it was all about economic empires and controlling them, but many of the ways and means of achieving goals remained the same. The country with the biggest stick made the rules and broke them when it suited, and Russia was not about to fall behind if it could help it. Zhilev felt confident everything in the forest was how he had left it all those years ago and that he would find what he was looking for. He had nothing to lose by carrying out a reconnaissance, and everything to gain if he was right.

Zhilev was not here for any political, economic or military gain. His motivation was an ancient one and second only to greed: revenge. Those who supported the people who murdered his brother were going to pay a terrible price for what they did. The whole world would know by the time he was finished, and, more than that, the entire world would be involved.

Zhilev had already found one of the markers as per the map: a centuries-old milestone, its engraved information long since eroded, located precisely 73 metres on a bearing of 271 degrees from the apex of the bend in the road, which itself was exactly 527 metres north of the northernmost entrance to a public picnic area. The milestone was one of three short-range markers which would lead him to what he was looking for. The markers were chosen for their location; surrounding the precise place he was looking for in a triangular fashion. If an imaginary line were drawn through each marker on the specific bearing written in the report, where the three lines crossed was the pinpoint he was looking for. There were also three long-range markers or landmarks, more prominent features several miles away, aimed at vectoring a searcher to the area of the short-range markers. One was a radio mast, the other a factory chimney, the third the centre of a roundabout, the bearings through all three crossed at the secret location; the smaller markers were the final and more accurate indicators.

Since Zhilev had already been to the location he did not need the long-range markers and could make do with just two of the short-range landmarks: one of them being the milestone, the other the southerly post of a five-bar metal gate, 150 metres on a bearing of 270 degrees from his position.

Lights suddenly appeared in the distance and seconds later the sound of a car approaching. He stood still as it drew closer and waited until it passed and continued out of sight.

Zhilev searched the immediate area and selected two long and robust sticks, breaking off the smaller branches to clean them up.

He took a compass from a pocket, held it in front of him and turned his body until the needle settled down and the thin luminous line highlighted his pre-set reading of 105 degrees. Then, holding it like a weapon, he looked for something in the distance he could aim for so he would not have to keep following the compass, but there was nothing but black wood. Not that it mattered. It would just have made it easier.

He set off in the direction the compass indicated, taking solid paces through the short firs that grew out of the acidic, pine-needle soil. Every time he had to move around a tree, he rechecked his bearing. It had to be precise. After 127 paces, he stopped and planted one of the sticks in the ground by his foot. As an afterthought, he removed his scarf and wound it around the top of the stick so it would be easier to find at the end of the next phase.

Satisfied he had been as accurate as possible, he retraced his footsteps on a back-bearing to the milestone. Here he turned the bezel of the compass to a heading of 270 degrees and marched off in the new direction. In Zhilev's experience one of his normal paces with a slightly added stretch was a metre long, and 150 steps later he was standing in front of the five-bar metal gate which immediately filled him with confidence as well as satisfaction, despite the fact there was a lot more to achieve before he could call it a success.

He adjusted the compass bezel once more and set off in the new direction, counting his paces and constantly reconfirming his direction. At 135 paces he stopped, placed the second stick in the ground beside his toe and looked up to see the stick with his scarf attached two metres away to his left. One more pace and he would have crossed the path from the milestone. He considered taking the distance and bearing from the third marker, but decided it would not be necessary since the first two sticks were quite close together. He could always use the third marker if he had trouble finding the exact spot.

He put the compass away, reached into an inside pocket and pulled out a slender, telescopic length of steel thirty centimetres long. Gripping the ends, he extended it to its maximum length of a metre, then a quick twist and the device was locked into position. One end tapered to a sharp point and Zhilev proceeded to insert it into the ground between the two sticks, pushing it firmly down two-thirds of its length without meeting resistance. He withdrew it, moved the point a few centimetres and repeated the procedure.

The third insertion a little further away met resistance after a third of the rod was in the ground, but it was shallower than he was expecting and he removed it, moved a few more centimetres away and pushed it into the soil again. This time it continued down unimpeded, suggesting the previous obstacle was a stone or a root.

Zhilev continued to work methodically in a line until he had passed the stick with the scarf, then changed direction to head back to the other stick at an angle. After a dozen more insertions the rod met solid resistance about halfway down its length. Zhilev moved it up and down a few times to confirm it was there then inserted it further along again and met the same resistance. A ripple of anticipation shimmied through him and he dropped to his knees, cleared the area of small firs, selected two small sticks and stuck them in the ground at the first two points of resistance. Now he changed direction, probing around to locate the edges of whatever was under the ground. Each time he identified an edge he placed a small stick in the hole. Ten minutes later he got to his feet and looked down at the fruit of his efforts. A dozen twigs formed a near-perfect circle a metre in diameter.

Distant lights indicated another car was approaching. Zhilev watched the beams flicker through the trees until they passed out of sight then removed his coat in preparation for some manual labour and hung it on a nearby tree. He got back down on his hands and knees and began to scrape away the topsoil of pine needles, placing them in a pile outside of the circle of twigs. He went back to his coat and took a military-style folding spade from an inside pocket. Zhilev unfolded it, screwed down the locking device that gave it rigidity, inserted the tip into the soil and, with a heavy boot, plunged it into the earth.

Fifteen minutes later Zhilev struck something hard with a solid clunk that suggested the object was large and metallic. The noise was loud enough to make him pause, his ears searching in every direction. He had not decided what he would do if someone appeared out of the darkness and discovered him. His mission procedure of old was to terminate any intruder and dispose of the body or bodies. He did not expect to meet anyone but he knew he had to have a definite plan in case he did. Up until when the spade struck the metal object beneath the soil, the mission was all so much speculation. But now things were beginning to look as if they might become reality, it was all suddenly deadly serious. If he wanted to proceed, he would have to kill. He did not honestly know what he would do were he to be discovered right at that moment, and he would only know if the situation arose. He decided to leave it at that and let things happen organically, but he felt in his heart that if this phase of the mission was successful, he would proceed as if he was here on behalf of his country.

Satisfied he was alone, Zhilev got on to his knees and reached down into the hole. He scraped around, pulling out handfuls of soil until he exposed what appeared to be a thick iron wheel a little smaller than a steering wheel. He lay on his stomach and, gripping the wheel with both hands, tried to turn it. It would not budge. He tried again, applying every ounce of effort, but the wheel was stuck solid.

He took a moment to rest and wondered when it had last been serviced, or if indeed it had been at all in the last few years. He remembered clearly from his original briefing that the caches were checked at least once a year by an agent whose sole job it was to maintain them and the equipment inside. Any sign of such a maintenance schedule would be an encouraging indication of the cache's operational status. If not it meant the option had been abandoned by the FSB some time after the end of the Cold War and, depending on how long ago that last service was, it would be a decisive factor as to whether or not his plan could continue to the next phase or end there and then.

Zhilev remained optimistic. He took the shovel, jammed it in the rings of the wheel and pulled with all his might. As his head began to shake with the strain, the wheel suddenly moved a little. With renewed vigour he readjusted the spade and took another pull at it. The wheel moved again, this time a little further. He repositioned it again, gave it another firm yank and the wheel turned half a revolution and the friction eased off. He could now turn it with his hands. It moved easily and after several revolutions practically spun, rising as it did so, then stopped suddenly as it reached the end of its thread. Zhilev felt around the threaded shaft beneath the wheel. It was greasy. His expectations rose once again.

He gripped the wheel and this time pulled it upwards. It moved slightly, with a grinding sound. He repositioned his body, gave it another tug, and a heavy, steel, submarine-like hatch opened sideways on a hinge aided by powerful springs designed to counter its weight. A thick, musky smell rose out of the dark hole like damp, rotten clothing. The hatch was half the diameter of the hole Zhilev had dug and wide enough for a full-grown man to climb down through.

Zhilev stood to take a breather and admire his work, and to ensure once again that there was no sign of human life anywhere nearby. Another car appeared and followed the road through the wood before carrying on out of sight.

Zhilev pulled on his coat, removed his scarf from the stick and wrapped it around his neck, then sat on the edge of the hole to search inside with his foot for the ladder he knew was there. He found the first rung, stood upright on it, and lowered himself down through the hatch. As he reached the bottom he took hold of the hatch's inside handle and pulled it down on top of him. What light there had been from the moon and stars disappeared as he closed and secured it with a half turn of the handle.

Seconds later, his granite face was bathed in the light from a small torch. He moved the narrow beam around the chamber and it swept over various objects, many he recognised, and he was relieved as well as excited to find the place pretty much as he remembered it. His hopes of finding what he had come for soared but he held himself from searching for it right away and ordered himself to be patient and to do this in an orderly and clinical fashion.

The first thing he needed to do was find the main power connection. His light scanned the far end of the chamber searching the steel wall but there was no sign of the leads he was expecting to see. Either he had forgotten where it was or it had since been relocated. As he stepped forward to begin a more thorough search, the gods decided to play with him and his torch grew suddenly dim as the battery power faded.

He cursed and slapped the torch in his palm in a futile effort to revitalise it. Cheap Chinese batteries he mumbled, searching his pockets for spares, then remembered he had left them in the car. He cursed his own lack of professionalism. It was a warning that he was not as proficient as he used to be and that he was going to have to start being doubly cautious and more attentive to detail. He chastised himself. Spetsnaz, the finest Special Forces in the world, and he couldn't even organise a working torch. Had one of his subordinates done as much he might have punched him to the ground for being so incompetent.

He blinked as the last drop of energy left his torch and it went completely dead. It was going to be very inconvenient if he had to carry out the rest of his task in complete darkness.

Stratton grabbed a couple of packs of sandwiches and two bottles of water from a shelf and walked over to the counter of the 24-hour BP garage on the A11 ten miles from the Mildenhall turn off. He paid the cashier, took his receipt and headed outside.

He walked to the car parked alone across from the pumps and looked inside, expecting to see Gabriel still sprawled across the back seat asleep but he was sitting up and pressing his skull with his hands as if in great pain.

Stratton opened the rear door. 'Are you okay?' he asked.

Gabriel didn't move as if he had not heard him. Stratton touched his shoulder and Gabriel lowered his hands and looked into his eyes, his own darkly drawn and filled with dread.

'What is it?' Stratton asked.

Gabriel shook his head. 'I don't know,' he said in frustration. 'I don't know . . . I can feel him. He's filled with excitement but at the same time there is guilt, but he's suppressing it . . . He has no doubts about what he wants to do. He's committed . . . I'm beginning to wonder if he's insane.'

'Do you know where he is?' Stratton asked getting down to basic tangibles.

'In a dark place. Cramped. Surrounded by things, objects. I can't make them all out. I saw beds, boxes, containers . . . There was some writing. Quick, give me a pen and paper.'

Stratton took a pen and notepad from his pocket and handed it to him.

Gabriel placed the tip of the pen on the page and then went still and closed his eyes. Stratton wondered if Gabriel was summoning up the image from memory or actually remote viewing it.

Gabriel started to scribble, eyes closed, and after drawing what looked like several squiggly lines he stopped and opened his eyes to see what he had done. Stratton leaned in to look. There were half a dozen separate markings but he could not tell if they were drawings or foreign letters. They looked Greek, or Russian perhaps.

'Is this happening now?' Stratton asked.

'It's now,' Gabriel said.

'Is this at the air base or the forest?'

'How can I know that?' Gabriel snapped. 'I told you it's in a small room . . . or perhaps it wasn't a room,' he said tiredly as he dropped his head into his hands again.

Stratton was beginning to see why this was such a low percentage success-rate intelligence-gathering programme. He wondered how many visions Gabriel had had that were never proven. It seemed too easy to say something was happening and expect to be taken seriously. The phrase 'con man' came to mind. Perhaps these characters had sucked everyone in. The CIA said the skill was real, put millions into it and, since they were committed, who could doubt them. It might be feasible and viewers might actually exist in the world, but who could tell if this guy was a fraud? Maybe the tanker was just a coincidence?

Stratton checked his watch. He decided that since they were here he would humour Gabriel a while longer before heading back to London.

'The ceiling was low and arched,' Gabriel then said. 'It was made of metal, steel, not brick or concrete. Like a submarine.'

Stratton gazed at the petrol station which was now empty. 'Now we're in a submarine,' he mumbled to himself. He wondered if he could lure him into a pub for last orders. A drink might help make this easier to deal with.

'What do you want to do?' Stratton asked.

'I want to find him, of course. That's why we're here.'

Stratton rubbed his face as if to push away the tiredness he was suddenly feeling, then closed Gabriel's door, opened the driver's door, climbed in and started the engine. He drove out of the garage and on to the highway, passing a sign to Thetford Forest.

Zhilev searched in the blackness under one of the bunk beds, his hands becoming his eyes as he felt around for what he knew had to be somewhere in the room. If it took him all night and the next day, searching every inch of the steel tube, he would find it. Zhilev was a patient man but his growing frustration was being fuelled by his own feeling of incompetence. The issue of the failed torch would never leave him, not for as long as he had a memory. As he cursed himself out loud, his hand brushed against what felt like a cable hanging below the mattress.

He pulled it through his fingers until it divided into two thinner cables and then he found the ends, both of which had crocodile clips attached. He followed the cable back in the opposite direction to where it disappeared inside what felt like a junction box. This was what he was looking for. Taking hold of the crocodile clips he stretched under the bed, fanning out his arm in search of the power source that had to be within the length of the cable, and hit a solid, heavy box. He felt the top and what seemed to be battery terminals, attached the crocodile clips to the nodules, and light from several bulbs in the ceiling and on the walls instantly glowed, illuminating the chamber.

Zhilev crawled out from under the bed, covered in dust, and as he stood he had to hold his head for a moment and support it as his neck began aching fiercely. He massaged the vertebrae, bringing his head back and then dropping it forward down on to his chest hoping for the click that usually brought some relief, but it did not come this time. He moaned loudly as he forced his head down, increasing the pain, and then it suddenly cracked. He released it slowly, enjoying the comparative relief, dropped his shoulders and exhaled to relax, then took a look around at the long, narrow, sombre, metal chamber. In shape and size it was similiar to the inside of a road-haulage fuel tanker. It was just high enough for Zhilev to stand up in although he had to lean forward to prevent his head scraping on the ceiling. The memories came flooding back and the cache grew more familiar to him by the second.

A military communication system sat on its own metal shelf welded to the wall beside the bunk bed. Zhilev turned the radio on and as soon as a series of LED lights glowed, he turned it off.

The length of one side of the cylinder was crammed tightly with shelving packed with durable moulded, black plastic boxes of various shapes and sizes. Two pairs of bunk beds took up most of the other side with a narrow walkway separating them from the shelves. At one end of the bunks was a toilet with no privacy panel or curtain, and a sump in the ground beneath it large enough to take care of four men's evacuations. Beside the toilet was the ladder welded to the wall directly below the entrance hatch. At the other end of the cylinder, beyond the beds, was a small table with an electric kettle on it as well as neatly stacked plates, mugs and cutlery. Beneath the table were several oxygen bottles. Everything was covered in a thin film of white dust which came from the air-scrubbers, a carbon-dioxide-absorbent powder which increased the life of the air inside the chamber in case it was unsafe to open the hatch for a long period. Like the submarines of old, if the percentage of oxygen dropped below a partial pressure of point two bars absolute, which affected most people's brains, causing an initial drunken-like state before unconsciousness, the oxygen bottles could be activated and a trickle flow of the live-saving gas would maintain the correct percentage.

On the floor beside the toilet was a camouflage disk the size of a car tyre, designed to fit snugly inside the entrance hole; it was secured in place from beneath prior to closing the hatch and intended to hide the hole from the outside. It would not sustain a close inspection or an adult standing on it, but then it would only ever be used in the event of a real operation and the odds on someone walking through that precise part of the forest during the short period it would be in use were calculated as acceptable. There were also contingency plans in the event the cache was discovered. If the alarm was not immediately raised by the discoverers and they could be captured before they escaped, they were to be killed and their bodies buried. If it was the British military that made the find, and the inhabitants of the cache had no chance of escaping to continue their task, then the final option, which involved explosives and the total destruction of the cache, was none too pleasant for anyone in the immediate vicinity. This was the only kind of operation Zhilev had ever been involved in that called for suicide in the event of the threat of capture, and he remembered his team accepting the order wholeheartedly, understanding the logic and necessity of it.

The placing of the chamber in the ground sometime in the early sixties had been an impressive operation, taking several years to plan and many months to execute. The bare cylinder, or habitat, was purchased from a company in Hull which made it to spec believing it was to be used as an underground fuel reservoir for a factory outside Glasgow. The ground preparation and digging of the hole was carried out by a small group of KGB agents masquerading as geologists, archaeologists and students. Their cover story was that they were on a joint archaeological and soil-sampling project for Exeter and Munich Universities and they had genuine documentation giving them formal written permission to carry out limited earthwork in the area, which was more than enough to satisfy any curious passing police patrol or forest official. The hole itself was dug in a few hours late one afternoon using a rented digger and the cylinder delivered by truck early the next morning, lowered into the ground by crane and buried the same day. This took place far enough away from the road to be shielded from view by the young forest, which was part of the reason for selecting the location. The young pine trees that had been removed to dig the hole were replanted once the cylinder had been buried. The displaced soil which was not redistributed around the area was taken away on the truck that delivered the cylinder. None of the KGB involved in this phase of the operation had any idea what the cylinder was to be used for. The rumour deliberately circulated suggested it was to contain electronic eavesdropping equipment to monitor aircraft movements in and out of various airfields in the region.

Several months later, after the empty habitat had

settled, the Spetsnaz took over the next phase, which was filling it with its various pieces of equipment and making it operational. The first stage was putting in the basic survival and living requirements such as toilet, beds, air-scrubbers, food and water. After that came the communications systems, and then finally the weaponry.

Buried cylinders were only one of the inventive ways the KGB used to provide operational war caches for the Spetsnaz. Some were in the sealed basements of town houses or farms owned by sleeper agents, others were in cleverly concealed caves. Their locations were limited only by the imagination, their main requirement that they could remain in situ without discovery for fifty years.

The last time Zhilev had been in this cache he had spent a week locked beneath the ground, the hatch sealed, with three of his comrades. It was classed as an exercise but deep inside his enemy's territory. The cache was not a surveillance post and never intended to be one. It was specifically designed as a saboteurs' hide, to keep four men in the most basic of comforts while they waited for the order to climb out and head for pre-designated targets where they would carry out their directives. That order would come via a one-way communication system, the signal received by pushing up an antenna through the soil using a specially designed telescopic system in the roof. If sensors under the ground around the cache detected movement by anything as large as a human, the antenna would be lowered. Twice a day, for half an hour each time, it was raised and the radio operative listened on three specific frequencies, each for ten minutes duration, for the Morse sequence that would precede the coded message that contained the vital signal to commence operations. It was a passive receiver device since the ever-watchful electronic ears of the British army intelligence corps might pick up a transmission and come sniffing in the woods for the source of the signal, for the British were well aware these caches existed, although as far as Zhilev knew they had only ever found one in England. He thought there were over two dozen in the British Isles, twice that number in Germany and several dozen more throughout the rest of Europe including Scandinavia. America had the largest number, understandably so, with over a hundred between the two coasts. The only other cache Zhilev had been to was in America, situated beneath a small lake in North Carolina a mile from a series of long-range nuclear-missile silos, and accessed by duck-diving down to a sump, like the U-bend in a toilet.

Zhilev turned to the shelving and looked at the numerous and varied cases spread in front of him, deciding where to start. He was looking for something specific, but also for anything that might be useful on his mission and therefore he decided he might as well search all the containers now that he was here. He moved to one end of the shelves and studied the catch on the front of the first container which consisted of a butterfly screw system that pulled the lid closed as it was turned. He unwound the first pair of latches and forced the halves apart. The hermetically sealed container popped as it opened.

Zhilev raised the lid to find it filled with a variety of canned foods, powdered soup, tea and coffee, hard tack biscuits, dried milk and sugar, chewing gum, chocolate and boiled sweets. There were six of these containers, enough food to last four men a month if they kept their calorific intake down to two thousand per day.

Zhilev took out one of the tins to read the label: Meat and Cabbage Stew. He smiled to himself as he remembered the jokes that always accompanied this infamous meal and the fear of being in the confined space after it was consumed, especially with such an exposed toilet. In practice there never was an inordinate amount of noxious methane produced and everyone suspected that was the work of the great National Scientific Research Institute of Experimental Medicine of the Defence Ministry who had toiled relentlessly and no doubt spent millions of roubles to find a way to reduce the foul gaseous odour. It was with much comic relief the men whiled away the time adlibbing the likely conversations between the scientists on the subject of fart reduction in the Russian military, on account of its multitude of tactical disadvantages including noise, smell and flammability.

Zhilev replaced the tin and examined the next and largest container which was filled with water. On top, neatly stacked, were boxes of sterilising tablets and filtration tubes. In the event the team was required to stay longer than two weeks, water could be collected, even from dirty puddles and ditches, and made fit for drinking. The instructions assured one that the filtration system would make their own raw sewage drinkable simply by pouring it in one end, and pumping it out the other, but no one was prepared to try it unless absolutely necessary.

The next shelf contained weapons: eight sub-machine guns with attached suppressors, four for the cache team and another four in case a second team joined them directly prior to the operation. There were also eight semi-automatic pistols, also with silencers, and several boxes of ammunition, the same calibre for both weapons, and a box of hand grenades, a selection of fragmentation and white phosphorus, the latter more useful as an instantaneous smoke-creating device than an incendiary. These were intended for use on target but their secondary purpose was as a replacement for cyanide tablets.

The next stack of cases contained plastic explosives with separate boxes of electrical and igniferous detonators. Another container above those held several hundred yards of detonation cord, slow-burning fuses and mechanical timing devices – mechanical because there were defensive systems that could disable electric timers over a wide area.

The next shelf held several ominous boxes with warning labels on them. Zhilev ran his hand along the seam of one with respect. He knew what was inside and had no intention of opening any of them. The lower box contained a dozen VX nerve-gas dispensers, and the one above, also daubed in warning slogans, contained cylinders of botulism, one gram of which could wipe out a million people if distributed correctly. Six thousand litres of the liquid was theoretically capable of wiping out the planet. Zhilev could never understand why they carried as much as a litre in total, enough to wipe out everyone in Europe let alone England. He was aware it had to do with the distribution system, which was not very effective, but still, Zhilev had a psychological problem with chemical and biological weapons. Perhaps it was his personal experiences at the hands of the experimental scientists. The nerve gas and botulism dispensers were attached to timing devices, the idea being to distribute them in inhabited locations, secured in trees, placed on the roofs of buildings, or dropped into storm drains. One sketch in the operator's handbook even suggested attaching a dispenser to a dog so that, on activation, the devices would discharge a fine mist of the chemical or biological agent as the animal trotted down the street. The weather would dictate the distribution and hence overall effectiveness, a good wind dispersing it over a wide area being the ideal situation.

Zhilev came to the end of the row and stopped in front of three ordinary-looking suitcases. His heart picked up the pace as adrenaline shot into his bloodstream. The silver-grey cases were unfamiliar, but that was only to be expected. There must have been advances and updates in the past fifteen years. For a moment he wondered if they were not what he was expecting to find and that there had been a policy change. But that did not make sense since the chemical and biological weapons were still here. No, he told himself. This is what he had come for.

He took hold of the handle of one of the cases

and pulled it towards him. It was heavy, a good sign. He had to take its weight with all his strength as it reached the end of the shelf and tipped forward. He had forgotten how deceivingly heavy the device was for its size as he carried it to the bunk and lowered it on to the mattress. His neck immediately complained after the effort and he took a few seconds to manipulate it.

There were no markings on the case. He inspected the latches: two on either side of the handle with combination locks set to zeros. A gentle push of both lock levers and they sprang open; the combination locks were intended for use outside and anyone qualified to enter the cache was qualified to see the contents of the case. Zhilev took hold of the sides and opened it, his eyes eagerly looking inside. Set into a sponge mould designed to fit it perfectly was a log; a large lump of wood, sawn cleanly on both sides and covered in bark. Zhilev slipped his hands down each side, took a firm hold, lifted it out of its mould and placed it on the mattress beside the case. Inside the mould, beneath where the log had been, was a pamphlet. Zhilev took it and sat on the side of the bed to read it. He glanced over the first page looking for a piece of very important information and sighed with relief as he found it. It was the date. It was recent, which meant the device was 'fresh'. The feeling of relief was accompanied by a creeping nervousness as the reality and enormity of his find sunk home.

The device, disguised as an ordinary lump of wood, was an RA 115, the latest version of the ZAV or

Special Nuclear Charge, better known as a suitcase bomb simply because it could fit into a suitcase. The date showed it had been replaced six months ago, which was the most important factor after actually finding the device. Pu 239, weapons-grade plutonium, and the intricate detonation system had a shelf life, which was partly built into it and not to be confused with its radioactive half life. That meant the cache maintenance programme was still fully operational. Someone regularly came and checked to keep it in working condition.

The log effect meant the weapon could be left in the open immediately prior to use, without drawing undue attention. There were a variety of disguises and their design depended on the country, terrain and meteorological conditions. The log was suitable for the targets for this cache: Mildenhall and Lakenheath air bases. There were three nuclear devices here in the event another target was designated by central command during hostilities.

Zhilev scanned the pages of the instruction booklet to make sure it covered everything he needed to know to detonate the device. When he was satisfied, he put it in his pocket. There would be plenty of time to read it in detail later.

He lifted the log off the bed, placed it back inside the suitcase and carried it to the bottom of the ladder.

He checked the hatch to plan how he was going to get the heavy suitcase out on his own since it was expected there would be more than one operative, and when he was satisfied he went back to the bunk bed, reached underneath and disconnected the cable from the battery. The chamber was plunged into darkness.

Zhilev went to the ladder, climbed it and pushed open the hatch. His night vision having been ruined by the light in the chamber revealed little even by the light of the stars, but his ears told him all was clear. He thought about waiting twenty minutes for his night vision to return, which was standard operational procedure, but chose against it. His confidence was high and he wanted to be out of the area with his atomic bomb as soon as he could.

He slid back down the ladder, grabbed the suitcase, raised it above his head and pushed it up the ladder ahead of him. A couple of steps was high enough to push it out and over the lip of the hatch and on to the forest floor. Within minutes Zhilev had climbed out, shut the hatch and was filling in the hole with the shovel. Once he had finished, he stamped the soil down with his feet, compressing it level, then covered it with the pile of pine needles he had scraped from the surface. As a final touch he replanted a couple of the small firs on top. He could not see his work perfectly well, but he felt he had done a more than adequate job. Within a week or so there would be no sign anyone had been here, and by then it would be too late.

Stratton arrived at a large roundabout. One of the exits led to Mildenhall, another to Lakenheath. He chose the A1065 to Lakenheath as a start. The road would take them in a large circle to Mildenhall and past the forest. His slender hope was that something might fit one of the images Gabriel had recently seen in his head.

Gabriel had remained silent in the back since they left the garage. Stratton kept checking his mirror to see if he had fallen asleep again but he had not and was looking out of the windows. Perhaps he was hoping this mysterious and frightening character might leap out in front of them.

Stratton drummed his fingers on the steering wheel contemplating the immediate future of this assignment. He decided to give it once around the block, so to speak, then head back to London. There was nothing to keep his interest here and he was feeling tired and looking forward to his bed at the Victory Club. The next thing to consider was the structure of his conversation with Sumners. He wanted out of this job as soon as possible, but he wanted another one in its place. The big question was, did Sumners give him this assignment as the bottom of the pile, the only thing they could trust him with, or was the man telling the truth when he said it was considered a most important task? Stratton knew he could never really trust Sumners, and Sumners would not be keen to let him off this case.

The road was quiet. A handful of cars had passed them, mostly from the opposite direction, and a glance in his rear-view mirror now showed no headlights behind.

'Stop!' Gabriel shouted suddenly, sitting forward in his seat and gripping the back of Stratton's.

Stratton slowed the car while scanning around to

see what Gabriel had seen. He pulled the car into the side of the road, his nearside wheels mounting the grass verge, and stopped, leaving the engine running.

'What is it?' Stratton asked, unable to see anything unusual let alone threatening.

Gabriel opened his door, climbed out and stood on the road looking at the skyline where the trees met the heavens. Stratton climbed out too, more interested in Gabriel than anything else.

Gabriel kept his head craned skyward and turned slowly all the way around until he was back facing the direction he began, and then he started to turn again.

There was a sound in the bushes a few yards away and a fat little muntjak trotted out into the open, studied the strangers for a moment, then decided it wasn't safe company and bolted away into the wood.

Stratton's initial fascination with the sudden excitement evaporated and he put his hands into his pockets wondering if this was all one big pantomime.

'Gabriel?' Stratton said.

Gabriel raised a hand to silence Stratton who was breaking his concentration.

Stratton played along. A sign on the road indicated a picnic area back the way they had and come and Gabriel was now staring at it.

Stratton could feel his night vision slowly kicking in, the cones in his retinas taking over from the rods, but it had a way to go before he would be able to make out anything inside the blackness of the wood. The headlights of a car appeared in the distance.

Stratton looked over at Gabriel who was still in the road.

'Gabriel? Car.'

Gabriel snapped out of his thoughts and looked over at the oncoming lights. He walked across the road then stepped a few yards off it towards the edge of the wood.

Stratton turned his back to the car and closed his eyes as it approached to preserve his night vision. He waited for a few seconds after it had passed before opening his eyes and looked over at Gabriel, but he had gone.

Stratton took his hands out of his pockets as he scanned around.

'Gabriel,' he called out, but there was no reply. Then came movement from the wood and Stratton crossed the road towards it.

'Gabriel!' he shouted again.

Gabriel was pushing his way through the slender, brittle pine branches that stuck out almost horizontally from the trunks, snatching glances up at the sky. He paused, looked around, then moved ahead in a different direction. He heard Stratton call his name but he was on the scent of something he did not want to lose and pressed on. Without a doubt, there was a familiarity about this place, a smell, the temperature, the light, the feel underfoot, as if Gabriel had been here before and quite recently, all the sensual memories still fresh.

Stratton entered the wood and paused to listen before readjusting his direction towards the movement. He was straining to look into the blackness as he walked forward, when his foot banged into something solid and he stopped to look down. He crouched to see it more clearly and found what appeared to be an old milestone. Then he heard a metallic clang some distance ahead followed by a crashing sound. As he moved quickly toward the sound, his senses began to tingle, a warning.

'Gabriel,' he called out against his better judgement. It was instinctive for him not to make more noise than he had to, especially when alone in the bush. Years of experience had ingrained in him the subconscious practice of reducing one's target profile, by movement, shape, silhouette, or sound. But they were not in a battlefield right now. This was Thetford Forest, England.

There was no reply to his call and Stratton moved carefully forward.

Another few yards and he paused to listen. The sound of movement he had been following through the trees had ceased. Then suddenly he thought he could hear it again, but it was a distance away, fifty or eighty metres. He moved forward once more, his senses tuned to the maximum.

A few paces further on Stratton stopped again, this time holding his breath so that he could hear more clearly. He picked up one particular sound, unnatural to the wood, rhythmic, like strained breathing, and very close by, then the sound of movement, metres away, low on the ground. Stratton moved forward until he saw what looked like a log until one of the limbs moved. He inched closer and realised it was Gabriel.

Stratton dropped to his side. Gabriel let out a moan. Stratton flashed a look in all directions, tensing for any attack. He heard movement again, this time further away. There was rhythm to it: walking, and fast, which was why it was louder. Gabriel's assailant was hurrying away. But the priority was Gabriel and Stratton crouched by his side and felt his head and face and then something wet which he assumed was blood.

'Gabriel,' Stratton said in a loud whisper. 'It's Stratton. You're okay. You're safe now . . . Can you hear me?'

Gabriel let out a moan and moved a shaking hand towards his head.

'Everything's okay,' Stratton reassured him. 'Keep still.'

Stratton felt along the back of Gabriel's neck to see if there was any damage to the vertebrae, then his face and jaw, his nose and forehead. It all seemed intact and dry, except for the back of his skull, which appeared to be intact although starting to swell.

'Gabriel? Give me some sign you can hear me.'

Stratton put a couple of fingers into Gabriel's hand. 'Squeeze my fingers if you can hear me,' he said.

'I can hear you,' Gabriel said, weakly.

'I'm going to sit you up,' Stratton said as he turned Gabriel carefully over, then, supporting his back, raised him up.

'Do you have pain anywhere else other than your head?' Stratton asked.

'I don't think so . . . Someone hit me. Did you

see who?' Gabriel asked, his hand coming up to feel the back of his head.

'No,' Stratton said, pulling his hand away. 'Don't touch your head. Can you get to your feet?'

'Yes,' Gabriel said, but then took a moment to respond as he gathered himself, and Stratton pulled him up. Gabriel almost lost his balance but Stratton held on to him.

'Take a step. I've got you.'

Gabriel took a wobbly step forward.

Stratton steered him through the wood and into the open.

They crossed the road and Stratton led him around to the front passenger side, opened the door and helped him in. Stratton climbed into the driver's side and within a few seconds had started the car and was pulling a U-turn in the road.

'Where are we going?' Gabriel.

'Mildenhall air base. They have a hospital there.'

'No. Go back. We need to find him.'

'He's gone.'

'We still need to go back.'

'I'm getting you to a hospital. You're in no condition to do anything.'

Gabriel leaned forward holding his head. Stratton glanced at him, wondering how badly he was hurt. RAF Barnham was nearby but Mildenhall was a US base and Gabriel was US government property on loan to the Brits.

Sumners was going to be pissed off about this. Stratton had been looking after Gabriel for just a few hours and he already had a dent in him.

This was really quite bizarre, Stratton thought. Was it possible the mysterious man Gabriel had been talking about had hit him, and had he really recognised a place at night just by looking through his assailant's eyes? It was a lot to believe but there were no other explanations at the moment. The fact remained that Gabriel had talked about a dangerous, angry man in a wood near a US air base in England, and he found one. That could not be ignored, no matter how sceptical a mood Stratton was in.

'Don't lose consciousness,' Stratton urged Gabriel. 'Stay awake.'

Several rows of bright lights in the distance looked like airfield landing lights. He applied the brakes gently and took the next corner tightly where a sign indicated the air base entrance.

Up ahead was the main gate and several armed US soldiers wearing helmets. Stratton reached inside his pocket for his identification. With luck, it would be enough until he could find Gabriel's ID.

Stratton decided to wait until Gabriel was in safe hands before calling Sumners. He had the feeling this was going to be a long and sleepless night.

6

Zhilev's Volvo was parked on the side of a quiet road at the highest point of the tallest hill for miles, the side of the car up against some thorny scrub growing out of the grey-and-white rocky landscape. Behind it the road twisted downhill for miles through the Ciceklibeli Pass to the ancient town of Mugla. Ahead, just about visible between a range of small hills, was a slither of blue water, the Gulf of Ceramus.

The day had begun chilly but the sun had broken through by mid-afternoon and Zhilev was enjoying its warm rays as he sat on a rock in front of his car dipping bread into a jar of local pine honey and eating it. In front of him, on a rock, was a picture of him and his brother, both wearing brightly coloured windproof jackets, arms over each other's shoulders, their straggly hair wet and matted, both clutching a bottle of beer and grinning broadly.

The picture was not there to remind Zhilev of his purpose, for that was now as much a part of his existence as was breathing. It was one of several photographs of Vladimir he carried in his pocket, inside a plastic bag to protect them, each from a different year and occasion going back to their youth. Zhilev was playing a kind of game with himself whereby each day he chose a new photo and tried to remember as many moments from that period as possible using the background, objects or clothing in the picture to help with the association. He was surprised just how effective the process was for conjuring up forgotten times. That particular day they had spent boating on the Dvina, the river that divided the city in two on its way to the Gulf of Riga. It was a major task for Zhilev to get his brother on the water simply because Vladimir spent all his working days at sea and insisted he preferred to spend his time off on dry land. Despite his complaining, Vladimir always ended up having fun and that day was no exception.

Zhilev looked up from the photo to find the glimpse of blue water in the distance. The journey from Ostende to Istanbul had taken him six days, which he would have enjoyed more if not for his neck although the vertebrae had been less painful than expected. He had started this day early, an hour before first light, just outside the town of Bursa, south of old Constantinople across the Denizi Sea, having spent the night on the back seat of the Volvo. It was the last day of driving and he wanted plenty of time at his destination to organise the next leg of the journey.

He had chosen to spend every second night sleeping in the car or on the ground immediately outside of it, not because he was short of funds, but as part of a self-imposed hardening process. He did not feel operationally fit yet and was determined to take advantage of the driving phase to toughen up as much as possible. He still considered himself too soft by Spetsnaz standards and felt the exposure to the damp and cold nights and rugged ground would help prepare him. Sleeping outside would also hone his senses and help him back into half-sleep, a resting mode where he remained constantly aware of every sound and movement around, a condition all Special Forces operatives had to achieve, ideally before an operation since the first night would be too late to begin developing it. But it was not always possible to create the right atmosphere in training and it usually took several days in a live operational environment with the threat of death or capture to unlock that particular sense. Judging by the way he had slept the night before, Zhilev felt he was close to getting the old form back, but he was also aware that too much exposure to the elements might weaken his immune system, which was why every second night was spent in a warm bed following a hot bath and a hearty meal.

Zhilev pulled a map from an inside pocket, folded to show his location, and studied it. He was satisfied with the distance he had covered so far that day. The sight of the Mediterranean was a welcome one and stopping to enjoy the view for a few minutes was essential psychological therapy. It was as important to look after his mind as his body. Stress could be more debilitating than a broken limb.

Zhilev had been to this part of Turkey before but many years ago. He liked it here where the Mediterranean lapped against the shores of Turkey, Greece and old Yugoslavia. He would spend the night in the open since he was feeling so well, and, besides, the next phase was the move into the operational area and the fewer chances he took the better. Staying in a hotel or bed and breakfast had to be regarded as a risk because it meant having to communicate with people, exposing his face and possibly providing identification such as his passport.

Zhilev dipped the last piece of bread into the honey pot and chewed it slowly before swallowing it. To top off his meal he reached into a side pocket and pulled out a chicken leg wrapped in paper. This was the last of a dozen he had bought from a village that morning as a snack while driving. It was a large leg, barbecued in the Turkish style and seasoned with herbs. He bit down on the bone halfway along it, his powerful jaws crushing it easily, and moved it around inside his mouth to trap the knuckle between his molars and pulverised it. It seemed excessive to eat the brittle bone as well, but it was another habit he had developed in the Spetsnaz where the philosophy of wasting anything edible while in the field was heresy. He chewed thoughtfully, masticating the bone, meat and skin until it was a poultice before swallowing it. Then he put the rest of the chicken leg in his mouth and crunched on it, like a hound, chewing it thoroughly.

A car approached from behind Zhilev's Volvo, a white Mercedes saloon that looked old but in fair condition. Zhilev stopped chewing and lowered his heavy head out of habit, avoiding eye-to-eye contact, and looked through his straggly hair.

Three men were in the car, two in front, one in

the back, all looking at Zhilev through closed windows as they drove by. They appeared to be locals but it was impossible to say at a glance. They continued up the road at an easy speed and drove over the crest and out of sight.

Zhilev continued chewing while he watched the spot where the car had disappeared. He wasn't feeling paranoid but there was a scent of trouble in the air and he could clearly smell it. There was something vaguely familiar about the car that niggled him. He was sure he had seen it somewhere before. Then it came to him. That morning in the village where he stopped to buy the chicken legs; after parking the car he had taken his backpack out of the boot and carried it to the barbecue stand. The Mercedes had been parked across the square. He did not remember seeing the men, but had they been there they would have seen him buy the food, return to the car, put the pack back into the boot and drive out of the town. Anyone treating a pack with such reverence was bound to attract the attention of people whose livelihood was banditry.

Zhilev swallowed his food, stood up, his heavy knees creaking, walked around to the boot of his car and pulled on the handle to check it was locked. There had been little danger getting the nuclear bomb through customs in England and Belgium. He had discarded the case in England and placed the block in the boot. The odds on being searched were low and no one would have taken notice of a block of wood that Zhilev would explain away as something used to hold up the car if a wheel needed changing.

As for radiation-detecting devices, there was little chance of the plutonium registering on them. The radiation was minimal at best, and inside its specially designed skin it was impossible to detect. The device had not left his side since he took it out of the cache. He had slept beside it, taken it to shops and cafés with him in his backpack and even carried it with him on the ferry.

Zhilev was about to head to the driver's door when he stopped. The white Mercedes was returning.

Alarm bells rang in his head and he quickly scanned around for a weapon, a piece of wood, anything he might use. In the business of survival, one did not consider coincidences. He thought about getting into his car and driving off but then decided that might not be the best tactical move available to him. They might try and block him and since the Mercedes was as strongly built as the Volvo, if they crashed, he risked injury or having to stop. Worse still, if they got to him before he could get out of his car he would be at a great disadvantage. He needed the freedom to make the first move. Taking the upper hand whenever possible was the prudent course of action, and that often meant starting the fight.

Zhilev stepped back behind his car and picked up a large rock. The Mercedes slowed as it approached. Zhilev kept the rock out of sight.

The three men stared straight at him as their car drew level and stopped on the other side of the road. The driver leaned out of his open window and said something that Zhilev did not understand and chose not to respond to. The one in the back, sitting forward in his seat, said something just for the other two to hear. The driver attempted to communicate with Zhilev once again, this time using hand gestures which looked like he was asking for directions. Zhilev remained like a statue, his sullen eyes reading theirs, waiting for the sign that would launch him into attack. He felt no fear, and was even beginning to wish they would climb out. He knew what he was going to do and unless they had guns, he felt confident. He'd had many fights during his military career, and because of his size, and being Spetsnaz, he was often a target for more than one man at a time. Fighting was a pastime in the Russian military and he'd never lost, even the day in Sevastopol when five sailors attacked him in the street when he was not expecting it. His success was partly because he never got drunk, and partly because he went for maximum damage with every blow and was prepared to wait for or create the opportunity. His problem was that he sometimes lost control, and on that day, because they had jumped him, he did not stop even after three of them had been laid unconscious and the other two were begging for mercy. He continued to stamp on and kick them, and when he walked away one had permanent brain damage, one a broken neck and the other three a dozen major bones broken between them.

The rear door of the Mercedes opened and a foot touched the ground. This was the moment Zhilev was waiting for and the furthest he was prepared to let things develop beyond what till then could possibly still have been innocent.

The door opened fully and the man's other foot

came out. Zhilev gauged his moment. He noticed the man was concealing something and, as he leaned out of the car to stand, Zhilev planted a foot forward like a javelin thrower, cocked the rock behind his head, and, with all the might he could muster, launched it. The rock left his hand as if released by a catapult and flew across the road with such speed none of the Turks had time to react. The rear passenger began to turn away as the rock hit the top edge of the door, bounced off and struck him in the jaw. He rolled back on to the rear seat and the driver pushed the accelerator to the floor and the Mercedes screeched away, the man's feet dragging along the road. At the same time the front passenger leaned across the driver and fired a single bullet from a revolver, which struck Zhilev's car a metre from him.

Zhilev picked up another rock as he considered his options but there were not any that did not call for him leaving his car, which he was loath to do. He could grab his bag and run but that would put him in the position of the hunted and he felt he was in the strongest position by his car. Besides, that would mean leaving behind the rest of his equipment without which he could not complete the operation as planned.

The Mercedes drove to where the road dropped out of sight, turned sharply, and headed back towards Zhilev.

Zhilev gauged the oncoming car, weighed the rock in his hand and decided on a more unpredictable tactic.

He stepped on to the rear bumper of his Volvo, on to the boot and then up on to the roof. Legs apart, he faced the oncoming Mercedes as it bore down on him. The passenger leaned out of his window with the gun in both hands and aimed with one eye shut while trying to hold it steady. It was plain the man had little experience with a pistol. He fired. Zhilev felt the bullet pass but held his ground, the rock raised behind his head. As the car came into range and before the man could squeeze off another shot, Zhilev hurled it through the windshield and into the driver's face. The vehicle careened out of control and Zhilev watched with horror as the Mercedes lurched towards his Volvo. He jumped the instant of contact, landed on the boot, and, as the Mercedes bounced away, swerved across the road and smashed into a pile of rocks, Zhilev hit the tarmac, falling heavily on to his hands and knees. He got to his feet, moving towards the Mercedes quicker than his legs could get under him; he fell down and ran on all fours a few paces, before getting to his feet to run forward.

The front passenger door opened on the other side of the car and the man with the gun climbed out groggily, stepping backwards, the revolver dangling heavily in his hand. As Zhilev got up speed, the man started to raise the gun. Zhilev jumped on to the bonnet, more athletically than seemed possible for him, pushed his feet forward and slammed them into the Turk's chest as the revolver went off wide. Zhilev followed through and landed hard on to the man's chest with his knees, knocking the wind out of him. Then he held his head, picked up a rock and brought it down with such force on the man's forehead, he split it. Despite the awful injury the man still struggled, purely a survival reaction as there was no fight left in him. Zhilev raised the rock once more and smashed open what he had already cracked.

Zhilev's eyes immediately searched inside the car for the other occupants.

The driver was lying across the seats, unconscious, his head gashed open, the rock sitting in his lap like a pet, but the back seat was empty and the far door open.

Movement caught his peripheral vision and he looked towards his own car. Shock flooded his heart. The boot was swinging on its sprung hinge, popped open by the impact with the Mercedes, and the Turk was running down the road.

Zhilev dropped the bloody rock, pushed away from the Mercedes and loped across the road to look in his boot in the vain hope the backpack with the log inside was there, but it was not. He broke into a run.

The Turk glanced over his shoulder to see the big man coming after him and suddenly he was no longer sure this was such a good idea. It quickly became obvious that running along the road was not going to lose the man who might be slower, but the Turk was weighed down with the backpack. To the right the landscape was rocks and harsh vegetation requiring even more effort and probably a broken ankle to cross. To the left the ground dropped steeply to a line of pine trees, which appealed to the Turk. He left the road, dropped over the lip and immediately picked up speed down the slope as gravity aided his forward momentum.

Zhilev left the road at the same time on a converging path, like a large, old cat, determination etched into every thrust of his powerful legs. He was running as if at the head of a charge of fierce warriors, the pedigree in his genes ten thousand years old, driven on by an unshakable force, focused, unswerving and unforgiving.

As the Turk swept into the wood, smashing his way through branches with little care for his eyes, a glance over his shoulder at the beast bursting through the trees just rows away confirmed his suspicion that this was indeed a very bad day.

The heavy backpack dropped from his hands as its priority withered, and as it bounced on the ground the log flew out ahead of him. The Turk found himself following it because they were both taking the natural line down the steep hill. For a second, part of the Turk's mind wondered why he had stolen a log, and why there was a maniac chasing him for it. Then something gripped the back of his neck brutally from behind and the various factions of his consciousness joined in a single screaming thought. But Zhilev did not pull him back. As the two men continued at top speed down the hill, his fingers wrapped themselves tightly on either side of the Turk's neck and squeezed, not to strangle but to control. If the Turk thought the next move was to be brought down, he was wrong. A shove pushed him slightly faster to match the speed of his pursuer. Then came a thrust to the side, a subtle change in direction at first, followed by a more aggressive push off course, and, for an instant before his head struck, the Turk saw the tree that was to kill him. There was a series of loud cracks, the sounds of his nose, jaw and forehead breaking, an instant of pain and then it went dark for ever.

Zhilev continued down the hill, releasing the body as it slammed against the tree, his eyes locked on to the log as it bounced ahead of him. It was unlikely the device would explode because of the safety features built into it, but as Zhilev watched it take the pounding he wondered how reliable those features were.

Zhilev was several trees behind the log when it burst out of the bottom of the plantation, rolled across a patch of open ground, hit a wickered fence and came to a stop. Zhilev put the brakes on and slipped on to his backside, skidding the last few feet to end up alongside his atom bomb.

He put a hand on it, fearing it might fly off again as he fell back to gulp the air. He could not remember the last time he had run so fast and so far, probably on his Spetsnaz selection course a thousand years ago. He rolled over on to his side, his face in the grass, gasping heavily, mucus and saliva dribbling from his mouth, then pushed himself up on to his knees. A bolt of pain shot through his neck to punish him further but he used it to mask the hurt of the exhaustion and forced himself to get up.

The sound of a goat bleating focused his mind. Goats were domestic and that meant humans could be close by. He looked around and saw several of the small, rugged animals the other side of the wicker fence munching calmly while looking at him.

A scan further afield revealed an old man outside a simple, run-down hut, and, like his goats, he was slowly munching something as he watched Zhilev.

Zhilev looked back up the hill to see if the Turkish bandit was visible. He could just make out the man upright behind the tree on which he was impaled, but the wood was too dense from the old man's perspective to see that far.

Zhilev picked the log out of the damaged wicker fence and glanced at the old man who was no doubt its owner. Zhilev pulled on the fence in an effort to put it back into place but when he let go of it, the section collapsed completely. He glanced at the old man again who had not moved. Zhilev chose to ignore him and the fence and headed back up the hill and into the wood.

A few minutes later, he emerged from the plantation carrying the backpack, the log inside, and climbed back on to the road. The cars had not moved and he walked at a brisk pace towards them, focusing on the open boot of his Volvo, praying the contents were untouched. The Turk with the smashed skull was still lying on the roadside beside the Mercedes. As Zhilev closed on his car he could see the top of a large bag and breathed a sigh of relief. The Mercedes driver was still lying on the front seat, unconscious. It was fair to assume no other car had been by, or, if one had, it had kept going.

Zhilev inspected the damage to his car. The back wheel was buckled and unusable. Changing the wheel would not be a cure. The Mercedes was also inoperable, not that he would have used it anyway.

There was no choice but to walk, a decision he accepted without a second thought.

He took his walking boots from the car, sat on the bumper and pulled them on, stowing his shoes in the backpack.

He pulled his pack on to his back, hoisted the large, heavy bag out of the boot, looped an arm through the carrying straps and hung it from his shoulder. It felt comfortable enough to walk with and he lowered it back down on to the road along with the backpack. He looked at the mess of cars and bodies. If he was going to ensure his security he would have to clean up before leaving.

He went to the driver's door of the Volvo, took the brake off, leaned his shoulder into the doorframe and, with a powerful shove, moved the old car forward. As it got going, he turned the wheel and steered it across the road and towards the lip of the hill. He increased his speed to get it up the slight rise on the edge of the road and then its nose suddenly dipped and carried on under its own momentum. Zhilev stepped away and watched his car trundle down the steep slope, picking up speed, then crunch heavily into the pine trees, coming to an abrupt stop a few metres into the wood. It could not be seen by anyone driving by in a car. Someone in a lorry or coach might see it perhaps, or a passer-by. There was nothing he could do about it now anyway and it would have to do.

He walked over to the Turk with the broken skull and knelt by him. The man looked dead. Zhilev prodded him in the chest and to his astonishment, he murmured. Zhilev never ceased to be impressed with the resilience of the human body. The man was probably a vegetable since there were tiny bits of his brain leaking from the crack in his skull, yet it was possible he might live, a chance he could not take. He was not following his own operational procedures for leaving witnesses behind as much as those of the Spetsnaz, and, since he was imposing those operating standards on himself, he could not divert from them. It had been a long time since he had killed a man, and never this cold blooded.

Zhilev reached for the man's jacket collar with both hands and placed his fingers inside, the knuckles against the man's neck directly below the ears, as if he was going to punch him from both sides simultaneously. With his thumbs outside the collar, he gripped the shirt strongly and twisted his wrists inwards forcing the knuckles of both index fingers deep into the neck using the collar as leverage. The move clamped shut the carotid arteries that fed blood from the heart to the brain thus depriving it of oxygen, which would lead to a speedy death. As soon as he applied pressure, the man began to choke and wriggle. Zhilev increased it further, his knuckles sinking deeper into the man's neck. The Turk's struggle intensified, his eyes opening in horror and his hands coming up to take hold of Zhilev's. Within seconds the Turk's eyes rolled back into his head, his tongue slid out of his mouth and his hands dropped to his sides.

Zhilev kept the choke on for a little longer, to make sure, before releasing him.

He got to his feet to look at his handiwork. It was a strange experience taking a life in that way, but he felt no remorse. He had rid the world of one more piece of scum. Zhilev urged himself to get on with it and, taking hold of the man's feet, dragged him around to the side of the car and, with some effort, rolled him on to the back seat. Zhilev took a moment to catch his breath and glanced at the driver lying across the front seats; the man was conscious and staring up at him.

The Turk guessed his partner was dead and knew he was next. He tried to get his arms and legs to move to pull himself out of the seat, and he might have managed it if he had all day to try. When Zhilev put a hand on him and held him down on to the seat, he gave up the effort knowing it was hopeless.

Zhilev leaned over and put his hands inside the Turk's collar as before. The Turk did not struggle. It was pointless against this powerful man. He stared into Zhilev's eyes and Zhilev stared back as he twisted his wrists and clamped the Turk's carotid artery. Like his comrade, he struggled for a few seconds, an involuntary reaction caused by oxygen deprivation, then it was all over.

Zhilev climbed out of the car, closed the doors, leaned in through the driver's window and pushed it to the edge. It rolled down the hill as gracefully as the Volvo, penetrating only a little further into the wood.

He took his map from his pocket and studied it. He had been heading for Marmaris, a good-sized seaport some thirty kilometres away, and he decided it was still his best bet. It would add another day to the planning if he did not come across an alternative mode of transport, but that was not a major concern as long as he was not on anyone's list of wanted persons, which he was positive he was not. As regards the recent incident, with the efficiency of the Turkish authorities, or lack of it, the cars could be discovered five minutes after he was gone and it would still take days, perhaps weeks, before the deaths could be linked to the man from Riga and any kind of manhunt organised. By that time he would be wanted in connection with a far more serious event.

He pulled a flat, transparent-plastic prismatic compass from a pocket and laid it over the map, placing the edge so that it formed a line from where he was standing across country to Marmaris. He turned the dial of the compass until it lined up with the north pointer on the map, pocketed the map and, holding the compass steady, orientated his body until the needle settled in its box. He looked directly ahead, in the direction the compass was pointing, and found the furthest object on the horizon, so he could walk towards it without constantly checking his compass.

He pulled on his backpack, picked up the heavy bag and was about to set off when he stopped and patted his breast pocket quickly as if he had forgotten something. His eyes darted to the rock where he had sat and ate his bread and honey. On it was the photograph of him and Vladimir. He walked over, picked it up, studied it for a moment, then placed it in the plastic bag with the others and pocketed it safely by his breast. He set off, leaving the road after a few metres and headed across country, trying to think what else Vladimir and he had done during that day.

In many ways this journey across country on foot carrying all he needed to complete the operation was quite satisfying. It had the feel of a real operation: weight on his back, map in pocket, compass hanging from his neck, blood on his hands and the objective within reach. The travelling part of the mission, the approach phase, was half over and, but for a handful of Turkish highwaymen, the trail behind him was clean.

As he trudged on the Mediterranean came into full view, filling the horizon and stretching as far as the eye could see. Somewhere between the furthest hills and the water, out of sight, was the harbour of Marmaris where he would get a boat and leave the land behind. How he longed to be at sea once more, a phase of the journey he had delighted in planning.

The ground gradually began to drop away. He was 880 metres above the sea, according to the map, which meant the journey was practically all downhill, and a rough estimation would have him on the outskirts of the town soon after first light as long as he had no more than four hours' rest. He wanted a complete day at the seaside town to carry out his next phase, reasoning he would be able to rest all he wanted when at sea. A good hearty meal on arrival, then to work. There was plenty of time. He suddenly felt very pleased with himself, a delayed euphoria after his victory in battle, made all the more pleasing because he had taken on three assailants and destroyed them without so much as a nick to himself. He was pressing on relentlessly, victoriously, and in complete control. And why not? He was Spetsnaz and, as long as he stuck to his plan, unbeatable.

Stratton sat in the departure lounge of Heathrow's second terminal, his feet stretched out in front of him, reading his Knights Templar book with a small backpack on the seat beside him. He sighed and looked up across the crowded hall unable to concentrate. Nearly two weeks had passed since the Thetford Forest incident but he was still feeling niggled by its outcome, specifically his failure to protect Gabriel. Sumners had indeed been angry, mainly because of how it reflected on him personally. Gabriel had been diagnosed with a severe concussion and forced to remain in a hospital until further notice, and Stratton had been sent back to Poole without another word on his immediate future. Asking for another assignment was obviously out of the question, and, after complete silence from London, once again Stratton began to give up hope of getting another call to return to work for MI6. Deep down he now realised it was what he wanted to do, despite the plethora of negatives. It was the most exciting game in town and even though some of the jobs, such as the remote-viewer gig, were boring and others unsavoury, there were always many good assignments as compensation. What annoyed Stratton was how unreasonable Sumners had been. He knew what a dead-end job looking after Gabriel was and how far removed from Stratton's particular skills. And Gabriel had not died.

Stratton urged himself to calm down and accept it was over. He was at the airport waiting for a flight to Norway and a three-week skiing holiday, taking some long overdue leave. To spend it mulling over his failure was pointless and the time would be far better spent planning the holiday.

He would start off in the north of the country, above the tree line, cross-country skiing, of course. He fancied the idea of revisiting some of the old routes he used to take with his team while shadowing the Russian Special Forces units that frequented the fjords during the winter months. Stratton had enjoyed those days working against the Eastern Bloc, especially when it involved diplomat surveillance. The Norwegian and Swedish fjords were favourite locations for Russian spies and diplomats to move documents, equipment and people in and out of the West. On one memorable operation Stratton and his team followed a Russian diplomat from Oslo to a lonely fjord miles from the nearest habitation on a route that covered hundreds of miles. The extremely paranoid man had taken months to house, or to discover his final destination, from the Russian embassy without him knowing. It had to be taken step by step, following him for only part of each trip, pulling off before he became even remotely suspicious, piecing together his various routes and dummy runs and recognising the tricks designed to catch would-be followers. The diplomat practised anti-surveillance at every opportunity, such as doubling back along a route, pausing periodically, taking loops to check if anyone was following, suddenly stopping and getting out of his car to scan the skies and horizon with binoculars, looking for aircraft or vehicles on mountainsides and regularly having his car swept for electronic devices which made it impossible to bug him. Such was the painstaking technique of surveillance.

Finally, one day, while Stratton was shadowing the diplomat's car from a hilltop using a skidoo, it stopped by the edge of the lonely fjord and he climbed out. It was a quiet road with hardly more than a vehicle an hour, less during winter. Stratton climbed off the skidoo and took out his petrol cooker and makings so he could have a quick brew while he kept an eye on his man several hundred feet below.

After a quick check around him the diplomat busied himself removing several items from his boot and set about constructing something. He was moving quickly and positively, having obviously rehearsed whatever he was doing. His next noticeable step was to start pushing something up and down with his foot that turned out to be a pump. Within minutes a rubber dinghy began to grow on the verge beside his car. When it was fully inflated, he placed a pair of paddles in it and carried it down a rocky bank to the water's edge a few feet away. He came back to the car, collected his briefcase and a fishing rod, and went back to the boat.

He climbed in, paddled into the fjord for several hundred metres, picked up the fishing rod and lowered a device of some kind on the end of the line into the water. He sat there for quite some time as if fishing, waiting for a bite, when eventually the end of the rod bowed to the water several times and the diplomat quickly reeled in his line, removed the device and replaced it with his briefcase, which he then lowered into the water. A moment later he retrieved the end of his line, now minus the brief-case, and paddled back to his car. Within a few minutes, he had deflated the boat, packed everything back into the boot and was driving down the road on his way back to Oslo.

The diplomat had obviously made a drop to a mini submarine and, as a result, two months later Stratton's team took part in the capture of a Russian subma-rine, a full-sized one, which was the mother ship of the mini-subs used to rendezvous with Russian spies and diplomats. It was not a complete success though. Two Russian mini-sub drivers, Russian Special Forces or Spetsnaz, got away after the trap was sprung. Stratton and several of his team gave chase along the bank of ankle-breaking rocks and ice but the Spetsnaz ran with a recklessness the SBS were not prepared to match that day. The Russians had far more to lose than their freedom if they were caught, and had the SBS closed in, the fight would have been a bitter one with survivors on one side only. They had an ambiguous respect for the Spetsnaz, mainly because hardly anything was known about them. It was assumed they were of a high standard although there was no evidence to support that. They were undoubtedly tough, illus-trated by the operations they mounted, and, like their British counterparts, preferred training in the worst possible conditions. Stratton had met members of most country's Special Forces but never a Spetsnaz.

As he pondered his route across Norway, his phone vibrated in his pocket. He took it out and checked the screen but there was no indication of the number. His first thought was the camp and one of the secure lines. Perhaps it was an operational recall. He was technically on standby, even though on leave, since he was attached to an operational squadron. It continued to ring. There was a time when he would never have considered not answering. It was indicative of his mood these days that he would forgo the opportunity of an operation just to go skiing. He might have continued to let it ring but he was cursed, and, like a drug addict, could never resist a fix.

He pushed a button and put it to his ear. 'This is Stratton,' he said.

'What do you think you're doing?'

It was Sumners. Stratton could only wonder what the man wanted. He had given him every piece of information during the debrief, at which he was cross-examined by Sumners and two other MI6 non-ops. Stratton had an urge to ignore him and turn off the phone, which would piss him off no end. He might be Stratton's superior but he was Military Intelligence and Stratton was SF field ops, and, frankly, Stratton could say what he wanted to the man without any real fear of repercussion. But the very same reasons that made him answer the phone in the first place pushed him to find out what Sumners wanted.

'I'm at Heathrow Airport.'

'I know where you are. You work for me now, and if you want to go anywhere you ask me first, or have you forgotten how the system works?'

'But I thought—'

'What? That you're off the assignment? Stop acting like some prima donna for God's sake. I'll tell you when you're off the assignment. Have you checked in yet? Or are you in the departure lounge?'

'I'm in the departure lounge,' Stratton said.

'I need you to get over to terminal one. You've got half an hour. You're booked on an Olympic Airlines flight to Athens then on to Rhodes. You know Rhodes?' Sumners asked.

'The largest of the Dodecanese islands. Rhodes is also the name of the old fortress city which was built by the Knights of Saint John in the fourteenth century.'

'I'm impressed,' Sumners said, though he might not have been had he known Stratton had just read as much in his Templar book which was still open at the relevant page.

Stratton was about to ask what the job was and decided against it. The message was clear. He was back in the game and he could not help feeling good about it.

'I'll have your baggage transferred to the Olympic flight.'

'Not my skis,' Stratton said. He did not want to look a complete wally walking around Rhodes carrying a pair of cross-country skis.

'That might be too much for the system but I'll try. I'm going to give you a ticket re-locater number,' Sumners said.

Stratton took out his pen and notepad and scribbled down the number.

'They're expecting you. They'll hold the plane but don't take all day.'

'Do I get to know what this is about?'

'Can't say anything on this means, other than you'll be meeting a familiar face who you recently had a little adventure with.'

Stratton's heart sank. He thought he had seen the back of Gabriel.

'Your friend's been in Turkey the past few days and now he needs to go to the Mediterranean. Stratton. Listen to me. I stuck my neck out for you on this. The Boss voiced doubts about you but I assured him you were up to it. I've never done that for any operative before in my life. The Agency assigned one of their own people to him in Turkey but nothing came of it. Despite your misgivings about him, it seems you made some kind of connection. He asked for you personally.'

This was not particularly good news for Stratton. He wanted to ask if anyone else could do the task, but it did not take much to work out that either he went on the assignment or he let the side down. The facts were obvious. He was familiar with the job and its linch-pin, namely Gabriel. Saying no to Sumners now would be saying no to any other MI job in the future.

Stratton stood up with the phone to his ear. 'I'm on my way,' he said sighing to himself.

'Stratton. One more thing. You still have your ID, don't you?'

Stratton automatically felt his pocket where his wallet was, not so much with his hand as with his mind. 'Yes,' he said.

'I don't suppose it ever crossed your mind why I never asked for it back?'

Oddly enough, it had not.

'When you arrive in Athens one of our people will meet you and give you some bits and pieces,' Sumners continued. 'I'll talk to you later.'

'Sumners?' Stratton quickly said.

There was silence for a moment and Stratton thought Sumners had gone. 'What is it?' he said, sounding as if he wished he had disconnected.

'I'd like some extra tools,' Stratton said.

'Tools?'

Stratton felt Sumners was being deliberately obtuse. 'You know what I mean. We're heading east. This job could end up anywhere. What if we have another incident like last time?'

'I see what you mean. I'm afraid I can't do much about that right now. Greece is a difficult one at the moment. She's being a bit of a bitch. I'll see what I can do . . . Anything else?'

Sumners hadn't even tried to disguise the insincerity in his voice. Greece wasn't the only bitch being difficult. 'No,' Stratton answered.

'Have a good trip,' Sumners said in the same tone, and the phone went dead. Stratton put it in his pocket as he dug out his MI6 ID and looked around for the security desk. He wondered why Rhodes and what Gabriel had seen in the time since they were last together. The remote viewer had obviously recovered from his concussion.

Stratton headed across duty-free to where he knew there would be a security checkpoint to stop arriving passengers from entering the shopping hall. Two guards in blazers and smart slacks were seated on swivel stools behind a desk in front of a set of doors that led to the gates. As Stratton approached, one of them, a large red-headed Gaelic type with a gut that hung over his belt, eyed him coldly from head to toe. Stratton held up his badge for the man to see.

'Hi,' Stratton said, forcing a polite smile.

The man maintained his 'I'm hard and important' expression.

'I need to get over to terminal one right away.'

'You need to do what?' the man said, as if he hadn't heard.

'Do you know what this badge is?' Stratton asked, the smile gone on hearing the attitude.

The man raised a hand to take it and Stratton pulled back the badge. 'I'll hold it as close or as far back as you need.' Stratton opened the flap to reveal the special enamel and silver crown that declared the badge owner was Military Intelligence on Her Majesty's Service and that all assistance was to be rendered to the bearer on request.

Stratton might as well have shown him a Blue Peter badge for all the reaction it got, other than the man picking up a phone.

'Who you ringing?' Stratton asked.

'Get verification,' the man said tiredly.

'Verification of what?' Stratton asked.

'Your pretty little badge, sir,' he said sarcastically.

Stratton put his hand firmly on the man's, pushing the phone down with superior strength, and stared closely into his eyes. 'When you got this job you were shown a slide of this badge and told that the bearer represented the Queen and you were to move the airport a foot to the left if that person asked you to. Now you're going to get off your fat arse and show me the back way to terminal one where a plane is being held for me right now, or I will thrash the shit out of you and have you slung in a cell for a week under the prevention of terrorism act for obstructing justice. Do I make myself clear?'

Stratton had to give credit to the man. If he was concerned, he didn't show it even though he got to his feet and straightened his jacket, all the while looking at Stratton.

'Be back in a bit, Fred,' he said to his partner. 'This way,' he then said to Stratton and headed across the corridor to an airport-staff-only door.

7

Stratton sat in the empty arrival hall of Paradisi Airport in Rhodes on the end of a fixed row of seats with his feet stretched out in front of him and looking as uncomfortable as he felt. It was six in the morning and the next connection from Istanbul was due in any time soon. The café and kiosks were shut for the winter by the look of them. It was off-season and hard to imagine that in the summer the large hall would be literally packed twenty-four hours a day with people coming and going from all over the world. This time of year the tourist resorts would be ghost towns since even most of the Greeks who lived on the island either left to find work elsewhere for the winter or the ones who had made a good income from the tourists were themselves on holiday until the start of the next season.

Stratton scrolled through the directory of numbers on the satellite phone his contact had given him on his arrival a couple of hours ago, along with a credit card, money and the request to keep receipts or he would be charged. Since the man did not offer Stratton a weapon there seemed no point in asking for one, but Stratton hinted at it anyway, getting nothing but a strange look in reply. The contact was a local runner for whoever ran the island's office and would know nothing about the operation anyway.

As Stratton read the phone list, many of the entries first names only, it became clear that the operative who had the phone last did not erase the directory, which was not an uncommon mistake. One of the names was Aggy, and Stratton wondered if it was Melissa – Aggy being her undercover name – a former partner from the Northern Ireland undercover detachment. She was beautiful and in many ways a perfect match for him. They had worked together for over a year and gotten to know each other well, though not intimately. What made Melissa special was that she knew the world of military intelligence and understood its influences on Stratton, since it affected her in the same way. They were very much alike, and in the world of undercover operations it made sense to be with your own kind. There was no need for their professional lives to be hidden from each other; they could discuss practically everything, and they did not have to put up a wall of secrecy when suddenly one of them had to leave on a job. He thought about calling the number, his finger hovering over the button, but stopped himself. It would not have been cool, not right now, and he would not have known what to say to her anyway. Despite genuinely missing her and often wondering if anything might have come from their relationship, he also knew his wanting to call was symptomatic of a desire for female company, a friend and confidante he could hold closely and be affectionate towards. Melissa could fill those criteria, if she was still available, but this was not the time or place.

Movement suddenly caught his eye. Staff in uniform, immigration or customs officers, were milling about, a good sign that the plane he was waiting for, and the only one scheduled to arrive for the next six hours, had landed.

There was also activity in the baggage hall and Stratton's expectations began to look justified. The conveyor belt started up and then a few seconds later died with a terrible crunching sound. Stratton looked through the windows to the taxi rank outside where just two cabs were waiting. As he turned back to face the doorway from the customs hall, Gabriel walked through it.

Stratton got to his feet, put his hands in the pockets of his old leather jacket and waited for Gabriel to find him, which was not going to be difficult in the empty hall.

Gabriel spotted him and as he closed in, Stratton saw he was wearing a slight smile.

'Stratton. How you doing?' he asked, as if they were friends.

'Fine thanks,' he said, surprised by Gabriel's joviality. 'How's your head?' he asked.

'I think it was more shock than injury,' Gabriel said. 'I'm not used to getting knocked on the head.'

Stratton could see the scab-covered bump clearly.

'You have all your baggage?' Stratton asked, looking at the one bag he was carrying.

'I'm set,' Gabriel said. 'So,' he continued, still wearing his smile. 'Where are we off to?'

Stratton had a sudden flashback to the first time they set off together. 'Don't get mad but I really don't have a clue,' Stratton answered. 'Do you mean accommodation? That won't be a problem. There's plenty of room this time of year.'

'No,' Gabriel said, his smile fading. 'I mean, where do we go?'

'Why would I know? I don't even know what we're doing here.'

Gabriel's smile was gone.

'Why don't you tell me why we're here,' Stratton said, trying to keep it together before it all fell apart.

Gabriel nodded, controlling his annoyance. He had vowed to act more like a partner this time, and, anyway, it was clear that this was going to be as much about them versus their bosses as it was looking for the mysterious demon. 'I had another image while in Turkey,' he said.

'I gathered that much,' Stratton said. His doubts about Gabriel went up and down like a big dipper. At this moment they were very high.

'I saw medieval walls and buildings, Knights . . . crusaders I suppose, and they were on a Mediterranean island.'

'Why Rhodes?' Stratton asked. 'There must be hundreds of islands with medieval buildings. European knights were all over the Med.'

'I saw thousands of homes crammed around a horseshoe harbour. Our people came up with this place. Apparently Rhodes' old city is medieval, densely packed with buildings and has a horseshoe harbour.'

Stratton was beginning to feel trapped on this assignment. 'The man you see, the one who hit you in the wood, is he here too?' he asked.

'If this is the right place,' he said.

'Have you actually seen him?'

'I've never seen him,' Gabriel said pressing one hand to his forehead with the other held up, stopping the conversation. 'Stratton, I want to apologise to you. This last week I've had time think, and I, well, I realised what a difficult position you must have been in when we first met. I never took a moment to consider it from your point of view. You were thrown in the deep end, with someone you didn't know, who claimed to do something that must've sounded wacky to you – and probably still does. I not only expected you to believe in me without question, but to help me as much as you could at the same time. I am arrogant and I apologise . . . Truth is, you did pretty good back there in the forest. You took me to the right place and you didn't block me. That's more than I've gotten from most decoders I've ever used. But asking for you to rejoin me was thoughtless. I didn't stop to think that working with me was the last place you wanted to be . . . If you want to go, I'll tell them it was my fault and I was unhelpful and impossible to work with.'

An apologetic smile crept on to Gabriel's face as he looked at Stratton. 'But I need help on this. I can't do it alone. I'd like you to stay on.'

Any anger Stratton had for the man dissolved in the face of such sincere contrition. It was nevertheless tempting to accept Gabriel's offer for him to get out, but he could not. It was a plea for help and it would be desertion. Like it or not, it seemed he was stuck with this old man for the immediate future.

'Okay . . . Partners. Just explain something to me. Why can't you see his features?' Stratton asked.

'I see into his heart, not his face,' Gabriel said. 'And through his eyes, but not like they are windows. I feel his emotional reaction to things. He's nostalgic. Something he saw allowed him to imagine himself as a knight, on castle battlements, fighting an enemy who came in wooden ships by their thousands. The knights did not lose the fight and the enemy left in their boats. That's the adventure he had and what I saw. I told that to our people, they decoded it and they sent us here.'

Stratton sighed. He was not enjoying this. 'Why don't we find a hotel and take it from there?' he suggested.

'Agreed.'

They picked up their bags and headed out of the airport to the waiting taxis.

Gabriel sat in the back of the car while Stratton sat beside the driver as they followed the coastline. Twenty minutes later they reached the twentieth-century outskirts of the city of Rhodes where they left the beach and climbed a hill. The modern houses gave way to a cluster of ancient remains signposted as the Acropolis and a mile further on they came to an imposing medieval wall with a vast moat in front of it. They followed the road in front of the wall for another mile, gradually downhill and back to the sea, then along the front of a harbour where ships lay at berth. Suddenly the taxi turned in through an arch and the road became narrow and changed from tarmac to cobblestone. They stopped in a cramped, sloping square with a fountain in the centre and shuttered shops on the higher ground facing the arched entrance and battlements.

Stratton asked the driver if he knew of a hotel but the man did not appear to want to spend any more time with them than he had to and shrugged ignorance.

A moment later they were standing in the square overshadowed by the heavily fortified ramparts on one side and two-storey buildings tightly packed together on the other, holding their baggage, the taxi gone, and looking at the narrow streets that led away in every direction. There were few people about and, in short, the atmosphere was ghost town.

'This isn't it,' Gabriel said.

Stratton said nothing but inwardly sighed. Why was he surprised, he asked himself. There were some sixteen hundred Greek islands, six hundred of them inhabited, and then there were the thousands of miles of mainland coastline and all the towns along that – not to mention places in Turkey that could match the description. The whole idea of detailed research was to avoid pointless journeys such as this. If they had got it wrong with all the databases at their finger-tips, what chance had Stratton and Gabriel of find-ing the place.

'Why's it wrong?' Stratton asked.

'There aren't any people.'

'It's out of season,' Stratton reminded him.

'What I mean is I saw hundreds and hundreds of houses, more than a thousand maybe, but no people. Just a few. The houses are nearly all empty.'

'Like this,' Stratton pointed out, holding on to his frustration.

'No. The houses in my viewing have been empty for a long time.'

'Was it an ancient town like Pompeii?' Stratton asked.

'No. That's too far back. The houses still stand but many are in ruin. Walls collapsed. No windows or doors. Overgrown.'

Stratton tried to think of any town destroyed by a natural disaster, or chemical or radiation attack which was still empty but nothing came to mind.

'I wish I could draw it for you,' Gabriel sighed, 'But I can't. All I can say is this place doesn't fit what I saw.' He looked away as if he did not want to think about it any more.

Stratton thought about reporting back to Sumners. Perhaps the boffins could draw up a list of possible towns for them to check out, or at least get pictures of to show Gabriel and save some travelling. He wondered why they had not done that in the first place.

'You hungry?' Stratton asked him, trying to think of something to help ease the tension he could feel rising in Gabriel.

'I haven't been very hungry lately . . . I don't think you realise how serious this is.'

Gabriel was right. Stratton did not.

'We're running out of time. Each day he gets closer

to his goal, whatever or wherever that is; he pushes relentlessly towards it.'

He could feel the change in Gabriel. Back in London and Thetford he was tired and frustrated, but now he looked more drawn, weaker and sounded much more desperate.

A man sipping a hot drink from a mug stepped from a shop nearby and looked at them.

'Hello,' he said in a charming manner. 'Can I help you?'

Stratton turned to him. He was middle-aged, small, comfortably dressed and as harmless looking as he sounded.

'You are English,' he said confidently, then, when Stratton did not answer immediately, he looked unsure. 'Françoise? German? My Dutch is not so good.'

'English,' Stratton said.

'Ah. I thought so. I am rarely wrong. I am Cristos,' he continued, remaining in his doorway with his free hand casually in his pocket. 'This is my travel shop. If you need anything: car, boat, flight, hotel, I can help you.'

Stratton thought about asking him for a hotel, but he was habitually untrusting of strangers and liked to find his own accommodation, especially when on the ground himself. 'We're fine, thanks.'

'Looks like a storm is coming,' Cristos said. 'Maybe tonight. A good time to find a cosy restaurant with a log fire and a nice bottle of wine.'

Stratton could go along with that suggestion, although he doubted it was what Gabriel had in mind.

'You look like you have just arrived . . . Would you like some tea or coffee?'

Stratton considered the offer. A cuppa would be nice and there wasn't a café open in the immediate area. He looked over at Gabriel who was staring at the battlements and the rooftops, shaking his head, compounding his belief this was not the place.

'Gabriel? Cup of tea? We need to take a moment to consider our next move.'

Gabriel looked at him, thought on it a few seconds and nodded his head.

Stratton looked back at Cristos with a smile. 'Tea would be great, thanks.'

Cristos beamed. 'Come in, come in,' he beckoned and stepped inside his shop.

The travel shop was long and narrow, and covered with posters displaying inviting beaches, advertisements for boat trips, maps, charts and souvenirs. Cristos was standing by a little table where there were half a dozen mugs and an electric kettle.

'Come in,' Cristos said. 'How do you like your tea?'

'Milk, one sugar,' Stratton said.

'And you?' he said to Gabriel.

'Black no sugar.'

'Ah. American, no?'

Gabriel acknowledged it with a forced smile.

'Please. Sit,' Cristos said.

A row of chairs extended from the door to the back of the shop, intended for people waiting to make bookings.

Stratton and Gabriel studied the premises. One

wall was practically covered with postcards from satisfied customers from all over the world.

'If you don't mind me saying, you looked a bit lost outside.'

'Not lost. We were expecting to meet some friends but it seems no one else has turned up.'

Cristos nodded understandingly as he handed them a hot mug each. 'Are you planning on staying long?'

'No. Just passing through,' Stratton said as he sipped his tea. It tasted good. 'Nice cuppa.'

'Where are you off to next?'

'Not sure.'

'If you need transport, you are in the right place.'

'We certainly are,' Stratton said, smiling politely.

Gabriel sat down and nursed his tea as he stared into space.

'We don't get many tourists this time of year. Usually the ones more interested in the island's ancient and medieval history prefer to come when the crowds of holiday makers have gone.'

'That's us.'

'Are you interested in anything in particular? This city was built in the fourteenth century, but we have places dating much further back.'

Stratton stared at Cristos as he considered something. 'You probably know the Mediterranean pretty well.'

'I am second-generation travel shop. My father and mother had this place forty-eight years ago. There's not much I don't know about this part of the world.'

'If I were to describe a town that had a

horseshoe-shaped harbour, that once had a large population – several thousand people, a thousand houses say – but only a few people now lived in it, where would you think I was talking about?'

Cristos grinned. 'Kastellorizo,' he said without hesitation. 'Have you been there?'

'No.'

'Well you have just described it as if you have seen it for yourself.'

'Kasta . . .?'

'Kastellorizo. It's an island. Kastellorizo means red castle.'

'It has a castle too?'

'Yes. The same knights who built this place built it. The soil is red so they called it *château roux*, which in bad Greek means Kastellorizo.'

'Where is it?'

'Off the coast of Turkey, about seven hours from here by boat and forty minutes by plane.'

'And this place is practically deserted?'

'Before the First World War it had seventeen thousand people on it. It was . . . how you say . . . when people are taken from a sinking ship?'

'Rescued?' Stratton offered.

'Yes, but . . . evak . . .'

'Evacuated.'

'Yes. It was evacuated during the Second World War by the British Navy before the Germans came. Then it was mostly burned down. Some say it was the Germans who looted it, some say the British. Who knows? Someone does, I suppose. Then, after the war, everyone was happy in their new countries, and so only a few people went back there. There was not much to go back to. There's a ferry every few days and not many people go or come from there.' Cristos smelt the potential business. 'You want me to check on flights or ferries for you?' he asked.

Stratton looked around at Gabriel who was staring at Cristos.

'Could you?' Stratton asked, looking back at Cristos.

'That's what I do for a living,' Cristos said, pulling a book from a stack on his desk and flicking through the pages. 'When do you want to go?'

'Today, if we can,' Stratton said, always preferring movement to stagnation.

Cristos paused to look at the two men, shrugged and carried on thumbing through the book. 'We will do our best,' he said.

Half an hour later, Stratton and Gabriel were heading out of the old city and along the waterfront towards the harbour. There were no flights scheduled from Rhodes to Kastellorizo for the next five days and even then there was no certainty it wouldn't be cancelled, but there happened to be a ferry leaving for the island late that morning. The boat's advertised departure and arrival times were not to be taken seriously, Cristos had advised, listing several factors that included unreliable engines and machinery as well as captain and crew lethargy. If all went well, bearing in mind the likely storm, it was expected to arrive at around seven in the evening, give or take an hour, which posed one other problem for them. Accommodation. The phone cable from the mainland was over eighty years old and for unexplained reasons foul weather affected transmissions, which was why, according to Cristos, he could not contact any one of the handful of faxes or phones on the island to book rooms for them, although he promised to continue trying.

As they approached the harbour and identified their ferry, the only large boat in the harbour, Stratton phoned Sumners to tell him about their move and to set in motion his idea about getting as many photographs of similar harbours for Gabriel to take a look at if Kastellorizo was a dead end. As they rounded the corner of the mole, the poor condition of their boat became apparent. Rusty streaks from the rails on the main deck covered it from front to back, a stream of hot, dirty water spurted from a hole just above the waterline and the hum and rattle of the ancient engines grew louder the closer they got.

As Stratton and Gabriel approached the rear ramp, a crewman appeared – an older man with a roll-up stuck to his bottom lip – took their tickets, said something unintelligible while indicating inside the boat and walked away. They took it as an invitation to board and entered the ship, which smelt of a mixture of gasoline and sewage. On the other side of the vehicle deck they climbed a stairway that led to the upper deck, then pushed through a door into a large room filled with what looked like old aircraft seats. There were a hundred or so, all bolted to the floor in neat rows as in a cinema, except in this case they faced a long, grey, drab, metal bulkhead.

'The passenger lounge I would guess,' Stratton said as he dumped his bag on the floor.

Gabriel wearily took a seat as Stratton went back into the hallway and found a door that led out on to the deck.

The crew were preparing to cast the lines although no one appeared to be in any kind of a rush. Half an hour later, a tug arrived to pull the ship into the middle of the harbour after which it slowly made its own way out to sea.

Stratton remained on deck until Rhodes disappeared behind a dark-grey sky which descended like a curtain around the ship. The storm that had threatened to hit all day had finally arrived, and the rain began to fall in heavy sheets.

Stratton moved inside before he got soaked and went back into the lounge, which was empty except for Gabriel who was asleep in his chair. Stratton took off his wet jacket, sat a few seats away, dug his Knights Templar book out of his bag and settled in.

The journey took longer than expected, no doubt due to the storm. They were served a pot of coffee and a pair of suspicious-looking pies a couple of hours after leaving, which Gabriel avoided and Stratton ate after inspecting carefully. At around nine o'clock there was a distinct change in the engine revs. Stratton had been dozing easily with his book on his lap and opened his eyes. Either the ship was breaking down or they were slowing to approach a port.

He grabbed his jacket and went out on deck to find the sea on the starboard side replaced by a mass of land. Mountains loomed high in the background, cupping the town as if in the palms of a pair of hands.

There were lights inside the houses near the water; the rest, creeping up the hillside, although in darkness were just about discernible. The harbour was as horseshoe-shaped as it could be and at one of its points were several official-looking buildings, a minaret and a medieval castle, not huge but large enough to hold a company of men, positioned to defend the entrance to the harbour.

The ferry began a slow, graceful turn to position its aft end facing the quay. The engines accelerated in reverse stopping all headway and the boat began to move slowly backwards, reducing speed to an absolute crawl until the back end bumped gently against the quay.

Gabriel came out to join Stratton and look at the island. Stratton waited for any sign that might suggest Gabriel thought this was the place, but he was to be disappointed.

'It's very pretty,' Gabriel said.

'Yeah,' Stratton agreed, suddenly wondering what the hell they were doing coming all the way here.

A loud metallic squeal came from the back of the boat as the ramp was lowered, followed by a thump as it hit the concrete quay.

A minute later they were walking down the ramp along with a handful of islanders who had been shopping in Rhodes for essentials, then stepped on to the gravel-covered quay.

Both men walked to the water's edge to look out over the harbour where lights twinkled in many of the houses that were packed tightly shoulder-to-shoulder all around it. The night was chilly but with barely a cloud in the sky, all sign of the storm had gone and the water rippled gently, lapping the stone quay several feet below the lip.

'I suggest we look for somewhere to get a bite to eat, which might also be a good place to ask about a hotel,' Stratton said.

Gabriel was staring out across the water and did not appear to hear him.

'Gabriel?'

Gabriel slipped out of his reverie and looked at Stratton tiredly. 'I could eat something, I s'pose,' he said.

Stratton wondered if Gabriel might 'recognise' this was the place come daylight and then sighed to himself. He was acting as if he had no doubts about Gabriel when in all honesty he did. His hope was only a response to the game of it all. He felt that even if Gabriel did announce that this was the island he had seen in his viewing, it would be like winning a stage of a board game: it meant nothing. The incident in Thetford Forest was already beginning to seem to him like little more than a strange coincidence.

Moments later they were alone on the quay; the people who had come off the ferry had disappeared into the town, and the crew had gone inside the boat where they were no doubt settling down for the night before their departure in the morning.

The two men set off along the quay, Stratton looking for any sign of a restaurant and Gabriel walking alongside him like a pet with little interest in anything.

Up ahead, where the quay began to bend away to

the right, there was what appeared to be a restaurant. A candlelit table was set out in the open, taking up practically the entire width of the narrow quay, and several people sat around it. Two barbecues were on the go with fish and chunks of lamb sizzling on the grills, and the table was adorned with various dishes as well as bottles of wine. Several men and a woman were drinking while conversing but as Stratton and Gabriel approached, they all stopped to look at them.

As Stratton and Gabriel tried to identify the appropriate person to ask about dinner, one of the men, a portly, gypsy-like character with every year of his long life etched into his craggy face, said something to them in Greek.

'Anyone speak English?' Stratton asked.

'English,' the same man said, appearing surprised but oozing confidence. 'You just come off the ferry?'

'Yes,' Stratton said. 'We were wondering if we could get a meal here.'

The man looked at one of the others across the table as if to refer the question to him, then looked back at Stratton and produced a smile. 'There are no restaurants open tonight, but you can join us if you like.'

'That's very kind,' Stratton said. 'But we wouldn't want to intrude.'

'No intrusion,' the man said, looking around at the other men for their opinions, neither of whom appeared to have any. 'You will be our guests. I am the Mayor of Kastellorizo,' he continued, not getting up or offering a hand. He then said something to one of the staff tending the barbecue who immediately went into the building and returned with two chairs.

'This is my wife,' the mayor said, introducing the short, ample woman at his side. 'She does not speak English, although she understands it.'

As Stratton and Gabriel nodded hello, the next person was introduced as the island's lawyer who lived most of the time in Athens and happened to be on one of his frequent business trips to the island. Beside him was a Greek Orthodox priest who did not speak English and looked quite trashed unless he had some kind of debilitating illness that caused slow blinking and a lack of co-ordination when bringing his glass to his mouth. The man across the table, who the mayor had first sought approval from for inviting the surprise visitors, introduced himself as the restaurant owner, which was becoming obvious since he was directing the staff in a familiar and harsh manner.

The remaining two men were in uniform, one the island's immigrations and customs officer who did not speak very much English, the other a Greek army captain who commanded the island's small garrison, which turned out to be no more than a dozen men. He appeared feminine in his deportment whereas the others were brusque and rural, except the lawyer who had a modicum of refinement. His uniform was immaculate as was his hair and moustache and he sat cross-legged most of the time, smoking a cigarette from a silver cigarette holder.

Gabriel was seated beside the mayor's wife with the customs officer on his other side who was stuck in conversation with the drunken priest. Stratton's chair was placed between the army captain and the lawyer and, when asked, introduced himself as Gabriel's assistant who in turn explained briefly that he was a geology lecturer from Stanford University. None of the others appeared to be interested in geology, certainly not enough to question them further although the lawyer said something in Greek that Stratton had the feeling was about him.

The early small talk covered the weather, fishing and the poor tourist trade, with the locals taking the opportunity to vent their disappointment at the drop in visitors the past few years, some of the blame being heaped on the Turks' apparent ambitions for the island. As the barbecued fish was served, Stratton asked why the island had so many homes and so few people, a question he expected would have a simple explanation. He was not prepared for the can of worms he opened.

'We are the cowards,' the mayor announced as if it were their group title. 'All of us.'

No one verbally disagreed with him although there were some looks that suggested there was more to the comment.

'We are the ones who ran away,' he elaborated. 'Forgive me, Captain, I did not mean to include you. The captain is an honoured guest from the army and not from the island.'

The captain smiled slightly, nodding forgiveness, then delicately brushed an imaginary piece of dust from his sleeve and cleared his throat.

Gabriel was staring at the mayor, which the Greek took for inquisitiveness.

'Before the war . . .' the mayor said, pausing to drain a glass of wine, 'the last one, the Second World's War. Before that war this island was seventeen thousand people.'

'Less,' the lawyer interrupted with the perfunctory certainty of someone who has the answer to everything. 'The First World War there was seventeen thousand people perhaps, but there was less by the Second World War.'

'Okay,' the mayor shrugged, indifferent to the actual figures. 'Fifteen thousand then.'

'Maybe less,' the lawyer interrupted again, much to the irritation of the mayor who tried not to let it show.

'It doesn't really matter,' the mayor went on. 'My point is there were thousands,' he said, pausing to look at the lawyer in case he had another comment to make. 'The Germans were coming and so the British sent some ships to take the people away. Everyone left the island. Every member of every family carrying what they could.'

'And then there was the fire,' the restaurant owner said.

'I was getting to that,' the mayor said. 'A fire spread through the town destroying almost all of it.'

'A fire started by the British,' the lawyer added.

'No one knows that for sure,' the mayor corrected, smiling at Stratton, his defence of the British a little obvious.

'They robbed the island first, don't forget,' the lawyer said.

'Rumours,' the mayor scoffed. 'There is no proof . . . Anyway, the point I am trying to make is everyone left the island.' The mayor refilled his glass.

'The entire island was evacuated?' Gabriel asked. 'Even the farmers and shepherds?'

'All of them,' the mayor said. 'It was completely deserted. Everyone vowed to return as soon as the Germans were defeated.'

'But since no one at the time believed they would be defeated, no one in fact said that,' the lawyer added.

'So what happened?' Stratton asked.

'Nothing happened,' the lawyer said.

'Everyone was comfortable where they were,' the mayor said. 'In America, Australia, England, wherever they ran away to.'

'This was an island with occasional electricity, occasional water shortages, occasional fresh food and half a mile from the Turks who say it is theirs and one day they will come and take it,' the lawyer expanded. 'And nothing has changed.'

'The Turks will never take it,' said the restaurant owner. 'Not while the army is here,' he said, indicating the captain, who nodded appreciatively.

'They will come if the population drops below one hundred and fifty people,' the lawyer said. 'That's the agreement.'

'It's already below that figure,' the restaurant owner argued. 'One hundred and five is all we have.'

'Then the Turks will come,' the lawyer said, unconvincingly.

'Never,' said the restaurant owner. 'All we have to do is bring more people back to claim their homes.'

'Huh,' grunted the lawyer. 'Big chance of that. It

will be the same problem. How can they prove which home belongs to whom?'

'The land registry was burned down in the fire,' the mayor informed Gabriel. 'Inside was all documentation of who owned what house on the island. People have come back to try to claim their house but have no proof.'

'There are even cases of more than one family claiming they own the same house,' said the lawyer.

'No one knows whose house is whose,' the mayor added.

'Which suits you and our fine lawyer here,' the restaurant owner mumbled.

'Not in front of our guests, please,' the mayor said.

'Why not? It doesn't matter if the whole world knows. No one can meddle in your affairs. You have it all tied up like a neat package.'

'It doesn't concern anyone,' the lawyer said.

'What are you afraid of?' the restaurant owner continued defiantly. 'No one can touch you or the mayor. You have the support of Athens, as long as you don't get too greedy. You already own a quarter of the island and you will own the rest before long.'

'And you have done okay by it, I might add,' the lawyer snapped, getting heated. 'I wonder who really owned your restaurant and your vineyard before you claimed them.'

The restaurant owner felt the sting of that attack; however, he was not to be silenced yet. 'Everyone at this table has done okay, and they might not all say it in the open but behind your back they all agree you have been too greedy.'

'We've all done okay,' the mayor said, trying to calm things. 'Don't ruin it for yourself.'

'Is that some kind of threat?' the restaurant owner asked.

'You're getting paranoid,' the lawyer said.

'Me? Paranoid! You are joking, of course. Everyone who sets foot on the island he quizzes in case they are here to claim a house,' the restaurant owner said to Gabriel. 'I can guarantee he is suspicious of you. You think he believes you are a university lecturer? And then they complain about the lack of tourists. What precious few we have are investigated by this man. And heaven forbid if they should hint they once had family on the island. Suddenly their water runs out or their electricity, or something happens to their baggage, like that Australian family who lost their wallets, passports and other valuables which strangely turned up on Rhodes, and you and the mayor ever so kindly bought them ferry tickets – one way tickets – to go to Rhodes to get their stuff.'

'That's absurd,' the lawyer said, suddenly starting to laugh. The mayor also fought a snigger as he remembered the incident.

'You laugh at us as if we are stupid. But not all of them are so frightened of you,' the restaurant owner said, grinning as he nudged the customs officer and then whispered to him. They both sniggered and the restaurant owner translated what he had said for Stratton and Gabriel's entertainment. 'What about that crazy Russian you tried to interrogate because he was being so secretive?' he directed at the lawyer.

The customs officer chuckled as the lawyer looked suddenly embarrassed.

'You kept on asking him what he was doing here and he didn't want to say,' the restaurant owner continued, then began to mimic strangling someone. 'Finally you asked him again what his name was and he grabbed you by the neck and threatened to break it if you didn't leave him alone.' The restaurant owner and customs officer burst out laughing, the mayor joining them.

'He would have crushed you like a snail if the army had not come to save you,' the restaurant owner added, guffawing loudly.

'And so he call army,' the customs officer said in broken English, almost in tears.

'Rubbish,' the lawyer said in a red-faced huff that only caused more laughter.

'Isn't that right, Captain?' the restaurant owner asked the army officer. 'He would have stamped our great lawyer into the ground and hit him with his big piece of wood.' The laughter got even louder and the mayor's wife joined in. It was so infectious Gabriel began to grin.

'You should have seen this Russian,' the mayor said to Stratton. 'He was huge. Hands like plates. And he carried a large piece of wood everywhere. You would have to shoot him several times to stop him if he attacked you.'

'The lawyer was right to call me,' the captain said, quite seriously. 'The man was a soldier and very dangerous.'

'How do you know he was a soldier?' the mayor

said. 'He told no one anything about himself. That's why our lawyer thought he wanted to claim a house.'

'Soldiers know these things,' the captain said in a superior fashion. 'You wouldn't understand,' he added, glancing at Stratton in a way that suggested it was a mystery to everyone at the table but himself. 'This man had seen war. That was why I got him to calm down. I talked to him as only a soldier can to another.'

'Yes, and our brave lawyer ran away from the island yet again,' the restaurant owner added.

'But this time only for a week,' the mayor said, raising his glass. 'Good to see you back.'

'But remember, don't stay too long, the Russian is back in a few days,' the restaurant owner added, setting everyone off laughing again.

Thoughts began to stir in Stratton's head. The words Russian and soldier jingled some bells. He looked over at Gabriel who was grinning at the customs officer mimicking the lawyer being strangled.

'Oh, look out,' the mayor said as he stood up, pointing along the quay.

Everyone looked. The restaurant owner uttered some Greek expletive as he threw down his napkin.

At the far end of the quay, near the customs office where the ferry was tied alongside, a small four-wheeled dumper truck was put-putting towards them.

'Why does Dimitri always have to drive home along the quay when we are having dinner?' the restaurant owner said. 'I think he does it deliberately. Come on. Grab the table,' he ordered.

Everyone, including the cook and waiters, except

Stratton, Gabriel and the mayor's wife, grabbed an edge of the table on the restaurant side – no one on the water side.

'Up,' the restaurant owner said and they all lifted at once. 'Go,' he then commanded, and they shuffled to the edge of the quay and held the table out over the water, carefully balancing the candles and bottles of wine.

The noisy dumper truck chugged by without so much as a nod or look from the old man at the wheel.

As the vehicle passed, the customs officer lost his balance and let his end slip a little, enough to send a bottle of wine rolling to the edge, which the priest made a grab for, missed, and the bottle dropped into the water closely followed by the wailing priest.

The priest surfaced immediately, spluttering and grasping for the edge of a small rowing boat tied alongside. The others quickly put the table down and the customs officer and restaurant owner scrambled over the edge of the quay and into the boat to help the panicked priest. They unceremoniously hauled him in and then all three sat down to recover from their efforts while the mayor and lawyer stood above them giggling like children.

The captain shook his head as he placed a fresh cigarette into his holder and lit it. Stratton joined him to watch the restaurant owner and customs offi-cer help the priest back on to the quay while the mayor graciously lent a hand.

'Have you been here long?' Stratton asked the captain.

The captain looked to see who was talking to him. 'Nine months with one more to go. A year for some, but ten for me, thank God,' he said. 'They're nice people, but, well, I'm from Athens, if you see what I mean.'

Stratton smiled as if he agreed. 'I should think island fever sets in pretty quick around here.'

'Yes. For sure.'

'Gets lively in the summer, this place, I suppose,' Stratton said.

'Sometimes. The tourists can fill up the handful of apartments, and the boats that arrive can help fill the restaurants too. Occasionally an interesting person turns up, but not often.'

'So no one comes here in the winter then?'

'No.'

'Except crazy Russians,' Stratton said, forcing a chuckle.

'Yes,' the captain said, puffing on his cigarette and forcing a polite smile of his own. Stratton obviously did not fall into his category of interesting people.

'What was he doing here?' Stratton asked matter-of-factly.

'Diving.'

Stratton pondered the comment. 'I do a bit of that when I can,' he said. 'Where's the good diving around here?'

'I understand there are some exceptional caves on the south side of the island. I've never seen them. I don't dive.'

'Is that what the lawyer is frightened of, the Russian being back soon because he's on the south side of the island?'

'I don't know where the Russian went. He rented a boat from a fisherman.'

'I think I'd like to do that while I'm here . . . Who can I rent diving equipment from?'

'I have no idea. As I said, I know nothing about diving.'

Stratton was digging too quickly with the Russian but felt justified in taking advantage of the opportunity. 'So, why did they call him crazy?' he asked.

'He was big, like a Frankenstein. That scares some people. He also kept to himself.' The captain then smirked. 'He carried a large piece of wood in a bag everywhere he went. He never left it in his room when he went out. That perhaps was a little crazy.'

'A piece of wood?'

'Yes. A small log. Why does someone carry a log everywhere with them if they are not a little crazy?' the captain asked.

Stratton nodded. Something about the story niggled him but he couldn't put his finger on what precisely. 'When did he leave to go diving?' Stratton asked.

The captain looked at him, at last wondering why Stratton was so interested in the Russian. 'Must be a week now.'

'I'm curious to know what the diving was like. I hope I'm here when he returns.'

The priest was finally hauled back on to dry land and he stumbled away with the help of the customs officer.

'Captain,' the restaurant owner called out, drying

his hands with a dishcloth. 'Would you like some coffee?'

'Yes, thank you,' the captain said. 'Excuse me, please,' he said to Stratton before starting to walk away.

'Captain . . . How do you know he was Russian?'

The officer paused and looked back at him. 'His passport. He was Latvian, actually. From Riga. It was needed for the hiring of the fishing boat. I helped with the paperwork.'

'I thought you were going to say you spoke Russian. I wouldn't have been surprised,' he said, turning away to look out over the harbour and cringing at his pathetic efforts to disguise his interest.

The captain's eyes lingered on Stratton a moment before he headed into the restaurant.

Stratton felt the officer watching him before he moved away. One too many questions, but then he did not particularly care what the captain thought. He was unlikely to have anything to do with whatever the hell it was Stratton was chasing. He reflected again on how absurd this assignment was and imagined handing it over to a fellow operative and explaining, or attempting to, what exactly they were doing and what they had to go on. It was a joke.

Despite all the negatives though, he had to admit it held an element of intrigue. He wondered if the Russian, or Latvian, played any part in all of this. Was he Gabriel's vision, the fearful demon on a mission? Was he the man in Thetford Forest? If so, where was he going in the fishing boat? And what about the log? Maybe the man was crazy.

Maybe that's all Gabriel had picked up on: a crazy Russian.

Stratton's peripheral vision caught movement to his side and he looked over to see Gabriel standing on the edge of the quay staring down at the water. The first thought that flashed into his head was accommodation, and then, as if he had read his mind, the mayor called out to Stratton.

'Where are you staying?'

'Ah. Glad you asked. We don't have anywhere booked. Could you suggest a place?'

'My wife will take care of you. Your friend looks tired. Perhaps you would like to get him to an apartment.'

'Thank you,' Stratton said.

The mayor called out to his wife, explaining what he wanted, and she came over to Stratton, beaming a smile, and invited him to follow her.

'Gabriel,' Stratton called out. 'We have an apartment for the night.'

Gabriel nodded and walked back to where his seat was and picked up his bag. Stratton collected his and stopped in front of the mayor. 'Can we contribute to the evening?' Stratton said, reaching for his wallet.

'No,' the mayor said. 'You are our guests. Besides, you'll pay through the nose for the apartment since it's the only one available tonight.' He grinned.

Stratton got the picture. 'Thanks anyway,' he said, and walked off after the mayor's wife and Gabriel who were waiting for him.

'This is probably the only place open for breakfast tomorrow so we'll see you then,' the mayor called out.

They walked away and the mayor's smile faded as he was joined by the lawyer, both watching the strangers go.

'What do you think?' the lawyer asked.

'I don't think the old man is a university professor, and neither is the Englishman his assistant.'

'I agree,' said the lawyer. 'But I don't think they're here looking to claim a house either.' He glanced at the mayor for his consensus.

'So what are we worried about then?' the mayor said, grinning. 'Let's finish off the wine.'

That was an attractive offer and they returned to the table.

Stratton and Gabriel followed the mayor's wife around the bend of the quay then up a narrow, dark, cobbled side street, past a tethered goat and along another street that headed steeply uphill.

She paused at a corner, indicated a three-storey house opposite, handed Stratton a large old key and remained where she was, smiling, and waiting for acknowledgement. It was clear she did not intend to go any further, obviously uncomfortable about going into the house with two strange men.

Stratton nodded thanks and crossed the alley; it could not be called a road since no car could pass along it.

The two men faced the front door which would have been in complete darkness had it not been for a light in the house opposite. It looked centuries old with ornate carvings around its edges and a lion's face in the centre. Stratton looked back to find the mayor's wife had gone and then glanced at Gabriel.

'This okay for you?' Stratton asked.

'As long as it has a comfortable bed, I don't care.'

Stratton put the key in the lock, turned it with a heavy clunk, pushed open the door and stepped inside. He felt around for a switch without luck, took a small button torch from a pocket and shone it around the hallway. There was a switch on the wall opposite, at the foot of the stairs, and he walked over to it and flicked it down. A bulb came to life above and Gabriel walked in and closed the door behind him. There did not appear to be much downstairs other than a cellar and so Stratton mounted the steps. The place looked as old as the door, the plaster in many places fallen away to expose stonework.

At the top of the stairs, across the landing, was a door. Stratton opened it and turned on the light to reveal a contrastingly clean and freshly decorated room, sparsely furnished with a bed and wardrobe, and net curtains framing a pair of French windows.

'Not bad,' Stratton said.

'I was beginning to wonder,' Gabriel said. He walked along the landing that doubled back on the stairs to another door, pushed it open and flicked the switch on the wall but it did not work.

'You need a flashlight?' Stratton asked, remaining in the doorway of his room.

'I can see a table lamp,' Gabriel said as he entered the room. A second later a dim light came on inside.

Stratton walked into his room, put his bag on the bed, and went to the French windows which had a small balcony beyond. He parted the net curtains to look at the view, which was quite stunning. Silver moonlight illuminated one side of the black mountain and silhouetted the edge of the town, a part that had long since been abandoned. Beyond was the Turkish mainland where tiny lights flickered, outlining the coastline.

There was a thump from the next room, not a very loud one, but at night in a strange house in a foreign land with unknown people, it was enough to warrant an inquiry.

Stratton went back to his door and looked up the landing. Gabriel's door was still open with the light on inside.

He walked along the landing and looked inside the room. It was larger than his, not as cleanly decorated, with plaster coming away in places around the edges of the ceiling, but the large, comfortable bed nevertheless made it inviting. Gabriel was standing with his back to Stratton, his bag on the floor beside him, no doubt the source of the thump.

'Gabriel?' Stratton said quietly, wondering why he was standing so still.

Gabriel did not reply.

'Gabriel?' Stratton repeated as he took a step closer to the old man.

'This is the room,' Gabriel said, almost in a whisper.

Stratton took another pass around the room, checking to see if there was something obvious he had missed. 'What room?'

'I didn't tell you because there was no point at the time, but he was in a room in the derelict town . . . It was this one.'

Stratton walked across the room, scrutinising every inch of it.

A wedge of light from the top of the lampshade washed the cracked plaster wall above the bed, high-lighting what appeared to be several lines of Greek writing in large letters across it. His eyes were drawn to the meaningless letters which suddenly reminded him of something. 'Remember the letters you wrote on my notepad, at the garage, on the way to Thetford?'

Gabriel looked at the wall. 'This is Greek,' he said. 'What I wrote was in Russian according to your people.'

The word Russian got Stratton's attention. 'What did it mean?'

'Nothing. Random letters, like a serial registra-tion.'

Stratton could sense some kind of connection or emerging pattern but he could not quite see it.

'He did not like being here and was anxious to leave, but he was forcing himself to be patient. He was suspicious of the locals, I feel . . . Do you think he's the Russian they talked about?'

Stratton didn't answer. He walked to the doorway and paused to look back at Gabriel. 'I'll talk to you later . . . If you think of anything else, come and tell me. Don't worry about waking me, okay?'

Gabriel nodded without looking at him. 'He was still very afraid of what he was planning to do, but also determined to do it . . . That was many days ago, Stratton. I think we will be too late.'

Stratton stared at him a moment then walked away.

His footsteps echoed down the wooden stairs and

a second later the front door banged closed. Gabriel sat on the edge of the bed and looked at a worn Persian rug on the floor, then at his hands. They were trembling.

As Stratton made his way down the street back towards the harbour he pulled his satellite phone from his pocket and scrolled through the numbers until he found the one he was looking for, pushed the call button and held it to his ear.

'Sumners? This is Stratton.'

Sumners was reading a newspaper on the sofa by lamplight in the small living room of his terraced house in Hampstead. As the satellite phone on the desk beside the sofa chirped and Sumners reached for it, his wife automatically got up out of the armchair to turn down the television and then without a word left the room to go into the tiny kitchen to make a pot of tea.

'Yes, Stratton,' he said, still reading the article.

'I think I have something. Not sure. Probably nothing,' Stratton said.

Sumners lost focus on the paper. He might have been irritated with most of his other agents for ringing with a comment like that, but Stratton would never call unless there was an underlying importance to his empty introduction.

'Nothing?' Sumners asked anyway.

'It's vague enough as it is, but since this isn't mauve you'll have to bear with me.' Stratton was referring to the mauve secure phone system. The system did not work on wireless systems such as mobile and sat. phones. That required an altogether different scrambling encryption, which was difficult to implement on an international grid.

'Understood,' Sumners said, putting down the paper. 'I take it you arrived at your planned destination.'

'Affirmative,' Stratton said, then paused to choose his wording. 'I need you to think of another team to relate this party to. Last week you stopped me from heading elsewhere. You with me?'

Sumners reached for a notepad and pencil as he considered the first of what he expected to be several clues. He wrote down the word 'Norway' since it was where Stratton had been going when Sumners redirected him to Rhodes. 'Yes,' Sumners said.

'That place is where our team used to play their team.'

Sumners' pen hovered above the page – where Stratton's team used to play their team. Play meaning to operate against. Their team meaning the only people they operated against in Norway – the Russians. 'I'm with you,' Sumners said as he jotted down 'Russians' on the notepad.

'My colleague gave you some letters written in that team speak,' Stratton said.

Sumners jotted down 'Gabriel' then 'Viewer notes in Russian??? – Thetford'.

'I have no meaning for that yet,' Sumners said.

'Understood. Reference the big fish I caught recently that prompted this party,' Stratton said.

Sumners wrote down the word 'Supertanker'. 'Go on,' he said.

'Find a connection between the fish and the team national,' he said.

Sumners drew brackets connecting 'Russians' with 'Supertanker'.

'A team national came through this location recently.'

Sumners scribbled the word 'Kastellorizo' then connected it to the word 'Russians'.

'My colleague believes the hare came through here recently. Reference where my colleague got a dent when I wasn't watching.'

Sumners scribbled down 'Thetford Forest'. 'Yes,' he said.

'Possibility it was the same national.'

Sumners connected 'Thetford Forest' to 'Kastellorizo' and 'Russians'. 'Understood,' he said.

'Here's the wild card,' Stratton said. 'The national is in possession of something portable. My friend's concerned about such a thing.'

'Unclear,' Sumners said.

'Me too. But there is a lot of reference to it. That national carried something here. Bear it in mind and maybe it'll fit in somewhere.'

Sumners scribbled down the words 'portable object???'. 'Anything else?' he asked.

'I'm gonna wait till morning,' Stratton said. 'See what daylight brings.'

'Understood. Speak to you later,' Sumners said, and disconnected.

He studied his notepad for a moment then got up, went to his writing desk and reached for a mauve-coloured phone.

Stratton pocketed his sat. phone and looked out over the water wondering if there was anything he had overlooked. He decided not to spend any more time concentrating on it. In his experience, unsubtle or not obvious connections tended to make their own way to the surface, and not always quickly.

He headed back towards the house.

8

Zhilev cut the boat's engine for the last time and it spluttered in the darkness for several seconds, resisting, holding on to life as if it knew its future was uncertain in these strange waters hundreds of miles from home and after an adventure its owner never intended it to have.

Zhilev felt relief in the silence, with the cessation of the vibrations that had been slowly making him numb. He let go of the wheel and squeezed and released his fingers repeatedly, getting the blood flowing around them again to relieve the pins and needles that came without fail at the start of each day of his journey. Ironically though, the vibrations appeared to stop the aching in his neck. Hour upon hour at the wheel in the small cabin, standing or slouched in the uncomfortable wooden seat with its lumpy cushion, should have left him in an agonising mess, but there was no sign of the pain as long as the engines hummed and his hands were on the wheel.

The boat rocked and bobbed gently in the light swell caused by the prevailing southeasterly wind which had been at his back all the way down the Suez Canal. The worst part of the journey from

Kastellorizo had been crossing the Mediterranean to Port Fu'ad, the entrance to the canal. Zhilev had topped up a dozen large cans with fuel for the non-stop journey and lashed them to the decks forward and aft of the small wheelhouse. Fortunately the weather had remained calm, a surprise for the time of year, allowing him to snatch a few hours' sleep while the wheel was tied in position, without straying too far off-track. The small marine GPS he had bought in Marmaris along with all the relevant charts had proved more than adequate. He had never used one before, having learned sea navigation in the Spetsnaz using a compass and dead reckoning. He was hugely impressed with the modern technology that told him where he was at any given time. It even calculated his average speed and distance to his destination, once he had read the manual several times and thoroughly understood the complicated device.

By day three he was so engrossed in the journey he began to daydream about other sea journeys he would like to do now that he had re-acquired a taste for the ocean, and then something horrific happened. A tinge of doubt had somehow crept into his head about his mission. The doubt was laced with a kind of fear that spread through him like fire in a field of wheat until he reached out for the key on the tattered control panel, turned off the engine and sat in silence in the choppy water, staring at nothing while his mind raced to find a foothold of sense amid the sudden panic.

Finally the Zhilev of the past emerged once again and stood tall to take charge, cursing the weak old man for allowing uncertainty to take a grip and demanding he find his spine. He reminded himself about one of the many lessons he learned in the ranks of the Spetsnaz, that it was during those times when a soldier felt at his weakest that he had to recognise the dangers of making decisions he would regret. This mission was revenge for the murder of his brother, but it was something else. It was an opportunity to put his glorious Spetsnaz on the map. Once Zhilev's mission was complete, the practically unheard of unit would be on everyone's lips and it would have the respect it had always deserved as the finest Special Forces the world had ever known. Even those among his peers of old who would not openly agree with his mission would grudgingly have to admit it was a deed few could have accomplished.

Zhilev took the photographs of his brother from his pocket and looked at the one on top inside the now wrinkled and worn plastic bag. Vladimir was standing alone on the deck of a supertanker, wearing his white engineer's boiler-suit and hard-hat, the wind tugging at him. He looked strong and at ease with the world. It had a controlling effect on Zhilev even though he could not remember when the photo was taken. Vladimir was wearing a slight smile as if he could see Zhilev. Zhilev asked himself what his brother would truly say about this mission. It was easy to imagine him disapproving, but Vladimir was quite capable of picking up a weapon and fighting to protect his beliefs, let alone his family. He could quite easily approve of Zhilev's actions and tell him to push on and destroy those who had killed him and left his family without a father. But it did not matter what Vladimir would have thought. He was not always right about everything. It was Zhilev's choice to avenge Vladimir's death, and this was the way he was going to do it.

Zhilev turned the key and ignited the engine. He put the photo away, took up his GPS to check the bearing and adjusted the wheel.

Zhilev's arrival at Port Fu'ad and his first contact with an Arab since working with the Palestinian Liberation Organisation more than fifteen years earlier reinvigorated his contempt and hatred for the race, and, combined with the inconsolable grief for his brother's death at their hands, only served to fuel him further. As he arrived at the entrance to the canal, a pilot boat, crewed by the pilot and his assistant, sped out to meet him. Zhilev slowed to nearly a stop as they approached, expecting to receive information about port fees, agents and where to get his boat measured for the canal transit fees. But the first demand the pilot shouted at him was the singular word 'cigarettes'. Zhilev did not have any cigarettes and informed them of the fact as best he could in English, the most common language between them although neither of them spoke it well. Zhilev was not prepared for the pilot's reaction to his apparent refusal to provide any baksheesh. The man threw his throttle forward and rammed the small fishing boat while at the same time shouting what were no doubt obscenities in Arabic. But neither was the pilot prepared for the fury he unleashed from the giant Russian as a result of his attack. The blood rushed to Zhilev's head, filling him with violence. He ran to the front of his boat, found an old shackle and launched it with such force it crashed through a window in the pilot's bridge, bounced off his control console and almost took out his assistant. If the pilot had been stupid enough to repeat his attack, Zhilev would not have been able to stop himself leaping aboard and smashing the pilot's and his assistant's skulls together. But the pilot must have sensed something of that order was probable from the hairy, bedraggled and enraged monster he had awoken and elected to back smartly away and depart altogether. All he dared offer in reply was another volley of abuse as he accelerated away.

Zhilev chastised himself, aware that his response had been a senseless one. Had he indeed boarded the boat he would probably have had to end up killing both men and sinking the boat, something he might have gotten away with since there was no other vessel close by, but had he been seen it would have meant the end of his mission. As it was, he still had to make port and run the risk of having to deal with the pilot on land.

The visit went smoothly. The man who measured his boat for the transit fees also asked for cigarettes and was content to receive ten US dollars instead. Zhilev resented paying that much but decided it was wiser not to cause any more trouble and keep as low a profile as possible.

Early the next morning he caught the south-bound convoy and spent the following night at the halfway point of Ismailia where he stayed aboard in the yacht club's marina. He ate from the ample supply of rations he had bought from the small grocery shop on Kastellorizo, practically emptying it of its tinned goods which he ate without heating, and ventured ashore only to refill his water containers.

On the evening of the second day of passage down the canal, he left Port Suez and headed into the Gulf of Suez where he moored for the night prior to cutting across the Red Sea and into the Gulf of Aqaba. The journey along the monotonous, mainly rocky eastern coast of Egypt had been uneventful. The only points of interest were the occasional clusters of barbed wire and dilapidated signs in Arabic and phonetic English warning against coming ashore.

That was yesterday and now the lights from the city of Aqaba, Jordan's most south-western town and only seaport, were to the north and less than a mile away. A short distance to the west of those lights, separated by a narrow dark area, was the even more brightly illuminated holiday town of Elat, across Jordan's border, and Israel's southernmost town. It was this cluster of brightness, formed by a dozen towering hotels and dense harbour life, that held Zhilev's gaze.

He studied the panorama for a long time, looking for any signs of security measures such as military vessels that might approach to investigate his little boat, and then looked at the waters to estimate the speed and direction of the current before finally turning to face his large bag which was on the deck. This was it, he told himself, the point of no return. Once this next phase was complete and he was on Israeli soil, there was no going back, not that Zhilev had any doubts now about completing his mission.

He crouched in front of his bag, cracked his neck which had begun to ache a little, and opened it. He removed various pieces of diving equipment, one by one, like a priest reverently sorting out his altar before a mass, and laid them neatly on the deck. He removed a black, rubber dry suit from a plastic bag; it was covered in talcum powder to prevent the thin wrist cuffs and neck seal from adhering to themselves, which would cause them to tear when pulled apart. Beside the suit he placed a pair of black fins, a face-mask and a black board the size of a small tea tray that had a depth gauge and compass fixed to it. He then removed a small oxygen cylinder the size of a water bottle and what looked like a coffee tin with Russian writing on it describing the contents as carbon dioxide absorbent powder. The last and heaviest item was an old Spetsnaz re-breathable diving apparatus which Zhilev had purloined while in service – along with all the other equipment. The diving set was some twenty years old but because of its basic design and solid construction it was as good as the day it had been made. It comprised of a large, thick rubber bag the size of a small backpack attached to a harness made up of a series of broad, heavy rubber straps. Fixed to the bottom of the harness, under the rubber bag, was an oxygen-flow regulator, and beside that was strapped a canister the size of a small cake tin. The mouthpiece of the apparatus was similar to a regular scuba's in so far as it was made up of two flexible rubber concertina hoses attached either side of breathing valves, one leading to the canister and the other fixed directly into the large rubber bag.

Zhilev unscrewed the side of the canister, which was empty, and then opened the sealed tin which contained white granules. Zhilev poured them into the canister until it was full, discarded the empty tin over the side and re-screwed the canister tightly shut again. He picked up the oxygen bottle, checking a small gauge on the side to ensure it was full, and fitted a short, high-pressure hose attached to the regulator, tightening it with a wrench, and then strapped it into its place on the harness. After checking all the seals were secure, he turned on the oxygen bottle and lowered it over the side into the water to check for leaks, and finally opened the bypass valve on the regulator partially inflating the bag. He took a couple of breaths through the mouthpiece to ensure the breathing circuit was functioning. Everything appeared to be working perfectly.

The system was ingeniously simple. High-pressure oxygen trickled from the oxygen cylinder, through the flow regulator and into the rubber bag at low pressure. With the mouthpiece in his mouth, when the diver inhaled fully he emptied the rubber bag containing the pure oxygen, which passed along the concertina hose and into his lungs. When he exhaled, the gases, which were made up of unused oxygen and a small percentage of carbon dioxide, travelled through a valve, along the other concertina hose and into the canister where the carbon dioxide was absorbed by the special powder. The unused oxygen continued through the canister and back into the bag where the spent oxygen was replaced via the regulator attached to the oxygen cylinder, completing the closed-circuit system. The result was a sealed breathing apparatus that did not release any bubbles and therefore did not betray the presence of a diver beneath the surface.

Zhilev looked around to see if any boats were approaching, and when he was satisfied he was alone made a final check of his breast pockets to ensure he had his passport and all his money.

He picked up the diving suit, sat down on the deck, removed his boots, pushed his legs inside and, lying on his back, wormed his way into it. Once he was inside up to his chest he got to his feet, pushed his arms through, being careful not to tear the cuff seals, then lifted up the front and pushed his head through the neck seal. After putting his boots inside the suit, one down each side, he made a quick adjustment of his clothes to ensure comfort and yanked tight the watertight zip across his back to create a seal. After slipping on his fins he picked up the diving apparatus, placed it over his head and buckled the rubber straps that criss-crossed his back so that the bag fitted snugly across his chest.

The nuclear device in its log-like casing was neatly wrapped inside a canvas bag and had a short length of line tied around it that he attached to one side of the diving apparatus harness. The atomic bomb was waterproof to a depth of one hundred feet, more than enough since he would not be going deeper than a quarter of that. The final items were a pair of rocks he had brought from Kastellorizo, which he placed in pockets on the thighs of the suit. Zhilev had carried out a ballast test in a quiet cove of the island prior to leaving, to ensure he had the precise weight including the nuclear device to keep him below the surface. He tied the line connected to the compass and depth gauge board to his harness and picked up his facemask. He was ready.

Zhilev checked around the deck one last time to ensure he had everything then put the facemask on. A quick turn of the regulator bypass valve filled the bag and then he switched the regulator to a trickle flow. He placed the mouthpiece in his mouth, checked his watch and began to breathe. Zhilev stood quietly for two minutes, the prescribed time to test the set and ensure it was working properly. If the gas was bad or the system faulty in some way, it was better to collapse on the deck than in the sea. He looked out over the water once more to check for boats then picked up the nuclear device, climbed carefully over the side and lowered himself into the sea.

As he let go of the boat and quietly drifted away he was suddenly filled with sadness for the little craft. They had not spent very long together but in that short time she had become a friend to him. They had had their ups and downs, such as the times the engine would die suddenly and for no apparent reason. He would curse and shout at it, but after a little tinkering here and there, patching a leaky fuel hose, or unclogging a filter, and always accompanied by words of encouragement, it would run once again as if all it really wanted was some love and attention.

In an odd way Zhilev felt the little boat had similar affections for him. They made a fine pair, both old and in their winter, but plodding on without complaint, needing little more than fuel to keep going. It was love, or the lack of it, that was the great sadness of Zhilev's life and one he was hardly aware of. He had never known it from, or given it to, anyone but his brother. Perhaps that was the deeper reason for his mission, the severing of his last emotional attachment to the rest of humanity, but he would never admit as much. Watching the little boat drift off into the darkness, he was alone again. He had thought about sinking her, and knew it was the wisest course if he was to maintain the strictest security, but his heart would not allow it. At least the boat had a chance if it did not founder, but both their fates were uncertain. Hopefully it would be discovered by a fisherman, the plight of its crew a mystery, who might love it as Zhilev did.

He turned away and faced the lights of Elat, putting the boat out of his mind, and concentrated once again on his task.

The air in his suit gathered at the top keeping him on the surface like a large float. He raised an arm, pulled the cuff away to allow the air to escape, and as it did so he sank slowly beneath the water.

The sea was pleasantly chilly around his head and he swam slowly to keep himself just below the surface while he felt for the line tied to his side and pulled the compass board attached to it into his hands. The nuclear device hung heavily from his waist several feet below but out of the way. He checked the compass that he had already preset, levelled off and started to fin gently along. He did not have to look at anything other than the compass and depth gauge to get to his target. The estimated time it would take him to cover the distance was somewhere around two and a half hours. His oxygen bottle should provide enough gas for three. The depth gauge was needed to keep him close to the surface and important for two reasons: first, the deeper he went the more oxygen he would use because of the increased pressure; and second, pure oxygen could become poisonous beyond a depth of ten metres. The one factor he had not been able to calculate was the tide. The charts were not accurate enough for that and he was going to have to rely partly on luck to get him to his target before he ran out of oxygen.

Zhilev had not swum with a compass board in almost two decades and he had forgotten how boring it was, like a pilot flying a plane at night with no visibility and nothing to look at but his instrument panel. The tiny fluorescent sea anemone glowed around the board, across his hands and along his body, streaming off him as if he were a spacecraft on re-entry into the earth's atmosphere. This was the time for silent thought while his feet beat a constant rhythm propelling him along slowly, and Zhilev went over his plan for the next phase of the operation. He had no doubt that he would come ashore, one way or another, in Israel.

After thirty minutes, Zhilev stopped his forward passage and headed slowly up. He controlled his ascent carefully allowing only his head to break the surface, hoping to see Elat directly ahead, but it was slightly to his right. That indicated a current pushing him to the left, but, thankfully, it was small. He had carried out dives such as this for thousands of hours in his lifetime and was confident he had maintained a true course. All he needed to do was make a slight adjustment to counter the current. The town seemed as far away as it had been when he started but he was aware this could be more illusion than fact. He studied the lights for a moment and decided some aspects had changed and he was indeed getting closer. He pushed himself below the surface using the board as a fin and checked the oxygen gauge. It was still three quarters full. Had it been much less, he would have turned the bottle off and risked swimming on the surface for a while, breathing air, but he felt that would not be necessary. There was enough O_2 in the cylinder, he was sure of it.

Now that he was actually crossing the Gulf of Aqaba, he wondered if he would have got away with swimming in from the Mediterranean, directly on to the Israeli coastline, but he was confident he had made the more difficult but wiser choice. Fifteen years ago he had been part of a team that had supplied the Palestinians with arms from one boat to another in the Mediterranean, and he remembered the briefing regarding the Israeli coastal defences and how good they were rumoured to be in places. The Gulf of Aqaba was much more difficult for them to secure because of the diving and water sports which took place in Elat harbour, as well as the many pleasure boats that sailed this Gulf. The defences here were weak against this kind of approach and the risks for Zhilev greatly reduced.

An hour later he stopped to check his position, gently breaking the surface once again, and this time he was pleasantly surprised to see that he was not only bang on target but quite close to the port. He could make out dozens of boats alongside the jetty and the windows of several towering hotels just beyond. He estimated the distance to be around six hundred yards and dropped below the surface once more. The gauge on the oxygen bottle indicated it was a quarter full, more than enough to complete the journey. He set off at a steady pace and spent the time going through the final surfacing procedures.

Twenty-five minutes later lights appeared above him, diffused and rippled by the water, and a few minutes after that they disappeared indicating that the jetty had cut them out and he was now very close. He slowed his pace and was about to reach in front of him for obstacles when suddenly his head slammed into something solid, the shock almost making him lose his mouthpiece. He dropped the compass board that sunk to the end of its line and felt the object. It was rough and barnacled, with a curve to it that dipped away below him. A boat. He followed it down, passing beneath it, and followed it up the other side.

Zhilev carefully broke the surface to find himself between a pleasure craft of some kind and the jetty. He pushed his facemask up on to his forehead and looked around. The rusty corrugated metal wall of the quay went straight up to a line of rails running along the top of it. A few yards away a ramp came down on to a floating platform that pleasure boats used to load and offload passengers. There were voices, the thud of disco music and then a burst of laughter that sounded like girls.

He made his way to the edge of the platform, keeping beneath the ramp and out of sight from the quay above. Once he reached it, he moved around until he was close against the wall of the quay and in the shadows, then held on to the side while he untied the device and attached it to a ring on the platform. He unbuckled the diving harness, pulled it off his shoulder and, with a firm yank, ripped the air hoses out of the bag. Oxygen gushed from it as it deflated and he released it to let it sink to the seabed. After dumping the two rocks from his pockets, he removed his fins and let them sink along with his facemask. He then took a firm hold of the top of the platform and hauled himself out.

Sitting on the edge of the wooden platform, he unzipped the suit and pulled it off as quickly as he could, placing his shoes to one side. Zhilev dug a penknife from a pocket, slashed the suit from toe to neck and lowered it into the water, pushing it under until enough bubbles escaped and it sank. He pulled on his boots, tied up the laces and stood up to sort out his creased clothes and smarten himself up as best he could. The bump on his head throbbed and he felt it to check for blood but the skin was not broken. His sleeves and collar were wet where water had seeped in but otherwise he was dry. He untied the device from the ring, hauled it out of the water and headed up the ramp and into the bright lights of the quay, acting as naturally as a worker coming off one of the boats.

As he stepped off the ramp, several young girls dressed sexily despite the cool air walked past talking energetically. The source of the thumping music was a building in front of him on the corner of the quay, the windows in the top floor washed in coloured lights flashing to the rhythm of a heavy beat. Zhilev hated disco music and did not understand the Western nightclub culture having never experienced anything like it in his life. Young people were everywhere, on balconies around the club, and walking up and down the broad exterior stairs that led to the entrance. None of them seemed to give him a second glance as he walked away.

In front of him, across a broad paved concourse, were several towering hotels vying for an ocean view with massive neon signs on top of each displaying such names as the Hilton and Sheraton. He headed for a dark area to the side of the nearest where a thick collection of manicured bushes grew.

As he walked towards the bushes he looked around to see if many people were about. Several couples were strolling casually, enjoying the night air, or moving to and from the disco in various directions, but none immediately close by. He slipped into the bushes and crouched by the windowless side wall of the hotel that towered above him. From his hidden position he could see the next hotel's car park which was almost full. He checked his watch. It was ten to eleven. His timing was perfect. Any later and it might have proved much more difficult to carry out the next phase.

A pair of headlights turned a far corner and headed along the road that ran along the back of the hotels connecting their main entrances. Zhilev hoped this would be his quarry, but as it passed the entrance and continued along the road, it became quite recognisable as a police Land Rover. It drove out of sight and another car turned the same corner in the distance and followed the road. When it reached the car park entrance it slowed, turned into it and came to a stop in a space. A moment later the lights and engine died, the doors opened and an elderly couple climbed out. Zhilev shifted his weight in anticipation, watching them unblinkingly like a leopard weighing his prey. The couple removed some plastic shopping bags from the back seat and unenergetically made their way along the back of the hotel towards the main entrance, the opposite side to the waterfront. Zhilev left the device on the ground concealed by the bushes and stepped out and on to the concourse. He looked back to see if the log was visible, suddenly feeling naked without it. It was the first time in almost two weeks it had left his side. He looked back for the couple and lost sight of them as they passed the corner of the hotel. He walked quickly through the car park and on to the pavement where he located them at the main entrance. A security guard was talking to them, and, after he had made a cursory check of their baggage, they entered the building.

Zhilev moved smartly off after them and as he approached the entrance the security guard turned to look at him. The guard was a young man in civilian clothing and had a metal detector in his hand.

'Hello,' Zhilev said with a broad smile as he headed for the single glass door. He must have looked an unlikely guest with his dishevelled clothes and hair, and matted growth of beard.

'Excuse me, sir,' the young man said in a heavy accent, holding his arm out to bar Zhilev's way. 'Are you staying in the hotel?'

'Not yet,' Zhilev said, smiling. 'I look for a friend here. If he is here, I stay.'

The guard looked Zhilev over from head to toe as if he was unsure about letting him in.

'Sorry for clothes,' Zhilev said in a friendly manner. 'I on boat, fishing. My friend has clothes.'

The young man stared into Zhilev's unwavering eyes, shrugged and held up the metal detector. 'I need to search you,' he said.

'Oh,' Zhilev said acting surprised, and raised his arms. 'I have nothing,' he said as if it were a joke.

The guard did not return the smile and ran the detector across Zhilev's body. It beeped loudly as it passed one of Zhilev's side pockets.

'Ah,' Zhilev said as if remembering what it was. He reached into the pocket and held out the small knife, his smile just as broad.

The guard ignored it since his prime function was looking for guns and bombs, and scanned the rest of Zhilev's towering frame. There were no other beeps.

'Okay,' the security guard said and stepped back to allow Zhilev entry. Zhilev nodded a thanks and headed through the door into the cavernous lobby with varying ceiling heights and floor depths defining a bar, restaurant and seating areas. Zhilev could sense the guard watching his back but ignored him as he scanned quickly about. The reception desk was the other end of the lobby and the elderly couple were in front of it talking to the receptionist.

As soon as he saw them, they moved off and headed down a corridor behind the reception counter. As they turned a corner and out of sight he set off briskly after them.

He walked past the receptionist who did not look up at him and followed the corridor to the corner where he paused to look around it. The elderly couple were standing quietly looking up at a line of floor numbers above a pair of elevators. The sound of a bell announced the lift's arrival and the doors opened. As the old couple stepped inside, Zhilev followed.

The old man pushed the tenth-floor button and as Zhilev jumped through the closing doors, the couple could hardly take their eyes off him. Zhilev went to push a button then acted as if the tenth was also his floor, nodded, smiled at them and then went back to staring at the doors. Zhilev could feel their eyes looking up at him as the lift gently ascended. He glanced at them for a second and they looked away but only until he faced the doors again, then they continued to stare at him, unsmiling, habitually suspicious. In the confined space Zhilev was suddenly aware of a foul smell and realised it was coming from him. He had not washed for a week or more and in the warmth of the hotel, with the sea drying in his hair, he must have smelt much worse to the old couple since he had grown accustomed to it.

The lift came to a stop and the doors opened. No one immediately moved and Zhilev smiled, motioning politely for them to alight first. They stepped out of the elevator and Zhilev followed, trying to walk much slower than them, which was impossible as they shuffled up the corridor. The old man turned to look at Zhilev who passed alongside his wife doing his best to act as if he was not sure where his room was. The couple stopped outside a door and Zhilev carried on.

The old woman had the key card in her hand, wiggled it into the slot and pushed down the handle but the door would not open, and after several failed attempts the old man forgot about Zhilev, put the bags down and took over, snapping at her in Hebrew. Zhilev glanced over his shoulder in time to see the handle go down and the door start to open. He turned round immediately, gauging his pace and, as the old man picked up the bags and the couple stepped over the threshold, Zhilev accelerated forward and brutally pushed them inside. He threw the door closed behind him and as the old man regained his balance and turned to face his assailant, Zhilev delivered a blow to the side of his neck so powerful it must have snapped a vertebra for the man's knees immediately buckled and he dropped to the floor like a puppet with its strings cut. The old woman watched her husband fall in horror and as she turned to Zhilev she let out a shrill scream. Zhilev reached out and placed one of his massive hands over her face and the other behind her head, squeezing them together as tight as he could. She continued to scream but it was muffled to near silence as he increased the pressure, her bifocals shattering against her face as if in a vice. The hold was airtight and she grabbed at his fingers to prise them off but for this feeble old woman it was an impossible task. Her nails clawed at his hands and broke against the leather skin leaving barely a mark. Her legs kicked out as the last vestiges of oxygen in her lungs were used, and her eyes bulged then turned up in their sockets as her life ebbed away. Her hands dropped to her sides and hung limply and only then did Zhilev realise he was holding her off the floor. He gently lowered her down and released his grip, and stepped back to look at his work.

He suddenly felt ugly and turned away so that he would not have to look at them. He had had to do it, he told himself. They were old and at the end of their lives anyway and there was no other way to complete the next phase of his mission. Then he saw himself in the large mirror on the wall above the bed and did not recognise himself. He looked far worse than he had imagined and appeared to have aged years in the last few weeks.

Zhilev removed his jacket, unbuttoned his shirt, removed the rest of his clothes and placed them on the bed. When he was naked, he walked into the bathroom and climbed into the bath. It took him a minute to figure out the shower and get it warm and then he immersed himself in the spray. He went through several bottles that lined the bath, unscrewing the caps and pouring the contents on to his head until they lathered, and began to wash himself thoroughly. He rinsed himself off, stepped out of the bath and grabbed a towel off the rail. As he dried himself, he searched through the washing bags, found a razor and shaving foam and set about removing his facial hair. After drying his face and feeling and looking a little younger again, he went to a cupboard outside the bathroom and sorted through the old man's clothes. He'd hoped there might be something he could wear but it was all ridiculously small. A pair of socks and underpants was all he could find to fit and he went back to his musky clothes on the bed and got dressed, leaving his old socks and underwear on the floor.

Zhilev searched the old man for his keys, picked him up, placed him inside the cupboard and went back for the woman. He packed her on top of her husband and closed the door, the intention being that the maid might not find them immediately the next morning, giving him as much time as possible before the search for him commenced. As a final touch he ruffled the bedclothes, making it look as if they had spent the night in bed.

Zhilev went back to the front door, listened against it for a moment then carefully opened it. The corridor was clear.

He closed the door behind him, walked to the elevator and pushed the call button. He checked his watch. Eleven thirty. The lift arrived and he stepped inside and pushed the lobby button.

The journey seemed to take an age and when the doors opened several young couples were outside, talking and laughing and barely giving him a chance to get out before they piled inside.

Zhilev headed across the lobby to the entrance and stepped through the door ignoring the young security guard who watched him as he walked away.

Zhilev went directly through the car park and into the bushes. A few seconds later he emerged carrying his bag, walked to the couple's car, opened the driver's door and climbed in. A quick search of the glove compartment produced a couple of tourist maps, which he quickly studied. The road system looked uncomplicated and if it was well signposted he would have no problems finding his way out of the town.

A minute later he was driving out of the car park and on to the road.

Despite the map it took Zhilev a good five minutes to find his way out of the confusing patchwork of streets that connected the dozen or so hotels in the resort, and when he finally found the main road a sign indicated the Taba Border crossing into Egypt was to the left. He turned right and headed north. Half a mile up the road he hit a junction where a series of signs indicated the Yitzhak Rabin Terminal into Jordan was right and Tel Aviv and Jerusalem were straight on. He continued over the crossing and left the town behind on the virtually dead straight road where there was one other car some distance ahead and nothing behind. He took a deep, relaxing breath and concentrated on removing the tension from his shoulders as the ache in his neck returned. The petrol gauge indicated the tank was over half full, ample fuel to get well away from the town without having to stop. He decided to give it an hour before looking for a petrol station and if it was not open he would park and wait until morning.

As he drove over the crest of a slight hill, a cluster of lights appeared up ahead and he tensed when he realised it was a military checkpoint. Adrenaline trickled into his veins but he remained calm and did not alter his speed until he was close, then he began to slow down.

A soldier with a rifle across his back was standing in the road by a barricade system that narrowed oncoming traffic to a single lane. As Zhilev approached, the soldier stood to the side watching him. Several metres from the barricade Zhilev slowed, preparing to stop alongside the soldier, but he waved him through.

Zhilev maintained his speed and waved as he went by the soldier, then kept an eye on his rear-view mirror as he accelerated up the road. The soldier walked casually away from the barricade towards a hut on the side of the road and disappeared from view.

Zhilev went through the relaxing process once more and concentrated on the road ahead. A couple of distant red tail lights showed that it continued straight for several miles and he suddenly felt a burst of exhilaration. He was in Israel, having covered thousands of miles from his home in Riga, by car, ferry, on foot, by boat and then swimming. Despite his belief in himself he was still impressed he had got this far and with an atomic bomb. It was not that he ever had doubts about the effectiveness of his plan, but there were so many things that could have gone wrong, even relatively small things such as a car accident, or the boat breaking down, any one of a dozen things that could have meant the end of the mission. But none of them had happened and he was within reach of his goal. The next couple of phases would be extremely tricky, with the added danger of the Israeli police and an extremely paranoid military defence force. But then, if the checkpoint he just went through was anything to go by, perhaps that was not going to be as much of a factor as he initially feared. Then again, Elat was a tourist resort. Things would be very different the closer he got to the West Bank and Jerusalem.

Despite his efforts to relax he could not release the tension in his shoulders and the pain in his neck increased. He felt his breast pocket for the small packet of painkillers and thought about breaking his rule, part of him arguing that under the circumstances it would be forgivable. This was not the time to show vulnerability, but as the pain increased, the temptation grew stronger.

Zhilev opened the window, removed the pills from his pocket and tossed them out where they bounced off the black tarmac and rolled into the barren desert.

9

Stratton heard the creak, opened his eyes and focused all his senses outside of the room. He was a light sleeper at home, but abroad he was overly sensitive to any change around him. He felt certain the sound came from within the house but was not completely sure. The creak came again – the stairs – and he sat up in the bed. It was getting lighter outside but dawn had not yet reached the island. He checked his watch. The time was a few minutes after six. It could be Gabriel looking for the toilet, which was the last door on the landing, or perhaps he was heading out of the house for some reason.

Stratton climbed out of the bed and quickly pulled on his trousers and shirt. The creak came again, closer, further up the stairs. He pulled on his boots and tied up the laces.

As he stepped to the door, he could feel someone on the other side of it. It was bred in him not to overreact and in situations like this, if a threat was on the cards, his actions would always take the form of a counterattack.

The door handle moved, then began to turn.

Stratton stepped behind the door as it slowly

opened and the tip of a head came into view, peering at the bed.

'Mr Stratton?' It was the Greek army captain.

'Morning,' Stratton said.

The captain looked around the door as Stratton stepped into view. 'Oh,' he exclaimed in a most apologetic manner. 'I am sorry to disturb you.'

'That's okay. What can I do for you?'

'I have come to collect you,' the captain said, looking as humble as he sounded, a stark contrast to his superior attitude of the night before.

'Collect me?'

'Yes, you and your friend Mr Stockton.'

Stratton did not remember Gabriel giving anyone his last name during dinner.

'It is very urgent. I have a vehicle waiting for us.'

'I don't understand,' Stratton said.

'I am simply obeying orders. I received a call a short while ago from my divisional commander, General Stanopis. I have never personally spoken to him before. In fact, I have only ever seen him once. He instructed me to tell you that a British air force plane has been granted permission to land on the island and that I am to personally escort you both to it.'

Stratton's mind raced. His eyes flicked to the satellite phone on the small table beside his bed. He had checked the signal before going to sleep and it was weak but workable. It was close to the French windows, which were open, and should have been able to receive a call. But then, why would the captain lie?

'I am told to tell you that a Mr Sumners will be meeting you on the aircraft.'

That instantly gave the captain full credibility and Stratton finished getting dressed, tucking in his shirt and pulling his jacket off the bedpost. 'Is there anything else?' Stratton asked, as he stuffed his ablutions bag into his small holdall, put the sat. phone in his pocket and scanned around in case there was anything he had forgotten.

'Nothing,' the captain said. 'I take it you know what it's all about,' he said, more in hope that it might be revealed to him. He had been completely overcome by the request. Nothing like it had ever happened to him in his career. It was obvious that this Englishman and his friend were of great importance for the general to call him personally. Not only that, the general was insistent that this small but important task was carried out with the utmost efficiency and safety.

Stratton went to Gabriel's door and knocked once before opening it.

To his surprise, Gabriel was fully dressed and sat on the edge of his bed looking out of the window. He turned to look at Stratton long enough to see who it was and then went back to contemplating his view.

'We have to go,' Stratton said to him.

'I know,' Gabriel said.

Stratton glanced around at the captain knowing he had not stopped at Gabriel's room before coming to his. 'You know about the plane coming to pick us up?'

'No,' Gabriel said, without any change in his voice or reaction. He remained still, without urgency, as if nothing else mattered in the world.

'I've seen how it ends,' Gabriel said.

Stratton walked into the room to where he could see Gabriel's face. He seemed the same, older perhaps, and tired as always.

'What are you talking about?'

'The end. You know what the end means, don't you?'

'How does it end?' Stratton asked, wondering if Gabriel had flipped.

'My end . . . My death.'

The urgency left Stratton as he focused on the situation. Whatever was going on, it had to be dealt with calmly. 'Do you want to tell me about it?'

'I saw it. A bright flash, like the sun itself. A loud boom. A rush of violent air. Everything tearing apart, ripped to pieces . . . But I'm not alone. The air is filled with souls.' Gabriel looked at Stratton. 'Do you really expect me to be enthusiastic about going anywhere?'

Stratton stared at Gabriel, wondering if he had indeed gone mad. 'I didn't know remote viewing was also about seeing into the future.'

'I've been telling myself that all night, but the image won't go away . . . Perhaps I'm going insane.'

Gabriel got to his feet and took a deep breath. 'You're right though. We must go . . . No one can escape their destiny.'

He picked up his bag, turned away from the window and walked to the door. Stratton followed him, past the captain who looked somewhat bewildered, and they headed down the stairs and out of the house.

The captain led the way along a street, away from the harbour and up an incline. A minute later they stepped out on to a gravel track where a Greek army Land Rover was waiting for them, a driver behind the wheel and two armed soldiers in the back.

Gabriel, still looking as if in a daze, climbed into the back, Stratton behind him, and the captain got in beside the driver. He barked an order and the vehicle moved off, circling the back of the town before leaving it behind to climb a steep hill.

The sound of an aircraft penetrated the noise of the Land Rover's engine and a second later Stratton saw a Hercules C130 transport aircraft turning low over the water before disappearing behind them.

The Land Rover crossed the island, the sea to the south coming into view, and followed the winding track back inland. A few minutes later they reached the top of an incline and the road levelled out. A few hundred yards further and the road quickly widened and a runway appeared in front of them. Up ahead, coming towards them, was the C130 having touched down and making its way to the end of the runway.

The Land Rover stopped and waited for the aircraft to come to a stop, whereupon the rear ramp began to slowly open.

The captain said something to the driver and the vehicle moved off and pulled to a halt under the tail. Stratton climbed out amid the feverishly loud engines and acrid exhaust fumes clotting the air and helped Gabriel to step down on to the tarmac.

The captain climbed out and straightened his uniform, his task at an end but hoping to be of further use if possible.

'Thanks, Captain,' Stratton said, as he led Gabriel up the ramp. The captain came to attention and threw up a smart salute, holding it until the two men were aboard.

The loadmaster, in full green air suit, stood at the top of the ramp, his hand hovering over a button in a box mounted on the bulkhead, and as Stratton and Gabriel stepped into the cabin, he said something into his headset while at the same time pushing the button. A high-pitched whine filled the back of the plane as the end of the ramp began to rise off the tarmac, while at the same time an opposing section of roof, hinged beneath the tail, lowered to meet the end of the ramp and close off the Greek captain and his soldiers from any further view inside the mysterious aircraft.

The engines gradually increased power but the pilot kept the brakes applied and the plane still, an indication the runway was short and that they wanted to catapult the craft off its blocks. The two sections of ramp met and locked into place, fitting seamlessly to seal off the tail section, and much of the engine noise was immediately muffled.

There were several rows of aircraft seats halfway along the cabin, and at the front, against the bulkhead that sealed off the cockpit, was a desk with three swivel seats fitted around it, all occupied. On the desk were several communication systems and three flat-screen monitors.

Gabriel was invited by a crewman to sit in the regular seats while Stratton headed to the front where he recognised two of the men: Sumners was sat on one side of the table, and on the other, talking into a phone, was Sumners' boss, the man from the Grenadier pub. In the middle seat was a young, nerdy assistant in an inexpensive black suit. The type was familiar enough, recruited young, usually straight out of university, because of either their family connections or their brilliance, and put to work in an administrative capacity to learn the ropes. This youngster was obviously one of the smart ones since his cheap suit suggested he did not come from wealth.

Stratton's first introduction to MI6 many years ago, and where he first met Sumners, was during an operational training session. He had been sent to the secret Military Intelligence training school in Portsmouth to teach a batch of young MI6 agents, all quite brilliant academically, most of them able to speak several languages, how to climb the side of a three-storey building using a caving ladder. It seemed basic stuff but it had to be technically sound so as to be adaptable to a variety of structures and conditions. Stratton discovered two of them were later selected for an espionage job in Eastern Europe from which one never returned, rumoured to have been killed in action. Stratton found the differences between Special Forces operatives and these types interesting. MI6 operatives' idea of light conversation was quantum physics, and sometimes for fun they would discuss topics in Latin or a mixture of several different languages at once. But practical things, such as instantly recognising the difference between a pull and tension-release booby trap, or how to quickly turn a semi-automatic pistol into a fully automatic machine gun, appeared to be beyond most of them.

'Take a seat, please,' the loadmaster said to Stratton in a perfunctory manner, as he headed into the cockpit.

Stratton dropped into one of the hammock seats against the bulkhead behind Sumners who appeared to be deliberately ignoring him as he scrolled through data on a computer monitor.

The engines screamed in a chorus of painfully high-pitched tones and the aircraft vibrated so strongly it seemed the rivets holding the skin together might pop. The brakes were suddenly released, and the bulky craft lunged forward and lumbered down the runway, quickly building in speed. Had it been carrying its full capacity it would have needed a far longer runway or a set of rocket boosters to achieve take-off velocity. Being relatively empty, a few hundred yards later the nose tilted up as the pilot eased back on the stick, the wings bit into the air and the craft rose gracefully off the tarmac. The ground dropped away as the wheels retracted and within seconds there was nothing below but sea and the island was a colourful mound in the green-blue water getting ever further behind.

The cabin tilted as the pilot banked the aircraft steeply on to its heading and Sumners' boss put down his phone and swivelled in his chair to face Stratton, wearing what looked like the same immaculate dark suit he had worn in the Grenadier. If the suit was a different one, the cold, empty smile he wore was not.

'Stratton. Are you well?' he asked.

'Fine, sir,' Stratton replied.

Sumners turned in his seat to face Stratton wearing his own stock smile.

'Good,' Sumners' boss said. 'Fine job, young man. Fine job.' Then, as if he'd had an idea, he leaned close to Sumners to say something privately into his ear. Sumners gave him an equally private and short reply and the boss picked up a phone, punched in a number and concentrated on his call.

Stratton could only wonder what he had done so well that resulted in the boss himself requisitioning such an expensive trip to pick him and Gabriel up from the island, and so rapidly too. They must have left the UK only a few hours after his call to Sumners.

Sumners got out of his swivel chair and sat in the hammock seat beside Stratton. 'Well,' he said, as if he had a lot to say and did not know where to start. 'Are you wondering why we're here, the boss included, and at great expense to the taxpayer?' He sounded like a children's talk-show host.

Stratton did not want to take part in Sumners' little panto and offered him only a smile. The man was evidently in a good mood about something and would no doubt reveal why in due course.

Sumners took Stratton's lack of interest as his usual, cold standoffish self. If he did not want to be chummy when the opportunity was offered, then that was his loss.

'The name Mikhail Zhilev mean anything to you?' Sumners asked, getting down to business.

Stratton wondered why the name had a familiar ring but could not place it. He shook his head.

'What about Vladimir Zhilev?'

An image suddenly popped into Stratton's head. 'The tanker engineer?' he asked, not entirely sure.

'Correct,' Sumners said like a schoolteacher. 'Mikhail Zhilev is Vladimir's brother. Your hunch about checking the tanker was a good one. Vladimir was the only Russian on board. Latvian to be precise. I immediately put the name through to our good friends in the FSB,' Sumners said, emphasising the words 'good friends' for its irony. 'They were surprisingly forthcoming, although I must say they have been recently . . . I made my inquiry sound as if it was nothing more than a next-of-kin search, of course. They provided a profile almost immediately but it only covered his youth and the last seven years or so, which immediately suggested something else – when the FSB omit large blocks of years in an adult's life it usually indicates those years were spent in some sort of government service. We made another more urgent request, this time suggesting Zhilev had some vague connection to terrorism, fictitious, of course, which produced a more detailed coverage showing his military postings. Judging by the department and locations Zhilev served, we could ascertain he was in a Special Forces unit or at least attached to one. The FSB did not confirm that but it's pretty obvious Zhilev was in this special unit from the mid-seventies. As expected, our interest sparked the FSB into doing some checking of their own and they offered to share some of their information with us. It seems Zhilev recently left his home in Riga and took a trip to England, arriving the same day Gabriel was attacked in Thetford Forest. The Russian lettering Gabriel saw prompted us to look at all of the recent viewings more closely. The big question was if this mysterious person – assuming that person was Zhilev – was indeed a serious threat and in some way linked to the tanker, and that it was him who attacked Gabriel, then what was he doing in Thetford Forest and at that precise location?'

Stratton hoped Sumners was not expecting him to come up with an answer because he did not have a clue.

'It was Chalmers who cracked that one,' Sumners said, indicating the nerdy assistant pecking away at a computer terminal. 'He reads everything. MI archives mostly. File after file. Packing his mental database, so he says. Has a photographic memory. There are different types of photographic memory. Most just see an image they can recall instantly as if looking at an actual photograph in front of them. Then there are those who can compare relationships between different images – cut and paste between them, if you like. Chalmers has that ability. Ever heard of Operation Kraken?' he asked.

Stratton had, but after so many years and so many operations, he had to think about it for a moment. 'Norway,' he finally said. 'The Russians coming into Europe and the UK through Norway and Sweden.'

'That's right,' Sumners said, again the ever-complimentary tutor. 'Spetsnaz. Your chaps once chased a couple of 'em who'd been flushed from their submarine in a Norwegian fjord. Remember that?' Sumners said, obviously aware Stratton had been on that operation.

Stratton nodded anyway.

'Didn't catch them though,' Sumners said, scoffing. 'Must've been fit chaps to outrun you lot, eh?'

Stratton couldn't be bothered telling him the poor bastards had much more to lose if they were caught than the SBS had to gain by capturing them. Sumners was a desk spy and would never understand ground operatives and their complex, unwritten rules of survival.

'Kraken,' Sumners mused. 'A Scandinavian sea monster. Did you know that? "Then once by man and angels to be seen, in roaring he shall rise and on the surface die." Tennyson. Expecting the Russians to die so easily was more wishful thinking than optimism, especially in those days . . . Those were the days, though, eh, Stratton? The Russian was an adversary to be sure . . . in some things. Toe-to-toe, compared to this terrorist malarkey these days . . .

'But OP Kraken was far bigger than merely observing the Russian infiltration of Europe and the UK,' Sumners went on. 'It's what they were doing when they got to the UK that was of greater interest. It turned out the buggers were busy setting up sabotage teams near military targets up and down the country. It wasn't until after the Cold War we learned they had at least twenty-two sabotage hides placed in various locations in England and Scotland, though we don't know where. We found one in the late seventies in Portsmouth in a public park – a children's playground, no less. Clever bastards used an abandoned sewage system. They were ingenious at concealing these hides. We have only ever found one other . . .

'Chalmers was the one who came up with a sabotage hide being the relationship between Zhilev and Thetford Forest, or, to put it another way, Russian Special Forces and the Mildenhall and Lakenheath air bases. The thought that Gabriel had managed to stumble upon Zhilev as he was actually looking for a hide was far too irresistible to ignore. The RAF has a piece of equipment called Gronar or ground sonar, designed to find underground pipes and communication cables, et cetera. Pretty useful at finding certain types of landmines too, so I hear. We found the hide close to the spot Gabriel was attacked. Unfortunately, when Gabriel disturbed Zhilev, he was on his way out of the hide, not going in and he had already taken what he wanted. We believe he's carrying a nuclear device. In fact, we're certain of it. Simple reason is there should have been three such devices in the hide but there were only two.'

Stratton could feel the words 'nuclear device' coming before Sumners said them. He knew about the hide in Portsmouth, or cache as the SBS called it. Stratton didn't see it for himself but one of the

303

older SBS lads at the time had been on the operation to secure and recover the cache and its contents. The fear was that there might have been Spetsnatz in the area so it was prudent to take a few operatives along, just in case. There was no interference from the Russians and the rumour was that three atomic weapons had been lifted from the cache along with an assortment of biological and chemical weapons.

So this Russian had a nuke, Stratton pondered. That changed everything. Suddenly the many things Gabriel had talked about over the past few weeks dropped into entirely different slots, the most troubling of all being his comment that he had seen his own death at the hands of whatever it was the man in his viewings possessed.

'We haven't told the Russians about the nuclear device, but we've created enough suspicion around Zhilev's suspected terrorist connections that they're doing all they can to track him down,' Sumners said. 'We haven't told them about Kastellorizo either. If we can find him on our own we will.'

Stratton could guess the reasoning behind that. If they could produce a former Russian Spetsnaz with a nuke the Russians had planted in Britain, it would be an immense bartering tool.

'Any ideas as to where he's headed?' Sumners asked. 'Stratton?'

Stratton snapped out of his thoughts. 'What?'

'Zhilev. Any thoughts on where he could be heading?'

Stratton looked at a map in his head, the Mediterranean, Kastellorizo, Turkey to the north, Egypt to the south, Libya to the west of that, and then Cyprus, Syria, Lebanon and Israel to the east. He considered the range of a small boat, but then there were plenty of places to pick up fuel. If it was one of the fishing boats he had seen in the island's harbour it could carry enough cans of fuel to cross the Med. In short, Zhilev could be anywhere. The big question was what did he want to blow up with a nuclear bomb?

'Did the Russians provide a psychological profile?' Stratton asked.

'Yes, and I'm afraid it isn't very encouraging. Zhilev was retired from the Spetsnaz for medical reasons. The report cites physical as well as psychological problems but it was unclear about the relationship between them. Chalmers suggested Zhilev might have been one of their medical experiments. It wasn't uncommon for them to use their own people as guinea pigs for various experimental mind and body enhancing drugs. Then again so did we until a few years ago. But we didn't use our best soldiers. Can't understand that one,' Sumners said.

Stratton didn't believe him. The person who gave the orders was someone just like Sumners except they'd been brought up by a regime with an historical lack of regard for the lives of its own people, especially its military.

Sumners leaned towards Chalmers. 'The picture,' he said to him. Chalmers looked up with an innocent expression, not understanding Sumners' request. 'The picture,' Sumners repeated sarcastically, outlining a small rectangle with his index fingers. 'Zhilev.'

Chalmers opened a file, removed a couple of photographs and stretched across the table to hand them to Sumners who passed them to Stratton. One of the pictures was a group shot of Zhilev with several Spetsnaz colleagues but not a good one of him. The other Stratton recognised from the tanker, the one he had found in Vladimir's wallet.

'That's him with his brother,' Sumners said. 'Apparently, when they forcibly retired Zhilev from the Spetsnaz, he threatened to blow up a government department. The facts regarding that side of it the Russians left deliberately vague but one thing is obvious: Zhilev appears to favour explosives as a form of revenge. The scenario we're most in favour of is he's avenging his brother's murder. Zhilev headed east from England. The killers were Islamic extremists and so I think it's safe to assume the target is therefore Islamic. Question is where? Saudi Arabia is a good bet, Mecca and the like, but obviously he is spoilt for choices in the Middle East. One option would be a landfall somewhere in the Levant in Syria or Lebanon. Perhaps Israel is also a possibility, but their coastal security is very tight both physically as well as electronically and one would expect Zhilev to suspect that given his background. But then Lebanon would be difficult too, for a foreigner anyway, and Syria is very tight since the Iraq conflict.

'The only other realistic option east is through the Suez Canal, which leads to a thousand miles of Saudi coastline, but that would be quite a trek in a small fishing boat. If he left Kastellorizo a week ago, he would be through the canal by now. We've asked Egypt and Jordan to report in if Zhilev makes port but that would take a month under normal circumstances and there's no way on earth we can tell them an atom bomb is possibly passing through their borders. The word would be out in a heartbeat and there'd be a mad rush by every Arab state and Islamic organisation to get their hands on it. If they found him, we'd be the last people to know.'

Sumners took the photos out of Stratton's hands and put them back on the table.

'One other thing,' Sumners said. 'Zhilev withdrew every penny he had in his bank account, the equivalent of several thousand pounds. He was a frugal man who spent little of his pension, which could suggest he's not planning to return home. He's committed. All in all, I think we have a rather serious problem on our hands.'

With all the talk about the Middle East, Stratton wondered where the aircraft was heading. The sun was shining in through the starboard window and slightly ahead of the plane. He checked the compass on his watch to confirm they were indeed flying southeast. 'Where are we going?' he asked.

'Tel Aviv. It's time to bring Mossad into the game,' Sumners said. 'We can't tell them about a nuclear device either, of course. Got to play the Israelis carefully when it comes to threats against Islam. They wouldn't exactly bend over backwards to prevent a bomb blowing up that lot.'

'Unless it was made to look like the Israelis did it,' Stratton said.

'Horrifying thought,' Sumners said as he got to his feet. 'I'm going to grab a nap. Been a long night.'

Sumners stifled a yawn and was about to head towards the seats when he thought of something else. 'How is he?' he asked, referring to Gabriel. 'Fit, you think?'

'He's tired.'

'I expect he wants to see this through though.'

Stratton gave nothing away, looking at the top of Gabriel's head just visible above his headrest.

'We're all believers now, aren't we, eh, Stratton?' Sumners said as he walked away.

Stratton watched him step into the row behind Gabriel and plonk himself tiredly into a seat, but his mind was fixed on the most important implication of this entire situation.

'Stratton?' a voice called out.

Stratton looked around to see it was Chalmers holding out a pamphlet. 'The specs on the likely device,' he said.

How apt, Stratton thought as he reached over, took the pamphlet and flicked through it. He knew a bit about suitcase bombs anyway. It was a requirement for senior operatives to understand at least the basics of them, just in case. It was a crazy world and one could expect to run into anything these days. Explosives were one of Stratton's fortes anyway.

The implication that remained a painful distraction was Gabriel's fear that he was going to die by Zhilev's device. Gabriel did not know it was an atomic bomb. Stratton had never been more than a few hundred yards from Gabriel's side while on the assignment and was hardly likely to ever be much further since his job was to protect him as well as help in the decoding. The device had a destructive radius of five miles, which did not include the fall-out. That clearly meant that if Gabriel was going to be killed by it then so was anyone else with him. Sumners would not tell Gabriel about the weapon in case it affected his will to continue in pursuit of it. The information could only have a negative effect on Gabriel's performance and so why take the risk? Gabriel was the most important tool in locating Zhilev and his life was entirely expendable in the light of the gravity of the situation. The same went for Stratton. Sumners was unaware of Gabriel's fears and was clearly optimistic about finding Zhilev and the bomb before it was detonated. Stratton could withhold Gabriel's fears from Sumners and refuse to continue with the assignment, but that would mean bringing in someone else to take over the operation and Stratton would effectively be sending that person to his death, along with Gabriel.

Stratton tried to tell himself that didn't matter as long as he lived, but it wouldn't stick. He couldn't send someone else to die in his place, nor could he turn his back on Gabriel. They were team-mates now and, like it or not, in this together.

'Chicken or chicken?' a voice said, interrupting Stratton's thoughts.

Stratton looked up to see the loadmaster standing in front of him holding a stack of polystyrene in-flight rations boxes. He was reminded of the standing joke in the SBS about the lack of choice regarding RAF flight meals, which always seemed to be a couple of slightly warmed Kentucky Fried Chicken drumsticks and a serving of soggy chips.

'I'll have the chicken,' Stratton said, and was handed a box.

As the loadmaster moved on to offer the selection to the rest of the cabin, Stratton went back to his thoughts. He had a dilemma to say the least. There were some hard choices to make, and not a lot of time in which to make them.

10

Abed's mother lay on a mattress on the concrete floor, a white veil around her pale, wrinkled face which was bathed in the light from several candles flickering in the drab, airless room. A tattered towel hung across a small window high in the wall to cut out the daylight and half a dozen old women, all in black, squatted or stood about, one chanting a prayer while another prepared tea on a small wood-burning cooker in a corner.

She was not dead, though no one expected her to survive for long. Her breathing was so shallow the women frequently used a mirror kept by her side to see if she was still alive. The doctor had said that as long as she did not have the will to live nothing would stop her from dying. Since the day Abed left Gaza, his mother had hardly eaten or gone outside of her house. Neighbours took to bringing food and some spent time with her, cooking and trying to be comforting, but their efforts had been in vain. All meaning had gone from her existence; now that Abed had left, never to return, life had become utterly pointless to her. For the first few months after his departure, she could not resist clinging to the hope that he might one day walk back into the house. She dreamed of the times he used to take hold of her as if she were his daughter, and stroke her hair while holding her face against his chest. Few men showed such affection for their mothers. She had been lucky. Abed was the finest son a mother could ask for. But their luck ran out that night the Israeli soldiers came to Rafah to round up all the men. Frightened as she was at the time, she had no idea it was the beginning of the end for them as a family. As time trickled by, she began to accept that she would never see Abed again and then, as if the truth had tripped something in her body, she began to die.

She knew the end was very near and her thoughts drifted more and more to her childhood, playing in the streets of Rafah, which at that time seemed a normal place to her, as it did to all of the very young. She recalled her days in school and the faces of the friends she had made that she no longer knew.

Then suddenly, despite her low level of consciousness, she sensed a change in the room. It was unmistakable, as if a powerful presence had entered. It was noticeable in the energy of the other women, and the chanting had stopped.

Her eyes flickered as she fought to open them, but it was incredibly difficult, as if she had gone far too deep beneath consciousness to ever climb back above it.

The presence felt neither good nor evil, but it drew her out of the depths.

She finally managed to open her eyes and fought to focus on the cracked, brittle ceiling where tiny stalactites formed along the lines where the rain leaked in.

The presence was at the door and she concentrated hard to turn her head on the pillow and look towards it. The light was bad as was her eyesight but there was a figure standing in the doorway, she could tell that much.

The figure took a step towards her, and she could discern it was a man but not clearly enough to make out any features. She wondered why any man would be in her house. The doctor had left hours before and would not return until she was dead. Women like her died in the company of women and no man would venture to enter her house even to say farewell, no man save one perhaps. Her heart suddenly fluttered and raced in expectation and she struggled to find the oxygen to fuel the strength she needed to push death away, if only for a moment. She attempted to raise a hand and move her feet but the effort was futile. Nothing worked. Her limbs had atrophied to the point of uselessness. She tried to utter her son's name but there was not enough breath to form a word or moisture to lubricate her tongue.

As the figure stepped forward, the other women in the room moved back as if in fear. The man reached the mattress. As he crouched by her side he came into focus, and Abed's mother stopped breathing for a moment as the shock hit her like the blow from a hammer.

Her eyes remained fixed on him as he got down on his knees and placed a hand on one of hers. She had recognised him instantly, though he looked much older than she would have imagined, but then it was almost twenty years since she had last seen him. The memory of those days flooded through her as she recalled them without effort, especially that very last day. He was holding Abed in his arms, talking to him, and then he gave him a soft toy he had brought as a present, hidden under his tunic so that none of the other soldiers would see it. She recalled the heart–breaking words as he explained that he could never see them again. As she lay there staring up at him she wanted to cry, but she was spent and could not summon one more drop of sorrow, as if a lifetime of pain and tears had finally emptied her of those resources. All she could do was look at the Israeli she had once loved, the father of her son, and accept that he was here at her side. He had come to say good–bye and despite everything that had happened over the years, she was glad.

She tried once more to say something, but the words would not come.

'Give me some water,' he said to one of the women who quickly obeyed, handing him a small cup. He placed the edge against her lips and allowed a little liquid to trickle into them.

'David,' she suddenly murmured, as if the word had come from elsewhere other than her lips.

'Don't talk,' he said softly and with deep affection as he took hold of her thin hand and gave it a gentle squeeze. 'It's been a long time,' he continued after a thoughtful pause. 'I never thought I would see you again . . . I'm glad I came.'

She thought about the other women in the room,

what they might make of this, for he was without a doubt Israeli, but then almost immediately she realised how pointless her fears were. It was not twenty years ago. What did it matter? David was old, Abed was gone and she was dying.

It felt strange being called David after so many years, for that was not his real name. He could never have risked telling her who he was for many reasons, but primarily because of his own survival. Israelis did not fraternise with Palestinians without great personal risk, especially Israelis like him. He wondered if she had an inkling of who he was now. His picture had been in the papers on occasion, which had never been wise considering his position, but it could not always be helped. But then again, she probably never read the Israeli papers, since they were unwanted and not sold openly in Gaza. Perhaps she was wondering how he had the ability to enter this camp since it was illegal for Israelis to cross into Palestinian territory. But she was so close to death, why should he expect her to be cognisant enough to consider any of that.

He looked at her, frail beyond her years, unable to see the beautiful girl he had fallen in love with all that time ago. She could not be much more than forty, if that, but she looked much, much older. He could only wonder at the life she must have led in this hellhole that had turned her into this pitiful wretch. He knew she was dying from utter despair. She was not the first in these camps and would not be the last.

'Abed,' she suddenly uttered. Perhaps it was a

question, or she was trying to tell him their son was not here. He knew Abed had gone from Gaza, and much more than that, for it was his business to know.

'It's okay,' he said softly. 'Don't worry about anything . . . Be at peace, my darling.' He smiled.

She was comforted by his words, why, she did not know, but he always had that power. Those nights, when she would meet him in secret, though she was always fearful of being found out, he would talk to her and make her feel at ease. When they were together it was just them, he used to tell her, and the whole world did not exist. She had believed him because she had wanted to, and she believed him now.

A slight smile formed on her lips and spread to her eyes, and at once he could see her, the little girl he had loved, and his heart was suddenly filled with sadness and pity. These were emotions he had managed to stifle his entire professional life and now he was unable to halt them. 'I am sorry,' he said. 'Sorry for everything . . . I have always loved you.'

She closed her eyes and drifted away but he knew she had not died. The slight smile remained on her face and he wondered if, like him, she was thinking of those days they had together. He had given her the only happiness in her adult life and she had been his only true love. Despite feeling the world was a vile place his smile remained as he watched her and realised it was people who brought true happiness and gave value to everything else that was good in life.

He remained with her for just a while longer; too

long would have been dangerous, and, besides, important work beckoned and there was somewhere he had to be. When he replaced her hand by her side, she exhaled, barely perceptibly, and he wondered if that was her last breath. He did not want to know and he stood and went to the door. He paused a moment, then without looking back walked away and out of the house.

11

The C130 banked high above Tel Aviv turning on to its final heading while gradually losing height to approach Ben Gurion airport. Stratton looked down on the city through the small window. This was his first trip to Israel and as he studied the sprawling, modern city that hugged the Mediterranean coastline, he thought about the crusades and how this stretch of land was once owned by European kings and princes. Coincidentally, the last chapter he had read of his book was about Richard the Lion Heart and his great nemesis, Saladin, the two military giants of their day: the Christian known for his tactical brilliance and reckless bravery, and the Muslim for his exceptional magnanimity as well as courage. Stratton wondered where Jaffa was, an ancient harbour the modern city of Tel Aviv was built on, for it was there, a little less than a thousand years ago, that Richard had stormed ashore, leaping into the water from a boat, to take back the town that had been captured by Saladin. During that battle, which on this occasion Richard had won, Saladin watched in angry admiration as the Coeur de Lion repulsed wave after wave of his Saracen hordes. Even then, on learning that Richard's horse had been killed under him, the paragon of Islamic chivalry dispatched two fresh steeds as a gift for the English king. Looking down on the sprawling metropolis with its towering glass-and-steel structures it was impossible to imagine how it looked in those ancient times or what it must have been like as a European soldier on horse-back wearing armour and wielding a heavy sword.

Saladin's famed chivalry in war was not lost on Stratton. Despite his own ignoble reputation, deserved or not, graciousness in battle was a more natural impulse in him than those who thought they knew him would have imagined, but, then again, he had made a conscious effort to appear to have dispensed with it. Fair play was as out of date in warfare nowa-days as the siege tower and if anything was seen as a weakness.

The loadmaster entered the cabin from the cockpit and signalled those he passed to buckle their seatbelts. Stratton watched him help Gabriel locate his belt and wondered how seriously Gabriel's dream of death had affected him. Under normal circumstances Gabriel's condition would have been enough to see him pulled from the field as an operational risk but since there was no one to replace him, Stratton knew Sumners would keep him on for as long as he could, to his death if need be. Considering the gravity of the situ-ation that was an acceptable price to pay and the CIA would concur in a heartbeat. However, there was a point of exhaustion beyond which Gabriel could become a liability and Stratton wondered if he was not already close to reaching it.

The cabin suddenly shook and jolted as the wheels

hit the runway and the engines immediately screamed louder as the pilot threw the propellers into reverse thrust. The craft lurched several times as the brakes were touched and the plane quickly decelerated. After taxiing for a few minutes, it came to a stop on the edge of the airfield far from the arrivals building and prying eyes, and the loadmaster opened the rear side door letting a thick beam of sunlight stream into the cabin.

Sumners climbed out of his seat, leaned over to Gabriel and said something, then walked up the cabin without so much as a glance at Stratton and began a conversation with his boss. Stratton expected to be called to attend a final brief any moment and was still in a quandary as to what to say or do regarding Gabriel's fear.

Stratton had not come up with an alternative solution to quitting the assignment but he had spent some time on the one major weakness of Gabriel's vision and a possible way through. Since it was in the future, and since it was not a viewing by the definition he understood, and Gabriel had supported that much, then surely it could be changed.

Stratton unbuckled his seatbelt and got to his feet to look out of the window. It was decision-making time and this was not an easy one.

A nondescript car approached with two men inside and came to a stop just beyond the wingtip. The men remained inside the car watching the aircraft. If they were customs or immigrations, they would most likely have been in uniform and walking over to the aircraft by now. The way they sat silently watching with the patience of those who do it for a living left Stratton with little doubt they were Israeli intelligence.

The aircraft's engines finally died, plunging the cabin into a relative calm and a welcome relief after the hours of constant drone.

'Stratton?' It was Sumners calling him over.

Stratton stepped to the table where Chalmers was still tapping away at his keyboard, Sumners' boss beside him on a phone.

'Well,' Sumners began with one of his thin smiles which characteristically masked something new and unexpected. Stratton was not to be disappointed. 'You'll be happy to know you'll be home before the end of the day and you can take that holiday you'd planned. You might need a new pair of skis though – we seem to have lost yours. You were insured I take it?'

'I'm off the op?' Stratton asked, taken by surprise.

'I think you've done more than enough, don't you?' Sumners said. 'You're probably relieved, I'm sure. Damned fine job, by the way.'

'The op's cancelled?' Stratton asked, confused, and at a loss as to what the new developments might be.

'Gosh, no. Op's still very much on. We'll be taking it over from here.'

'We?' Stratton asked, looking around as if he had missed someone on the plane capable of running the operation in the field.

'Well, me, actually,' Sumners said, his smile starting to wane as Stratton's expression clearly telegraphed his disdain.

It was immediately clear to Stratton what was

going on. Sumners had been a desk operative since he joined the firm God knows how long ago; he had not been promoted in years and had been passed over for several younger, better-connected players, a trend that had no reason not to continue. If he wanted to move any further up the ladder the only way he was going to do it was to broaden his experience base. Sumners had obviously decided this was a perfect opportunity to get his field wings. Stratton was appalled at the timing and lack of thought this supposedly intelligent and experienced man had put into the move. He wanted to say as much, and on any other occasion he would have voiced his disapproval, but something was holding him back and he knew what it was. Survival. Sumners' move was the simple and convenient God-given solution to his problem. It was proof Sumners knew nothing about Gabriel's fear. Stratton would sit back, let him take over the op, and, if Gabriel were correct, Sumners would die in Stratton's place. Even if it was discovered that Stratton knew about Gabriel's viewing, he had been ordered off the op and that was that. There would be no comebacks.

'That's fine,' Stratton heard himself say almost immediately.

Sumners' smile regained some of its vigour as if he had misread Stratton's initial look and that this response was one of approval. 'I was going to have you come along as an assistant,' Sumners said buoyantly. 'But let's be honest, you are rather headstrong, and since you're used to working alone it might not be such a good idea . . . Make sense?'

'Perfect.'

'Good. Well, you stay aboard and make yourself comfortable and go home knowing you're on a recommend for a job well done.'

Sumners' boss was wearing one of his cold smiles as he put down the phone and stared at Stratton as if examining him. Stratton gave nothing away.

Chalmers got to his feet holding a small canvas bag and Stratton watched him walk down the cabin to chat to Gabriel, then after a minute he came back to the table while Gabriel waited by the door holding his bag.

Stratton felt he should at least say goodbye to him but could not bring himself to be so duplicitous. A part of him believed Gabriel was heading to his death and he would not be able to look him in the eye, shake his hand, congratulate him on a job well done, tell him how much he had enjoyed working with him and wish him well for the future. Gabriel would see through him as if he were a sheet of glass. Stratton wished that just for one moment he could be the cold-hearted bastard everyone thought he was, but he could not turn his back on Gabriel, not like this.

Strangely, in the end, it was not just his conscience that changed his mind about letting Sumners take over the op, but an ingrained belief in himself and his destiny. Ultimately, he could not accept that if he continued the assignment his end would come at the hands of a mad Russian with an atom bomb. It felt ludicrous and impossible. Fate had many more things in store for him, and perhaps a more horrible finale, but not this. It was more than simple optimism.

Stratton believed his life was written and that he had some kind of an insight into his future. He did not know when his time would come but it was not now, not on this operation. Of all the beliefs Stratton possessed, this was his most valuable. He believed he had a life worth living beyond this moment.

He came to a decision, turned his attention to the problem and focused on the tactics required to achieve his goal. The answer was immediate, simple and based entirely on intuition. He believed Sumners to have a high degree of self-preservation, enough for him to drop the ball once he learned of Gabriel's fear, but Sumners also had pride and the trick was going to be how to manipulate it. The success would hang on the execution.

'Sumners,' Stratton said.

Sumners was talking to his boss and did not appear to hear him. Stratton stepped over to the table and leaned closer. 'Sumners,' he repeated.

Sumners was annoyed at the interruption. 'What is it?' he said.

'Something you need to know.'

'You'll be fully debriefed by Chalmers on the flight back and I'll receive your entire report,' he said.

'That may be too late.'

Sumners exaggerated a sigh. 'What is it?' he asked like a tired parent.

'You're pretty sold on Gabriel, aren't you?'

'Sold?'

'You suggested earlier you had become one of the converted, a believer.'

'Hard to be sceptical under the circumstances. He got us this far, didn't he? What's your point?'

'You're going to be with Gabriel all the way?'

'Of course,' Sumners said. 'He's our golden goose.' Sumners suddenly felt he had detected Stratton's true worry. 'Don't worry,' he added. 'I'll look after him. I must say I'm touched if not a little surprised at your concern.'

Sumners turned away to continue talking to his boss.

'It's not him I'm concerned about,' Stratton said. 'It's you. Gabriel has seen his own death by the device. He believes he's going to be blown up by the nuclear bomb. I thought you should know.'

The words dropped like a ten-ton weight through the thin roof of the aircraft, and although Sumners did not face Stratton immediately, he had stopped in mid-sentence, and his boss's eyes had moved from Sumners to look directly at Stratton – he could smell a game afoot if Sumners could not. Chalmers stopped tapping the keys of the computer and looked between the men. They all instantly understood the implication of the statement that anyone within five miles of Gabriel would also be vaporised. It seemed to rock Sumners to his very foundations though probably only Stratton and his boss could see it.

The blow was a multiple one for Sumners. Every plan and dream of glory he had fermented in the hours since his boss had given him his blessing to take over the assignment were shattered like a stack of crystal ten-pins.

There was a long silence which served only to

emphasise Sumners' astonishment as his mind worked like a computer calculating the various angles he might employ to get out of this predicament, unable to find a single one.

'When did he tell you this?' Sumners' boss asked Stratton, breaking the silence.

'Yesterday. Obviously the implications weren't apparent to me until I heard about the nuclear device when I came on board.'

'Why didn't you say anything right away, as soon as I told you?' Sumners asked.

'I didn't know you were taking over the operation.'

'Why are you telling us this now?' Sumners' boss asked, curious.

'You just heard Sumners say he believes in Gabriel's viewings,' Stratton said. 'If he didn't find out now he'd find out later and, since he's a believer, it might affect his command of the situation.'

Stratton and Sumners stared at each other unblinking. If their positions were reversed, Sumners would not have said anything. The operation could go forward on Gabriel's viewings, but it certainly could not halt because of a daydream about the future. Nevertheless, that wasn't why Stratton had offered the information. He was not trying to do Sumners any favours either. On the contrary, Stratton had had his operation taken away from him and he was obviously manoeuvring to take it back. But the implication remained that whoever was with Gabriel was going to end up being blown up. It would be easy to prove. Gabriel was right at the door and a lie like that would be the end of Stratton's career. There was something devious behind it, Sumners was sure of it.

Sumners' boss remained coldly relaxed in his chair with his legs crossed and fingers intertwined in front of him. 'Do you believe Gabriel?' he asked, switching his gaze to Sumners.

Sumners didn't answer right away, his mind still going like the clappers weighing the various implications of his answer.

Stratton was impressed with the heartlessness of Sumners' boss. The man had the charm of a rattlesnake and the personality of a lettuce. He was coldly twisting the knife that Stratton had shoved into Sumners, pushing his subordinate into a corner. Stratton almost felt sorry for Sumners. It was his first attempt to step into the field and he was about to be metaphorically blown out of the water before his foot touched down. Since Sumners admitted believing in Gabriel's unusual abilities, it disqualified him from taking over the ground operation because it would influence his decision-making process. If he now changed his tune, his credibility would be in jeopardy.

Sumners suddenly found himself hating Stratton for putting him in this position, even more so because it was in front of his boss. Stratton could have taken him aside and discussed it first, which would have given him time to manoeuvre. But no, not him. This mere thug of a labourer had conducted himself in the callous and brutal manner he was famed for. The ungrateful sod had turned on his master. This was Stratton's revenge for the cold-shoulder he had received all those months prior to this operation.

What's more, he had correctly estimated and then ruthlessly attacked Sumners' weakness, which was his sense of self-preservation, and exposed for all to see that it was greater than the desire to further his career. What Stratton did not know, and what made it look even worse for Sumners, was that Sumners had confided in his boss and Chalmers that his doubts about Gabriel would always remain. The reason behind that revelation was that he simply felt foolish admitting otherwise. He was an intelligence officer of the old school and it was impossible for him to accept that the advancement of this case, of which he was the operations officer, had so far relied entirely on the mystical viewings of a mind reader. The tormenting truth was that until Stratton's comment, Sumners did not realise how much of a believer he had become. He *was* now afraid to take over the operation and everyone knew it. Stratton had exposed him, not only to his boss and young Chalmers, but also to himself, and he hated him for it. However, having put everything through the mental scrambler, Sumners still could not understand why Stratton was placing himself in a position to take over the op if everyone on the ground was going to die.

'Sumners?' his boss said, still patiently waiting for an answer to his question.

'I'm afraid I . . . I, er, Stratton is right. It would affect my judgement, sir.' Sumners looked down at the floor to hide his embarrassment. But there was still some fight left in him. If he were going down he would at least bring Stratton with him if he could. He looked up at Stratton, regaining some of his posture.

'Are we to understand you want to remain in command of the ground operation?'

'Unless you have anyone else in mind.'

'But you're a believer too,' Sumners said accusingly.

'Am I?' Stratton replied coldly, looking him in the eye like a poker player, pushing the knife even deeper into Sumners. Stratton's rock steady gaze had convinced everyone, even Sumners, of his doubt in Gabriel, and further illustrated his strength of character and power of leadership and Sumners despised him even more for it.

Sumners capitulated. He removed the photograph of Zhilev from his pocket and placed it on the table.

Sumners' boss could see the private battle between the two men and although he did not entirely comprehend the politics behind it, it was now time to intervene. In truth, he had harboured doubts about Sumners' ability to see this operation through almost immediately after he had given him his blessing. Stratton's credentials for the job were obvious and he now understood why he used to be a favoured operative. The answer was simple. Sumners had been a desk agent all of his career and was meant to remain as such.

Sumners' boss pushed the photograph across the table towards Stratton. 'Right then,' he said. 'Shall we get on with this operation?' He thought about letting Sumners brief Stratton on the further details then decided against it. He got to his feet. 'Stratton,' he beckoned as he walked down the cabin fastening his jacket and smoothing out the sides.

Stratton unlocked his gaze from Sumners and followed.

Sumners looked down at his hands to find them both formed into tight fists. He unclenched them and then sensed Chalmers looking at him. Sumners forced a smile as if to shrug the incident away but Chalmers' only response was to go back to his typing.

Sumners' boss reached midway of the cabin and folded his arms as he faced Stratton. 'Let's appraise the situation so far,' he said. 'We don't know where Zhilev is or where he's heading, but I think the Middle East is as good a place to start as any, and our Israeli friends are the regional experts. We've told them we're on the trail of a former Russian Spetsnaz operative who we believe has been employed by an Islamic terrorist organisation to instruct them on how to improve their bomb-making capabilities. We're holding back Zhilev's name for as long as we can because once the Israelis have that they'll soon discover his brother was killed by Islamic terrorists, and then, of course, our story won't hold much water – unless their imaginations run away with them, which Israeli intelligence is not famed for . . . We're taking a risk by not telling them about the device but I believe it is justified for the moment. We'll lose all control for one. The bottom line is there will be hell to pay if we screw this up . . .

'You will be acting as our intelligence liaison offi- cer while you're here. The Israelis will not want you running around carrying on your own investigation. They won't trust you, of course, and you should expect them to monitor you. They know we won't have told them everything, which is why they will give you some leeway to move about in the hope of gaining information. I've suggested you be based in Jerusalem to start with because it's the most central location and a good jumping-off point for all borders. Another reason for choosing Jerusalem is you need to be in the town of Ramallah by dawn tomorrow, which is about half an hour away by car. You need to be there without the Israelis knowing. In case you are not aware, Ramallah is the seat of the Palestinian authority and is surrounded by Israeli security forces, checkpoints, et cetera. Chalmers will fill you in on the details.'

Stratton looked over his shoulder to see Chalmers standing out of earshot halfway along the cabin waiting to be beckoned, holding a small canvas bag.

'In Ramallah you'll make contact with a man,' Sumners' boss went on. 'He'll be waiting for you at the lion wearing a wristwatch – apparently that will become obvious to you once you are in the town. He is a member of Islamic Jihad and is also working for us. I cannot advise you on the level of trust you can give this character. It's Sumners' idea. The man has played a rather large part in this saga and he may be of use. That will be up to you. His motives are convincing though. I think that's about it.'

'I don't know Israel or the West Bank. How do I get into Ramallah?'

'You'll have some help, hopefully. At such short notice we've not been able to get in touch with our local agent, but we should manage by tonight. Any other questions, ask Chalmers. The little swot knows just about everything . . . Good luck,' he said with a smile and walked back up the aircraft.

Chalmers took his cue, approached and took out the contents of the bag, handing them to Stratton as he described them. 'This is a BBC press identity card that allows you to operate as a member of the press in the West Bank. It'll make it easier for you to move through IDF checkpoints. There are two main checkpoints into Ramallah – there's a third but it's not advisable. Kalandia checkpoint is the only route Palestinians are allowed to drive through. The checkpoint on the other side of the town is known as the DCO and they will allow you in on the press pass, depending on the mood they're in. The soldiers on the checkpoints are usually conscripts and therefore tend to carry the psychological baggage of the pressganged. Kalandia closes around six p.m., the DCO is open twenty-four hours a day. One credit card. Five thousand US dollars. Do you have receipts for the last twenty-four hours? I'll take them off you now if you have.'

Stratton dug into an inside pocket of his jacket, produced a pile of paper and handed it to Chalmers who took it with a frown.

'I take it these have not been itemised?'

'When do you think I had time to do that?'

Chalmers pocketed the papers and handed Stratton the cash. 'Gabriel doesn't know about your visit to Ramallah and we should keep it that way. One satellite phone with numbers pre-programmed . . . One passport . . . Give me your other one.' They exchanged passports. It was obvious they did not want the Israelis knowing where Stratton had been in the past. 'And a précis on the Israeli intelligence services, which you should read and leave on the plane . . . Any questions?'

'I was hoping I'd get a gun.'

'The Israelis won't let you carry one. Anything else?'

'Yeah. What was the name of the pope who started the first crusade?'

'Urban the Second. Anything else?'

'. . . No.'

'Good luck then,' Chalmers said and turned on his heels to head back to his perch in front of his computer.

Smart arse, Stratton thought. With the personality of a turnip he'll probably go far.

Stratton glanced through the paper on Mossad and Shin Bet. He knew a little about both services having worked on a case two years before of an IRA sniper hired by the Palestinians because their own were so poorly skilled. The sniper hit fourteen soldiers in twenty-five minutes at an Israeli checkpoint in El Arik near the town of Ofra killing ten of them before making his way out of the country using a well-planned escape route. Because of the expert shoot-ing and high-quality design of the hide which had been carefully prepared over several days, and, more damningly, the fact the sniper left his weapon behind, not a Palestinian habit but certainly an IRA modus operandi, Israeli intelligence directed their suspicions towards the Irish Republican terrorist group. British intelligence eventually narrowed it down to two suspects but there was not enough evidence to pin it solidly on either. No further action was taken. A few weeks later, a rumour surfaced that the IRA had warned the Israelis if they attempted any kind of retaliatory assassination, a standard Mossad reaction, it would be brutally answered by a campaign against Jewish interests in Britain. No retribution against the IRA was made.

Stratton put the paper down on a seat, picked up his bag and joined Gabriel at the door.

'You get any sleep?' he asked.

'A little.'

Gabriel looked much the same: tired, red-eyed, stressed. Stratton was almost getting used to the sight of his unhealthy condition and thought of it as normal.

'You know, if you wanted to pull out of this, you could,' Stratton said quietly, checking they were out of earshot of everyone.

'I have to see it through.'

'Why? If it's written, if you've seen the end, why do you have to go? Let the end come to you.'

'I don't claim to understand everything about this phenomenon. We're here to stop this madman from doing whatever it is he feels he needs to do, and we must continue to try.'

'But you said you saw the end. What does it matter? We will fail.'

'You obviously understand this better than I do,' Gabriel said harshly.

'Then tell me.'

'I did see the end. An end. My end. And it will come, and soon. But that is all the more reason why we must find him. Why do you look so worried, Stratton? I did not see your end.'

Stratton wanted to tell him that where Gabriel went, he went, and that if he saw the light, heard the pop and felt the wind, then he would too, but Stratton didn't want to even hint at the calamity. 'As long as you're okay to continue . . . Let's go.'

They stepped down out of the aircraft and on to the tarmac. It was sunny but not as warm as Stratton had expected, even for a Middle East winter.

Manachem Raz sat beside his driver, both watching the two men leave the aircraft and walk towards them. Raz climbed out of the car and his driver did likewise.

Raz had been told he would be meeting two men, one British intelligence, the other American, and the Brit had the seniority. As Raz watched them approach, however, it was an unexpected picture. He had an image in his head of a slick pair of polished prep-school types but that was completely erased as this odd pair walked towards him, one old and the other more like a field operative than an intelligence officer. Raz's eyes never left Stratton, dissecting and gauging every aspect of him, and continued to do so even when his face broke into a smile and he offered his hand.

'Welcome to Israel,' Raz said in strongly accented but confident English. Stratton shook his wiry hand.

'My name is Manachem Raz.' The words rolled off his tongue as if through a gorse bush. 'I am head of Shin Bet, Islamic Division, Jerusalem.'

'John Stratton, and this is Gabriel Stockton.'

Raz shook Gabriel's hand and immediately noted how unwell and distracted he looked. 'Can I have your passports, please?'

Stratton and Gabriel dug their passports out and handed them to Raz who quickly flipped through them, examining the pictures and details and finally checking the stamps. He looked at Stratton as if he knew the passport had just been manufactured on the C130.

'Are you carrying arms or anything that could be considered as contraband?' Raz asked.

'No,' Stratton replied.

'Please excuse me, but we all have rules to live by.'

The driver stepped forward holding a metal detector and moved the device over Stratton, then did the same to Gabriel. He checked each time the bleep went off before continuing, finding nothing illegal. Raz kept his smiling eyes on Stratton, both aware he was merely pissing on his territory and ensuring Stratton understood who was in charge. When the driver finished, Raz stepped aside and gestured towards the car.

'Let's go,' he said brusquely. 'We can talk in the car.'

Gabriel was about to follow Raz when Stratton put a hand on his arm to stop him. 'We'll be there in a minute,' he said, looking Raz in the eye. Gabriel looked between the men.

Raz understood the move was simply intended to snatch the control away from him, if only for a moment, to make a point. He admired anyone who took a stand against him but only if they could carry it off. It remained to be seen if this younger man had any metal to him.

Raz stepped away and stood beside his car out of earshot while the driver climbed inside.

'Did Sumners ask you not to confide in the Israelis about any aspect of this operation?'

'Yes,' Gabriel said, then he turned to glance over at Raz who was watching them. 'This a power-pissing contest?' Gabriel asked, seeing through Stratton's reason for holding back a moment.

'Something like that.'

'He's a pushy-looking son-of-a-bitch,' Gabriel agreed.

'I did want to say something to you,' Stratton said. 'I think you're a brave bastard for continuing with this op, in the light of what you know. A lot of people would have folded. I'm still not sure why I'm here.'

'Don't bullshit me, Stratton. Anyway, this might be a bit premature. I'd like to run for the hills, and I just might yet.'

'I'm coming with you if you do.'

Gabriel smiled, this time looking Stratton directly in the eye. Whatever he felt about Stratton, he knew he was not the kind of man who would desert a partner under any circumstances. That was no small thing. In fact it was pretty damn big in his eyes.

'We pissed on him long enough?' Gabriel asked, good humouredly. 'I'm looking forward to a nice bath and a comfortable bed.'

'Yeah,' Stratton said, tapping him on the side of his shoulder, and they headed for the car.

As Manachem Raz watched them he wondered

how he was going to deal with this unexpected and, frankly, strange development. That morning, during the weekly meeting between senior members of Mossad, Shin Bet, the army and police, he had been handed this assignment which required him to look after two characters from MI6 and the CIA arriving in Israel on the scent of a Russian mercenary explosives expert. The unofficial feeling of some of the council members was that the visit was another example of the post-9/11 programme of commitment by the West to combat international Islamic terrorism and show solidarity with Israel. Not that there was anything wrong with that, nor did the Israelis not take it seriously. All and any help was appreciated. However, the general ignorance and insensitivity of the Europeans, British and Americans to the Israeli cause never failed to astound Raz, and, more often than not, anger him. But he was forced to suffer it, not only because Israel needed the West's support, but also their approval, more so now than ever, and Israel had to accept the various pros and cons that came hand-in-hand with that support.

Things had changed a great deal in Raz's twenty-one-year career in Shin Bet, and the army before that. In the early days of Middle East terrorism, it appeared to most other nations to be primarily an Israeli problem and so they were left pretty much alone to deal with it as they saw fit. But now that the West was as much a target as Israel, the big two in the fight, namely America and Britain, wanted to show Israel the correct way to deal with the situation, as if they suddenly knew what they were doing and possessed all the answers. The British should have been the easiest to deal with since they were the most experienced in terrorism and the Middle East, but that was not always the case, as far as the Israelis were concerned. Ironically, the Israelis had modelled Mossad on British military intelligence after spending several years as their bitter enemy. It was no secret that the current international intervention was due in part to the perception that Israel, with its heavy-handed tactics, was in many ways as much a part of the problem. Israel had little choice but to bow to outside pressure or at least to be seen to, since the country practically depended on an annual three and a half billion dollar handout from America, and much more than that in recent years. There was also the perceived increased threat to Israeli national security due in no small part to the stirring of the terrorist pot caused by the American-led invasions of Afghanistan and Iraq, Western threats against Iran and Syria and the 'occupation' of the Middle East and North African oil states by Western companies. Mossad and Shin Bet had enjoyed a great deal of assistance from British and American intelligence over the years; however, any help these days often came at a price in the form of concessions to the Palestinians and Israel's other Arab neighbours. That ran counter to everything the average Israeli had been indoctrinated with from childhood concerning the threat from its neighbours to their very survival. This resentment of Western tampering was even stronger in Shin Bet because of its more right-wing politics. It was Raz's nature, as well as a prerequisite of his employment, to be suspicious, but when he laid eyes on this odd pair, he became convinced that the American and British story about a Russian bomb-making instructor was bullshit.

Raz had lived his whole life on his intuition and he was no ordinary man. He was ruthless but not exceptionally so by Shin Bet standards. Planning and selecting targets for execution was a regular activity which had dulled his conscience over the years and Shin Bet was very much behind the force that maintained the right to torture suspects for the purpose of gathering information. Raz had spent years as an interrogator in Lebanon and had become adept at interpreting the four prescribed legal methods of torture in Israel, namely shaking, sleep deprivation, music and cramped positions. The interpretations of these guidelines were broad and many prisoners had died from exhaustive combinations of them, although Raz could say, with his hand on his heart, none of those were his direct responsibility. Many of his comrades regarded the Palestinian as a low form of life and therefore brutalising them was not a human-rights issue. Raz did not feel the same way but he could never share the reason for that sentiment with any of his colleagues.

Most traditional Hebrew names for people have meanings and Raz's was tailor-made for him. Raz means secret and, living up to the reputation of the family name, everything about him had some mystery attached. His wife of twenty-one years and his two children, both now in their late teens, knew he worked for Shin Bet, but that was the extent of their knowledge. He told them nothing of what he did or where he did it, and they knew better than to ask. There was very little routine in his life, which was essential for his personal survival; he left his house at any time of the day or night and returned hours or days later. One of the many rules of Shin Bet is that an agent cannot work near where he lives, and since Raz's patch had been Jerusalem for nearly a decade now, he had chosen to live with his family in the town of Kokhav Ya'ir, east of Tel Aviv, on the border with the West Bank. Selecting Kokhav was not just because of its convenience. Raz had always been keen for promotion, as were most Shin Bet agents, and the competition was tough. Kokhav was populated by many high-ranking army and security members and considered somewhat exclusive to those fraternities. His promotion to head of the Islamic division in Jerusalem was in no small part due to careful fraternisation with selected neighbours.

Raz was an Ashkenazi Jew from a third-generation middle-class family of European roots. It was practically unheard of to get into Israeli intelligence without hailing from a second-generation family at least. He was the only son of a schoolteacher and recruited into Shin Bet after serving three years' mandatory service in the army. The examination of his past went back the standard two generations although, it was rumoured, to reach the higher echelons of intelligence, that examination went much deeper.

Raz had spent most of his three years as a conscript in the Gaza Strip and it was during his last couple of months that a senior member of intelligence approached him to join the Sherut Bitachon Klali, shortened to Sha-bak or, more commonly, Shin Bet. Raz's father had wanted his son to follow in his footsteps, and Raz might well have become a teacher since although life in intelligence appealed to him, he did not believe he had the slightest chance of gaining entry because of what he had done as a young man which was far worse than any ordinary crime. It was while he was serving in Gaza and even though he had been careful to hide it from even his closest friends, he fully expected Shin Bet to find out once they investigated his past. He could have declined the offer to join and avoid the possible consequences, but he did not. Perhaps it was the gambler in him, or the fatalist, or perhaps it was something as simple as his conscience as the discovery of his secret would have freed him from many years of mixed feelings that included guilt.

The vetting of recruits into the intelligence community was historically intense for obvious reasons, the most important one being the fear of enemy infiltration. Many potential recruits never learned why they failed to gain entry. They were simply invited to leave without explanation. All through the selection period, while he carried out various aptitude tests and examinations including foreign languages such as English and Arabic, he expected at any time to be asked to pack his bags and never darken their doors again, and possibly even receive some form of retribution for his past crime. And if they never told him why, he would know. He became so convinced they would find out he remained extremely blasé throughout the selection programme, right-wing and even at times aggressive towards his teachers, which, ironically, began his reputation for being self-assured, arrogant and unflappable. Add highly intelligent to the mix and his reputation spread.

It was not until he was given his first posting that it dawned on him they had not discovered his secret. His first thought was that perhaps the rumours about the effectiveness of Israeli intelligence were greatly exaggerated. It took several years on the job before he appreciated how he had slipped through the cracks due to the complex rules of intelligence compiling and how the three basic means of the process of information gathering were applied. The first was to direct precise interrogatives towards precise focuses for precise answers, usually because those answers were already known. In Raz's case, no one in Shin Bet had considered if he had ever had an affair with a Palestinian woman and so there was no specific investigation of that nature. The second was the collation of data, which needed to be sorted, cross-referenced and placed in correct acquisition pools with the correct links. There were countless stories of Israeli soldiers fraternising with locals, but, again, in Raz's case, since he had called himself David and was just a regular conscript, the spies inside Rafah had produced nothing that pointed a finger directly at him. Finally, piecing together information from the multitude of sources to form a picture relied on many things and one of those was luck, and Raz appeared to have had an adequate amount of that. His past, or that one small part of it, had been overlooked. The information was there somewhere that could link him to a Palestinian woman and her son, but it had not been pieced together.

By the time he received his first promotion and had taken up a new posting on the Lebanese border, one of the most dangerous and interesting offices of all the divisions that assured promotion if successful, he was confident enough to once more make contact with the girl and open up a bank account for her and their child. Despite his politics and, since being in Shin Bet, developing an unhealthy hatred for the Arab in general, his sense of honour and duty to the child he had seen only a handful of times was startling and ensured he watched over the young Abed as best he could. Raz did many vile things throughout his career in the name of national survival but, strangely, the hand he reached out to Abed and his mother remained a precious redemption of his soul and served in part to forgive him some of his sins.

Raz monitored Abed for over twenty years and not once was he disappointed in the boy who had managed to grow up so wise. Because of Abed's strength of character, due to or despite his difficult existence, he had become far more fascinating to Raz than his Israeli children had ever been. Raz's marriage was one of convenience, arranged by his and his wife's families, which Raz went along with in his inimitable way – it was not important enough for him to go against. Raz believed he would never again have the love he shared with his Palestinian girl, and a normal family life was important for his chosen career.

He went to extraordinary lengths to keep his son safe, even placing his name on a secret intelligence list as a potential spy, which saved him on more than one occasion from being brutalised during incursions. The day Raz learned of the death sentence placed on Abed by the IDF officer he found himself fearing for the life of his Palestinian son more than he imagined possible. He went immediately into high gear as he considered various ways of getting the death sentence removed. His options included abducting Abed and his mother and placing them in a safe house much like a witness protection programme, but even in his high position within Shin Bet that would be too difficult to engineer and maintain for long without drawing suspicion. Another option was to place Abed on record as actually being an insider, a confirmed spy for Shin Bet, but that was fraught with danger too. It would expose Abed to other agent handlers and then create all kinds of complications if Raz was ever asked to 'loan' him out, since Abed was not really a spy. When the day came that Raz learned the officer had decided to carry out the assassination of Abed himself, he was motivated into taking action that was drastic but unavoidable if he was to save his son's life.

Raz took full advantage of his senior position to mount a relatively small operation aimed at establishing a covert observation hide in the attic of a derelict building that just happened to be next to Abed's new metal shop. The operation required Raz to be driven into Rafah late one night through an IDF checkpoint and dropped off where he could walk to the proposed hide carrying a nondescript case of observation equipment. It was more normal for a police agent to carry out such a task for Shin Bet, but neither was it unheard of for a department head to get his hands a little dirty now and then to keep in touch with the realities of field operations.

Raz did not know where the IDF officer intended to position himself for the shoot although the options were limited if he wanted to kill Abed while inside his shop. However, he did know roughly when to expect the hit which would be on Abed's arrival at his metal shop. The biggest problem for Raz was locating the officer's hide. Raz knew he would probably have to wait for the first shot to give away the officer's location. The question was, would the officer play with his mouse first as he had done so often in the past, or would he kill Abed at the earliest opportunity. The first bullet that slapped into the metal shop took Raz by surprise even though he had been as vigilant as possible. It was the second shot, hitting a sheet of steel inside the shop, that gave the sniper's position away, a hint of smoke and movement in the shadows of a distant building. Raz could only pray that Abed had not yet been hit. Fortunately, the officer was not a professional sniper and as he exposed the barrel of his weapon to squeeze off his next, and probably deadly shot, Raz carefully took aim through the scope of his own rifle and fired. The bullet flew down between the houses that lined the market road, across the open stretch of no-man's-land that ran along the edge of Rafah, past the Israeli watch tower, over the three layers of fifteen foot high fence topped with razor wire, in the second-floor window of the derelict house on the edge of the Egyptian border and through the officer's head, flinging him back across the room, killing him instantly.

Raz left his hide almost immediately and did not find out until the next day that his son had survived unhurt. Shortly after that, Raz lost track of Abed and assumed he had gone to ground in fear for his life.

It was not until a year later he learned the name and description of the leader of the team of Islamic Jihad which had hijacked a supertanker off the coast of Spain, murdered all the crew and set the boat, filled with crude oil, on a collision course with the English coastline.

There was a time before that when Raz fantasised about one day meeting Abed and revealing himself as his father, not that he was under any illusion it would be a loving reunion. Perhaps it would be nothing more than closure between them. But it was a pipe dream, for their races could not be more polarised. In truth, it was both their stated doctrine that the other be denied the right to exist. There used to be a chance things could change on a personal level between the two of them, but now that Abed had joined the ranks of the arch terrorists, Raz's fantasies were forced to give way to the grim reality that Abed would probably die at the hands of an Israeli or British assassination squad. He did wonder what he would do if he happened to become involved in such an operation even though that was unlikely.

In his heart of hearts, he knew he would pull the trigger, even if that only meant giving the order.

His thoughts went back to Abed's mother, the image of her on her deathbed still fresh in his memory, and he was filled with sadness at the outcome of it all. The human story was indeed more often than not an unhappy one.

Raz snapped out of his daydream as Stratton and Gabriel walked towards him and he opened the rear door of the car for them to climb in. As they drove across the airfield and out of the airport, Raz looked over his shoulder from the front passenger seat. 'We will be in Jerusalem in forty-five minutes or so,' he said. 'Will that be okay for you?' he asked in his typically insincere polite manner that was only barely detectable.

No one answered him. They were looking out of the window at the country neither of them had seen before. It did not look as clean as it did from the air. The land was dry and dusty. In the distance was a hint of green but no evidence of the soil that produced the lush fruits and vegetables for which Israel was famous.

Raz considered asking them about the Russian to get the ball rolling and start searching for any cracks in their supposed mission but decided against it and turned back to face the front. He was not in the mood for subtle conversation at that moment, and, anyway, he got the impression from the thuggish-looking Englishman he would learn more from watching than discussion.

Stratton stared at the back of Raz's head and wondered what kind of man he was and would he pose any problems for them. His thoughts drifted to the meeting in Ramallah and what light it might throw on the mission, if any. Zhilev was somewhere here in the Middle East with his atom bomb, of that he was certain. The question was, where did he want to detonate it. A more detailed profile on Zhilev could have been useful and might shed some clue as to what his goal was. From what little Stratton knew, and thinking as a Special Forces soldier himself, he had boiled it down to two options. Zhilev either wanted to destroy an Islamic symbol and as many Muslims as possible along with it, or start a fight between the East and the West. For the latter, initiating the bomb in Europe would have been better, but only if he could somehow blame it on Islam, which would not be easy. For the former option, the two most important Muslim sites were Mecca and Medina. After that came Jerusalem, but inside what was perhaps technically or symbolically the West, i.e. Israel. That certainly made it interesting, but the big disadvantage was the degree of difficulty. It would be much harder to get a bomb into an Israeli city than into an Arab one. But then, from what little Stratton knew about Zhilev, he was certainly ambitious and did not lack tenacity or planning abilities. The truth was Zhilev had been faultless so far and was only being hunted thanks to a psychic remote viewer.

Stratton suddenly felt eyes on him and looked up to the rear-view mirror. Like most civilianised police-type vehicles, there was a second rear-view mirror for the passenger to use and Raz was looking directly at him.

12

Zhilev pulled off the tarmac road scarred by countless tank tracks and eased on to a sandy, stony verge, stopped the car and killed the engine. He looked ahead through the dirty windscreen up the road that climbed steeply to a permanent Israeli army checkpoint a hundred yards away. A large sign close by announced the entrance to the city of Jerusalem. Jericho, the lowest dry point on earth, was some twenty miles behind and to the east on the northern tip of the Dead Sea and over two hundred miles north of Elat. He had spent the night outside a petrol station, south of the Dead Sea, waiting for it to open, and the drive to Jerusalem had been eventless with no other checkpoints after the one outside Elat.

The traffic heading into the city at this checkpoint was light; however the lethargic soldiers who ran it were slow and managed to maintain a constant line of half a dozen or so waiting cars. Beyond the checkpoint, lining the high ground a mile away like medieval battlements, were new Israeli housing estates, their stone-clad buildings and red-clay tiled roofs standing defiantly, proudly occupying their captured ground. The land in front of the city on all sides was barren, rocky desert with sprinklings of hardy shrubbery growing out of the arid soil.

Zhilev had considered bypassing the Israeli outpost on foot but after studying the land decided against it. There was hardly a stick of cover for a daylight move and at night the likely approach routes to the city were undoubtedly monitored by a variety of night vision, trembler and movement detection devices. Attempting to pass through the checkpoint with the stolen car was obviously out of the question. He had to assume the owners had been discovered by now and the car reported missing.

He watched a handful of Palestinians approach the checkpoint on foot where they were questioned, asked to show identification and searched before being allowed through into Jerusalem. The checkpoint was his only option but Zhilev's concern was not so much the device he was carrying. The young soldiers would hardly be suspicious of a block of wood even if it did appear to be a little bizarre. The obvious cover story would be that the wood was a souvenir from the Holy Land. His problem was identification; his passport had no entry stamp in it. He did not know if the carriage of identification was mandatory for tourists, and whether or not they would ask him to present it. He was beginning to feel apprehensive. Considering all he had gone through to get this far, the checkpoint could turn out to be the most difficult obstacle. All it needed was one vigilant young soldier to demand proof of official entry into the country and he might find himself locked up and waiting for an immigration officer to arrive and interrogate him. The justifiably paranoid Israelis would undoubtedly make a closer inspection of his belongings in that event and the game would be up.

As he mulled over the problem he watched a taxi drive through the checkpoint from the Jerusalem side and, since it was leaving the city, continue without being stopped. Zhilev watched as it came to a stop a short distance down the road and a Palestinian, wearing the black-and-white patterned kaffiyeh headdress of his tribe, climbed out of the back seat dragging several large bags with him.

Zhilev's mind raced through the possible scenarios as he studied the dented vehicle with its cracked windscreen, wondering if it would turn around and head back into the city. Inspired more by intuition than any firm plan he quickly opened his bag on the passenger seat and took out a bottle of water, unscrewed the top, dug his passport out of his pocket and carefully poured water down one edge of it, partially wetting the pages. He put the bottle down and opened the passport to check the effect. A good portion of each page had been soaked causing the fine anti-forgery patterns to run. He found the page that contained his UK entry stamp and carefully rubbed moisture over it until it became smudged and illegible. His aim was simple and surprisingly desperate considering his planning so far but the momentum was taking him along and having decided to go for it, he chose to ignore the obvious risks. If the soldier asked for his ID Zhilev would offer the passport with the explanation that it accidentally got wet in his bag and he was heading through Jerusalem on his way to Tel Aviv and the Russian embassy to have it renewed. Not completely satisfied with the plan but committed, he climbed out of the car as he watched the taxi pull away and turn in the road to join the back of the line of cars entering the city. Zhilev shouldered his pack and headed briskly up the hill. The taxi was three cars from the checkpoint as he approached it from the back, opened the rear door and climbed in.

The driver, a large, unshaven, gruff-looking man in a sweat-stained t-shirt with a cigarette in his mouth, turned to look at him and said something in Hebrew which Zhilev did not understand.

'Jerusalem, old city,' Zhilev said, expecting that was the answer to the question.

The driver said something else but when his passenger did not reply he realised it was because he was not being understood.

'English?' the driver asked in a harsh accent.

'A little,' Zhilev said.

The driver studied his passenger a moment before removing his cigarette to smile, revealing a bad set of brown teeth that still had food in between them from his last meal. '*Gavaritye pa-russki,*' he said, more a statement than a question.

Zhilev looked at the man again who was deeply tanned with black hair. Now that he was speaking in Zhilev's native tongue and asking him if he was Russian, it was suddenly obvious the driver was neither Arab or Israeli.

'*Da,*' Zhilev replied, deciding it made no difference

if the man knew he was Russian or not. He had not spoken a word of his language since leaving home and Russians were not famously suspicious characters in Israel. On the contrary, thousands escaped Russia during the communist era by pretending to be Jews and were shipped to Israel.

The man was pleased to have a fellow countryman in his cab and began to rattle on as if they were old friends.

'Where are you from?' he said in Russian. 'I'm Moscovite.'

'Latvia,' Zhilev said. It was pointless saying otherwise because of his accent.

The taxi driver nodded although his smile waned as his eyes checked out Zhilev more closely. Zhilev suspected a hint of discrimination in the man's look but ignored it. In his younger days, he would have baited anyone who acted derisively regarding his so-called impure Russian blood. More than one fellow Spetsnaz had suffered crushing blows from his massive fists for making disparaging remarks about his nationality, but this was not the time or place.

A slam on the bonnet startled both of them and they looked up to see an Israeli soldier in full combats and carrying a Canadian M16. There were no other cars in front of them and the soldier had obviously become frustrated with his attempts to wave the taxi forward to his cubicle.

As the driver wound down his window, the young soldier began to complain but the driver, obviously the short-tempered type and not remotely intimidated, interrupted heatedly in what appeared to

Zhilev to be an offensive tone. The car behind honked its horn and the taxi driver immediately switched his attention to that driver, shouting back from inside the car. Zhilev looked behind to see an irate Israeli family packed inside a small car with the man at the wheel gesticulating abusively. The soldier banged the roof again to get the driver's attention, which he got in the form of further abuse. The young soldier was becoming increasingly agitated and pulled open the door, raising his voice and demanding something of the driver. The driver climbed out of the taxi, obeying the soldier, but without interrupting his own vitriolic dialogue. They walked to the back of the car and the driver opened the boot. A moment later, he slammed it back down but the catch did not operate and the boot bounced open. The driver then proceeded to take out his anger on it, repeatedly slamming it shut until the catch finally hooked. He returned to his door continuing his verbiage as if in chorus with the soldier and climbed back into the car. It seemed he was talking more to himself than the soldier as he slammed his door shut hard enough to rattle the glass, put the engine into gear, revved it far too high and jerked away out of the checkpoint and up the hill.

Zhilev remained silent in the back, revelling in his good fortune. He had been completely ignored in the heat of the exchange. It occurred to him he might have been overly concerned in the first place. Whatever, he was through the checkpoint and on his way into Jerusalem.

'Goddamned soldiers,' the driver continued in

Russian. 'It makes my blood boil to be talked to like that by a twelve-year-old with a gun. I hate the Israelis. I hate the fucking Arabs too. Where did you say you were going?'

'The old city.'

'Hmmph . . . Fucking Israel,' he went on. 'My stupid father and mother came here thirty years ago. They lied about being Jews. Russia was a shit hole. Now Israel is a shit hole and I'm stuck here. I have cousins in Russia who are rich. They make ten times, a hundred times more money than I can earn all my life in this shit hole. The economy is fucked. No one comes because of fucking war. Shit hole . . . You a tourist, eh?'

'Yes.'

'First tourist I've had in a week. How's a man supposed to keep a wife and children alive?'

The driver went on for a while, castigating the Israelis and Arabs, pausing only to hurl abuse at other cars which impeded his selfish, aggressive driving as he made his way through the colourless city that appeared to be built of either concrete or stone.

'I'm going to get into prostitution,' the driver announced. 'I've been saying it for years but I'm going to do it soon. What do you do?'

'I'm a postman,' Zhilev said.

The driver glanced at him in his rear-view mirror. 'Postman? How can you live as a postman, even in Latvia?'

Zhilev didn't answer.

'These Jews are horny people. Especially the Hasidic. There is no law against slavery here. They bring in whores by the truck load. The Hasidic is so ugly he has to pay for his pussy, and he likes his pussy. Fucky, fucky, fucky all the time. And most of the women come from Russia and Eastern Europe. I have contacts. I could open a whorehouse with the best pussy from Russia and clean up. Soon, I tell you . . . You live in Latvia?'

Zhilev didn't answer and the driver glanced at him again.

'Why don't you make some money and round up some women when you get back home and send them to me. I'll make you rich. Eh?'

'How far are we from the old city?' Zhilev asked.

The driver was miffed at being ignored. 'Five minutes,' he said. He then pulled a bottle of vodka from under his seat, unscrewed the top, took a swig and offered it to Zhilev.

'You want?'

'No,' Zhilev said.

The driver shrugged, screwed the top back on and replaced it under his seat. 'Which gate you want?'

'What?' Zhilev asked.

'Which gate? I can't drive into the old city. You must walk. Which gate? There are eight.'

'Any will do.'

'Where you staying? You need a hotel? I know a good hotel. Cheap.'

Zhilev could only imagine what this man's hotel recommendations would be like. 'No, thanks,' he mumbled.

The driver shrugged as they pulled to a stop at a set of traffic lights and he pulled his bottle from under the seat and took another swig.

Zhilev had not thought about staying in a hotel, but now that the driver had mentioned it, it sounded like a sensible idea. There was no rush. He had originally planned to plant the bomb as soon as he arrived, but there were several good reasons why a delay of one day made sense. He wanted to make a final check of the device to ensure he had bypassed the protection protocols, and run through another arming rehearsal. He would need complete privacy for that. There was also the possibility that something might prevent him from carrying out his plan right away and he would need a base. On top of all of that, the thought of a hot bath and spending the night in a comfortable bed with clean sheets was very appealing.

'I want a good hotel,' Zhilev announced.

'Good? How good?'

'The best.'

'The best?' the driver said with a smirk. He had already begun to smell Zhilev and was wondering if the man could pay his taxi fare. He looked in his rear-view mirror and this time Zhilev was looking him in the eye. The driver's smirk melted as he saw something in the big Latvian's eyes that was clearly a warning.

'What kind of hotel you want?' the driver asked. 'Israeli or Palestinian?'

Zhilev considered the question. He cared for neither in particular, but the Palestinian was closest to his enemy and the thought of bedding down amongst them before he ended their lives appealed to him. 'Is there a good Palestinian hotel?'

'We are coming to it,' the driver said. 'And it's just a five-minute walk to the old city.'

They approached a roundabout, took the first exit and a few yards up a slight hill the driver pulled the car into the kerb and stopped. Zhilev looked out of the window at a bronze plaque on a wall by an entrance that advertised the American Colony.

'It's called American Colony but it's Palestinian,' the driver said. 'Expensive.'

Zhilev opened the door.

'Thirty shekels,' the driver said, holding out his hand and putting on his mean expression just in case Zhilev thought of running.

Zhilev pulled a US five-dollar bill from his pocket and put it in the driver's hand.

'That's not enough,' the driver said.

'It's enough,' Zhilev said as he climbed out of the vehicle with his bag and closed the door.

The driver rolled down his window and called out an expletive as he drove away. Zhilev ignored him as he walked to the entrance and stopped to look inside the grounds, the hotel being mostly hidden by trees and groomed vegetation. It was inviting and he could already feel himself soaking in the hot bath. He looked down at his feet, his trousers and the sleeves of his shirt. They were grubby and worn. If he was going to clean up, he should not do it by halves. Some new clothes were in order, the question was, should he buy them now before he entered the hotel, or after, when he was refreshed. The obvious answer was to have something clean to put on after his bath.

He looked up and down the street. There were no

shops in the immediate area, but further up the hill, at the top of the road, there were what appeared to be several stores. Perhaps others were around the corner.

He shouldered his bag and walked up the hill.

As Zhilev reached the top of the hill and the first of the shops, a car turned into the road at the bottom, past the spot where he had alighted from the taxi and drove in through the old stone entrance of the hotel. It slowly navigated a sharp turn around an ellipse of dense foliage that led into a tight-fitting portico where it stopped outside the main doors of a three-storey stone colonial building. Tastefully over-grown creepers and huge-leaved plants hugged the pillars, portico and walls of the building and much of the entrance and driveway were in the shadow of a variety of tall trees. The hotel, in exceptional condi-tion, was a marriage of old European walls and Middle Eastern windows.

A bellhop stepped through a pair of modern heavy glass doors set behind what appeared to be the orig-inal oak doors and opened the rear passenger door where Stratton and Gabriel sat together.

'This is where the East meets the West,' Raz said.

Stratton glanced inside the lobby at its highly polished stone floors covered in rich Persian carpets and bedecked in a tasteful collection of Eastern and antique European furniture. It looked very chic and very expensive.

'You will be comfortable here,' Raz said. 'It's more popular among Europeans and Americans than other hotels. Just be careful what you say or where you say it. Nearly everyone here is either a spy or a member of the media. It's Palestinian and one of the best hotels in the city . . . and the most expensive. I know how cheap your English bosses are,' he smiled. 'You can tell them you had no choice since I would not take you anywhere else.'

Stratton wondered if there was a meaning behind the gesture, and why he had not taken them to an Israeli hotel.

Gabriel climbed out of the car with his bag and Raz watched him walk into the hotel. His eyes then fell on Stratton.

'Your friend. Is he okay? He doesn't look well.'

'He just needs some rest.'

'If he needs a doctor, let me know. I don't want anything happening to my guests.'

As Stratton opened his door, Raz stopped him. 'I'm going back to my office,' he said. 'When would you like to give your brief?'

Stratton paused, trying to decide how best to stall him. Of course they would expect a brief but no one said anything about it to Stratton on the aircraft. Sumners would have prepared one. He probably deliberately omitted to mention it after Stratton cut him off. He wondered what else the petulant bastard had forgotten to give him.

'Can I get back to you tomorrow on that? Just between us, we're a little ahead of ourselves. I need to catch up on the paperwork.'

Raz smiled insincerely, his suspicions increasing that these people were playing some kind of game with him. He was not concerned though. He was used to it. The CIA were always coming into town on their fact-finding tours and then secretly, or so they thought, meeting with Hamas and other terrorist groups, negotiating behind the Israelis' backs. The Americans' partners, the British, usually preferred more clandestine methods, disguising themselves as members of NGOs, non-governmental organisations such as the Red Cross and UN, or as human rights observers. But they were on Raz's turf and therefore vulnerable. Raz had his own extensive spy network that included the NGOs, hotels, media organisations such as the BBC and CNN, and, of course, the various Palestinian terrorist organisations. He thought about inviting Stratton to dinner as was customary when a fellow intelligence operative came to town, but decided against it. He could detect a level of tension in the two men, which suggested their concerns were more immediate than long term. It would be prudent to give them as much room as they wanted and set up a surveillance team right away.

'Fine,' Raz said. 'Why don't you get settled and I'll come by in the morning.'

'Sounds good,' Stratton said, and climbed out of the car.

Raz and his driver watched Stratton walk into the hotel. The two men shared a look, then, on Raz's nod, the driver pulled away and they left the grounds.

Darkness fell around 7 p.m. and three hours later Stratton was in his sumptuous ground-floor room in an annexe building situated the other side of a large garden from the main hotel. On the coffee table was a tourist map showing the main roads across Israel and the West Bank, and on the reverse side a gaily illustrated guide to the old city. He had spent the past few hours considering how he was going to get into Ramallah and then back to the hotel by the morning. Getting there and back was not the problem. Taxis were in ample supply in the city, and from what he could gather from talking to the receptionists, disguising his intent with dozens of questions about all aspects of travel in the West Bank and Gaza, there was also no difficulty in finding one in those places either. His problem was getting out of the hotel without being seen. He had found at least one reason why Raz had chosen this place. It was surrounded by a high wall on all sides that backed on to well-lit streets, private gardens and a school that was in itself surrounded by a high-fenced wall. Basically, it would need only a small surveillance team to watch all possible exits and there was little doubt Raz would have that covered. It was beginning to look as if it might require something radical to get out of the area. That category included ruses such as calling in the emergency services, the fire department or bomb disposal, or anything that brought a lot of activity with it and required people to leave the hotel grounds. Stratton would rather avoid going that far but his choices were beginning to look limited.

As he sat on the bed studying the map, the patio light outside the French windows went out, plunging the immediate area into darkness. There were lights across the other side of the garden but none strong enough to illuminate Stratton's garden entrance. The light switch was inside the room on the wall near the door, which meant the bulb must have gone. Stratton remained still, his eyes fixed on the small gap in the curtains, when something moved across the window.

There were a couple of light taps on the glass and he got up and moved to the side, away from the gap in the curtains.

The tap came again.

Stratton looked at the door handle, the key in the lock beside it. Someone obviously wanted him to come to the door but did not want to be seen themselves. If they meant him any harm, all they had to do was knock at the front door as he would have been less suspicious. There was only one way to find out who it was.

Stratton walked to the front door and turned off the light inside the room. He went back to the French windows, turned the key, pushed down the handle and opened the door. He waited behind the curtain a moment but no one ventured inside. He moved to the door, opened it fully and stepped through it.

'All right, mate?' a voice said in a forced whisper from the darkness across the patio where there were several large bushes. 'It's me – Morgan.'

Stratton checked to see there was no movement in the gardens and walked towards the bushes.

''Ow you doin', mate?' Morgan said. Stratton moved to where he could see his big friend's beaming face.

'What the hell are you doing here?' he asked.

'Long story. Tell you later. I'm here to take you to Ramallah.'

Stratton was surprised to say the least and had he a few minutes to think about it, he might have been able to figure it out, but now was not the time. One thing he had no doubt about and that was Morgan was on his side.

'I'll grab my coat,' Stratton said as he walked back into his room.

He met Morgan at the corner of the block, where he was scanning the ground ahead which was in darkness.

'There's a door in the back gate over there just behind those bushes,' Morgan said.

'And it's got a huge padlock and chain on it and it opens directly on to the street,' Stratton said.

'I broke open the bottom of the street lamp and killed the light, one of the links on the chain is broken and simply unhooks and I've got a car parked tight up against the door so no one will see you climbing in,' Morgan said matter-of-factly. 'That good enough for you?'

'That'll do nicely.'

'Good. Shall we?'

Morgan led the way to a large red gate used for bringing heavy supply trucks into the back of the hotel and unhooked the chain as he described. He carefully opened a door in the gate enough to look out on to the street.

'All clear,' he said. 'I'll go first, open your door and you can jump in,' he whispered.

And with that, he walked casually to the driver's

side, climbed in and a second later the passenger door opened to touch the wall. Stratton closed the gate door behind him, moved quickly to the car and climbed in. He closed the door quietly as Morgan started the engine and, without turning his lights on, moved up the road. Stratton kept down and out of sight as Morgan turned on to the main road and headed away from the hotel. He turned his lights on as he accelerated up the hill and into a street, then quickly turned into another, all the time keeping a watchful eye on his rear-view mirror. A minute later they were on a major artery and mingling with the light traffic.

'You're okay, mate,' Morgan said. 'No one's backing us.'

Stratton sat up and reclined the chair a little just to be on the safe side. He took a look at Morgan who was wearing one of his familiar broad smiles.

''Allo, me old mate. How are you?' he said.

Stratton smiled, enjoying the surprising company. There was definitely something about being with your own kind, he thought. 'Let me guess. They called you in to work against Al Qaeda.'

'Did you put a word in for me?'

'I wouldn't do that to a friend,' Stratton said, somewhat seriously.

Morgan's smile dropped off a little as he glanced at him.

'It's good to see you, though,' Stratton added. 'How long you been out here?'

'I'm supposed to do a six-week course but they

needed me out here right away. I got the call the day after you left. They said they'll pull me back in for the course when I'm burnt. D'you know a bloke called Sumners?'

'Yeah, I know Sumners.'

'Seems like a good bloke.'

Stratton kept his eyes on the road ahead and gave nothing away. He used to think the same about Sumners in the early days.

'What's your job?' Stratton asked.

'Go between. Handling intelligence from field agents. Quite interesting really. Got four fuckin' apartments and four cars. One in Ramallah, Jenin, Gaza and Jerusalem.'

'How's your Arabic?'

'Comin' along. Trick is to keep a low profile. I reckon you can last a couple months before getting burnt. Israelis have people everywhere. No one knows where I'm from when they see me. They know I ain't local when they 'ear my fuckin' gash Arabic,' he said, ending with his famous guffaw.

Morgan checked the rear-view again. There were several headlights but it was impossible to tell if they were being followed.

'Don't know 'ow good these Israelis are at surveillance,' he said. 'I expect they're all right though. Been doin' it long enough . . . We'll be out of the city in about ten minutes, then a couple of long stretches of road with hardly any traffic this time of night. We'll know if we're being backed. Couple a places we can lose 'em if we think we are. Can you say what you're doing?'

'Looking for a bloke. A big Russian. Former Spetsnaz. Possible connections with Al Qaeda.'

Morgan wouldn't know anything about the operation but there was always a slim chance he'd run into a big Russian. He obviously had not or he would have said something.

They drove in silence for a while until they had cleared the checkpoint on the outskirts of the city and headed out into the black desert. There was always a point in a conversation between operatives on different tasks, even when they are friends, when shop talk ceased. Then it was idle chit chat about the lads in the Service and things back home. The road to Ramallah was long and straight and although there were a couple of headlights behind, they were in the far distance. By the time they turned on to the Ramallah circular that led to the DCO checkpoint, they were alone.

The checkpoint was uneventful and after a brief stop to inspect their press passes, the soldiers let them through with only a cursory search of the vehicle.

As they headed into Ramallah it showed all the signs of a town that had endured a major conflict of conventional war proportions. Many buildings had been turned into rubble, the roads and pavements were chewed up by tank-tracks and there were a number of cars flattened where they were parked. On one street corner the locals had created a bizarre sculpture out of a dozen cars flattened by tanks, placed neatly on top of one another and painted white. Few houses had electricity and there was little sign of life this late at night. Some roads were blocked, either by locals trying to screw with the Israeli patrols, or the Israelis screwing with the locals. There was no road discipline for cars and if there was a clear route, no matter what side of the road, even against oncoming traffic, it was taken.

Near the centre of the town, Morgan pulled over to the kerb and turned off the lights and engine.

'The main square is just down there,' he said, indicating straight ahead. 'There's a small roundabout with four lions pointing outwards. Your man will be near the one on the right and closest to you as you approach.'

'The lion with the wristwatch.'

'That's right.'

'Do you know who I'm meeting?' Stratton asked.

'All I know is he's Jihad or Al Qaeda and works for us. Sumners said it was a real coup to get this bloke but if you ask me I think it's a bit dodgy.'

'Why's that?'

'You don't work for Al Qaeda unless you're real committed, do you? Know what I mean? They fuckin' 'ate us. Enough to top 'emselves. So why does one of 'em suddenly want to work for us?'

'Money?'

'They ain't into that. My point is they totally 'ate us. We represent everything that goes against what they believe in. They 'ate the Jews and they say the Jews own America and so they 'ate America. You know what this lot believe around 'ere? They believe the nine-eleven attack was planned and carried out by the Israelis and CIA. I 'eard that from the mouth of the president of a university in Gaza. If someone as intelligent as him believes that, then what do the thousands of 'is students believe? Na, I'd watch me back, mate. I mean, you obviously know what you want 'im for, but just watch your back, that's all.'

Stratton wanted to say he wished he did know what this guy was about. It was obviously something to do with Zhilev the Russian but the connection was eluding him thus far. Sumners' boss never said anything because he was protecting his source in case the meeting didn't happen. That was fair enough. It's one thing that operatives know there's a tout within Al Qaeda working for MI6. If it got out what his connection was, it would provide a clue to who he was. They were giving the terrorist to Stratton because this operation was big, but if it fell through, if Stratton could not meet him, then the spy was still protected.

'He won't be there before first light,' Morgan said. 'If you wanna get your head down for a bit I'll stay on watch.'

That wasn't a bad idea, Stratton thought. He felt more tired than he should have, and in this game you took your sleep when you could. 'Maybe I will,' he said, reclining his seat fully and closing his eyes. 'It's been a long day.' And a new day was coming, he thought, and no doubt one full of surprises. The most frustrating thing about the assignment was he had no idea what his next move was going to be. He couldn't imagine how a member of Al Qaeda would be any help and made an effort to clear his head of thoughts so he could rest for a while. He did not expect to get any real sleep but a long rest, thinking of nothing, was almost as good.

Stratton quickly drifted off, and what seemed to be only minutes later he felt a nudge in his side, but for some reason he could not respond as if he was confused about its origin. It came again, this time stronger and he fought to find himself and take control of his limbs and pull himself together. He opened his eyes and light streamed into them, and for a couple of seconds he did not know where he was. Then it came rushing back like a freight train.

'Stratton,' he heard a voice say, recognising it was Morgan's.

It was daylight. He sat up and checked his watch. Nearly 7 a.m.

'You were gone, mate,' Morgan said.

Stratton rubbed his face to push the sleep away.

'Time you checked on your man.'

Stratton moved the seat back into the upright position.

''Ere you are, mate,' Morgan said, holding a bottle of water for him.

'Thanks,' Stratton said as he took it, poured some into his mouth and splashed his face. He handed the bottle back to Morgan and rubbed the water around his neck. Consciousness had almost fully returned and he focused on the street ahead that was already looking busy.

At the end of it, a couple of hundred yards away, he could make out what appeared to be some life-sized stone lions but they were too far away and it was too crowded to pick out any particular individuals.

'You carrying?' Stratton asked.

'Na. Ain't worth the risk. The Israelis'd slap you in jail in a 'eartbeat if they found it. Maybe worse if they caught you at night and there were no witnesses.'

Stratton did not particularly care about those risks at the moment. He was beginning to feel more and more naked without a weapon the deeper he got into this operation. The no weapons policy of the MOD was political and getting worse each year. As usual, it would continue its trend until operatives started dying before the powers that be reviewed a change, and even then that was no guarantee. That didn't help him right at that moment. He just hoped he would not be the operative who inspired the policy change.

Stratton glanced at Morgan to nod farewell and paused to study his face, seeing him for the first time in any proper light since meeting him the night before.

'What?' Morgan asked, wondering why Stratton was staring at him.

'You've been putting in a lot of hours since you got here, haven't you?'

'Yeah . . . Why?'

'Your nose and ear hairs stick out like rose bushes. You normally pluck 'em bald when you've got nothing to do.'

Morgan adjusted the rear-view mirror to have a look for himself, examining both ears and deep into his large nostrils. 'Bloody 'ell. You're right. Give me som'ing to do while I'm waiting for you.'

Stratton opened the door. 'See you later,' he said as he climbed out. Morgan didn't reply, already busy gripping a large clump of hair sticking out of his nose which he ripped out with a small yelp.

'Been a while,' he said, his eyes watering.

Stratton closed the door and headed for the centre of Ramallah.

It was market day in the town. Barrows lined each side of the street stacked with all kinds of produce and sundry items. The smell of fresh bread filled the air and the traffic was increasing by the minute as vans arrived from both ends of the street to unload their goods. Stratton gave up trying to walk down the pavements strewn with crates and boxes and moved out on to the road.

As he reached the circle, he focused on the nearest lion on the right. Sure enough, it had a wristwatch carved on to its front leg. People and vehicles milled around the circle, moving in and out of the five roads that led from it like spokes on a wheel, but no one was waiting beside the lion with the wristwatch.

Stratton looked for any faces among the sellers and buyers that might be watching him but nothing was obvious. He was the only white man in the area and there were the inevitable curious looks from passers by. Nearby vendors offered him their wares but they were not pushy. A news crew appeared from a side street, three Westerners, and set up a camera to film the market, their presence making him feel less conspicuous.

Stratton's gaze moved back to the lion, still sat by itself, and just as he was about to cross the road to stand beside it a man in jeans and a black leather jacket walked around the roundabout and paused by the great stone cat. He was in his twenties, dark skinned, handsome, with long jet-black hair and a neatly trimmed goatee. He raised a foot, planted it on the base of the lion, and proceeded to retie his shoelace. When he put his foot down, he stood up straight, put his hands in his pockets and looked directly at Stratton for a moment, his eyes intelligent and piercing.

Abed had not been given a description of the man he was to meet other than he would be white, and apart from the media crew this was the only white man around, and, what's more, he was at the circle at the right time and without a doubt looking for someone. Abed stared at him long enough to make it obvious he was the one and then walked away. If it were not the right white man then he would not follow.

Abed did not check back to see, hoping they had sent someone smart enough to play the game and follow him without giving it away to anyone who might be watching. A lone white man in a notorious West Bank town would get some attention and the odds that someone in this square reported to Mossad or Shin Bet were high.

Abed crossed a busy junction and walked down a steep road that had shops either side. Halfway along it he turned off the pavement and up a short flight of steps that led into a small, low-roofed shopping precinct lined with dusty, dilapidated, glass-fronted kiosks. A short distance along the hall he climbed a flight of stairs that doubled back on itself. Abed glanced below, through the rails into the hall, but there was no sign of the white man. At the top of the stairs, at the end of a short corridor, was a set of double doors that he pushed open and walked through. He let them close behind him and stood inside a spacious, dirty room cluttered with odd pieces of dust-covered office furniture that looked like they had been there for years. Much of the false ceiling had collapsed adding to the litter on the floor.

He walked across the room towards the windows that lined one of the walls, the crunching of his shoes on the dirty concrete floor echoing in the room, and stared out across the rooftops. Ramallah was built on a series of steep hills and the northern edge of the town bristled on a crest half a mile away. On the highest point a tower block with sand-bags stacked on its roof, commanded the heights, evidence of an Israeli lookout post, the Israeli flag flying on top as a reminder to the local populace who the masters were.

This was his first time in Ramallah and he was eager to leave. He was looking forward to getting back to Lebanon, not only because it was dangerous for him to stay in this country, but he had a house in Beirut, and although it was not his own and was paid for by the sheiks, it was home. But for how long, he wondered. If the path he had taken to join the Jihad was a deadly and historically short-lived one, then this new alliance, working for the British, was certain to be suicide. But he had no choice now. He was committed.

There were several reasons Abed had turned against

the Jihad. The most powerful was his conscience. What he took part in on the supertanker had horrified him, and it was only a matter of time before they asked him to do something like it again. He believed in the fight against Zion and its allies, but not in the form of a worldwide Jihad, and quitting the organisation now would be difficult, if not impossible. He did not have the funds or documentation to go anywhere outside of the Middle East, and if his masters knew his intentions they would turn on him. If they could not get to him themselves, the West would soon track down the man who led the attack on the tanker once they had a name and photograph, which would be mysteriously provided. The only option left to him was the one he was now pursuing, and that was to sell himself to his enemy. All he wanted was to live in peace somewhere far from the madness of the world he had been born into.

The idea that changing sides was his only option came during the attack on the tanker, but he did not have a clue how he would go about it. The masters kept a tight rein on their men for a variety of security reasons and he did not have the freedom of movement to make contact with an embassy or consulate. The vile killing spree was enough to convince him he had to get out of the Jihad even if it required desperate measures. What affected him most about the attack was the hate and enthusiasm with which his men cut the crew to pieces. None of the murdered men was asked his nationality, religion, or beliefs. The fact that they were on a

Western ship was enough. He watched throats slit, bowels sliced open, hearts ripped from chests and flesh literally slashed from the bodies of men as they ran. Blood was everywhere, on the walls, ceilings, stairways and in large pools in rooms and corridors. Being the leader, directing his men, Abed had avoided taking part in the actual carnage until the big engineer in the bosun's locker. As Abed's men charged down the long metal stairs in pursuit of the two Asian crewmen, the engineer had managed to give them the slip at the bottom and scramble up the ladder. Abed was standing on a midway landing, alone and the only obstacle to the open deck. He would have let the man get past if he could but the stairway was narrow and the engineer was fighting for his very life having seen his two comrades cut to pieces below. He was much bigger and stronger than Abed and came at him with great ferocity, eyes wild and determined. At the last second Abed held his scimitar above his head and as the man lunged across the small platform, he brought it down with such force on to the side of the man's neck, it cut halfway through it. Had he not done so, the engineer would surely have thrown him over the rails.

Looking down on the dying man as the blood poured from a severed artery he saw a pen and notepad poking from his breast pocket and an idea immediately came to him as to how he might be able to contact the West. He tore a page from the pad, scribbled his name on it, wet his thumb in the man's blood and pressed it on to the paper. As his men came back up the stairs, Abed stuffed the note into engineer's wallet, pushed him under the lower rail and watched him fall to the bottom of the ship.

Abed was surprised how quickly the British had found him and was impressed by the subtlety of the contact. His handler was Lebanese, or so he said, and treated him like a son, giving him friendly advice and always begging him to take care of himself. Abed did not expect them to use him for any kind of assignment as soon as this, and so it came as a surprise when, the day before, he was told to come to Ramallah to meet with a British agent. It was not an inconvenience since he was already on his way to Palestine on personal matters with special permission from his sheiks. Not an inconvenience yet, but then he did not know what the British wanted him to do. He knew he was going to have to pay a price for his freedom and that would not come cheaply, or even soon. Perhaps never, he was realistic about that. But it was something he would look forward to anyway. At least he had a guarantee they would not exact retribution on him for the tanker, if the British were to be trusted, that is. They had not yet asked him to identify the others on that mission but they soon would. But saving his skin by sacrificing his associates did not sit well with him and he was not sure how he would handle that yet. He knew that at least one of them was already dead. Ibrahim. A few days after the tanker he left to join the fight in Iraq and was killed by the Peshmerga, the Kurdistan border guards, while crossing over from Iran to join the battle in Fallujah. Abed expected that he would be ordered into Iraq eventually. It was the nexus of the fight against the West. The world was the battle-field, but Iraq was the central battleground. If it fell to democracy, a wedge would have been driven right through the heart of the Middle East and Islam. Abed did not know what he would do when that order came. He was playing it day by day. Perhaps that was the place he could earn his freedom working for the British. But that could be weeks or months away and too far in the future for an Ansar Islam, a supporter of the Jihad. Tomorrow was far enough into the future for him to look.

Abed did not know how much control the British had over the Israelis. He told the British he would not work on behalf of Israel, but if the Israelis discov-ered who he was, what would happen to him then? The British might barter for his life as long as they had a use for him. It was a difficult and complex game and one that Abed knew he was not equipped to play, but he would do his best to learn quickly and find a value for himself that the British would appreciate. Hoping to be free one day was possibly naïve but if he could just stay alive, it might become a reality. He would eventually be too old or spent to be of any value and perhaps they might allow him to slip away into the mist. The odds were stacked against him but that was the way of his life for now. He was a double agent and that probably meant it halved his chances of survival. He was playing the most dangerous game there was, working between the East and the West.

The door opened and closed behind him and he

turned to look at the white man standing in the room.

'*Salam alaykom*,' Stratton said.

Abed could not see him clearly in the shadows but he appeared to be somewhat scruffy: unshaven, tousled hair, his brown, leather jacket older and more worn than Abed's.

'*Alaykom salam*,' Abed replied.

'*Ana issmi* Stratton. *Wa issm hadritak?*' Stratton said in halting Arabic.

'My name is Abed,' he replied. 'Would you prefer to speak in English?'

Abed had learned English in school and although he had forgotten much of it by the time he left Gaza, his masters had encouraged him to take it up once again. English was the most common language of the enemy and if the fight was to be taken to his lands, the warriors had to be able to speak it. Several of those Abed worked with had been educated in England or America and for months he had spoken nothing else. This was the first time he had spoken it to an Englishman.

'Sure. My Arabic's a bit rusty anyhow,' Stratton said.

'What do you want of me?' Abed asked, getting to the point.

Stratton did not have an answer to that question just yet. All they had told him about this man was that he had played a part in this operation. The only part Stratton could think of was the beginning.

'Does the Orion Star mean anything to you?' Stratton asked.

Abed heard the words as from a prosecutor, and

for a moment he considered the possibility the British had set him up and that this man had come to execute him. Abed had accepted the probability of one day paying for his crime and was strangely prepared for it.

'I led the mission,' Abed said firmly but without any hint of pride.

Stratton walked across the room and joined Abed at the window as he pondered this information, searching for a use for Abed. One thing immediately struck him. Abed might have seen the engineer; Zhilev was virtually his twin. It was always difficult to identify a person from a photograph unless that person had some highly distinguishing features. Zhilev and his brother were large, powerful men, but someone who had seen them in the flesh, the way they moved, their features from angles other than that in the photograph, would have an advantage when it came to recognition. He was clutching at straws, but he could see no other use for Abed at the moment.

Stratton reached into his pocket and took out the photograph of Zhilev. 'Do you recognise this man?'

Abed took the picture, studied it, then handed it back to Stratton.

'He looks like the engineer on the tanker. Is that who it is?'

Stratton stared into Abed's eyes, looking for something, and he was sure he had found it when Abed could not hold his gaze. A picture flashed into his head of the engineer, draped over the pipes, his neck cut to the bone and almost beheaded. A feeling of disgust grew in him but he could not bring himself to feel hate, which he should have done. It was more than just the guilt in Abed's eyes that mellowed Stratton. Even though they had exchanged but a few words, Stratton could sense a strength in him. He stood confidently, but not defiantly, and he spoke softly without guarding his words, as if he had nothing to hide. It was an honesty that came only with youth. The Arab did not appear to be a cold-blooded, fanatical killer. But then again, Stratton asked himself, what did he know about these people? He fancied himself a good judge of character in the business of soldiering and terrorism. He had had enough experience. But he had also made mistakes in the past.

It suddenly dawned on Stratton Abed's true value, and why Sumners' boss had brought him so hurriedly on to the assignment. Abed had killed Zhilev's brother and was the reason why the Russian was walking around with a nuclear bomb looking to blow it up somewhere in the Middle East. If the opportunity arose, Zhilev might take the Arab in exchange for the bomb. Abed was a tool, and in the right circumstances, a very useful one.

'This man is the engineer's brother,' Stratton said. 'I need your help in finding him.'

Abed looked at Stratton, suddenly curious about him on a different level. He looked tired, but not for lack of sleep. It was the fatigue of someone old who had seen enough of life, but this man was young. The eyes were a window to a man's soul, and Stratton's were strong and unwavering, those of a man who led rather than followed; but there was something else in them that he had seen in only a few men before. He was inviting and approachable, but there was an undeniable warning not to cross his line. Everything about him, his strength, his spirit, the way he stood, threatened to ruin anyone who tried.

'Why?' Abed asked.

'Because of what you did to his brother he has become very dangerous.'

'How is he dangerous?'

'I believe he wants to start a holy war between Islam and the West.'

'He's too late,' Abed said, without intending to sound flippant.

'This isn't a war. It might be the beginning of one, but it's not war. Not yet. This man can start one.'

Abed believed what the Englishman was saying and wanted to ask how one man could achieve such a powerful thing, but he knew he would not find out now, not here at least. He had no choice, no matter what this man wanted of him. He was here to barter for his freedom, and that meant servitude. They held his life in their hands and he had to do their bidding whether he liked it or not, trusted them or not, whatever the task.

'Can I see the picture again?' Abed asked.

Stratton handed it to him and Abed studied it more closely.

'His name is Zhilev,' Stratton said. 'He's a little broader than his brother and far more dangerous.'

'More dangerous?' Abed said. 'I hope you have a gun when you meet him.'

No, but I have you, Stratton thought to himself.

Finding this man was obviously of great importance to the English and if Abed could help them, he would be helping himself. 'Where do we start to look?'

'We have to get to Jerusalem first.'

Abed ignored the fears he had of staying in this country where he was exposed to his greatest and most dangerous enemy, and concentrated on the positive aspects of succeeding in this mission.

'Where do you live?' Stratton asked.

'Lebanon.'

'How did you get into Palestine?'

'I have false papers.'

'You couldn't have known about this meeting more than twenty-four hours ago. What are you doing here?'

'My mother has been ill. She died yesterday,' Abed said, unable to conceal his sadness. 'I could not risk trying to get into Gaza but friends are bringing out some things from our house and I came to take them home with me.'

Stratton did not care about Abed's loss and paused to consider his next move. 'Let's go,' he finally said, and headed for the door. Abed followed.

Five minutes later they were back at the car where Morgan was waiting for them. Stratton climbed in and did not introduce Abed who got into the back.

'We need to get back into Jerusalem but not through the checkpoint,' he said to Morgan.

Morgan glanced over his shoulder at the Arab just long enough to be able to recognise him if he saw him again.

'There's only one way I know of,' Morgan said. 'Through the old quarry. It comes out right behind the Kalandia checkpoint – the Jerusalem side of it.'

'Problems?' Stratton asked.

'I've never done it but I know people who have. A couple of Brit peace nuts who are banned from Ramallah by the IDF got in a few nights ago. The soldiers don't watch it because it passes right under a settlement. Those fucking settlers are more danger-ous than the soldiers. They shoot first and don't even bother to ask questions later.'

'Anyone done it in daylight?'

'A year ago four Frog journalists tried it. All of 'em were shot and they only lived because the IDF came along to check on the settlers' handiwork and found 'em.'

This was not sounding encouraging. 'Any other options?' Stratton asked.

'None that I know of. I could find out.'

'We don't have time. Let's take a look.'

Morgan started the engine, turned the car in the road to avoid the busy marketplace and cut down a rugged, trash-strewn side street, scattering several skinny dogs fighting over a chicken carcass.

Five minutes later they arrived on the edge of the northern part of the town. Morgan killed the engine and they remained in the car.

'That gap in the wall,' Morgan said, indicating the other side of the road with a jut of his chin. 'Go through it and just follow the track and after a couple hundred yards you'll find yourself overlooking the quarry. Head down into it soon as you can and follow the lowest line through. You can't miss the settlement. It'll be right above you surrounded by a big fuck-off wall and razor wire. That's your main problem. Once that place is out of sight you're laughin'.'

Stratton looked at the gap in the wall, then over his shoulder at Abed who stared coldly at him.

Stratton opened the door and paused to look back at Morgan, studying his nose and ears. 'Nice job,' he said.

'I saved 'em for you,' Morgan said, indicating a chewing-gum wrapper on the dash with a pile of curly black hairs in it.

'You're a pig, Morgan.'

Morgan grinned.

'Let's go,' Stratton said to Abed and climbed out of the car. Abed made his way across the road to the gap in the wall to take a look.

Stratton paused before closing the door and crouched to face Morgan, something on his mind. 'You said you had a place to go in Gaza.'

'Yeah.'

'Why don't you go down there. Today . . . like, now.'

Morgan looked deeply into Stratton's eyes and saw something he had never seen there before. Fear was probably over the top but if not fear, it was the look of someone who had grave doubts about their business, and Stratton's business was not just the job, but also staying alive to do it. Concern for his friend rose in Morgan but he knew better than to ask why Stratton was worried.

'All right, mate,' Morgan said.

Stratton nodded and was about to stand up when Morgan put his hand out.

'Stratton.'

Stratton looked down at the big, black hand and took hold of it. Morgan leaned over and placed his other hand on top of Stratton's, who did likewise. They held on to each other for a moment, no words spoken but everything being said.

'You take care, mate,' Morgan eventually said.

'You too. And remember, nothing in this business is what it seems and there's always more than what they tell you. Don't trust any of 'em, Morgan . . . Better still, get a fucking real job.'

They smiled at each other.

'I'll see you back in Poole, mate,' Morgan said.

Stratton released him, closed the door and crossed the road to join Abed. Seconds later they were gone. Morgan stared at the gap in the wall for a moment, unable to guess why Stratton had told him to leave the West Bank. He would not allow his imagination to run wild but one thing was certain: when Stratton looked you in the eye and told you to get out of town, you had better do it. He started the car and headed away.

Stratton and Abed reached the top of the old stone quarry and crouched by several jagged boulders to view the area. The route through looked obvious; with a sheer wall of rock on one side and a steep craggy climb on the other it had to be along the bottom. The settlement was out of view from their position but no doubt they would see it from where the track disappeared around the side of the quarry.

Stratton glanced at Abed who was concentrating on the area ahead and wondered what he would be like if they ran into a problem. He looked athletic and alert, and anyone who could climb a supertanker at night in rough seas and murder the entire crew was undoubtedly capable. However Abed was the leader and Stratton's concern was whether the man would take commands from him. He had to rate Abed's value on this op as high, if for no other reason than he was all he had, after Gabriel. If there was contact of any kind in the quarry they would have to go either forwards or backwards. Backwards meant having to find another way out, which would also burn up time and possibly increase the risk since the authorities would know that someone was trying to avoid the checkpoints out of Ramallah. Going forward meant moving quickly into unknown territory, and that was always a high risk and inadvisable. This was one of those situations where there was no point in hanging around since no further information would be forthcoming.

'I'll lead off. Give me some space, okay?' Stratton said.

Abed nodded and Stratton moved around the boulder and headed down a steep, loose track. Abed gave him a good distance before he followed.

Stratton kept his eyes ahead, his ears telling him Abed was behind.

They reached the bottom and carried on along the track that tightly hugged the quarry wall. Within minutes, they reached the furthest point they had been able to see from their start point and Stratton squatted to take a look at the ground ahead. The route looked obvious enough, keeping to the lowest point of the valley. The tough part was, as Morgan had said, the settlement on the top of the hill. It lined the ridge like a fortress, its battlements made of sheer plates of concrete fifteen feet high and knitted together to form an impregnable defence against a human assault, the tops of the ramparts fringed with razor wire just in case anyone was crazy enough to get that far and put up a ladder.

Abed joined him and looked at the route for himself.

'You up for it?' Stratton asked.

'If you are,' Abed said, matter-of-factly.

Stratton concentrated on the route again, taking stock of his senses that were working hard but not reporting back anything in the way of danger. He got up and walked forward. Abed let him get a dozen yards ahead before following.

Stratton repeatedly switched his gaze between the path ahead and the settlement above. There was no sign of life in any direction. As always, he automatically scanned for immediate cover he could drop behind in the event of a contact. The bad news was that as they moved around a gentle bend protection from above slimmed and the route was highly exposed. If they were going to be hit from the settlement this was the ideal place.

He increased speed across the open stretch, his eyes on a crop of boulders ten yards ahead. Suddenly something whistled through his jacket sleeve and struck the ground a few feet away with tremendous force, kicking up stones. It was accompanied by the loud report of a gun firing from above that echoed around the quarry. Stratton lunged forward and dived for the boulders, immediately looking back to see Abed sprinting across the open space towards the foot of the hill to dive and roll behind a collection of small rocks.

Abed could not get more tightly against the rocks but he still felt highly exposed. He looked over at Stratton who held up a hand indicating Abed to stay where he was. Abed had seen the round strike close to Stratton and if the man was wounded, he gave no indication of it.

Stratton pulled up his sleeve to find a bloody crease across his forearm but not deep into the muscle. That was too close for comfort.

He took stock of their tenuous situation. At first take they were pinned down by a sniper with nowhere to run and a good eleven hours before darkness. However there was some useful information to be gathered to help form a strategy other than waiting for nightfall. The first and most obvious point was that the sniper was a lousy shot. The ground immediately in front of the battlements of the settlement, the most likely place for the gunman, was no more than two hundred yards away. An average sniper, using the term as a military qualification, with a 7.62 rifle, was expected to hit a man at six hundred yards every time. A good sniper could do the same at a thousand yards in ideal conditions: good light and no wind. The next point was the type of weapon. If it was an automatic or semi-automatic rifle the sniper had plenty of time to take another shot at Stratton or adjust his aim and shoot at Abed, but he had not. That would suggest the shooter had a proper sniper or hunting rifle that required a manual reload. The best sniper rifles had as few working parts as possible to improve accuracy, the main parts being the barrel that floated in a wooden stock, the scope fixed on top and the breech. The only parts that actually moved during the firing process were the trigger mechanism and firing pin. As few working parts as possible meant each round had to be loaded manually. That meant moving the scope off the target, reloading the breech and then relocating a target. A good sniper would have had ample time to reload and squeeze off another shot at Abed as he was exposed for several seconds, but this one could not manage it, another indication of his amateur status. Looking around at the hill and surrounding ground Stratton found one more indication of the sniper's inexperience. A few yards further on up the track was a small gully that looked like it ran all the way up the hill. The lowest point of the gully would be dead ground to the sniper, out of his view. If Stratton could get to it, he might be able to make his way up. The main glitch would be if there was more than one sniper.

Stratton looked back at Abed who had not moved. 'Abed,' he called out, just loud enough for him to hear. 'You're gonna have to draw his fire.'

Abed understood what the Englishman wanted and although it crossed his mind that it might be a ploy to allow Stratton to escape, his instincts said to trust him. The Englishman was a soldier and calm under fire, and, more compelling than any other reason, he had no choice.

Abed nodded and looked around for some better cover. He did not like where he was anyway, with his face in the dirt, and a safer hiding place would be very much appreciated. But there was nothing close by. His best bet was to move up the hill where there were larger rocks and some foliage. Cover from view in this case was as good as cover from fire. But it was closer to the sniper.

Abed gathered himself, took a breath and sprang like a cat, rolled over the rocks towards the sniper and scrambled forward on all fours. The sniper fired hitting the ground inches in front of Abed, smacking him in the face with gravel. At the same moment Stratton leapt from his position and ran as fast as he could to the gully. He had estimated it would take him three to four seconds to get there and if his estimation of the sniper's abilities was correct, that would be ample time.

He dived across the last few metres, rolled into the gully without a shot being fired at him and lay there for a few seconds. One other thing now seemed certain. The sniper was working alone.

Stratton could no longer see Abed and wondered if he had been hit, but there was no point in thinking about that right now. He could not waste another second and began to crawl up the gully as quickly as possible. Several yards up the hill, the cover increased and he got to his feet to move more quickly. Suddenly a shot rang out and he hit the deck. A second later he realised it had not been aimed at him but at Abed. Stratton pushed on and made his way to the crest.

The ground was almost flat at the top for a few yards before rising steeply again to meet the impregnable wall. There was no sign of anyone on the wall but then only a complete idiot would fire from that position since they would be silhouetted against the sky.

Keeping as low as he could without getting on to his knees he made his way towards the probable location of the sniper. Another shot rang out, again aimed below, and Stratton got down on to his belly and crawled to a crop of boulders from where he could see the likely sniper position. Since the gunman was still firing he was obviously confident his other target had run away. As he scanned for any sign of Abed, he saw him move quickly between a pair of boulders. The sniper fired again hitting the rocks inches from Abed. The Palestinian went up a notch in Stratton's estimations. He was continuing to draw fire, allowing Stratton to get closer and at the same time find the sniper's location, and judging from the last shot he was just the other side of Stratton's cover.

Stratton moved swiftly and rounded the boulder to see a man squatting in what looked like a shell scrape with stones neatly arranged around the edges, his rifle in his shoulder and scope in front of his eye. The man heard Stratton step behind him and as he scrambled to turn and pull his rifle around, Stratton dropped a foot on to the weapon where the man was holding it and brought his fist down on to his jaw with such force he shattered several of the man's teeth. The man yelped, giving up immediately, and released the rifle to hold his face, bringing his knees up into the foetal position in an effort to protect himself from further punishment while he cried some garbled words that could have been in any language. Stratton pulled the weapon away from the man, ripped out the breech, tossed it away, then jammed the end of the barrel between two large rocks and stamped on it fiercely enough to put a kink in it, rendering it inoperable.

The man looked between his fingers at Stratton and his whimpering slowed as he noticed his assailant's Western features.

'You ain't Palestinian,' he said in what sounded like a New York accent.

Stratton ignored him and moved to where he could see Abed looking up between some rocks. When he saw Stratton, he got to his feet brushing the dust from his clothes.

'Where you from, man?' the sniper asked in a pathetic tone, blood seeping from his mouth, the broken teeth giving him pain. Stratton did not answer. 'If I knew you weren't Palestinian I'd a never shot at ya. Honest, man.'

'Why didn't you ask?'

'I'm . . . I'm sorry.'

Stratton threw down the gun, his anger melting at the sight of the pitiful creature, a flask and sand-wich box beside him. 'Where you from?' he asked.

'Brooklyn. I'm American.'

'What are you doing here? Hunting out of season in New York?'

'I'm Jewish, man.'

'You speak Hebrew?'

'Some words . . . No.'

Stratton scanned the walls of the settlement in case the shooting had attracted any of the sniper's friends. There was no sound or movement but prudence dictated that they move on as soon as possible.

Abed climbed over the edge and stood the other side of the sniper, looking down on him. The sniper rolled on to his back to look up at Abed and grew even more frightened at the sight of the Arab. He looked between the two men frantically trying to gauge them.

'What are you gonna do to me?'

'You got any other weapons?' Stratton asked.

The man hesitated before deciding this was not a man to lie to.

'I gotta semi,' he said, indicating the left side of his torso.

Stratton leaned down and pulled open the man's jacket to reveal a steel-coloured semi-automatic pistol in a shoulder holster. He pulled it out of the spring-grip and inspected it. Afghanistan was the last time he had held a Russian 9mm Tokarev. The date on the side was 1938, the same age as the one he had taken off a dead Taliban in Kabul. He removed the magazine to find it full of the peculiar long Tokarev 9mm copper-coated bullets. He pulled back the top slide to find the breech not loaded and repeatedly slid it back and forth to test the return spring, the mechanism designed to pick up another bullet and shove it into the breech after the previous one had been fired – the return spring was one of the weaknesses of old semi-automatic pistols and this one was almost twice Stratton's age. It felt strong enough. Perhaps it had recently been replaced. Stratton slid the magazine back into the bottom of the pistol grip, cocked it, putting a round into the breech, and let his arm fall to his side, the barrel, perhaps coincidentally, aimed at the man's crotch. The man knew his weapon well enough. The Tokarev had no safety catch and when the hammer was back it was ready to fire at the touch of the trigger.

'Spare clips?' Stratton asked, using the American word for magazine.

The man kept one eye on the pistol and one on Stratton as he quickly reached into a pocket to produce a spare magazine filled with bullets.

'These nine mil. longs are hard to come by. Where'd you get them?' Stratton asked.

'A guy in the settlement. He can get any weapon you want.'

Stratton placed the magazine in a pocket.

'What are you gonna do to me?' the man asked again, this time expressing more concern.

Stratton looked at Abed as if to ask him for an answer. Abed looked away. It was not his place to say, but if it were up to him he would leave the man alone. He no longer had the stomach for killing. He would never kill again unless he had no choice, he was sure of that.

Stratton had no intention of harming the sniper

any further. For some strange reason he felt something of a hypocrite even considering it. He was not like this man who was here for the fun of it. There were several places in the world where humans could be hunted and shot with impunity, and the Israeli settlements were just one of them. Another was working for Western intelligence, but it was a far more exclusive club.

Stratton aimed the pistol at the man's heart, placed the pad of his index finger on the trigger and pulled it; at the same time his thumb caught the top of the hammer as it sprang forward, and let it gently fall into its seat against the back of the firing pin.

The man flinched, then exhaled slowly, feeling a little giddy as Stratton placed the gun in his pocket.

'Go home,' Stratton said, and then turned and walked away.

The sniper switched his gaze to Abed, wondering if he might harm him, but Abed stepped over him and followed Stratton.

They walked at a brisk pace down the gully and on to the path to leave the settlement behind. Ten minutes later they headed up a track to find themselves amid the bustling throng of cars, trucks and people lining up to pass through the Kalandia checkpoint into Ramallah.

They had covered the distance in silence but Abed had hardly taken his eyes off Stratton, wondering what kind of man he was. What fascinated him was Stratton's complexity. The man was clearly troubled by something, but Abed felt certain it had nothing to do with the problems in this country. He was

Abed's first contact with the West, he was the enemy, and in a very short time he not only believed he could trust him, he had to admit he liked him. That troubled Abed even more.

They climbed into one of the many taxis dropping Palestinians off at the checkpoint and Stratton told the driver to take them to the American Colony.

13

The block of wood sat on the writing desk in Zhilev's room with the instruction booklet lying open beside it. Zhilev's gnarled finger moved down the page and when he reached the end of the paragraph, he studied the diagram pertaining to it. He took the knife off the coffee table that came with the complementary bowl of fruit and placed the tip of the blade into a thin slot barely visible in a knot in the wood. He pushed it down exactly a centimetre and levered it slowly to one side. A small section of the bark popped open on a cloth hinge to reveal a small panel of coloured buttons and a numeric pad.

Zhilev turned to the next page of the booklet detailing how to adjust a timer that could be set in increments of fifteen minutes up to thirty hours. He had already calculated three hours would give him ample time to get a taxi out of the city and on the road to Haifa. That was the minimum time he needed to get away from the danger area, allowing for unforeseen delays and without leaving the device alone too long and risking it being found. He chose Haifa because it was a seaport, a boat being his best bet out of the country since he did not have an entry visa and could therefore not use the airport. He did not know precisely how he was going to manage that but he was confident, after achieving so much, that he would find a way. The second and more important reason for heading towards Haifa was because it was in the north. The prevailing winds in the region blew from the north-west and any nuclear fallout after the explosion would head south-east.

After setting the timer he studied the next paragraph which explained the arming sequence. He had the option of pre-arming or arming on site, and he chose the latter simply as a precaution. He would have plenty of time to carry out that phase when he reached the target. Satisfied with the procedure so far, he turned to the last chapter in the book which dealt with the safety protocols. This was the part that had bothered him most throughout the mission. None of Russia's nuclear devices could be detonated without the permission of the Kremlin. This was in the form of a special code transmitted only with the consent of the head of state and, combined with the operator's own code, allowed the activation of the arming mechanism. This rule applied to every nuclear device in Russia's arsenal, except those hidden in secret caches abroad and used by the Spetsnaz for international sabotage. A bypass had been built into the bomb's arming sequence so it could be detonated in the event the chairman and his immediate subordinates were killed in an unexpected nuclear assault by the West. In those circumstances all Spetsnaz in operational areas had orders to continue with their assignments regardless, and to achieve that end they needed to be able to remove all safety protocols so they could initiate their bombs manually. Needless to say, overcoming the protocols was crucial to Zhilev's entire mission.

Zhilev read the instructions carefully, as he had many times before, but this time he actually pressed the buttons on the numeric pad in the order stated. A small LED screen reacted favourably to each button pressed, and when he got to the end he expected the procedure to be complete, but, to his horror, a message came up on the LED strip stating: ENTER 6-DIGIT CODE.

Zhilev stared at it in disbelief. The book had said nothing about any code. He hurriedly searched the document once more in case he had missed something, but knowing he could not have read anything as important as that and not noticed. He started from the beginning, this time focusing on any numbers that could be interpreted as a code, but as he reached the end of the book without any obvious six numbers, panic set in.

He placed the booklet on the desk and stepped back, rigid with frustration and anger. Suddenly the room seemed to shrink to the size of a prison cell and he felt claustrophobic.

He had no code.

He grabbed his straggly hair wanting to pull it out. Without the code the bomb could not be detonated. The device was too sophisticated to be tampered with, and he would not have a clue what he was doing anyway. How could he be so stupid?

His mind flew back to the cache, scanning his

memory for any hint of a code. He wondered if it had been written on the box somewhere, or if he had left some crucial part of the instruction papers in the packaging. He contemplated going back to England and the cache to look for it but he wrenched the thought from his mind as ridiculous. He had failed. The entire journey had been wasted. The only other way he could detonate the bomb was with the consent of the President of the Republic of Russia and there was not much chance of gaining that.

Zhilev wanted to bang his head against a wall to punish himself for being such a useless fool. He clenched his fists, shook them and let out a scream. He had not only failed himself, his heritage and the Spetsnaz, but his brother too.

He crossed the room and raised a fist to slam it through the wardrobe then looked back at the bomb and decided to take it out on that. He walked back to the desk raising his hand, and brought it down on to the block with great force in a momentary suicidal hope of detonating it and putting him out of his misery, but all he managed to do was break the panel cover and send it spinning across the room in pieces. He raised his hand to hit it once again but was stopped in mid-strike by a thought flashing across his head. This system had been designed for field conditions in the event of an all-out war. Every weapon built for the Spetsnaz took into considera-tion the worst conditions a soldier could operate in, including physical disablement due to health or battle. In other words, it was designed to be simple. But this had not been simple. Had he been an operative in a war situation he would have failed due to a code he did not have. It did not make sense.

He lowered his hand to think about that in more detail. The people who designed the operating procedures must have considered a scenario where an operative would have to grab the device and the instruction book and hurry to a target to set it up for detonation. Designing the device was one thing, but the people whose job it was to think of the practical applications were professional soldiers like Zhilev. It was precisely the kind of job he might have had if they had kept him in the Spetsnaz instead of forcibly retiring him.

He picked up the booklet to feel the pages. As he had discovered on the boat, it was not made of paper but a thin material, hard to tear and which could suffer soaking and soiling without the ink running. Both the bomb and the booklet were made of relatively indestructible materials because they were the two essential elements to success. The key had to be in them somewhere.

He studied the instruction sheet with a new eye, looking for any kind of pattern, but not until he reached the back page did he find a clue. All the main headings were placed in rectangular boxes, and on the back of the booklet there was a pattern of different-sized rectangles made up of lines of varying thicknesses, but the one at the bottom-right corner of the page was the same size and design as the ones used for the headings.

He needed to think in practical terms, which was not difficult for him. If something was written on the page that was normally invisible, it had to be activated, and if that was the case the catalyst had to be something the operative carried on him all the time, even when things became desperate. Water was an obvious one, but the booklet had gotten wet many times while at sea and nothing appeared different about it. Blood was something the operative would always have, and urine. Zhilev went for the easy option first and spat on the rectangle. He rubbed it in and almost immediately the area began to darken. It was changing, that was for sure. Something in his spittle, a hormone perhaps, was reacting with a chemical in the paper. Zhilev spat on it again and rubbed it in further. The area began to turn black and numbers appeared in white on the dark background, six of them. He could hardly believe it.

Zhilev tapped in the numbers, slowly and methodically, not wanting to make a mistake. As he hit the last number the LED bar went blank and a second later a word appeared: ARMED.

He had done it.

He was frozen to the spot, staring at the device, his heart thumping with excitement. He had overcome the security protocols. All he had to do now was press the three trigger switches, one after the other, and the device would detonate three hours later.

Zhilev realised he was short of breath and his joints were tingling with the adrenaline that had surged through them when the code appeared on the page.

He slumped into the chair to unwind and pull himself together. He now had all the time in the world for the last phase. Jerusalem was his for the taking, and he was going to destroy it. He was not a God-fearing man but if there was such a being, then Zhilev had surely been given his blessing.

He checked his watch. Breakfast was still being served in the restaurant downstairs. He would put on his new clothes, have a hearty meal and head for the old city. He would not bother to check out. What was the point? By lunchtime the hotel would not exist.

Stratton asked the taxi to pull over a hundred yards from the road that led to the entrance to his hotel.

'That's the hotel to the right of the minaret,' he said to Abed, pointing at the stone tower. A small chamber at the top had been designed originally for a man to stand in, blasting the area with calls for Muslims to come to prayer. Now it concealed a set of tiny speakers. 'It's watched,' Stratton added. 'Understand?'

Abed nodded. He did not need Stratton to tell him to be aware of people watching and following him. He had been looking over his shoulder since the day he left Gaza.

'Above the hotel, further up the road, are some shops. There's a store where you can get something to eat. It looks a busy place. Find a way around from behind. Don't go past the front of the hotel. I'll see you inside the shop in an hour.'

'Okay,' Abed said as he opened the door and climbed out. Stratton tapped the driver on the shoulder and as the car drove away, Abed walked off in the opposite direction.

The taxi pulled up outside the hotel, Stratton paid the fare and the car drove away. He paused in the street long enough to glance up and down it, checking to see if there was any obvious evidence the entrance was being watched. There wasn't and he didn't expect there to be. The Israelis had had plenty of time to master the art of surveillance, and if they were here, he didn't expect he would see them, even with his experience.

He walked into the hotel and asked for his key at the desk. The receptionist took it from a hook and plucked a piece of paper from a pigeonhole above it.

'There's a message from your friend Mr Stockton,' she said with a pleasant smile. 'He asks that you go to his room as soon as you get in. Number twelve. You can take the elevator through there or walk up to the first floor.'

'Thanks,' Stratton said as he took his key and headed through a stone arch and to the foot of the stairs. A minute later he was outside room twelve and knocking on the door.

Gabriel opened it and stood in the doorway looking accusingly at Stratton. 'Where have you been?' he demanded.

Stratton closed the door quickly, not wanting the rest of the hotel to hear whatever was upsetting Gabriel. 'What's up?' Stratton said, emphasising his calmness to offset Gabriel's vexation.

Gabriel walked to the dresser and leaned heavily on it as if he could no longer support himself.

'You okay?' Stratton asked.

'No, I'm not okay.' Gabriel said, looking defiantly at Stratton. He then noticed the streak of dried blood coming out of Stratton's sleeve and down the outside of his hand, but it was nothing compared to what was troubling him.

'Why didn't you tell me?' Gabriel spat, pushing himself off the desk and walking across the room away from Stratton. He stopped by an antique wardrobe near the balcony and held on to it as he looked through the patio doors.

'Has anyone said anything to you about me being a faker?' Gabriel asked.

Stratton did not answer. No one had, but Gabriel appeared to be heading off somewhere and needed no encouragement from him.

'Well, I am. Surprised? Or not? You know how I got into this business? How I became a so-called psychic spy? I was a teacher. Mathematics. Not a very good one either . . . It all ended, or began if you like, fifteen years ago after a car crash. I was in hospital for weeks. They thought I was going to die . . . or maybe it was just me who thought that. I can't remember. During rehabilitation, I started to become eccentric. That's not true, I was always eccentric. But unlike the English, Americans don't appreciate eccentricity. Far from it. They don't like it. They don't understand it. The habitually unusual unnerves them. But after the accident, I felt strangely free. I'd escaped death and I could be myself. I had a new start in life and I didn't care what people thought about me any more. I had become brave. They say that often happens after a near-death experience. I've always had strange thoughts, daydreams if you like. Mostly fantasies about things I wanted to be or do. There was nothing psychic about them. But as I got older I daydreamed less and less, as if I had lost hope. There seemed no point to dreams anymore. My life was dull and I had no future and so why bother fantasising? But after the accident, the reborn eccentric in me started to enjoy those dreams once again. Freedom to think what you want is a wonderful thing. When you are dull and unambitious, you restrict your thoughts when they become absurd and unhealthy. I used to feel guilty about having them. Well I got rid of all of that. I allowed myself to think what I wanted, and even shared them with others, anyone who cared to listen. Sometimes I shocked people and I began to like doing that. The nurses thought I was mad. My psychiatrist spent a great deal of my medical insurance money listening to my thoughts. What I didn't know was that *he* was fascinated with them. I would freethink away while sitting back in his armchair, enjoying an audience that even wrote down my ramblings for forty-five minutes a session.

'A week after they sent me home, someone came to visit me. A man from the state department, or so he said. He was never very clear about that, although I remember he had great difficulty trying to avoid saying who he specifically worked for. I think he really wanted to tell me. You know how Americans are. Always wanting people to think they are special. Unlike you British who seem to revel in pretending to be nobodies. You can't fool us though. We know you do it in the hope people will think you really are somebody . . . The man wasn't the best communicator. It took some time before I realised he was actually trying to recruit me. Eventually he spelled it out and asked if I would attend an interview with a secret government intelligence department. He never said the words Central Intelligence Agency or Defence Intelligence but it was quite obvious.'

Stratton moved to the desk and sat in a chair beside it. Whatever it was Gabriel had to say he was taking the long route, talking more to himself it seemed, and Stratton didn't feel like interrupting him.

'A few days later,' Gabriel went on, 'I found myself in a sterile room in the Federal building sitting in front of several people who I later discovered were a mixture of psychiatrists, spooks and military personnel. Whatever it was they were looking for, I was apparently in ample possession of, and at the end of the interview they offered me a job that was considerably easier than teaching and far better paid. Basically, I was invited to spend my time sitting with a group of like-minded people searching the universe for matters concerning national security. It made no sense to me whatsoever and even sounded a little absurd but, being the pragmatist I am, I signed on the dotted line as soon as I could.

'And so I became a remote viewer, a psychic spy. I couldn't believe how my luck had changed. From a tiring, daily ritual teaching ill-disciplined children I did not respect, nor them me, to a revered position within the country's national security advisory. And the job was very easy too. All I had to do was spend my time perusing the id and declaring my thoughts, no matter how bizarre, and collect a cheque at the end of each month. Sometimes a subject or person was introduced, a name or a picture, and we would go into session, and, at the end of it, after our thoughts were transcribed, they were taken away for evaluation. We didn't always know what became of the transcriptions.

'I took it quite seriously at first, even started to believe I could actually do it, but eventually I had to admit, to myself at least, that I was faking it. Of course, I wasn't about to tell any of them that. It had become too attractive a lifestyle to throw away just because of an attack of honesty. So I kept schtum and worked on a technique of feeding off the others, importing strings of their thoughts, building on them and exporting my own versions. I must have been very good at it because one day I learned I had received the largest portion of the credit for finding the Lockerbie bomb. I expect there were other fakers in the group but it was near impossible to tell. Who could judge you? From our point of view the answers were all there somewhere in our ramblings, and it was up to the decoders to find them; if they could not, it was their fault, not ours.

'Then one day some people from Stanford University arrived who believed they had found a way of accurately evaluating our abilities. The CIA had been spending a fortune on the institute's research department. I was horrified. The lifestyle to which I had grown accustomed looked as if it was about to fall apart. Worse still, I was about to be exposed as a fraud. Iraq was the turning point. When we couldn't find any weapons of mass destruction, the hierarchy came down pretty hard on us and I came clean and told them I couldn't do it any longer. And that's when it happened. Perhaps it was because I had broken free of so many chains that restricted my clarity. I don't know. But there I was, sitting alone in the viewing room, a tranquil place designed to be alpha provoking, waiting for the department head to call me upstairs to sign my release papers, when I saw the tanker and the horrors that were taking place on it. It was so real it frightened me. I automatically did what we always did during viewing sessions so that nothing was lost to memory and I wrote down what I had seen and drew sketches and doodled images; everything, no matter how trivial or bizarre, was placed on paper. I was called upstairs to the office and so I left the report on the table, completed my leaving routine and went home. In the early hours of the following day an agent banged on my door with orders to take me back to the agency. My papers had been processed as routine, and, to the decoders' horror, everything I had seen had been happening as I was writing it down.'

Gabriel moved from the wardrobe and slumped on to the edge of the bed as if he no longer had the energy to stand up.

'It's a nuclear bomb, isn't it?' Gabriel asked, raising his eyes off the floor to look at Stratton. 'That's what the madman found in England and what he is now carrying.'

There was obviously no further point in lying to Gabriel. In fact, there was every reason to tell him the truth since this operation was far from over. If Stratton had any doubts about Gabriel, they were now gone. But he did not need to confirm Gabriel's accusation. Gabriel could see it in his cold, dark eyes.

'He's here,' Gabriel said. 'But why are you? Aren't you afraid?'

Stratton wanted to say it was his job, but that would have sounded pathetic. It would also have been a lie. Stratton was not about to die for anyone. It was his instincts that kept him chasing the Russian, but to analyse that any further would place him in the same confused netherworld as Gabriel.

'I don't like you, Stratton . . . No, that's not entirely true. It's your kind I don't like. You're the same as that man carrying his bomb. You may be the antithesis, but together you are one. You create each other and feed off each other. If you didn't exist, he wouldn't either.'

Stratton could not agree with Gabriel. He wanted to say that for every force there had to be an opposing force. The concept of good could not exist without evil. If there was a question it was who were the good guys and where did the true evil lie. Perhaps Gabriel was right and that was why Stratton's life often felt meaningless to him.

'How big is the bomb?' Gabriel asked.

'Five miles.'

Gabriel shook his head sadly. 'My God,' he murmured. 'It's not just you . . . We're all mad.'

A heavy knock on the door startled both of them, and Stratton got to his feet. Another energetic knock and Stratton opened the door to see Abed in the hallway.

'He's here,' Abed said. 'I saw him.'

'The Russian?'

'Yes.'

'Where?' Stratton asked with urgency as he stepped out of the room.

'I was at the top of the road, opposite the shops, when I saw him leave the hotel. It was not until he passed me that I recognised him.'

'When?' Stratton asked as he headed down the hall.

'I came straight here but it took me a while to find you.'

'Stratton,' Gabriel called out from the door of his room.

Stratton stopped at the corner to the stairwell and looked back to see Gabriel holding on to the doorway.

'Number seven,' he said.

'What?'

'Seven,' Gabriel repeated. 'I don't know what it means, but it's important to the Russian . . . It's today, Stratton.'

Stratton stared at him, a myriad thoughts crashing through his mind, including how to get away from Jerusalem as quickly as possible. He forced that to the back. 'I thought viewers could only see the present.'

'That's true.'

'Then the future. If it hasn't happened yet, it can be changed?' It was more of a question than a statement, and his immediate actions depended largely on the answer.

413

'Not mine,' Gabriel said darkly.

Stratton stared at him a moment longer, then he ran down the stairs at the sprint, Abed close behind him.

A minute later, they were running out of the hotel entrance and up the road.

'Was he carrying anything?' Stratton asked.

'A bag, a sack, over his shoulder.'

Stratton clenched his teeth and increased his pace up the hill, past the shops and towards the bend at the top.

They passed a van outside a photographic shop, daubed in various colourful slogans advertising photographic equipment. There was no one in the front of the vehicle and the interior was concealed from view by a panel behind the front seats with a mesh screen in it. The Shin Bet agent inside videoed Stratton and Abed running towards him, then he moved to the back of the van and operated another camera and recorded them heading around the bend and out of sight.

14

Manachem Raz sat in the cramped press office that dealt with international media, which was situated on the third floor of the government building beside the busy Ben Yehuda precinct known for its cafés and tourist boutiques. He was scrolling through data on a computer screen, the smell from the Chinese restaurant on the floor below wafting in through the window. As he scanned through the most recent applications for press passes he had to wonder why a government building had rented one of its largest rooms to a private catering business, and a Chinese one to boot, when there was a general shortage of office space. It was indicative of the country's poor economy where every avenue to making money was being explored. He wondered how many other governments rented out public buildings to private shops. It was all the more annoying because he didn't like Oriental cuisine.

Raz received copies of new press-pass applications at the beginning of each week which included a colour photograph of the applicant, but the next batch was not due for a couple of days and he was curious about something. He had received a report about a member of the BBC entering Ramallah late the night before, and the soldier on duty at the DCO checkpoint remembered the date on the pass showed that it had been issued that very week. The soldier could not remember the man's name, but then it was not the checkpoint's task to record the details of media personnel passing in and out of Ramallah.

Raz reached the end of the list and leaned back to think. Only one member of the BBC had applied for a pass in the last two weeks and that was a female assistant producer. What had prompted Raz's curiosity was Stratton's early arrival at the American Colony that morning, yet he had not been seen leaving. If Raz showed a picture of Stratton to the soldier, he was confident it would fit the description of the BBC journalist. The driver with him had a press pass from the Ramatan studios in Ramallah, a Palestinian media group, but it would be more difficult to identify him since there were so many of them. If the BBC journalist was Stratton, then the driver was no doubt a member of the British spy network in the West Bank. That was no surprise to Raz. He would find the Ramatan spy eventually but there was no urgency. Besides, he did not have the manpower to spare, and the spy would be replaced before he was exposed. The British were always the most difficult to work against, but then they should be. They had been doing it longer than anyone else. The foundations of their intricate spy network had been set up during the days when they owned a quarter of the world and much of it was still in place today, even in countries they no longer had any influence over, including Israel.

Raz was interested in Stratton and what he was doing here, and his gut instinct warned him something was in the wind, but that hunch did not come from Stratton, who gave little away, but from his companion. He had looked stressed and nervous during the drive from the airport and appeared half-dead from worry. Raz had authorised a costly surveillance operation against Stratton and would soon have to provide his bosses with his reasons, and a hunch was not good enough to maintain it. He planned to keep up the watch at least until he had received Stratton's brief and then he would re-evaluate the situation.

He looked at the clock on the wall. It was ten thirty. Time to contact Mr Stratton and hear what he had to say, although he was not expecting very much. Whatever the Englishman was up to, Raz was no doubt going to have to find out for himself.

His mobile phone rang in his pocket and he dug it out, hit the key and put it to his ear. 'Raz.'

As he listened, he got to his feet and headed for the door, knocking papers off a desk and not stopping to pick them up. Seconds later he was running out through the entrance, past the building's security guard and down the broad stone steps, waving for his driver who was waiting outside reading a newspaper.

Stratton and Abed hurried along the street, passing a school on one side and a heavily secured government building on the other, and closed on a Y-junction which was the start of a densely populated shopping area. Stratton paused on the triangle in the road to study his options, Abed behind him, both men panting heavily.

'Why are we chasing him?' Abed asked.

'He has a bomb,' Stratton said. There was still no point in anyone knowing what kind of bomb, and, besides, he needed Abed and did not want him taking off in the opposite direction.

'The Al Aqsa mosque in the old city,' Abed said. 'If he wants to attack Islam that is the place. Is he of the Islam faith?'

Stratton had not thought about that. It was an interesting question, but did not appear on Zhilev's profile. 'I don't think so.'

'If not, he will not be permitted into the square. Only those of the faith may enter.'

Zhilev did not need to put the bomb in the mosque to raise it to the ground, but the old city would be a good place for the explosion. It would read better in the press reports.

'The old city straight ahead?' Stratton asked, indicating the road crammed with shops, barrows and swarms of people.

'I don't know,' Abed said. 'I have never been to Jerusalem before.' Abed asked a passer by who pointed down the street.

They moved quickly into the throng, slowed by the density of the crowds, and headed down the steep, snaking road that became narrower as it divided into a fork. They paused at the split. Abed looked around for a sign, found one, and confirmed some information with a passing shopper.

'That leads to the Damascus Gate,' Abed said to

Stratton, indicating the right fork. 'And that one to Herod's Gate.'

'You take that one.'

'What do I do if I see him?'

'Stay with him,' Stratton shouted as he continued down the busy hill. Without communications there was not much else he could do. If Abed did find Zhilev, he had a better chance of following him unnoticed since he wasn't white. Stratton did not think he needed to tell Abed to tackle Zhilev if he thought the Russian was about to detonate the device. He had a feeling Abed would have a go if he thought there were no other options.

The bottom of the street got even narrower and became crammed with mini-buses, obviously the local bus depot, and Stratton pushed through and broke out into a broad street that ran across his front. Beyond the street the ancient white stone walls of the old city spread in front of him, the great, gold, bulbous dome of the Al Aqsa mosque rising out of the city in the distance.

He crossed the street, dodging traffic, and stopped at the top of a broad, jagged semi-circle of steps that formed an amphitheatre in front of a large fortress façade with battlements on top and an arch at the centre that led into the city. Stratton paused to scan the people milling around the amphitheatre where several traders had set up shop on the steps offering shoes, clothes, cheap electronics and fruit and vegetables. There was no sign of a big white man so Stratton ran down the steps to the floor of the amphitheatre and followed it across a stone bridge over a moat that once helped protect the gate from being stormed. The entrance led immediately into a hall packed with vendors, and beyond was the entrance into the city proper, around a tight corner guarded by half a dozen Israeli police and soldiers, the police armed with pistols, the soldiers with M16 assault rifles. They were watching everyone who passed in and out, occasionally selecting someone to search. Stratton was suddenly aware of the gun in his pocket, but the need to press forward and find Zhilev was greater than avoiding the risk of being searched. Stratton reduced his speed to a normal pace as he approached. One of the soldiers studied him as he passed. Stratton could feel the man's eyes on his back as he walked into the city but no one called after him.

A few yards in Stratton stopped at a fork in the walkway. Vehicles could not navigate this part of the city. In fact, all but a couple of the central roads were closed to wheeled traffic except the numerous barrows. The walkway straight ahead was crowded with people and tightly lined with kiosks and one-room shops, their wares spilling into the walkway leaving barely enough room for the barrows and people to move along. The path to the left dropped steeply away and led into a less crowded residential area. There was trash everywhere and grey water, thickened by filth, trickled along gutters and formed stagnant pools in the cracks and depressions of the stepped walkways. Every surface was stone: the walls, the road underfoot and the surrounding battlements, disfigured in places with patches of modern concrete sloppily applied, and graffiti could be found everywhere, some of it hundreds of years old. Only the older men wore traditional Arab dress, black-and-white, or red-and-white *kaffiyehs* which defined their tribes, held on to their heads with black *aggals*, their bodies covered in *dishdashas* or *abayas*, long one-piece outfits which reached the ground. Most of the younger men wore plain, or sometimes colourful, Western clothes. The women were also divided between Western and traditional dress but not so much by age, with many young girls wearing scarves over their heads and *thawbs*, a traditional gown sometimes decorated with colourful sequins.

Stratton took the map he had picked up from the hotel reception from his pocket and studied it. He decided on the busy route through the market and headed down the widely stepped walkway that had a narrow central path levelled out for the barrows. There was a loud shout behind him and he stepped out of the way just in time to avoid a young boy navigating an overburdened barrow down the path through the crowd, using his sandal on the wheel as a brake and looking as if he was only barely in control.

All the while Stratton scanned in every direction and inside the shops for the giant Russian. The Palestinians were not a tall race and he hoped it would be easy to spot Zhilev, but there was no sign of him.

The crowded walkway threaded into the central mass of buildings where it became a low, narrow tunnel still lined with shops. It was well lit with electric lights but there were nooks, crannies and even tighter alleyways branching off on both sides into residential areas, a veritable labyrinth.

After a hundred yards or so Stratton paused at a junction and looked at his three new options, comparing them quickly to the map. The right path led to a flight of stairs, left led downhill in the direction of the great mosque and straight ahead, through the thinning crowd, led deeper into the city, where a group of soldiers approached on patrol. Stratton chose the left path.

A few yards down the walkway he passed under a low arch and back out into sunlight. The shops gave way to homes where washing and small children were in abundance. Frustration began to creep over him as he realised how overwhelming the endless alleyways and tunnels were becoming. The old city was only half a mile square but the miles of walkways turned it into a maze. The horrifying truth was dawning that the only way he was going find Zhilev was through luck, and that was not a good basis on which to mount a search operation. A boy grabbed his arm in an effort to persuade him to buy something from his shop and Stratton pulled away so aggressively the boy almost toppled over.

Stratton could feel the stress rising in him along with mounting doubts about what he was doing. He stopped to look back at the junction he had just left as the tail end soldier passed through it along the walkway he had taken from the city entrance. The urge to turn around, head out of the city and get as far away as possible grew, threatening to corrupt his commitment. Fear was also beginning to nibble at him, fear of failing, as well as dying. He suddenly felt pathetically helpless. It had been a long time since he had experienced any kind of panic and it was starting to rise steadily inside of him. He took control of it and pushed it out of his stomach where it was massing, and concentrated on himself, who he was, what he had achieved in his life and the many dangers he had survived when he should not have. He walked on down the hill, his efforts working, but it still did not affect the source of the problem: to believe in himself he had to doubt Gabriel. If Gabriel was right, he was wrong and Zhilev was going to detonate his nuclear bomb, and he was going to die.

Stratton broke into a run, unsure where he was going. It was the worst feeling in the world.

Zhilev stepped through the Zion Gate and stopped to look around. To his surprise there were no soldiers in sight. He had originally planned to enter by the Damascus Gate after completing his reconnaissance the day before, but as he walked through the entrance hall, he saw a group of Israeli soldiers and police checking people's bags. He stopped dead. Zhilev could not afford to let anyone inspect the log now that the panel cover had broken off. He turned around, pushed through a crowd and made his way back out on to the street. Entering the city was probably the final obstacle to his target and he wanted to avoid all risks where possible. He consulted his map of the old city and considered the eight gates. It was worth checking the other seven.

He headed east towards the Herod Gate, decided to ignore it because it was too close to the Damascus

Gate and turned the corner of the city walls towards the Golden Gate. That entrance was closed and so he continued south to the next corner and then west towards the Dung Gate.

A couple of soldiers were sitting outside the gate enjoying a smoke and although several people passed through without being stopped, Zhilev decided to carry on and check out the last four. If they were fouled, he would head back to the Dung Gate and try his luck with the smokers.

At the southernmost point of the city, the Zion Gate was practically deserted. He had not reconnoitred this section but the map was detailed enough to lead him to where he wanted to go. It showed he was in the Armenian quarter and he set off, following the walkways east a few yards then turned north for several hundred more until he reached the Holy Sepulchre, the church built around Calvary and where Jesus was nailed to the cross.

Zhilev stopped to check his map, completely ignoring a man trying to get him to step into his shop to look at his selection of carpets. Zhilev did not have far to go. He looked ahead to where the short walkway disappeared around a corner and set off, leaving the carpet salesman, already depressed by the scarcity of tourists, to limp back to his shop. This was a quiet part of the city with no one else around and as Zhilev turned the corner, he literally bumped into a couple of soldiers coming in the other direction, nearly knocking one of them over.

'*Izvinitye*,' Zhilev apologised immediately, as surprised as the soldier who was half his mass.

The soldier regained his composure as his two friends looked on, one somewhat accusingly at Zhilev, the other grinning at his friend's misfortune.

'*Gavaritye pa-russki*,' the soldier said, looking up cockily at the giant in front of him.

'Yes,' Zhilev replied. 'I'm sorry,' he repeated. 'I did not see you.'

'Where are you from?' the soldier asked in a guttural accent. It was obvious to Zhilev this boy had not learned his Russian in the Motherland and was no doubt the son of one of the many immigrants who had come to Israel.

'Latvia,' Zhilev said.

'So you're not real Russian then,' the soldier said with an attitude.

It did not faze Zhilev in the slightest, and not just because he wanted to be on his way as soon as possible and without any fuss. He hated being talked to rudely by children, especially when they carried guns, but his contempt for this little one was such that he was not inclined to waste any anger on him.

'I feel Russian,' Zhilev said, forcing a smile which did not produce a likewise response from the soldier.

'Where are you going in such a hurry?' the soldier asked.

'I'm not in a hurry. I was reading my map and did not see you.'

'What are you looking for?'

Zhilev glanced around at the other two soldiers who had continued on their way behind him and did not appear to share their friend's interest.

'Nothing in particular,' Zhilev said. 'I'm just enjoying the city.'

'What's in the bag?'

Zhilev's temperature went up a notch though his eyes remained steady. He took the bag off his shoulder. 'Memorabilia.'

'You know there are some things you cannot take out of Israel,' the soldier said, being a pain.

'No, I did not.'

'Holy relics. Everyone comes here expecting to take something home but for some pieces you need special permission. What have you got?'

'A piece of wood,' Zhilev said, his smile appearing again.

'Wood?'

'Yes. I picked it up from a forest by the Dead Sea. My sister likes to carve and I thought it would be nice to have something carved from a piece of wood from the Holy Land.'

The soldier was untouched by Zhilev's efforts to portray himself as a sensitive individual.

'Let me see it,' the soldier demanded.

Zhilev held the neck of his bag open. The soldier leaned over to examine the contents but was not satisfied, that or he was being deliberately obtrusive.

'Take it out,' he said coldly, transferring his Uzi sub-machine gun to his left hand so that he could wipe his nose with the sleeve of his right.

Zhilev didn't move, staring into the soldier's eyes.

'Yoni, let's go,' one of the other soldiers called out from behind Zhilev. They had moved further around the corner and were only just in view.

'One minute,' the soldier said to them. 'I want to see it,' he said to Zhilev.

Zhilev slowly bent over and put the bag on the floor, glancing to his side long enough to see the other two soldiers inching away around the corner, engrossed in their conversation. He reached into the bag with both hands, gripped the log, slowly pulled it out and stood upright.

The soldier looked at the log and then at Zhilev with a smirk. 'You're carrying around a block of wood,' he said, emphasising the stupidity of it.

The soldier put his hand on the log and rubbed the bark then pulled on the bottom of it to turn it over, but Zhilev held it firmly. The soldier looked at him with an annoyed expression.

'Turn it over,' he said.

Zhilev glanced over his shoulder to see the other two had moved out of sight and he did not waste a second. With lightning speed his hand gripped the soldier around the throat so strongly the man's tongue flew out and he dropped the Uzi on its harness to grab Zhilev's hands. Zhilev walked quickly forward, pushing the soldier ahead of him who stumbled backwards trying desperately to pull the vice from his throat. Zhilev held him like a rag doll and shoved him round a corner into a narrower walkway. The soldier could feel the life draining from him as his brain screamed for the oxygen that was being restricted because of the grip on his carotid artery. His hands flicked down to his Uzi and fumbled to get a hold of it but they were torn between removing the hand around his neck and gripping the gun.

Before he could wrap his fingers around the weapon grip, Zhilev raised the log and brought it crashing down on to the soldier's skull with tremendous force, splitting the skin open and severing the artery that runs around the outside of the skull. The blow cracked the log open and a chunk of it flew off to expose a dull metal sphere. Blood immediately spurted over Zhilev and he raised the device to hit the soldier once again, but he felt the man's weight increase as his knees gave out. The soldier let go of his weapon and his hands dropped to his sides as the nerves ceased to send signals to his muscles.

Zhilev had to move quickly. He let the soldier drop unconscious to the ground, blood seeping from the wound on his head, and unceremoniously yanked the Uzi strap from around his neck, then ran past the walkway where the other soldiers were standing, and through an arch that led to the market beneath the buildings.

The soldiers, who had returned to see what was keeping their colleague, saw the walkway empty, then Zhilev run across the end of it. Their instincts immediately cried alarm and they hurried to the junction. On seeing their colleague lying on the ground they ran to him to find he was not breathing. One pulled the soldier on to his back to try and revive him while the other set off in pursuit of Zhilev.

The soldier ran into the market tunnel, the M16 in his shoulder ready to fire, and stopped to scan about. The tunnel ran straight in both directions and was not very crowded in this section, a handful of

Palestinians going about their business, but there was no sign of the large Russian. It seemed impossible in the short space of time, but he had disappeared.

Raz's car arrived at the street above the Damascus Gate and pulled to a stop, blocking traffic. Ignoring the honking horns he climbed out and made his way to the top of the steps. He was met by one of his agents who quickly explained how Stratton and the man he was with had split up, and that he had followed Stratton, who was running, and lost him outside the gate, believing he had entered the old city.

Raz could not think what to make of it. He had no information of any specific threat and was angry that British intelligence was conducting its own operation on Israeli territory without consulting him. On the other hand he was experienced enough to recognise that whatever it was they were up to had rapidly developed into something urgent, and that Stratton was reacting to what was no doubt an emergency. The British argument would be that Stratton intended to brief the Israelis but events suddenly got ahead of things. That would come later. Right now, he had a British agent in pursuit of something that was obviously important or they would not be here, and the man was operating unsupported, except for the mysterious Palestinian.

'Go through Herod's Gate,' Raz said. 'Call me as soon as you see him but don't stop him. And get some people here,' he shouted as he ran down the steps and hurried towards the entrance to the city.

★ ★ ★

Stratton jogged along a broad walkway that was practically deserted, the frustration of looking for Zhilev eating away at him. With every passing minute he was growing closer to quitting the assignment, the voices in his head urging him to find a gate and get out of the city and as far away from it as possible. Deserting was not in his nature but his devil was pressing him to save himself, reminding him he didn't owe anyone anything, that he had done his best and although it was not good enough, that's how things went sometimes. No one ever won them all. Gabriel would not be around to point the finger at him. The question would be asked why he had not brought Gabriel out with him, and it would be a difficult one to answer. Everyone would know Stratton had run, but so what? Who wouldn't have? The simple answer was, he could not save the city and so why die just to prove he had tried? The only thing that was keeping him on the search so far was that he believed he still had some time.

It had to be assumed that Zhilev was not on a suicide mission and would most likely set the device timer to give him the leeway to escape the blast. What was eating at Stratton was the growing belief that Zhilev had already planted the device in a secure location and was on his way out of town. Finding it would be an impossible task. If Zhilev had left himself enough time to get away, that meant Stratton could also escape, but only if he left now.

He paused to check the map. Every path eventually led to an exit and the one he was on headed back towards the Damascus Gate. He made up his mind. He would search as far as the gate, and if he did not find Zhilev, he would quit. As for Abed, since he no longer knew where he was, the Palestinian was on his own.

Stratton jogged up an incline and paused at a right turn that led towards what looked like a monastery on the brow of a rise where several monks were having a conversation. Straight ahead, in the distance, was the main market again. Both paths led to the gate. He was about to take the less crowded monastery option when something caught his eye. In front of him, protruding into the street and attached to the corner of a large building at a crooked angle, was what appeared to be a small mausoleum. The entrance was protected by an iron fence linked to a pair of ancient pillars, their tops broken off just above the level of the gate, which was chained shut. What caught his attention was the carving in the stone above the door. It was of Christ lying on the ground with his cross over his back, but above that was written the number three in Roman numerals. The last thing Gabriel had said to him as he left the hotel was the number seven without knowing what it meant. Beside the number three were the letters STA. The meaning hit him like a freight train. He had read the short blurb on the back of the map about the fourteen stations of Christ's journey with his cross through the streets of the old city to his eventual crucifixion. STA was short for station. A sign on a wall named the road as the Via Dolorosa, the Path of Pain.

He quickly opened his map and searched the list on the back of it. Station three was where Christ fell for the first time. Station seven was where he fell for the second time. Stratton turned the map over hoping to see the stations indicated, but they were not.

A Palestinian stepped out of a shop a few yards away and Stratton hurried over to him. 'Where's station seven?' he asked urgently.

The Palestinian did not appear to understand him. Stratton took his shoulder with the minimum of politeness and directed his attention to the mausoleum.

'Station three. Three,' he said, holding up three fingers. 'Station seven,' he said, holding up seven fingers. 'Where is it?'

The man still appeared confused. Then the penny dropped and he repeated the number in horrible pronunciation while holding up seven of his own fingers.

'Seven. Yes. Where?'

The man pointed towards the market area and before his hand had levelled in that direction, Stratton was off at the run.

He grabbed the Tokarev in his pocket, not only to stop it bouncing about, but in anticipation of meeting the Russian although the feeling remained that he was too late. Much as Stratton wanted to get away, it was his nature that if there was even the most slender of chances of succeeding, he could not resist pursuing it. There might be life yet left in this hunt. If there was ever a time to start praying, this was it. It was certainly the right place.

He sprinted around a gentle curve to see people milling about the marketplace ahead and slowed to search for station seven.

He concentrated on the walls hoping to find something written above a door or a plaque on a wall. A woman in traditional dress approached carrying a bag brimming with assorted vegetables and Stratton blocked her path.

'Station seven? Seven?'

As soon as he asked her it was obvious she could not speak anything other than her native tongue and she looked at him as if he were an alien and moved around him without uttering a word. He turned to ask a man passing the other side of him who did not understand either.

Stratton carried on along the walkway which grew steeper. Up ahead it passed through an arch to burrow inside the city. Traders' tables lined one side of the tunnel which was illuminated by strip lights fixed to the low, arched stone ceiling.

Suddenly shouts came from inside the tunnel but Stratton was too far away to see what the commotion was. As he moved under the arch, he could see the walkway ended at a T-junction some forty yards ahead. More shouts echoed through the stone tunnels and people scurried away to avoid a couple of police officers running across the end of the junction.

He closed on it just as a soldier, clutching his M16, followed the police officers, pushing his way through the people and shouting at them to move.

Stratton did not care what the fuss was about and concentrated on searching for station seven.

Before he reached the end of the walkway he stopped dead in his tracks. Directly in front of him, twenty yards away, at the end of the T-junction and facing him, was a pair of doors set into the stone wall, and above them, on a large brass plaque, was the number seven in Roman numerals and the letters ST.

The black doors were shut. Trash was strewn about the ground, and Stratton was suddenly positive he was looking at the place where an atomic bomb was ticking away. When he had first learned it was a nuclear device, he had considered what he would do if he found the bomb armed and ready to go. The brief report he had read on its probable type and construction had provided no hope of dismantling it. The only plan he had come up with was to warn the authorities of whichever country he was in and let them deal with it, while he got out of there as quickly as he could. Now that he was possibly faced with that option, he could not improve on this choice of action, but before he could do anything, he had to see the bomb.

He was about to take a step forward when one of the doors started to open inwards. He stopped dead in his tracks and his hand shot to his pocket, pulled out the Tokarev and held it down against his thigh, partly covered by his other hand. He did not move any further nor did he even blink as the door opened fully and a large figure took a step through it.

Zhilev saw Stratton immediately and froze in the doorway. There was a handful of locals in the vicinity but this white man, in his battered leather jacket, standing some twenty yards away and staring directly at him, stood out like a tree in a field of snow. Zhilev did not miss the gun in his hand held low by his body. He looked into the man's eyes and knew instantly that he had come for a fight, a fight to the end, and he also had the distinct impression the man was no stranger to such situations. He was smaller than Zhilev, and alone as far as he could tell, but his cold, unswerving eyes revealed everything he needed to know about him. He had come for Zhilev, there was no doubt of that, which meant the man knew what he was up against, and yet he was there, standing like a rock, his feet apart and shoulders square. A hint of fear cracked through Zhilev's body, shooting from the pit of his stomach to every part of him, but he maintained control as his mind raced to consider his options. He had only two as far as he could see: continue out of the crypt, or go back inside. His aggressive nature wanted to push forward and take on this foe, but something in his heart warned him that at this precise moment he would lose, if for no other reason than he had left the Uzi on the table inside. The man was waiting for Zhilev to make his next move.

Zhilev stepped back into the crypt, shut the door and looked at the device on the table, now completely exposed, the wood discarded. He considered his next action. Whatever it was going to be, it needed to be immediate. It might already be too late, but soldiers do not think like that. The wisdom in a developing situation is to strike quickly. To hesitate could be to lose. The decision he had to make was about the bomb. There was a panic sequence on the three arming buttons. Hitting them in one direction set the device to fifteen minutes, and then each hit of the last button reduced it by a further five minutes. Three strikes, five minutes each, and it detonated immediately. His hand hovered over the buttons, the pressure mounting to make a decision. Was fifteen minutes enough time to get away? From here on he would be doing everything at the sprint. If he could get through the man standing outside, he could get out of the city in less than five minutes. If he could grab a car, any one in the street, wrench the driver out and drive like the devil, he could get five miles away in ten minutes if he drove over pavements, through traffic lights and through people if they got in his way.

Zhilev did not waste another second thinking about it and hit the buttons in sequence. The device bleeped twice indicating acceptance of the change. Zhilev snapped up the Uzi, checked the safety was off, held it firmly in one hand and gripped the door knob with the other.

Stratton held the pistol in two hands and moved to one side, away from the position his enemy had last seen him in, and started to walk slowly forward. His enemy had three options: to charge out and fight, or stay inside and wait for Stratton to come in and get him. The third option did not bear thinking about and that was the man committing suicide and taking everyone with him.

Stratton sensed movement behind him but dared not turn to look in case Zhilev came out at that precise moment. It sounded like running. He concealed his gun under his jacket in case it was more soldiers, and he was right. A police officer ran past, closely followed by another. As the third and last officer passed him, Stratton saw the door to the crypt open and Zhilev emerge at the charge, a weapon in his hands. The following seconds were a mass of noise and confusion and seemed to last far longer than they really had.

Machine-gun fire filled the tunnel as Zhilev unleashed a hail of bullets in short, accurate bursts. The copper-coated lead rounds hammered into the first officer's flak jacket before tearing open his throat. His colleague close behind him took a round in the arm before two smacked into his head killing him instantly. Stratton brought his gun up, but the third officer sidestepped in front of him while fumbling with his own sub-machine gun, overwhelmed by the shock of the surprise onslaught. Stratton fired between the falling bodies and a bullet slammed into Zhilev's side. But the Russian was in full fury and only death would stop him now. His next burst travelled up the third officer's body, from his crotch, across his flak jacket and into his face, sending him backwards into Stratton. They fell back together, Stratton's head one side of the officer, his gun the other. The way was clear for a shot but Stratton was falling. As another burst from Zhilev went wide and hit the wall and ceiling in front of Stratton, something hammered into Stratton's chest with horrifying force and immediately began to burn. Stratton fired repeatedly until he hit the ground on his back, the weight of the officer knocking the wind completely out of him. But as he fell his bullets ripped into Zhilev – one of his kneecaps flew off, his left hip exploded as the bullet bounced off the bone, a round penetrated his stomach, another his chest, two struck the wall behind him, and the last three shattered Zhilev's jaw, drilled through his neck and ripped a piece of the side of his head away.

Zhilev stood for a moment in a daze, the world spinning, his vision blurred, images from his life that he had not remembered for years flicking in front of him like an erratic slide show. The only conscious thought he had, which lasted less than a second before the lights went out, was that it was over. The Uzi clattered across the stone floor, and Zhilev dropped back in front of the doorway to the crypt, hitting the ground like a felled oak.

Stratton released the gun to pull himself out from under the police officer's body with what felt like all the strength he had left. He took a deep breath before trying to sit up and the pain, like a bolt of electricity, seemed to ignite his entire chest and forced him to lie back. He reached a hand under his jacket and felt around his body, his mind unable to pinpoint the pain, and withdrew it to find it wet with blood. He had been hit by a bullet, a ricochet off the wall. He started to feel giddy and fought to control his mind. This was not the time to go unconscious. The will to live and win remained iron in him and the fight was not yet over. While the bomb remained unexploded there was a chance left, be it a desperate one, but that was what this fight had come down to. He knew Zhilev had set the bomb's timer to detonate. Why else had he made his last desperate charge? The problem was Stratton did not feel he had the strength to carry on.

He looked towards the sound of moaning nearby and saw a Palestinian woman on the ground holding her bleeding arm, a dead trader beside her.

Stratton rolled carefully over, every inch of effort causing a searing pain, and got on to all fours. He reached for a table and, calculating each move and preparing himself for the sting, pulled his feet under him and pushed upwards. He immediately became dizzy and gripped the table to steady himself. It was obvious he was not going to stay upright without support and quickly planned a route to the entrance of the crypt using the line of traders' tables. He heard more running behind him but this time the boots slid to a halt. Stratton looked over his shoulder to see soldiers taking cover in doorways or on their bellies where the walkway curved out of sight, their weapons pointed at him. He ignored them and pressed on. He did not have a gun and hoped they would at least try to identify his role in the carnage before they shot him.

He reached the last table and considered the gap across the walkway to the crypt entrance. It was only a couple of yards but seemed a long way without help, and so he took a moment to gather himself before he made what was going to be a very painful effort.

Abed had heard the gunfire from outside an old antique shop not far away and had ducked inside after seeing several soldiers running up the walkway towards him. They ran past the entrance and he remained hidden, concerned about the sudden increase in police and military activity in the old city. As the echo of gunfire subsided, he cautiously looked out of the front door and could see a man lying on the ground. He could not be sure, but it looked like the big Russian, and he was not moving.

Abed checked in the opposite direction where traders and shoppers were slowly emerging from shops and doorways, none daring to come any closer, and thought about getting away before the place was crawling with soldiers when he saw a white man casually making his way through them and heading in Abed's direction.

Before the man reached the shop, Abed ducked back inside and watched him through the dirty window as he passed by. He looked dignified, like a professor, and he was not young.

Abed went to the door and watched the man approach the scene of the shooting.

Stratton heard footsteps coming along the walkway on his right this time, but they were unhurried and sounded like only one pair. He looked up to find Gabriel walking towards him.

Gabriel stopped beside him and took a long look at the carnage. 'My God,' he mumbled. His eyes finally fell on Zhilev. 'Is that him?'

'Yes,' Stratton said weakly.

'And the bomb?'

'Inside there, I think. Your number seven.'

Gabriel looked at the writing above the door and nodded. 'That's what I saw,' he said. Gabriel had not noticed Stratton's condition at first and showed immediate concern when he realised how much pain he was in. 'Are you okay?'

Stratton took a short breath and held it while a bolt of fire surged through him. His hands trembled on the table until he brought it under control. 'Do I have a hole in my back?' he asked.

'What?' Gabriel said, as if he had not heard correctly.

'Is there a hole in my back?'

Gabriel stifled his shock and moved behind Stratton to take a look. 'I don't see any blood.'

'Give me a hand,' Stratton said, letting go of the table to grab Gabriel's shoulder. They shuffled across the walkway and then, unable to stand the pain any more, Stratton dropped to his knees and fell with his back against the wall beside the entrance to the crypt. The fall was excruciating and he almost lost consciousness. He groaned as he fought the urge to cry out, his breathing growing shorter and more rapid, and then the pain slowly became more manageable once again and he looked around.

Soldiers were making their way carefully forward along all three walkways towards them.

'Tell them there's a bomb and to stay back,' Stratton said.

Gabriel looked at the soldiers and then back at Stratton.

'Why?'

'Tell them,' Stratton said as forcefully as he could.

'What difference does it make? They're all going to die anyway.'

Stratton looked at him coldly. 'Do what I said.'

Gabriel could not see the point, but faced the walkways anyway, suddenly unsure how to say what was really not a difficult thing to communicate.

'There's a bomb,' he said, nowhere near loud enough for them to hear. He could not remember the last time he had raised his voice and it felt awkward. He cupped his hands over his mouth. 'There's a bomb,' he said louder. 'Stay back . . . A bomb,' he repeated along all three walkways. 'Stay back.'

The soldiers who understood English relayed the message to those who did not or could not hear. They were well experienced with bombs and quickly moved to more solid cover while an officer and a radio operator in the centre walkway moved back until they were out of view.

'What was the point of that? It's going to explode and kill everyone for miles.'

'Gabriel,' Stratton said. 'Can you see the bomb? Inside.'

Gabriel walked to the door of the crypt, grimaced at the sight of Zhilev's bloody corpse, and stepped over him to lean inside. 'It's on the table.'

'How's it look?' Stratton asked. 'Any sign of life?'

Stratton did not know what to expect but any information would be welcome at this stage.

Gabriel stepped inside the small, dank, dark room, the stone walls and domed ceiling darkened by centuries of candles and oil lamps. The only furnishings were an icon and crucifix on one wall, a chair and a small table with a dull metal sphere on it, slightly oblong, similar to a rugby ball but a little bigger. He stepped to the table and leaned over it to see the control panel. There were no flashing lights, dials, or digital countdown clock. The only indication of life was the grey LED bar which Gabriel had to lean closer to see. A thin black line was passing slowly along it from left to right.

He stepped back through the door and into the walkway.

'It appears to be doing something,' Gabriel said.

That's all Stratton needed to hear. There was nothing more for it but the final Neanderthal phase of the operation. 'You need to break it open,' he said.

'Break it open?'

'Yes.'

Gabriel looked confused. 'Why? It's going to explode. We're all going to die anyway.'

'I want you to break it open and remove the plutonium core.'

Gabriel was dumbfounded. 'But there's no point,' he said.

'Now you listen to me,' Stratton said, anger creeping into his strained voice. 'I don't give a damn what you thought you saw in your daydream. I had a daydream too and it was me, walking out of here and going home, and it wasn't as a ghost. That atom bomb is little more than a ball of plutonium surrounded by explosive. The explosive sets off the nuclear chain reaction. The device is designed not to initiate by accident or tampering. Its most important features are its safety protocols. Now I don't know for certain, but it seems to me you could break it open and remove the plutonium without detonating it. You have more chance of stopping it blowing than you do of setting it off.' Stratton stopped to deal with a bout of intense pain and concentrated on Zhilev's Uzi on the ground beside him. When the pain reduced, he picked up the Uzi and pointed the barrel at Gabriel.

'If you don't I'm going to upset your plans of dying in a nuclear blast by shooting you through the fucking heart, right now.'

Gabriel looked at the weapon in Stratton's hand, unaware the magazine was spent.

'Which is it going to be?' Stratton said. 'If I have to blow you away, I'll go and do it myself.'

Gabriel believed the bastard would do it too. But he was unfazed. He did not believe Stratton could save the day and did believe that his viewing had been accurate. He was strangely serene by the time he had walked to the old city. All the fears and depressions of the past few weeks had melted away as he came to terms with his destiny. The one beautiful thing that had come out of it was that he finally believed in himself and it felt good. He was not afraid of death now, and therefore Stratton's threat was meaningless to him. He even had the courage to smile.

Stratton could see the change in the man and the genuine contempt in his eyes for Stratton and his gun. His threat to try and defuse the bomb himself was a bluff. He would try, but he did not think he would have the strength to succeed. He maintained his determined gaze, but he felt his control of Gabriel slip away.

'What difference does it make?' Gabriel finally said.

'Tell you what, Stratton. Since it's your last wish, I'll grant you it, but you have to do something for me in return.'

'What's that?'

'Pray to God and ask him for forgiveness for all you've done in your life. I don't know what that is, but I'm damn sure a lot of it didn't please him any.'

Gabriel stepped into the crypt.

Stratton dropped the Uzi, unable to hold it any longer, and contemplated Gabriel's words. The man had a point, but asking God for forgiveness now, just before he was likely to die, seemed to him like the actions of a creep. Apologising for a wrongdoing when all other options had gone was not a real apology in his eyes. Apologise when you don't need to and it means something.

Stratton took a shallow breath and felt dizzy. He was not getting enough oxygen. He found the bullet hole in his shirt and, biting on the pain, tore it open to reveal the hole in his chest. The blood bubbling out of it with every exhale of breath was frothy. The only good news about a bullet through the chest was that there were no major organs or arteries in front of or behind the lungs, only ribs and muscle. Bleeding to death would be unlikely and as long as one lung was working properly, life was sustainable. The bad news was that the lung could collapse and come to rest against the heart causing it to spasm and stop beating. He could lie on his side but that guaranteed nothing. The only way to ensure survival until he could get to a hospital and be patched up was to re-inflate the lung.

Stratton looked around on the ground for anything he might be able to use and saw a photograph. His eyes moved on and found another that he could not ignore. It was a picture of Zhilev and his brother, standing in the snow, arms around each other and smiling broadly. A stab of pain reminded him of his immediate needs and he disconnected from the photo and picked up a small piece of plastic wrapping beside it. As he took a breath, the frothy blood immediately around the hole was sucked back inside. He placed the plastic over the bloody hole to seal it. It did not matter how filthy it was since dying of infection was a low priority. But placing the plastic over the hole was not enough. That only blocked it; he needed to get air back into the deflating lung and that required a valve. He noticed a piece of masking tape on the side of the Uzi with the owner's name and number on it. Using the tape, he stuck the piece of plastic to his chest, the tape placed above the hole so that the plastic flapped down over it. As he breathed in, the plastic blocked the hole, and as he exhaled, it allowed some of the air in the chest cavity to escape. With each breath, the lung would eventually inflate again. He dropped his hands to the ground, the effort exhausting him. It was all now up to Gabriel.

Gabriel stood inside the crypt looking at the device that appeared every bit as evil as it was. He wondered what kind of sick mind had invented such a weapon, and what even sicker one would use it. Zhilev had such a mind, but he had paid the price.

Gabriel ran a hand over it. The dull metal was

cold. For some reason he had expected it to be hot, such was the stigma of the weapon. On reflection, cold suited it better. The worst killers were always cold.

He rolled it over carefully and was then amused at his own stupidity. He had come to break it open and here he was treating it with reverence, a forgivable reaction perhaps for a thing of such power.

He picked it up, surprised to find it heavier than it looked, and rolled it over in his hands searching for an obvious way of opening it, but there did not appear to be one. It was made of two semi-spheres riveted together. After a thorough inspection Gabriel could not see any way into the device other than penetrating the seam and prising it apart.

He looked around for a tool of some kind and saw a large nail on the floor. As he bent down to pick it up, he found a stone under the table that looked like it might serve as a hammer. It fitted nicely in his hand and he got up, positioned the nail on the seam and tapped the nail head gently as a test. It made a small dent in the seam. He tapped it harder and the nail went in a few millimetres. Encouraged by his success he moved the nail along a couple of millimetres and repeated the process, this time prising the edge of the seam up a little by levering on the nail. Another puncture and he paused to inspect his work. To go around the entire seam would take a long time. What he needed was something bigger to jam into it and lever it apart. He was suddenly amused again, this time at the enthusiasm with which he was going about his task. He was reminded of his younger days when he used to enjoy helping his father fix his car in their garage. He always liked to tackle the simple yet awkward jobs, such as undoing the nut that didn't want to budge, or attaching the hose that did not appear long enough, but since it had come off, it had to go back on.

As he scanned the dusty floor without luck, he moved his search to the walls, and his eyes came to rest on the metal crucifix on the wall beside the icon of the Madonna. He took it off its nail and inspected it, testing it for strength. It was made of brass and felt sturdy enough. God was going to help out after all, he mused.

Gabriel jammed the bottom of the crucifix into the small gap he had made with the nail and pushed down on it, but it would not penetrate. He picked up the stone, turned it in his palm until it was snug and raised it up. 'Forgive me, oh Lord,' he said and brought it down heavily on top of the crucifix. It plunged into the sphere and Gabriel wiggled it around until he could pull it out easily. A thick, white, flaky substance oozed from the tear and crumbled on to the desk. Gabriel did not know for sure what it was, but since Stratton had described the device as explosive material surrounding a plutonium core he suspected it must be the explosive charge itself. He worked the crucifix along the seam, bending it back and forth, gradually widening the gap until the two halves suddenly popped apart. Both semi-spheres were filled with the white substance which surrounded the core, a sponge-like material no bigger than a tennis ball. He put down the crucifix and pulled at it. The surface broke apart easily to expose another sphere the size of a golf ball made of a dull silver metal. He pulled it out and held it in his hand and only then did it occur to him it was the radio-active nucleus, the plutonium. Gabriel realised he had effectively done what Stratton had asked of him. He had neutralised the device. But that could not be.

His mind raced over the images he had seen regarding his own destruction and began to wonder if they had been wrong. But how, since the other viewings had proven to be so accurate? To describe Zhilev well enough for anyone else to finger him in a line up would have been impossible, but after seeing the giant on the floor, he knew instantly it was the beast he had been frightened of all these weeks. Now it would appear he had been wrong about the explosion, but he still could not believe it.

Gabriel regarded the device on the table long and thoughtfully, the two pieces filled with the white substance, the crucifix and stone beside it, and realised he had seen the exact image before. He looked at the walls of the room, the icon, chair, the domed ceiling, all as he had seen it. As he looked back down at the bomb he saw a flash and heard the beginning of a loud explosion and then silence, and his heart leaped into his throat. It was not déjà vu. It was his viewing. He had not been wrong after all.

The device gave a single, short beep.

The explosion was thunderous and blew the doors clean off the crypt walls and into the walkway.

Stratton was close to the entrance and only survived because he was not in the direct line of the blast. It was like standing beside the muzzle of a huge cannon as it went off. The shockwave threw him over and the explosion rocked his brain. The entire walkway shuddered and went black as pieces of stone and mortar fell from the ceilings. The traders' tables directly in front of the crypt were shredded and blown away, the lighter debris flying out of the end of the tunnel like feathers from a burst cushion, followed by bellowing smoke. It seemed as if the ancient building complex would cave in. However, having survived so many wars over so many centuries it seemed it was not about to crumble now, as if Christ and Allah had agreed to protect their interests. The shaking quickly subsided and the buildings remained intact.

Stratton lay on the ground with his hands over his head, his ears ringing and mind spinning, but conscious enough to ask himself if his time had finally come. As he opened his eyes, blinking rapidly to clear the grit from them, he could see a distant light penetrating the thick dust.

He eased himself back up into the sitting position and coughed painfully, surrounded by smoke. The walkways were in near darkness, the dead neon lights dangling from their wires, making the daylight at the ends of the three tunnels contrastingly bright.

His recollection of the previous few minutes began to reassemble and he suddenly thought of Gabriel. There was no point even considering the possibilities of him surviving.

Stratton spat dirt from his mouth and thought about checking the plastic over the hole in his chest to see if it had fallen off but right then he did not

care. His prediction of walking away from this operation alive, which was nothing more psychic than a
wish, looked as if it might come true after all. He
considered actually attempting to walk but quickly
decided against it. Why bother, he thought? The place
would be crawling with troops in a moment, and he
would be carried off on a stretcher to a hospital. His
thoughts went back to Gabriel and he felt sorry for
the old guy. He realised he had to go into the crypt
to check, just in case. Stranger things had happened,
although he did not expect to find anything.

He gathered himself and prepared for the pain.
Anger was always a good tool at times like this, like
the final charge into the jaws of death, and, without
wasting another second, he gritted his teeth and rolled
on to his hands and knees. The pain was almost
unbearable and for a moment he could not pull in
a breath, then his diaphragm kicked in and his lungs
took in the air stabbing him once again. He crawled
up the wall, got to his feet and shuffled to the hole
where the crypt doors once hung.

He expected it to be dark inside but a shaft of
light beamed in through a hole in the roof where
there was once a dome. The walls were scorched and
anything that had not been made of stone had disin-
tegrated, including Gabriel, except for one of his
shoes. He started to feel giddy and was about to turn
around and rest his back against the wall when he
saw something on the floor in the middle of the
room. He slid down the wall until he was sitting on
the step then leaned forward on to his hands and
reached out. He picked up the small metal sphere,

rested back against the wall and inspected his find. It had to be the plutonium core – Pu 239, if the paper he had read on the likely device was accurate. If it was any higher than 239 he would suffer radiation poisoning and probably die, even if he had not touched it. But 239 was safe, a piece of paper was enough to protect from the rays.

He could hear footsteps approaching, mingled with the ringing in his ears, and he put the plutonium in his pocket.

A man stopped in front of him. The trousers were not that of a soldier's and Stratton looked up to see it was Abed.

Abed crouched to look at the Englishman who appeared to be in a bad way, but he could judge his condition more accurately by looking into his eyes. They were as bright and determined as before and Abed knew this man was not so near to death.

'You'd . . . better get away from here,' Stratton said, finding the breath to speak. 'This . . . place will . . . soon be crawling with soldiers.'

'It's already too late for that,' Abed said.

Abed had wanted to leave soon after he saw the older man help Stratton to the floor, but the arrival of several soldiers at the other end of the walkway had made the prospect a risky one. He decided to wait until the place had become busier; despite the fact that would mean cordons and more police and soldiers, it would also mean more Palestinians converging to see what had happened, and he could say he was just another shopper caught up in the incident.

But after the explosion that had brought down most of the shelves in the shop on top of him, he made his way to the doorway to take a look and as the dust cleared saw Stratton lying on the ground with his hands around his head. After watching him struggle to sit in the doorway of the crypt, he felt compelled to go to the man and see if there was anything he could do for him. It was the Arab way.

'You will live, *habibi*,' Abed said, using the phrase of friendship.

'That's the plan for now,' Stratton said. 'Get out of here.'

'When I have helped you,' Abed said, opening Stratton's jacket enough to see the blood on his torn shirt and the wound beneath it. 'We must get you to a hospital.'

'There'll be plenty . . . of people here for that, soon enough.'

'Look at it this way. By helping you out of the city, I could be helping myself.'

Stratton eyed him with a slight smile. 'Maybe that would work . . . Okay. Let's give it a go.'

Abed nodded and stooped to help Stratton up, when they both heard footsteps crunching on the debris and looked around.

Raz was standing a few yards away with a pistol in his hand levelled at them.

'You're not going anywhere,' Raz said, calmly and assuredly.

'I'm just a tourist,' Abed said, standing up. He knew immediately that the older man in civilian clothes had to be Israeli police or military intelligence. 'I was in a shop just down there when the explosion happened and I came to see if this man—'

'Your name is Abed Abu Omar,' Raz interrupted. 'You're from Gaza, and you are a terrorist.'

Abed could hardly believe what the man had said. His dreams of freedom immediately evaporated and were replaced by the image of a prison cell, with him inside, rotting in a corner.

The urge to run, no matter what the danger, took a grip of him.

Raz had been several streets away when he heard the shooting and had little doubt it was something to do with Stratton and his urgent dash into the city. As he hurried to where the sound had come from, the explosion was a shock that filled his mind with visions from so many bomb blasts he had been to in his city. As he broke into a run, in his mind he could already see the blood, severed limbs and struggling wounded. He arrived on the scene to see Stratton lying in the dust, and, again, he felt a mixture of anger and concern at the Englishman's presence in his country which had somehow led to the explosion. But when he saw the man who was talking to him, every other thought left his head, brushed aside by the incredible possibility that it was Abed, his son. Only when Abed turned to look at him was he certain. His gun was already in his hand from when he first heard the shooting, and a part of him was thrown into confusion when Abed saw it aimed at him. Raz wanted to lower it, but he took a firm grip on himself and checked his resolve, knowing what he had to do.

'Your presence here would suggest you have something to do with this,' Raz said, accusingly.

Denying his involvement in the explosion was pointless. Abed was a wanted man anyway, and that was that. He could feel the walls closing in on him and hear the door to his cell clanging shut, filling him with dread.

'I'm not going anywhere with you,' Abed said. 'You will have to shoot me.'

'If that's what you want, I will oblige you,' Raz said, hearing the words come from his mouth, but not believing he had said them. He had already accepted Abed's untimely death since learning of his connection with the Islamic Jihad, he just never dreamed he would be the one to pull the trigger. His son had become an enemy of the worst possible kind, and the need to eradicate him was greater than any bond of blood between them. Alive in a prison was better than death, but Abed was not going to accept that, and Raz knew he would be haunted for the rest of his life if he killed him. He had brought Abed into this world and then left him to live a vile existence in a shanty town, short of food and basic amenities, like an animal. And yet he had grown into a handsome, intelligent and good man, until he was given no choice but to turn against his own sense of right and become a terrorist. Everything about him was Raz's creation and responsibility, and every pain and hardship Abed had endured was because of him. This was the final injustice, for both of them.

'Why don't you pull the trigger?' Abed said, arrogantly. 'Don't you believe I would rather die than let you take me? After so many of us have killed ourselves? Death is not just a weapon for us, it is our only escape from you. I supposed it would ease your conscience if I went to jail instead. Well, I have lived in one of your jails all my life, surrounded by a wall of hate and death in every direction, and always in fear of my jailers' visits to beat and torment me. Even if you threatened to send me back to Gaza, I would rather die. So pull the trigger. Please.'

Raz could only stare at him. He wanted to tell the young man that he not only believed him, he also understood. For in many ways, he had lived the pain with his son.

'What are you waiting for?' Abed asked, raising his voice. 'Are you afraid? Let me make it easy for you.'

Abed took a step towards Raz who tightened his grip on the gun.

'Wait,' Stratton said. 'Wait,' he repeated, then broke into a painful cough.

Abed paused to look down at Stratton who was raising a hand as if asking them to hold on while he got through his choking session.

'He . . . he works for us,' Stratton finally said after taking a deep breath.

Raz was initially thrown by the revelation, but then it explained some recent events. The two of them being here together did certainly raise a question, and Stratton was no doubt a member of MI6. He would certainly not be trying to save Abed's life otherwise, who was now obviously the man seen running from the hotel with Stratton.

'He works for British intelligence?' Raz asked.

'Yes. We need him,' Stratton said.

Raz suspected the last comment, but then why else was Stratton trying to help Abed? He could not have known him for very long. In fact, if it was Abed who Stratton had met in Ramallah the night before, it would have been for the first time. That was also why there was no report of Stratton leaving the town, because he never went through any of the checkpoints. He couldn't because he was with Abed who could not take the risk. No doubt they went through the old quarry. Shin Bet deliberately left that area unguarded for the times when they needed to monitor specific characters moving through it so that they could mount surveillance operations from a solid start point inside Ramallah, or entering Jerusalem. The only reason Stratton could possibly be helping Abed was loyalty. It was that warped British sense of fair play; even though Abed was a wanted terrorist, he was in the old city helping Stratton and therefore did not deserve to be captured. He would be fair game only when he was off and running again.

'Don't waste your breath,' Abed said to Stratton. 'You don't know his kind. He wants to take me away and interrogate me, for weeks if necessary, until they have every piece of information they can get out of me, and then, if I survive, they'll toss me into a stone room and leave me there until I can find a way to kill myself. He will kill me. He just needs a little help.'

Abed took another step towards Raz.

'Stand still,' Raz commanded. But Abed did not obey him.

Raz stepped back. 'Stand still, I said,' he shouted, but Abed ignored him, his expression calm, his hands moving out from his side ready for the shot that he hoped would kill him.

'I've saved your life too many times to want to kill you now,' Raz said, standing firm, the gun levelled at Abed's heart.

Abed did not understand, and although the comment slowed him, he took another step closer to Raz, who was now within reach of him.

'I am your father,' Raz said.

Abed froze.

Stratton was equally stunned.

Raz stared at Abed, shaking with the effort to control his finger on the trigger, desperate not to have to pull it. 'Do you remember the time you were hit by a car leaving your university?' Raz said. 'You thought you had damaged your hip so badly you would have a limp. Did you ever wonder why you received better care than all the other patients in your ward?'

Abed remembered it well, but he never thought he had a mysterious benefactor.

'And during the many incursions into Rafah, the times you were released while others were taken away. You were on a list of people not to be harmed. Did your mother ever tell you where the money came from each month while you were growing up? And do you remember that day in your metal shop, when you were shot at by the soldier who had threatened one day to kill you? The last shot you heard came from the building beside you. That shot killed the soldier, fired by me.'

Abed was rocked to his very foundations, even more so than the night his mother revealed his father was an Israeli. The shock was tenfold now that he was facing the man he had thought about all his life and never believed he would ever see.

Raz was no longer looking at Abed but at the ground in front of him, his eyes seeing only his own youth and remembering Abed as a baby in his arms in a derelict building in Rafah camp. He lowered the gun and his arm hung limply by his side.

Raz finally looked up and the two men stared at each other, unable to do or say anything.

Abed had heard the anguish and sincerity in Raz's voice and it had touched something inside of him. The man he had hated with all his heart only seconds ago had disappeared but he could not understand who had been left in his place. Abed could not reach out and touch him, nor could he back away. He could not hate him, nor could he embrace him. He did not feel love of any kind, but neither did he feel fear any more. Time and space had momentarily stopped for both men.

The sound of running snapped them out of their trances and Raz glanced over his shoulder to see several troops approaching. He took his identification badge from his pocket, raised it for them to see and shouted something in Hebrew.

The soldiers stopped and did not come any further.

Raz looked at his son, then over at Stratton.

'What happened here today?' Raz asked Stratton.

Stratton could not tell Raz the whole truth, not about the atom bomb, but if Raz was going to let

Abed go he needed to be able to tell his bosses why. Abed was on videotape, and there were witnesses to Raz conversing with a young Arab at the scene that would need explaining if the Arab was suddenly gone.

'This man,' Stratton said, indicating the dead Russian. 'His name is Zhilev. He's former Russian Spetsnaz. Stockton's in there . . . what's left of him. If Zhilev had succeeded with his plan, you, me and a lot of other people, we would all be dead. Abed played a major role in preventing that.'

Raz could only guess at what Stratton was trying to tell him and it did not sound encouraging, but that was not the point of the Englishman's revelation. He was offering Raz information that would help him let Abed go.

Raz put his gun into his pocket. 'Since you work for MI6, you are a guest in this country. It sounds like I must thank you,' he said to Abed. 'One word of advice before you go . . . Never come back.'

They held each other's gaze for a moment longer, then Abed slowly stepped towards Raz to move past him.

'I'm sorry about your mother,' Raz said softly.

Abed paused alongside his father.

'I was by her side yesterday,' Raz said. 'She went peacefully. I told her I was sorry and that I always loved her.'

Abed could feel a lifetime of emotion churn inside of him, all too much for him to digest. This man had represented everything that was vile, but he could see none of that now. He was his father. He had given him his life, and had now done so again. He must have felt something for his mother to have been by her side when she died. He was saying sorry to Abed and to his mother in the only way he could, and Abed could not hate him any more.

The tension eased from Abed's eyes and as he walked away, Raz turned to watch him go, past the soldiers and down the walkway until he rounded the corner out of sight.

Raz looked back at Stratton, who was watching him, and wondered what the man was thinking.

'Will you report this?' Raz asked, without making it sound like a plea or request.

'Report what?'

Raz believed him. He turned and shouted something to the soldiers and they started to move in.

'We'd better get you to a hospital,' Raz said. 'You don't look so good.'

'To tell you the truth, I feel like shit,' Stratton said.

'And then we'll talk and maybe you can tell me what happened on my patch.'

'Absolutely,' Stratton said.

Raz knew Stratton would fabricate enough of a story to explain Abed's release, but perhaps they could also do some dealing. That was the true fun of the intelligence world. It was like a marketplace where things were bought and sold and exchanged like anything else.

Raz looked back to see if Abed was perhaps still there, but he was not, and he knew he would never see or hear from his son again.

★ ★ ★

Sumners sat behind a desk in his tiny office on the tenth floor of MI6 headquarters on the south side of the Thames, a stone's throw from Vauxhall Bridge. The one window overlooked the river and was some consolation for the size of the room, which was, in fact, not exceptionally small for the building. His boss's office, on the floor above, was only marginally larger and did not have a view. The room was clean, tidy and as lacklustre as one might expect for a civil servant's office.

Chalmers walked in without knocking, placed a file on Sumners' desk and left without either men saying anything, which was quite normal. On the surface, life in the firm hadn't changed for Sumners. From a psychological point of view, he had dealt with his situation back in Israel and succeeded in putting it behind him. Two months had passed since that horrible day on board the C130 on the tarmac of Tel Aviv's Ben Gurion airport but, as time went by, he thought about it less and less. Even the presence of Chalmers and his boss evoked few memories of that day, other than perhaps the slightest of fleeting images. It was simple enough for a man like Sumners to put it out of his mind. He had taken the logical approach and reasoned that he was never going to get another crack at running a field operation, and it was wise to believe so for the healing process to take effect. To that end he re-accepted his long-time role as a desk officer – and a damned good one at that – and continued to exert the confidence and authority he had enjoyed before the incident, which was considerable. A handful of people in the building might have had an inkling of what had taken place, but the majority would not. If it had been a major scene and Sumners had lost control and thrown a wobbly then perhaps that much of the story might have got out. But since it was a top-secret operation, explaining Sumners' little moment would require far more detail than would be deemed acceptable. Sumners was as aware of that as anyone and it aided his rehabilitation.

There was a knock and Sumners asked the caller in without looking up from his computer monitor until the door opened, whereupon he instantly stopped what he was doing and stared at his visitor. There was, of course, one person who would always remind Sumners of his folly, and as he walked into the room the memory of that day, as well as the intense embarrassment and implications of his character flaws, came flooding back.

Stratton looked remarkably well, which was not a surprise since he had not been involved with work since Jerusalem save for a couple of debriefs where the debriefers came to him. After two days in Israel he flew home, and a week later was walking around looking normal. In less than a month he went on his first long jog and a week after that his first workout in the gym. A Navy surgeon had told him that he could expect to be barred from diving but that would depend on how well his lung healed, and in the same sentence he suggested an operational necessity might supersede such a barring unless he was drastically impaired. He had spent much of his time off kicking back in the South of France, enjoying the quiet off-season, eating well, exercising and catching up on his reading. He should have been feeling depressed considering his mindset throughout the operation and the months prior to it, but the explosion and the injury had been a kind of cleansing. For reasons he could not precisely put a finger on, Stratton felt better than he had for a long time and the nearest explanation he could find was that he was more in control. Walking into the MI6 headquarters only confirmed the feeling. No one he passed in the labyrinth of corridors knew him, although there was a glance and a subtle nod from two senior-looking suits as he walked through the high-security entrance that suggested they knew who he was and approved of him. A few months prior, had he walked into Sumners' office, much as he hated it he would have felt as if he had his cap in his hand. Now he felt strangely superior. He was not, and he didn't approve of it because it was far too egotistical for his liking, but nevertheless that's how he felt and he could not help it.

'Stratton. To what do I owe the pleasure?' Sumners asked, looking as businesslike as always and masking any animosity he had towards his subaltern.

'I came by to drop off some things,' Stratton said as he placed his MI6 ID, credit card and some receipts on Sumners' desk.

Sumners looked at the ID and then at Stratton, wondering if there was more to this than met the eye. He had wanted to ask for them back but refrained for a number of reasons. First and foremost, he did not want to talk to or even see Stratton again, even though he knew it was unlikely such a wish would be granted, he felt that the longer he could delay such an encounter the better. Another reason was that asking for the return of the ID might have suggested he was cancelling Stratton's secondment and look like a vengeful act to those in the know, namely his boss, which would have been augmented if Stratton was suddenly required for something and it was discovered he was no longer on the assignment-standby list. Stratton was the one aspect of Sumners' rehabilitation that he had no control over. He could only pray the man did not recover or lost interest in the job. But that was obviously too much to hope and his sudden presence proved it, for here he was, standing in front of him in his office, his hands in the pockets of his grubby, old leather jacket and looking at him in his usual expressionless, cold manner as if nothing had happened between them. The only positive thing that Sumners could think of regarding the visit was that Stratton had come to quit.

'How are you feeling?' Sumners asked, chirpier at the thought that this might well be a farewell visit. It was also possible it was a subtle move by Stratton to announce his fitness, declaring himself ready to return to work, and wanting Sumners to ask him to pick up the ID and await a call. Sumners put that thought aside because it did not give him any pleasure to contemplate.

'I'm fine. Feeling better than ever. First good rest I've had in years.'

Sumners groaned inwardly as Stratton began to sound very much like someone who was looking forward to returning to work. 'You spoken to anyone else?' he asked.

'Chalmers, outside,' Stratton said, as he went to the window and looked down on to the river. 'He was surprisingly chatty. I still think he's a walking computer but he sounded quite human just now.'

Sumners wasn't sure about Stratton's mood. He sounded chipper enough all right, but that really meant nothing. 'You had a post-op report?' he asked, knowing Stratton had not. Stratton was entitled to a closing summary of the operation but Sumners' only reason for offering it was a personal interest in one major aspect of it.

'No. Any fallout?' Stratton asked.

Sumners sat back and exhaled deeply as he thought the summary through. Talking operations was his favourite pastime and he could do it with anyone, even Stratton. 'The Russians have been put under immense pressure from Downing Street to reveal the whereabouts of their sabotage hides in Britain. Washington has been doing the same regarding the hides in the US. The Russians have unsurprisingly refused to give the locations but then came back with a promise to remove the dangerous contents, a damned stupid suggestion that has created an enormous furore. How on earth they expected anyone to agree that they be allowed to transport nuclear and biological weapons across sovereign states without the assistance or even knowledge of the home government, I don't know. Anyway, that's where we're at at the moment, but Russia is in an untenable position and will have to concede something, and soon.

Interestingly, Israel has also brought some pressure to bear on the subject. Question is, how did they know about the nuclear device?' Sumners stared at Stratton, watching for his response to the last comment, which was the subject of his greater interest.

Stratton glanced over his shoulder at Sumners, giving nothing away. 'Smart cookies, those Israelis,' he said. Stratton had handed over the plutonium to Chalmers who met him at the trauma unit of Jerusalem's Ein Karem Hadassah hospital on his arrival, leaving no real evidence among the debris that followed the explosion in the old city. It was possible their forensic experts could have put something together that might have suggested it was a nuclear device, but without the plutonium it was a tough one to prove. Stratton had no guilt about bartering Abed's safety with a clue about the seriousness of the event the young Palestinian had helped avoid. It was only fair. Besides, he could not see what harm there was in Israel supporting the removal of Russian nuclear bombs from secret arsenals around the world. Sumners would no doubt have a good reason against it, but Stratton did not care to hear it.

'What happened to Abed?' Stratton asked, steering the conversation away from the nuclear device.

It made Sumners even more suspicious that Stratton had something to do with the Israeli interference. If he could find out how, he could close the door on Stratton in an instant, but short of the man admitting it himself, it was unlikely Sumners could prove such a thing. Manachem Raz sure as hell would not be of any help. Sumners decided to table it for now but he would never forget.

'We brought the Palestinian back here where he co-operated in a detailed debrief of the tanker operation. Because of that, and the assistance he gave you in locating Zhilev, he was placed in a protection programme. He's currently living in Glasgow under a new name and working as a bartender with class-one restrictions.'

A class-one restriction meant Abed could not change accommodation or employment without permission, or travel more than twenty-five miles from his address. Reading between the lines, Stratton assumed they were not finished with Abed yet and that he was still employable. Stratton got the feeling, during their short time together, that Abed wanted to be free from it all. The young man had a long way to go before that would be the case, if he ever made it at all. But it was out of Stratton's hands. He could do nothing more for the man and he put him out of his thoughts.

'Good . . . Well,' Stratton said, bringing his visit to a close as he stepped from the window to the door. 'I'm gonna head out. I lost most of the cash advance. Don't know if it was in the blast, the hospital, or the hotel.'

'Under the circumstances I'm sure it will be overlooked,' Sumners said. He was being deliberately charitable in case Stratton should make the leap he hoped was coming.

Stratton nodded and opened the door. 'See ya,' he said as he started to head out, but it was not enough for Sumners. He wanted to know what Stratton wanted to do about his MI career.

'Stratton?'

Stratton stopped in the open doorway and looked back at Sumners.

Sumners decided to push it. He did not have the patience, nor did he want to spend any time wondering. One way or the other. 'What about your ID?' he asked, jutting his chin at the MI6 badge on his desk, Stratton's picture looking up at him.

It was obvious to Stratton Sumners wanted him to quit the game. It was oozing from the man. The truth was Stratton still did not know. He could not make his mind up, or, more to the truth, find the strength to walk away from something he knew deep down was not the ideal life for him. For the past year or so, it had all been about him waiting for the phone to ring, wondering if they wanted him back, if he was still good enough. Now it was the reverse. Sumners could no longer ignore him. Stratton was, for the time being at least, top of the pile. He had saved Jerusalem, and, perhaps more importantly, averted what could have been a catastrophic conflict between East and West. Sumners no longer had the power to remove him from the agent list.

Stratton stared at the ID. Quitting at this level was permanent. No one walked in and out of MI6 of their own volition. If you volunteered to say goodbye it was pretty much written in stone. Stratton could feel Sumners willing him to close the door and walk away without a word, which, finally, was perhaps why he did not.

Stratton walked over to the desk, picked up the ID and put it in his pocket. 'Thanks,' he said, rubbing salt into Sumners' anxiety, the thanks a suggestion that Sumners had invited Stratton to pick it up. Sumners could only stare at him.

Stratton walked out the door, closed it behind him and headed down the corridor towards the elevators. He could quit next week, but for now he was staying in the game.

The Hostage

DUNCAN FALCONER

When an undercover operation monitoring the Real IRA goes horrifically wrong, British Intelligence turn to the one man who can get their agent out: Stratton, SBS operative with a lethal reputation. It's a dangerous race against time: if the Real IRA get to the Republic before Stratton gets to the Real IRA, his colleague is as good as dead.

But the battle in the Northern Ireland borders is just the beginning. For there can only be one way the Real IRA knew about the British agent: someone within MI5 is tipping them off. Then the surveillance mission in Paris to identify the mole ends in disaster: Hank Munro, US Navy SEAL on secondment, is captured.

Munro's wife Kathryn is distraught, and turns to priest Father Kinsella for support. Kinsella, though, is not the holy man he seems, and Kathryn becomes an unwitting part of a deadly Real IRA plan, a terror attack the likes of which London has never seen . . .

First Into Action

DUNCAN FALCONER

They are the most elite and mysterious special forces unit in the world – but they are *not* the SAS.

The Special Boat Service is a small, clandestine and highly professional unit whose team-based ethos and exemplary combat record has created an intense rivalry with the SAS. At the age of nineteen, Duncan Falconer was the youngest man in recent years to join the unit and rose quickly to become one of its most skilled undercover operatives.

Through his own extraordinary experiences, Falconer recalls his leading role in SBS operations in Northern Ireland, the Falklands and the Gulf. He recounts the missions that have contributed to the unit's astounding success in the fight against terrorism and drug-smuggling, and charts the long-standing power struggle between the SBS and the SAS.

A fascinating insight into the secret world of the special forces, *First Into Action* is the *Bravo Two Zero* for the SBS.